Praise for *Love Amid the Ashes*

"Andrews re-creates the biblical story of Job through the eyes of the women who remained loyal to him. She has interwoven Job's steadfast faith and his willingness to lead others to God amidst devastation and restoration. This classic story will speak to readers in new ways and ignite the passion for the ways God brings love into our daily lives."

—*RT Book Reviews*, 4½ stars

"Andrews's research shines through on every page as she delves deeply into the cultural, historical, and biblical records to create this fascinating and multilayered tale surrounding the OT hero Job and his family. Full of drama and overflowing with fresh biblical principles of finding forgiveness, hope, and healing."

—*CBA Retailers+Resources*

Praise for *Love's Sacred Song*

"Andrews weaves a beautiful tale and takes readers to an ancient Jerusalem rich with history and customs and a culture that struggles to follow the one true God. This novel is well researched and well told."

—*RT Book Reviews*, 4½ stars

"Andrews breathes life into her characters, portraying Solomon, who was known to have over 700 wives and 300 concubines, as a very human man whose love for one woman stands above all others. Recommended to readers who enjoy biblical retellings that focus on male/female relationships, such as those of Jill Eileen Smith and Francine Rivers."

—*Library Journal*

D1545545

Praise for *Love in a Broken Vessel*

"Andrews guides readers to fully grasp the ministry of Hosea. She creates biblical characters who are lively and vivacious and hold our attention. Their lives become a rich tapestry to find the one true God. The author is undoubtedly passionate about a believer's quest to reconnect with God. This read exquisitely brings the Bible to life."

—*RT Book Reviews*, 4 ½ stars, Top Pick

"Mesu Andrews has pieced together Scripture's truths with historical supposition through her masterful, research-based writing and captured the spiritual climate of those ancient days. Biblical fans will find it a powerful story of God's redeeming love and forgiveness that's as relevant now as it was then."

—*CBA Retailers+Resources*

IN THE
SHADOW
OF JEZEBEL

Books by Mesu Andrews

IN THE SHADOW OF JEZEBEL

A NOVEL

MESU ANDREWS

R
Revell

a division of Baker Publishing Group
Grand Rapids, Michigan

Published by Revell
a division of Baker Publishing Group
P.O. Box 6287, Grand Rapids, MI 49516-6287
www.revellbooks.com

Printed in the United States of America

Library of Congress Cataloging-in-Publication Data
Andrews, Mesu, 1963–
    In the shadow of Jezebel : a novel / Mesu Andrews.
       pages cm
       ISBN 978-0-8007-2170-1 (pbk.)
       I. Title.
    PS3601.N55274S53 2014
    313'.6—dc23   2013037318

This is a work of historical reconstruction; the appearance of certain historical figures is therefore inevitable. All other characters, however, are products of the author's imagination, and any resemblance to actual persons, living or dead, is coincidental.

14 15 16 17 18 19 20   7 6 5 4 3 2 1

To my mothers:

The mother who gave me life—thank you for loving me unconditionally. I see Jesus in you every day.

The mother of my heart—thank you for choosing to love me. I learn to give by watching you.

The mother who gave me her son—thank you for teaching him to love well. I'll see you again someday in glory.

NOTE TO THE READER

Israel demanded a king, and Yahweh gave them Saul. When Saul failed them—as Yahweh warned he would—1 Samuel 13:14 says the Lord "sought out a man after his own heart." David was that man, and Yahweh expressed His favor with a threefold covenant: David's lineage, kingdom, and throne would endure forever (2 Sam. 7:16), even if his descendants needed discipline from time to time.

The first discipline came after David's son Solomon died, when civil war split the kingdom into two nations. The northern ten tribes retained the name Israel, with its eventual capital in Samaria. The southern nation became Judah, maintaining David's descendants on the throne, with the capital in Jerusalem and the worship of Yahweh in His holy Temple.

Israel's King Ahab married the daughter of a Phoenician Baal priest, bringing pagan worship to the forefront of Israelite society. Though Judah's King Jehoshaphat remained true to Yahweh, he couldn't afford to make Israel his enemy, so the good king agreed to his son's treaty marriage with Ahab's daughter—a decision that shrouded two generations *in the shadow of Jezebel*.

CHARACTER LIST

Ahab	eighth king of Israel; married Jezebel (Jizebaal) to seal treaty with Phoenicia
Ahaziah/Hazi (king)	ninth king of Israel; son of Ahab and Jezebel
Ahaziah/Hazi (prince/king)	sixth king of Judah; son of Jehoram and Athaliah; Sheba's half brother
Amariah	high priest during Jehoshaphat's reign and beginning of Jehoram's reign
Anna	Jehoiada's first wife (fictional)
Asa (king)	third king of Judah; Jehoshaphat's abba
Athaliah/Thaliah/ Thali	daughter of Ahab and Jezebel; married Jehoshaphat's son Jehoram; Hazi's ima; Sheba's guardian
Elan	priests' assistant (fictional)
Eliab	helpful priest during Jehoiada's early high priesthood (fictional)
Elijah	Yahweh's prophet in Israel; died approximately ten years before Jehoram's reign
Elisha	Yahweh's prophet in Israel after Elijah's ascension
Gadara	midwife from the City of David (fictional)
Hobah	Sheba's favorite widow (fictional)

11

Jehoash/Joash (prince)	Hazi and Zibiah's son
Jehoiada	second priest during Amariah's high priesthood
Jehoram (king)	firstborn son of Jehoshaphat; fifth king of Judah; Athaliah's husband; abba of Hazi and Sheba
Jehoshaphat (king)	fourth king of Judah; Jehoram's abba
Jehosheba/Sheba	Jehoram's daughter; Hazi's half sister
Jehozabad	Zabad's best friend and fellow Korahite (fictional)
Jehu	Israel's general under King Joram
Jezebel/Jizebaal	daughter of Phoenician King Eth-Baal; wife of King Ahab; Gevirah of King Joram; ima of Queen Athaliah; mastermind of Baal's rise to power in Israel/Judah
Joram/Ram	tenth king of Israel; son of Ahab and Jezebel; Athaliah's younger brother
Keilah	young widow who is friends with Sheba (fictional)
Mattan	Baal high priest for Queen Athaliah
Nathanael	second priest to Jehoiada (fictional)
Obadiah	nobleman in Ahab's administration; Yahweh's prophet
Zabad	young guard made chief keeper of the threshold under Jehoiada (fictional)
Zev	captain of Judah's royal Carite guard (fictional)
Zibiah	Hazi's wife; Prince Jehoash's ima

In the Shadow of Jezebel
Family Tree

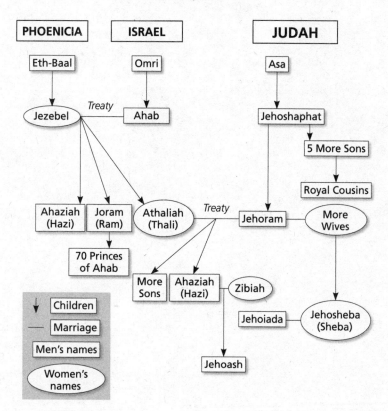

PHOENICIA

Eth-Baal

Jezebel — *Treaty* — Ahab

Ahaziah (Hazi)   Joram (Ram)

70 Princes of Ahab

ISRAEL

Omri

JUDAH

Asa

Jehoshaphat

5 More Sons

Royal Cousins

Athaliah (Thali) — *Treaty* — Jehoram — More Wives

More Sons   Ahaziah (Hazi)   Zibiah

Jehoiada   Jehosheba (Sheba)

Jehoash

Legend:
- ↓ Children
- — Marriage
- Men's names
- Women's names

13

Prologue

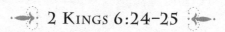
Some time later, Ben-Hadad king of Aram mobilized his entire army and marched up and laid siege to Samaria. There was a great famine in the city.

SAMARIA, ISRAEL, **843 BC**

From Jizebaal, Queen Mother—Gevirah—of Ram, King of Israel.
To My Revered Daughter, Athaliah, Queen of Judah, Wife of King Jehoram.

Greetings with blessings from almighty Baal Melkart, Rider of the Clouds.
Our plan to expand Baal's dominion will fail if your brother Ram continues to be duped by Elisha. Yahweh's prophet convinced him that his god ended Aram's recent siege on Samaria. Ram pledged his loyalty to Yahweh and destroyed my Baal temple and sacred stone in Samaria.
I warned him that almighty Baal would have his vengeance, Athaliah.
But he laughed.

Now Elisha is building prophet schools and teaching others to blaspheme Baal Melkart, while our nation falters under Ram's weak leadership.

If the fear of Baal Melkart won't bend the will of Israel's king, perhaps the fear of Jizebaal will. Ram must know that every king is replaceable—even my son. It's time I met my grandson Hazi. He's proven more pliable than Ram and seems more courageous than your husband.

I believe it's time to involve your daughter Sheba as well. I know her preparations as Baal's high priestess are nearly complete, but she may prove more useful in an alternate role. Bring her to me so I may judge her myself.

Come quickly to our spring palace in Jezreel.

Written by my own hand.

PART 1

1

Jehoram received a letter from Elijah the prophet, which said: "This is what the LORD, the God of your father David, says: 'You have not followed the ways of your father Jehoshaphat or of Asa king of Judah.'"

Late for the evening meal again, Princess Sheba hurried down the grand stairway, embers of fury still white-hot. A bumbling maid had dropped her favorite ruby earring and, after an enduring search, found it under Sheba's couch. In order to make an example of the careless girl, Sheba denied all her handmaids their evening meal. Queen Athaliah would commend her strict discipline. She might even forgive Sheba's tardiness when she noticed how beautifully the ruby earrings matched the scarlet head covering Abba had given her.

Sheba was usually afforded these little indiscretions since she was King Jehoram's favored daughter, but the looming pall in the dining hall made her wonder if she'd pushed too far. Keeping her head bowed, she tried to walk softly, but her new sandals clicked with every step across the marble tile.

Finally reaching the dais, Sheba took her customary place at the women's table beside Ima Thaliah. She kept her head low but felt every eye focused on the royal tables. Surely the eerie silence didn't hinge on her late arrival.

"You're late, Jehosheba." Ima Thaliah leaned close, whispered, and used Sheba's full name—three sure signs of her anger. But the queen always maintained control, considering emotions a luxury of the weak. Her ochre-stained lips, now pressed into a thin red line, resembled a wound against her alabaster skin and screamed their warning.

I'll probably have to help the servants clear the tables.

Ima often disciplined publicly if the offense was public in nature. Sheba's hidden bruises were testimony of her private errors.

Tonight, as on most other nights, two tables graced the elevated dais. Abba Jehoram sat at the head of the men's table, his closest advisors on his left, and Ima Thaliah presided over the royal women. The remaining tables formed neat rows in the expansive dining hall, every place filled with the king's council members, secondary wives and children, royal tutors, and Sheba's cousins—sons of Abba's deceased brothers. Three new tables had been added to make room for the cousins and their guards soon after Abba's brothers died. The thought of clearing all those dishes made Sheba bristle even more about her lost earring.

Perhaps my maids will lose two meals.

"Well, are you going to read it or not?" The queen's shrill voice split the silence, her eyes focused on a sealed scroll in Abba Jehoram's hand.

Sheba leaned close to whisper, "What's happening?" but fell silent at Ima's glare.

"You read it." Abba shoved the scroll back at his queen, bridging the small space between their tables. His hand trembled, the gold rings on his fingers clinking intolerably.

While Ima broke the seal and unrolled the parchment, Sheba scanned the tables of the king's royal guard. Her favorite brother, Hazi, sat among the hulking Carite soldiers, his eyes wide and staring, which sent her heart into a gallop. If even mischievous Hazi looked anxious, this scroll must be of grave concern indeed.

With a huff, Ima Thaliah cast a disparaging glance at Abba

Jehoram and cleared her throat. Sheba sat a little straighter, proud to be seated at the queen's right hand. She wondered not for the first time if Abba realized his good fortune at marrying such a capable woman. Athaliah, like her ima Jizebaal, had been trained as Baal's high priestess before her marriage, learning not only the religious rites but also how to read and write in three languages.

"The letter begins like this," Athaliah said. "'You, King Jehoram, have not followed the ways of your abba Jehoshaphat or of Asa king of Judah. But you have followed the ways of the kings of Israel, and you have led Judah and the people of Jerusalem to prostitute themselves, just as the house of Ahab did.'"

She slammed the scroll onto the table. "Really, Jehoram. I refuse to read any more. This scroll could not have been written by Elijah. He's been dead for ten years. This is obviously a ploy of his student Elisha, trying to deceive you as he's deceived my brother Ram. He wants to control the kings of both Israel *and* Judah."

Abba Jehoram grabbed the scroll from her and read the remaining message aloud. "'You have murdered your own brothers, members of your own family, men who were better than you. So now Yahweh is about to strike your people, your sons, your wives, and everything that is yours, with a heavy blow.'" His voice faded, the last words barely a whisper. "'You yourself will be very ill with a lingering disease of the bowels, until the disease causes your bowels to come out.'" The scroll dropped from his hands, clattering to the marble floor.

Sheba's thoughts raced with her heart. *What prophet would dare threaten the king of Judah and his entire household?* She glanced at Ima Thaliah, expecting the placid, granite calm.

Instead, her red, mottled neck showed raw fury. "Obadiah!"

The old nobleman rose with effort from the tufted cushion at his designated table, his gait labored, his back bent with age. "I am at your service, my queen," he said, kneeling, head bowed. Sheba noticed he'd attempted to comb his thinning white hair over a bald spot.

Ima regained her composure, her voice a dangerous purr.

"Are you at my service, Obadiah, or do you still serve Yahweh's prophets as you once served them in my abba Ahab's court?"

Obadiah lifted his gray head to meet her gaze. "I was given the scroll by one of Yahweh's prophets, it is true, and I delivered it to my lord Jehoram. But I serve King Jehoram and his family faithfully, my queen. King Ahab sent me to Judah to save my life, and I will not betray his favor."

"He sent you to Judah because my ima Jizebaal planned to kill you with the rest of Yahweh's conspiring prophets."

"Enough, Athaliah! Enough!" Abba Jehoram slammed his hand on the table, startling everyone in the hall and overturning his glass of wine. A thin film of sweat formed on his upper lip and forehead, and he was trembling head to toe.

Obadiah slowly resumed his bow, the only one in the hall seemingly unaffected by the prophet's message.

Abba Jehoram stood, thrusting the parchment toward the nobleman. "Look at the scroll, Obadiah. Is it the writing of the prophet Elijah or not?" Abba's purple robe dragged through the spilled wine.

He didn't notice, but Sheba did. The red stain soaked upward—like blood. Was it a bad omen? She cast a glance at Baal's high priest, Mattan, who sat on Abba's left as his primary advisor. He was also responsible for Sheba's magical arts training as a Baal high priestess. He'd taught her to read signs in everything—a bird's flight, bug bites, even spilled wine—but the bald, beady-eyed priest seemed as preoccupied with the mysterious document as was the king.

Obadiah rose, reached for the scroll, and studied it. "I saw Elijah's writing only once, but as I recall, these markings look similar."

"Similar or the same, man? Is this message authentic? Will the prophecy be fulfilled?"

The nobleman's features softened as he returned the scroll. "I believe the message is authentic, King Jehoram, but Yahweh is merciful and forgiving. Would you like me to summon *His* high priest? Amariah can speak with you about seeking Yahweh as your abba Jehoshaphat did."

"How dare you!" Ima Thaliah stood, placing a protective hand on Abba's shoulder. "He does not need advice from the priest of the god who is trying to destroy him! Now leave—before I do to you what Gevirah Jizebaal should have done years ago."

Obadiah resumed his humble bow, quickly backing out of the hall, while Ima coaxed Abba back to his embroidered cushion and knelt beside him. "I will not have you bullied by these Gileadites. These prophets from east of the Jordan can't be trusted, and their Yahweh is no match for Baal Melkart. Yahweh has battled the gods of Canaan since the days of your abba Jehoshaphat, but Yahweh's power is waning." Ima glanced in Mattan's direction. "Tell him there's nothing to worry about."

The high priest nodded his agreement, and Abba chuckled, then addressed those in the dining hall who'd grown awkwardly silent. "It appears my queen wishes to assuage any lingering fears. Tell us, Mattan, how we can be sure Yahweh's power is waning."

Sheba focused on the creeping stain on Abba's robe, his overturned goblet. Hadn't Mattan taught her such unsettling images foretold unsettling times? But her mentor and high priest rose with puzzling calm.

As he nodded first to the king and then to the gathering, Mattan's deep, resonant voice echoed off the stone walls. "Many of you will remember when King Jehoshaphat trusted Yahweh to bless his joint shipping venture with Israel, but the almighty storm god Baal destroyed Jehoshaphat's ships before they left the port of Ezion Geber."

"Yes! I remember!" shouted a white-haired nobleman. "Almighty Baal reigns!"

Mattan offered a condescending smile but lifted his hand for silence. "And remember that even Moab's god bested Yahweh when Elisha led Israel and Judah against King Mesha's rebellion. Israel still languishes without Moab's wool tribute because Yahweh couldn't secure the victory after King Mesha offered his son to Chemosh." Mattan reached for his goblet and lifted it high. "Stand, all of you, and bless your king and his queen in the name of almighty Baal Melkart!"

The dining hall erupted with shouts of praise for the Rider of the Clouds, but Abba turned to Ima Thaliah and spoke in a hushed voice. "What if the letter is right and Yahweh takes *you*, my love? I'd die if Yahweh took you from me."

Sheba's heart nearly melted. Of all Abba's wives, Ima Thaliah was the only one Sheba had heard him declare his love for.

The queen cupped his cheeks and drew him close. "I am the daughter of Jizebaal. Yahweh wouldn't *dare* touch me." She released a throaty laugh and pulled Abba into an impassioned kiss.

Applause transformed their evening meal into a celebration. Men shouted from every direction, "Long live King Jehoram! Long live Queen Athaliah!"

Sheba stood, joining the chorus, reveling in her parents' embrace. *Oh, how I long for a kiss like that.* She turned away, unable to bear the growing yearning in her heart. *Blasphemy!* she accused herself, unwilling to let a romantic thought take root.

In only a few weeks, she'd be initiated as a high priestess and vow a lifetime of service to Baal Melkart, dedicating her body to the prince of gods alone. Celibacy was a small price to pay to become the only high priestess presiding over her own temple. She'd endured the intimate Astarte training with full knowledge she'd never need the seductive skills. But on lonely, moonlit nights, she often wondered how she'd bear a lifetime without a man's love.

At least I won't be one of many in a harem. She had only vague memories of her birth ima, Naamah. She had died when Sheba was very young, but a little girl remembers her ima's tears. "Celibacy is better than a life of rejection," Sheba whispered, watching the crowded dining hall become more raucous.

Hazi's fellow guards grabbed serving maids for pleasure, and Abba's other wives danced while keeping their eyes on the king—undoubtedly hoping to gain his attention. But Abba Jehoram grew more passionate with his beloved Thaliah.

Sheba stood awkwardly, focusing on her new sandals. She felt Mattan's gaze on her. Why was she avoiding him? *If I'm going to become a high priestess, I can't blush like a child when the revelry begins.* Taking a deep breath, she squared her shoulders and raised her chin. Mattan grinned, his eyelids at half-mast, brows slightly raised as if challenging her somehow. She tried to look away but couldn't. Her breath became ragged as his eyes grew bolder, raking over her.

She'd heard rumors among the Astarte priestesses that Mattan had broken his vow of celibacy, but no one was foolish enough to accuse him. He'd come to Jerusalem as part of Athaliah's dowry from King Ahab, and he'd worked his way into Abba Jehoram's inner circle of trust. Sheba squeezed her eyes shut, retreating into darkness rather than facing her ruthless tutor. She dared not offend him. He was the key to maintaining favor with Ima Thaliah.

Balling her hands into fists, she dug her nails into her palms. *Stop this, Sheba. You have the power to create your own destiny. No man can steal your future.* She repeated Ima Thaliah's relentless mantra, words hammered into a thin gold plate covering Sheba's thoughts, words, and deeds since she had come under the queen's care. She'd been a whimpering brat when Ima Thaliah began training her.

Not anymore. Independent. Capable. Strong. These words described Sheba now.

So why did her insides shake like curdled milk when Mattan looked at her that way?

You have the power to create your own destiny. No man can steal your future.

She opened her eyes to meet Mattan's stare again. This time she lifted her golden goblet, toasted him, and found the courage to turn away with a smirk. Since before Sheba's first red moon, Ima Thaliah had taught her to humiliate men with a glance—but she'd never dared use it against Mattan.

From the corner of her eye, Sheba saw the high priest tap Abba Jehoram's shoulder, interrupting the royal couple's before-dinner passion. Her heart skipped a beat, rattling her fragile courage. Had the condescending smirk been too disrespectful? Would he tell Ima and earn Sheba more bruises? Or worse—days of silence from the woman whose approval meant more than life's breath?

Abba Jehoram leaned toward Mattan's hushed voice, and then he listened to Ima Thaliah's whisper. The king seemed troubled by Ima's words, but Mattan's obvious approval gave Abba pause.

After studying their faces for a long moment, the king lifted his hands to quiet the dining hall. "To show our disdain for the Yahwists' attempts to influence Judah's throne, I'm sending our youngest son as delegate to affirm Judah's parity treaty with Israel."

Sheba glanced at Hazi and found his expression chiseled stone. Hazi hated politics, as evidenced by his choice to join the royal guard rather than govern a fortified city as a Baal high priest like Ima Thaliah's other sons.

Abba Jehoram seemed oblivious—or impervious—to Hazi's displeasure. "Prince Hazi will lead his detachment of Carites to guard my lovely wife, who has demanded a visit with her ima, the Gevirah Jizebaal, in Jezreel." He lifted a newly poured glass of wine in Hazi's direction, and the usually charming prince offered a begrudging toast in return.

Sheba watched Ima Thaliah nudge Abba and whisper again. He cleared his throat and turned his attention to Sheba. "And you, my dear, will accompany Queen Athaliah to meet Jizebaal." Mischief crept into his handsome features. "May the gods help you."

Sheba gasped with delight—drawing a chastising glance from Ima for her lapse in etiquette.

A rumble fluttered over the gathering, and Sheba noted the impatient grumbling of the guards as they pulled the serving maids close again. Why were men so feral?

Abba Jehoram chuckled and extended his hand as an invitation for Mattan to address the gathering. "I can see our evening has whetted your appetites for celebration, but we must allow our maids to serve the evening meal." Disapproval threatened to delay the lovely meal Sheba smelled wafting through the hall. With good humor, Mattan raised his voice above the din. "Take heart, my friends. We'll open our temple gates for special offerings through the Astarte priestesses this evening." Roaring support erupted as the men released the maids to their appointed tasks. Mattan lifted his goblet again, signaling the meal to be served, while those at the head tables resumed their seats.

Sheba glanced at Hazi, his previous alarm replaced with a confident smile. He winked at her and bantered with his comrade Carites. As the youngest of Jehoram and Athaliah's sons, Hazi had been given the chance to choose his future, and he'd chosen a soldier's life. He was as tall as any of the paid mercenaries and more skilled with his dagger than most. Hazi and Sheba had always been the queen's favorites, the "chosen ones," as Athaliah's other sons had called the pair. Hazi's brothers hadn't been as appreciative of their roles as Baal's high priests—nor as committed to celibacy—as Sheba.

Ima Thaliah's hand gently enfolded Sheba's. "Are you pleased to finally meet Gevirah Jizebaal, Daughter?"

More than anything, she wanted to hug her ima and squeal. Instead, she met the queen's penetrating gaze and offered a slight bow. "I am pleased to do anything you ask of me, my queen."

The answer won her ima's approving smile. Respect. Decorum. Compliance. Queen Athaliah was as gentle as a lamb when people met her expectations.

2

The duty of the Levites was to help Aaron's descendants in the service of the temple of the Lord: to be in charge of the courtyards, the side rooms, the purification of all sacred things and the performance of other duties at the house of God.

Jehoiada let the warm, honeyed wine soothe his parched throat and eyed Amariah, his old friend and high priest. He looked bone-weary, his eyes heavy, head nodding. Perhaps he could get a short nap before the meeting.

The meeting. *Yahweh, will enough priests and Levites arrive to do the work?* It had become a weekly concern. Fewer men from outlying villages reported to the Temple for duty, which meant a smaller number of men must complete the same required tasks. Everyone fought exhaustion.

The downward spiral had started years ago when King Jehoshaphat toured the cities in Judah, appointing Levites as judges and scribes. Upon returning to Jerusalem, he established a central court, assigning two supreme judges. The high priest ruled on matters concerning the Temple, and a Judean tribal leader decided civil cases. Jehoshaphat intended to limit the power of his successor—the current King Jehoram—but the sweeping changes demanded more service from the priests and Levites.

While King Jehoshaphat reigned, Jehoram and his wife shrewdly integrated Baal worship into some of Yahweh's celebrations, but when Jehoshaphat died six years ago, the new king and queen set aside all subtlety. Pagan altars polluted every high place, and the people's commitment to Yahweh faded amid promises of Baal's freedom and pleasure.

How can we restore Your worship, Yahweh?

As if sensing Jehoiada's prayer, Amariah stirred, and Jehoiada reached across the table to wake him fully. "Are you ready, my friend?"

Amariah roused with a snort and a sheepish grin. "I suppose the Levites have put away their harps and lyres by now. I wonder why, among all Yahweh's instructions to David, He excluded a tidy work schedule for weekly assignments?" He chuckled, clearly amused with himself, and then stretched his back, joints popping like pebbles under new sandals.

Jehoiada hurried from his own cushion to Amariah's low-lying couch. He held out a steadying hand. "Let me help you."

Amariah stared at the proffered hand, grabbed it, and then turned it over and back, examining Jehoiada's smooth, brown skin. The high priest compared his own gnarled fingers and blue-veined hand. "How is it that you're almost as old as I am, but you look like a man half my age?" Jehoiada grinned and drew a breath to answer, but Amariah added, "And how many animals did you sacrifice today? I don't mean how many slaughters did you *oversee*. I mean how many did you *yourself* actually place on that altar?"

Jehoiada answered with a wry smile. Amariah wouldn't believe the numbers if he confessed. He'd offered three bulls, five rams, and fifteen lambs to Yahweh this day, and only one very young priest had kept pace. "You want to know why I look younger than you?" The high priest furrowed his brow, and Jehoiada knew he'd piqued his curiosity. "It's because the priests' assistants like me better than you and give me the best portions of sacrifice for evening meals."

Amariah cackled, good-natured as always, accepting Jehoiada's help to stand. "Well, let's go see if those priests' assistants have everything ready for our meeting." Laying his hand on Jehoiada's arm, he leaned in gently. "One day you'll be high priest, my friend."

"What? No. I'm your second, and seconds are never promoted to high—we choose by lot, someone younger, Amariah. Like you said, I'm almost as old as you are. A high priest serves for a full generation. It wouldn't make sense—"

"You have the qualifications, Jehoiada. You're a firstborn. You're a priest of Aaron's line and the family line of Zadok."

"But I'm old!" he said as they emerged from Amariah's chamber to the Temple's inner court. Several passing Levites issued sidelong glances, and the two top priests regained their dignity and returned respectful nods.

"Yes, you are old," Amariah whispered, allowing the Levites to gain a safe distance. "But the Lord has placed on you the spirit of Moses, Joshua, and Caleb. Like those wilderness fathers, you haven't aged and declined as normal bodies do. Yahweh doesn't offer that kind of blessing without a godly purpose—a holy calling."

Shame colored Jehoiada's cheeks. "How could I ever be Yahweh's high priest? My wife—may the Lord bless Anna's soul—never bore children during our forty-year marriage. Surely if I wasn't fit to be an abba, I am not fit to be high priest."

"Our good King Jehoshaphat proved that siring sons doesn't ensure God's blessing. He was a faithful king, sought Yahweh with his whole heart, and had *seven* sons. But when he died, his firstborn killed all six brothers and holds his nephews hostage in the palace to dissuade retribution. We priests are faced with the very real concern of keeping the lamp of King David's descendants glowing on Judah's throne."

Jehoiada felt his temper rising—as it always did when they discussed Judah's reigning king. He glanced behind them to be sure he wouldn't be overheard as they walked past the brazen altar and bronze lavers toward the large gallery behind the Temple. "King Jehoram is David's descendant in name only. He put Judah at risk by killing his brothers in cold blood—men who were loving husbands and abbas. Jehoram's brothers followed Yahweh and—"

"And that's what got them killed."

Jehoiada squeezed the knots at the back of his neck. "Their faithfulness got them killed, but their leadership kept Judah's borders safe. When Jehoram replaced his brothers with his pampered, pagan-priest sons as governors, it weakened the fortified cities, which weakened the whole nation—the military, the worship, and the morale. How can you stomach this king, Amariah?"

The high priest stopped walking and pulled Jehoiada into one of the storage chambers in the northern gallery. He, too, checked the hall to be sure they were alone. "I tolerate King Jehoram because I want our wayward king to know there's always a way back to Yahweh. You and I remember him as a boy—before he fell under Athaliah's spell. We knew his abba Jehoshaphat and the godly training invested in Jehoram and in this nation. Jehoram would never have killed his brothers without Athaliah's evil influence. And now *her* sons build temples in the fortified cities they govern, as Jehoram built high places on every hill." He straightened, adjusting his breastpiece, calming his tone. "For now, Jehoiada, Yahweh asks us to wait."

"Wait for what?" Jehoiada's shout echoed in the chamber.

Amariah's single raised eyebrow tamed Jehoiada's temper, reminding him of the high priest's authority. An effective muzzle.

Jehoiada inhaled, closed his eyes, and regained his composure. "Will we wait for another of King Jehoram's disastrous decisions—like going to war when Edom rebelled? The king and his commanders barely escaped with their lives, and now we've lost a third of Judah's top soldiers in a fight we shouldn't have fought. If Jehoram hadn't killed his brothers, Edom wouldn't have rebelled."

"*Should haves* and *would haves* mean nothing, my friend. We wait for Yahweh's decision through the Urim and Thummim to know what *will be*." Amariah patted his sacred breastpiece, indicating the two stones hidden within it. "They've been Yahweh's mouthpiece since the days of Aaron. We wait until we have a question with two alternatives—black or white, yes or no, guilty or innocent."

Jehoiada sighed, bone-weary, unsettled by the question nipping at his conscience. *Are the Urim and Thummim* always *right?* "You see, my friend?" He squeezed Amariah's shoulder and guided him out of the side chamber, refusing to voice his doubts. "Your wisdom makes you a better high priest than I could ever be."

They continued down the hallway and into the rear gallery, the only part of the Temple complex large enough to muster a full week's course of priests and Levites—sometimes as many as a thousand men. Yahweh's servants awaited their assignments for the coming week, but what normally sounded like a beehive in the sprawling space sounded more like subdued echoes in a tomb.

Amariah's puzzled gaze mirrored Jehoiada's words. "Where are all the others?" They stood gawking at the four hundred who'd completed their week and maybe another hundred who'd reported for their upcoming duties.

At the height of King Jehoshaphat's reign, his census of priests and Levites numbered thirty-eight thousand men aged thirty years or older. Every priest was a Levite, born of Levi's tribe, but not all Levites were priests. The priests, all direct descendants of Moses's brother Aaron, offered sacrifices before the Lord and were divided into twenty-four families. The Levites, divided into three clans, served within their specialized ministries as musicians, gatekeepers, and scribes.

Jehoiada knew most of the family leaders and many of their sons. A quick perusal of those present told him more Levites than priests had reported for duty, but they still might be unable to muster a full choir with the musicians.

Jehoiada lifted his hands for silence. "Quiet down! Quiet down!"

Sullen faces met his plea. Most of Yahweh's servants lived on small plots of land interspersed throughout Judah and viewed their three to five weeks of Temple service each year as sort of a family reunion. Disappointment undoubtedly colored their reaction.

"Where are the rest?" Amariah's reedy voice dissolved into the now echoing expanse. Those who stood before him stared at their feet, the ceiling, the walls—anywhere except the kind eyes of their gracious leader.

Jehoiada leaned close, trying to keep the panic he felt from seeping into his whisper. "I knew we faced steady decline since tensions with the Edomites, but this is serious. What do we do?"

Amariah stepped forward, ignoring Jehoiada's question. "Thank you, brothers, for your willing and eager service of Yahweh. May I ask if any of you know the reason your fellow priests and Levites have not joined us?"

Accusations launched from every direction, angry priests and brother Levites stabbing the air to stress their complaints.

Amariah lifted both hands. "One at a time, brothers. Please, one at a time."

A tall, slender Levite from Tekoa stepped forward as spokesman. Normally he was quite a reserved man, but now his leather-like skin was the color of his red-desert home. "My brother and nephews stayed to protect their families from invasion. The Judean troops in Tekoa spend all their time drinking wine and making so-called offerings to Baal's shrine prostitutes." Others began jeering, coaxing him to continue. "Judah's military wouldn't know we'd been invaded unless the marauders threatened their wine supplies."

"Is this true of others?" Amariah asked, shouting over the general agreement spreading through the crowd. Quieting them again with lifted hands, he said, "Then, my brothers, the burden—and privilege—of service falls to us. We will work harder because we are fewer, but we will serve joyfully because we come willingly."

Amariah's gentle spirit seemed to sweep away their outrage. *Serve joyfully because we come willingly.* Indignation fell from their faces like leaves from an autumn tree. How could a man's heart be so untarnished after serving all these years?

Awed, Jehoiada reached for the baskets of lots to begin assigning tasks. The first basket contained larger stones with all the Levite clan symbols, and the other baskets were designated by family, holding stones marked with specific men's names.

"In keeping with the Law of Moses," Jehoiada began, "Yahweh will now assign by lot your weekly service in His holy Temple." He released a deep sigh, preparing himself for the long process. With so many men absent, the selection process could take hours.

The scribe poised his stylus over the parchment, ready to record results as Amariah drew out the stones. "For the task of baking the holy showbread, I call forward the clan of Nadab, the families of Harim and Seorim."

A low hum began as men discussed their various assignments for the coming week. Trimming wicks, baking showbread, tuning harps, choosing Psalms, planning morning and evening sacrifices—a name was drawn for every task. Not once did Amariah's hand draw a lot with the name of a priest or Levite not present in the room. After over half the duties had been filled, realization spread among them and wonder hushed every sound. Yahweh knew them by name and was actually *choosing them.*

With the final duty assigned, Amariah raised his voice, tears streaming down his weather-wrinkled cheeks. "How can we express our praise, O Lord? You used the common lots to convey Your holy presence and prove You have chosen us by name. May Your overwhelming majesty crush Your enemies and empower Your priests. May we serve You well and be faithful guardians of Your covenant forever."

Jehoiada stood in hushed wonder beside his friend and high priest. Moments ago, he'd silently questioned the reliability of the sacred Urim and Thummim, but now God had spoken through *common* stones. *Perhaps Yahweh is more reachable than I thought.*

3

Early in the morning . . . Gideon and all his men camped at the spring of Harod. . . . The LORD said to Gideon, "You have too many men. I cannot deliver Midian into their hands. . . . Now announce to the army, 'Anyone who trembles with fear may turn back and leave Mount Gilead.'"

Sheba had ridden from dawn until dark, jostled and pitched atop this galloping camel. Now she must endure a second day of torture. *Prince Baal, rescue me.* Surely Mot's underworld was the origin and destination of all camels. They were stinking, spitting, insulting creatures, and if she never rode one again, her life would be much improved.

Had it really been only two days since Abba Jehoram's public ruse to reaffirm Judah's treaty with Israel? Everyone knew the treaty was built on his marriage with Queen Athaliah—just as the enduring treaty between Israel and Phoenicia had been established by Queen Jizebaal's marriage to King Ahab years before.

Their journey to Jezreel was prompted entirely by Ima's whisper that night at the banquet, and Abba had wasted no time with long good-byes. Before dawn the next morning, he'd bribed Hazi's cooperation with an Egyptian black stallion and shouted orders to his youngest son at Jerusalem's north gate.

"The faster you travel to Jezreel, the less chance of trouble along the way." Abba's full royal regalia hinted that he'd been awake for some time, perhaps choosing the fine black stallion himself. "Ride hard and change horses at each fortified city. Overnight at Tirzah, and you'll arrive in Jezreel by midday tomorrow. You can pick up the black in Tirzah on your way home."

King Jehoram often gave extravagant gifts to soothe his children's tempers, but Hazi was still piqued at playing Abba's delegate to Israel. "What about Ima and Sheba? I'd planned four or five days for travel with the women."

"Your ima can ride her camel to Aram and back before the sun sets, and you let *her* worry about Sheba." Abba had given his wife a conspiratorial wink and then grew suddenly serious, motioning Hazi closer. Sheba wished she hadn't heard Abba's caution. "Keep watch, my son. Moab's rebellion is still a freshly salved wound, and Yahweh's prophets are becoming bolder. Aram's siege on Samaria is over, but there's always danger, and you guard my most precious treasures." He slapped the stallion on its hindquarters, hurrying Hazi and half the royal guard out the northern gate.

On this, their second day of travel, Hazi remained their fearless leader, proudly perched atop his fourth stallion, having traded mounts at each fortified city as Abba instructed. A third of Hazi's Carites escorted Ima Thaliah, the curtains of her sedan tied back for a full view, and a third of the guards attended Sheba's camel. She'd unfurled her rear curtain so that Mattan, who rode his camel behind her, couldn't stare for the duration of the journey. The remainder of Hazi's troops provided rear guard, keeping bandits, wild beasts, and those dreadful Yahweh prophets at bay. The caravan had stopped yesterday at Bethel, Shiloh, and Shechem, refreshing their animals and eating quick meals of bread and hard cheese. Sheba asked for a little time at the city markets, earning a foul look from both her brother and Ima.

When they had arrived at Tirzah last night, the watchmen had already closed the city gates. Ima Thaliah demanded, "In the name of Gevirah Jizebaal and King Joram, open these gates!"

Hazi reminded her that she should have given Uncle Ram's name first. Regardless, the guards promptly complied. Ima ranted that they'd better reopen the gates before dawn and then added, loud enough for everyone to hear, "Anyone in *my* party found lagging in the morning will stay with these fine soldiers until we return for you on our way back to Jerusalem—if I've forgiven you by then." At the first shades of pink in the eastern sky, everyone in Judah's procession—and Tirzah's watchmen—were waiting at the city gate.

Sheba grinned at the memory. Her ima was a strong and powerful woman. Men feared and respected her because she acted on her word. *I will command that kind of power when I am high priestess in my own temple.*

She watched Ima Thaliah whip her camel, repositioning herself with grace and determination. She'd maintained the pace effortlessly, swatting the beast and gliding in rhythm with its long strides. Sheba, on the other hand, had been slammed from corner to post, feeling more like a kernel of wheat in a hand mill than a princess on her way to meet Gevirah Jizebaal.

But she knew better than to complain. Ima was too skilled with a whip to make her cross. The bruises on Sheba's arms were finally fading. *Just in time for my whole body to ache from this cursed camel ride.* On the only other occasion she'd ridden a camel, it had been a short ride to the healing springs in southern Judah. *I'd give a thousand shekels for a dip in En Gedi's springs.*

Her inner grousing suddenly vexed her. Why was she whining about a silly camel? She straightened her shoulders and watched Ima Thaliah with renewed appreciation—the woman who had taught her to dress, to speak, and to eat like a queen. Today Sheba would meet the woman who had trained Ima Thaliah in such things. *My muscles will heal, just like my bruises.* With rekindled excitement, she swatted her mount, imitating Ima Thaliah's riding techniques.

Sheba leaned into a turn, rounded a bend in the road, and caught her first glimpse of the Jezreel Valley. "It's beautiful," she breathed. No one heard her, of course, over the thudding of horses' and camels' hooves. A wide, green plain yawned between mountains on the left and gently sloping hills on the right. Orchards and groves sprouted from rich, black soil and offered late winter figs, and almond blossoms spread their lovely scent through the valley. To ride through it at this speed seemed almost irreverent.

"Sheba, come!" Ima Thaliah motioned her forward, and she tried desperately to obey, guiding her one-humped beast in the general direction of Judah's queen.

Looking ahead to the right, she eyed a copse of trees and beyond it a walled city with a lofty watchtower. Ima Thaliah seemed to be pointing to the oasis and yelling something to Hazi. Sheba hoped the royal guards would catch her camel's reins and lead her to the right spot.

Mercifully, the whole procession soon slowed, and she saw with relief that their destination was indeed the green trees—and hidden behind them lay a beautiful natural spring. It couldn't compare with En Gedi, of course, but crystal-clear water cascaded over rock formations, creating natural fountains around a deep, translucent pool.

"It's Gideon's Pool!" Hazi shouted, leaping off his horse, the first to run toward the inviting waters. "Look, Mattan! Saba Jehoshaphat told me the story of Gideon, how Yahweh winnowed his army to three hundred men." High-stepping through wheatgrass, Hazi stopped short of the pool and waited for Baal's high priest. "They say Yahweh won that victory over the Midianites."

Mattan slid from his camel and followed Hazi into the grassy marsh. "It's a legend, as are most stories of Yahweh, made more fantastic through years of retelling. No army of three hundred could defeat an entire nation."

Sheba waited impatiently for the lead herdsman to aid her dismount, but she noticed Ima's gathering storm. The queen had abandoned her sedan, but the two men completely ignored her. And worse, they'd impeded her progress to the pool. She was in her battle stance. Feet planted. Arms folded. They were about to reap the wrath of their disregard.

May the gods help you both. Sheba smiled wickedly.

Hazi untied his belt, and Mattan lifted his turban-like cap off his shaved head.

"Don't. You. Dare." Ima Thaliah pronounced each word succinctly.

Both men turned to stone. Not a flinch. Not a sound.

"Sheba and I have first rights to this pool."

The men exchanged a dejected glance and retraced their steps toward the animals. "Of course, Ima. I'm sorry." Hazi kept his head bowed and paused beside her, placing a hand on her shoulder. "Let us know if you'd like us to check for eels before you go in."

Sheba's heart leapt to her throat, but Ima shoved Hazi's shoulder. He nearly fell to the ground laughing.

"I'll show you the first eel I find," she shouted, laughing at the two men scurrying toward the camels. Hazi had always been the only one capable of diverting Ima's wrath.

A servant finally tapped Sheba's camel down for dismount, and she began questioning the queen while running through the wheatgrass. "Is that Jezreel in the distance? I saw the watchtower. Did you live here as a girl? If that *is* Jezreel, why did we stop here when we're so close to our destina—"

A sudden splash halted her questions and stole her attention. Two of Athaliah's handmaids held a large sheet open between them at the water's edge. "Ima, what are you doing?" She glanced back at Hazi and Mattan, but their backs were turned. Sheba seemed to be the only one amazed that Judah's queen would take a bath in the middle of a crowd.

Ima Thaliah giggled like a little girl, splashing, coaxing from the other side of the sheet. "I'm taking a bath, Sheba, and you will too. Now, tell your handmaids to bring another sheet and scented oils. Today you will meet Jizebaal, daughter of King Eth-Baal, priestess of Baal, wife of King Ahab, Gevirah of King Joram. She is a formidable woman, Sheba, and the waters of Gideon's Pool will give you the courage you need to face her."

Two maids appeared with the requested items, but Sheba hesitated, glancing at the men lined up near the animals. Mattan peered over his shoulder, chewing on a piece of grass. The familiar shiver worked up her spine. She looked again at the pool, reassuring herself that she couldn't see Ima behind the raised sheet. She left her sandals in the grass before her courage fled. The maids unfurled the sheet as they walked, and Sheba kept her eyes on the squishy ground, tiptoeing to the water's edge. She dipped her right foot in the pool.

"Come, Sheba. Jump in! Seize what you desire. It's cold at first, but plunge ahead. You won't be sorry."

Sheba closed her eyes and rushed in up to her waist, feeling the mossy pebbles slippery beneath her feet. She gasped and giggled, opened her eyes—and then saw Ima.

She wore only her seamless tunic, and her hair was wet, unplaited, and streaked with gray. Her face was free of paints and powders, her lingering beauty enhanced by delicate creases around her eyes and mouth. Sheba stared at the most powerful woman she knew—amazed at the first glimpse of her humanness.

"You're gawking, Sheba." Ima's grin was sharp as a flint knife. Her voice low, she held out her hand, inviting Sheba nearer. "You will see me differently after today, my little one. Come closer so we can speak of important things."

Sheba slid her toes on the mossy bottom, entering Ima's inviting embrace, bending her knees to meet the queen at eye level, remembering it was ill-mannered to ever stand above royalty.

Ima squeezed her shoulders, seeming pleased at their nearness. "Jizebaal trained me as I have been training you—to embrace the destiny of queens, an honor bestowed on our family by Prince Baal Melkart. The Gevirah began as a priestess, then became a queen, and when King Ahab died, she became the ima of King Ram—the Gevirah of Israel. She will judge you today to determine if you are the keeper of our trust. Don't disappoint me." She grabbed the long braid under Sheba's headpiece and pulled her backward, submerging her completely, and then released her.

Water rushed up Sheba's nose, and she came out of the water sputtering, coughing, and wiping her eyes. "Ima! What was that for? I won't dis—"

Ima Thaliah reached out to steady her on the slippery rocks, cradling her shoulders and wiping the water from her eyes. She pulled Sheba close again, her warmth in the cool water comforting, her tender smile and bright eyes seeming almost playful. Sheba crouched low into Ima Thaliah's embrace, gathering her wits, listening carefully.

"You see how quickly things can change, Sheba? One moment we're talking, and the next you're nearly drowning." She laughed, a lilting, agreeable sound, and Sheba relaxed, nodded. "Hazi called this pond Gideon's Pool, but it's also called the Pool of Trembling. It's where Ima Jizebaal brought me when I was a little girl to teach me not to be afraid of the water." Ima gently removed Sheba's headpiece, stroking her hair, and then pressed her head against her chest as she reminisced. "But you're not afraid of water, are you, my little princess?" Sheba shook her head, and Ima continued. "No, because I taught all my little ones how to swim in the waters of En Gedi. But Gevirah Jizebaal taught me another reason not to fear. Do you want to know why I fear nothing?"

"Nothing?" Sheba raised her head, questioning.

"That's right, Sheba. Gevirah Jizebaal said as long as I obeyed her, I should fear nothing." Without warning, she kicked Sheba's legs away and dunked her head underwater, this time holding her beneath the surface until Sheba began to thrash and panic.

Moments passed—days, it seemed—and finally Ima lifted her out of the water, both hands around her neck. Sheba came up gasping, frantic, sobbing. "Ima, please. Stop. Why are you—"

"What is going on?" Hazi shoved the handmaids aside but stopped short when he saw the state of his ima and sister. "Ima, no. Leave her be."

Sheba sobbed quietly, lowering her gaze, but Ima stared hard at Hazi. "I'm preparing your sister to meet the Gevirah, my son. Go, tend the animals. When we're finished, you and Mattan may enter the pool. You, too, must be spotless before you meet Gevirah Jizebaal."

Hazi cast a helpless glance at Sheba and returned to his men. The handmaids resumed their positions as a visual wall, and

Ima Thaliah continued her lesson. "Remember this moment, Sheba. Your life has always been—and will always be—in my hands, to do with as I please. Royal women may speak publicly of jewelry, pottery, and the gods, but today you will learn the destiny of queens, the purpose of Jizebaal's daughters. Kings sit on thrones, but queens rule their nations. If you ever disobey me, you will wish I had drowned you in Gideon's Pool of Trembling."

4

Then the LORD said to Moses, "Make a bronze basin, with its bronze stand, for washing. . . . Aaron and his sons are to wash their hands and feet with water from it. . . . This is to be a lasting ordinance for Aaron and his descendants for the generations to come."

The moon's eerie glow shone through Jehoiada's chamber window, waking him just before dawn. The Temple would soon come alive with priests and Levites making final preparations before the gates opened at day's first light. He pulled a corner of lamb's wool over his head and groaned. The thought of doing again today what he'd done yesterday and every day before that—it seemed more than he could muster. *Does Amariah ever feel overwhelmed?*

He'd lived on Temple grounds since he was a child, but these bleak days were more discouraging than any he remembered. During the flourishing days when Asa and Jehoshaphat reigned, almost forty priests' *families* were permanent residents on Temple grounds. The high priest, his second, the chief gatekeeper, and several other officers of the Temple remained on-site year-round, their wives living in a designated city house during their monthly uncleanness or prescribed child-bearing separation.

After observing the stress of such separations, King Jehoshaphat added a grand outer courtyard with living quarters built into the outer walls, where families could dwell together regardless of the women's state. The outer courtyards themselves served as overflow for the thousands of worshipers who had sacrificed daily at Yahweh's Temple.

Now, worshipers numbered less than the weekly course of priests, and the outer court family chambers were empty. Offerings provided barely enough food to support the priests and Levites who served.

With a sigh, Jehoiada peered from beneath his lamb's wool. How did Amariah maintain his cheerful spirit when the future looked so bleak? How could he continue to judge at the palace's central court when a pagan king sat on Judah's throne?

Amariah! We must hurry!

Jehoiada leapt out of bed, reached for two flint rocks, and ignited the wick on a clay lamp. Amariah moved a little slower lately, requiring more time for Jehoiada to dress him. The high priest's pained expression on the ascent to the raised altar had been a hushed topic among the Levites last week. Jehoiada had issued a deadly glare and heard no more about it.

A quick peek out his window revealed a faintly reddening sky. He must wake Amariah and get them both to the Molten Sea for purification. After a single knock on the adjoining door, he lifted the iron latch and let himself in, offering the usual morning greeting. "All right, my brother priest. Enough dreaming. It's time to begin a new day."

The flickering flame barely cast a shadow on the wall, but even the dim light made Amariah squint. "I keep hoping I'll wake up to words from Yahweh's lips and open my eyes in paradise."

Jehoiada chuckled. "Sorry. Instead, we get to wash our hands and feet in the ice-cold waters of the Molten Sea."

Amariah slipped into his woolen robe. "It is an honor, isn't it? To serve Yahweh each and every day of our lives?" Wonder laced his voice as he leaned on Jehoiada's forearm, and the two walked toward the door.

"It is an honor indeed." There it was. That inner joy. That undaunted eagerness to serve. *Let it be so in me, Yahweh.*

Jehoiada and Amariah finished their purification and donned the high priest's golden garments well before the morning service began. Blaring silver trumpets announced the Temple gates' opening, and Jehoiada stood at the eastern entry, watching the faithful worshipers straggle in. His heart sank. *Fewer than yesterday.*

Since King Jehoram had completed Baal's temple four years ago, offerings to Yahweh had steadily declined. Positioned south of the palace and closer to the city's market, Baal's temple greeted travelers entering Jerusalem's busiest gates. The mysterious-looking citadel of Baal beckoned those visiting the Throne Hall, which meant any foreign dignitaries arriving from south, east, or west met Baal's abomination before they glimpsed Yahweh's splendor.

Jehoiada breathed deeply, trying to calm his rising anger, but the stench of Baal's sacrifice already wafted on the northerly breeze—a lamb or goat, just like Yahweh's sacrifices. The similarities confused Judah's worshipers, and when the royal household vowed the New Moon celebrations were equally beneficial at either temple, offerings to Yahweh plummeted in favor of the pleasure-based rituals of Baal's shrine prostitutes. How many worshipers had entered Baal's court this morning? Was the high priest Mattan dissecting some goat's liver to predict the next battle, or were they reenacting some dramatic story of the pagan gods' antics?

"Shalom, Jehoiada." A man walked by, clutching a lamb, concern creasing his brow. "Is everything well? You look ill."

Kicking himself for his obvious scowl, Jehoiada wrapped the man's shoulders with a comforting embrace. "All is well, my friend. I overslept and didn't have time to break my fast. A time of worship will brighten my day and make me forget my empty stomach."

The sound of rhythmic marching approached, and Jehoiada pulled the man aside as palace guards streamed in the gate designated for royalty, though no king had entered it since Jehoshaphat fell ill years ago.

"Make way for King Jehoram," one of the guards shouted.

Almost immediately the king rounded the corner, surrounded by the elite Carite guards entrusted with his care—one of them leading a year-old male goat through the gate, toward the inner portico.

The priests in the inner court bowed as King Jehoram marched his goat to the altar. Amariah received his offering and directed the king toward the upper porch, where royal guests were invited to participate in Temple services. Before retiring to the porch, the king whispered something to the high priest.

What is our pagan king up to?

Jehoiada nodded greetings to the sparse worshipers in the other courts, making his way toward the portico. He had almost reached the steps when he felt a firm tug on his arm. "Obadiah?" Lowering his voice, Jehoiada guided the king's advisor to the portico, where they could whisper without being overheard. "What is going on here? Why is Jehoram bringing the sin offering required of a leader to a routine morning sacrifice?"

"He seeks forgiveness from Yahweh."

"You mean he wants a *favor* from Yahweh. What game is he playing?"

"It's no game, Jehoiada. I delivered a letter from Elijah to King Jehoram last night—"

"What? That's impossib—"

"Please, Jehoiada. I don't understand it myself. Either the prophet wrote it before he died and his students knew the right moment to deliver it, or . . ." He shrugged, leaving Jehoiada to consider the supernatural alternative. "But there's more. The letter condemned King Jehoram's murder of his brothers and his adoption of Ahab's practices and gods, but what really frightened him was the prediction of a wasting disease of the bowels. Jehoram remembers his saba Asa's death—the lingering disease of his feet."

Jehoiada released a disgusted sigh. "Obadiah, both you and I know *feet* was just a kind word for a very private and humiliating affliction."

Obadiah wiped both hands down his weary face. "That's the point. Jehoram is terrified that something just as demoralizing will happen to him. He's willing to pledge *anything* in hopes Yahweh will relent on his judgment."

"What do you mean, 'pledge anything'? That's not the way it works, Obadiah." Every word escalated, drawing attention from those nearby.

Jehoiada pasted on a smile, as did Obadiah, and the men resumed a calmer conversation. "He sent messengers this morning at dawn to collect the royal princes from the fortified cities," the nobleman said.

"You mean Athaliah's sons."

Obadiah nodded, sweat dripping from his brow though the spring morning was cool. "None of Jehoram's other sons would dare make a play for Judah's throne. Athaliah has made certain hers are the only sons given the title *prince*."

The thought of Athaliah's blood mingled on the throne of David piqued Jehoiada further. "What does Queen Athaliah think of Jehoram's sudden offerings to Yahweh?"

Obadiah glanced around them and kept his voice low. "Prince Hazi escorted Queen Athaliah to Jezreel to meet Jizebaal—or Jezebel, as she is so deservedly called, that pile of dung."

Jehoiada grinned for the first time, enjoying the nobleman's momentary lapse in decorum.

"I'm not sure why King Jehoram has summoned his royal sons or what restitution he has planned, but it seems he hopes to accomplish something of import while Athaliah and her Baal high priest are gone. Perhaps it has something to do with the Awakening Festival of Melkart."

"We shouldn't even be having this conversation," Jehoiada whispered between clenched teeth. *Breathe. Breathe.* "King Jehoram is a coward. Let him make his restitution while his wife and high priest are in Jerusalem! They should cancel the Awakening Festival and participate in the *true* Feast of Passover."

"Shh, Jehoiada. Keep your voice down."

"Might I also suggest his restitution include the Day of Atonement seven moons from now?" Jehoiada covered a sarcastic gasp as though a thought had just occurred. "Wait! I guess he'll *never* make restitution to the six brothers he murdered in cold blood."

Obadiah squeezed his eyes shut and let out a sigh. "Jehoiada, set aside your anger long enough to appreciate this moment. Yahweh's prophet has spoken to the king of *Judah*! Granted, we enjoy Yahweh's presence through His Temple, but we've had no direct word from Him since King Jehoshaphat's reign. Yahweh is at work again in our midst, Jehoiada. This is exciting news!"

Unconvinced, Jehoiada folded his arms across his chest. "I'll lead the rejoicing when Yahweh regains His rightful place in Judah, but I don't believe King Jehoram will make long-term changes because of a single letter from a dead prophet." He fell silent, awaiting Obadiah's next round of excuses.

Instead, the stately nobleman met his gaze, eyes glistening. "I don't believe Judah's fate ultimately lies in Jehoram's hands. The Yahweh I serve is bigger than Jehoram's failures and Athaliah's influence."

Before Jehoiada could utter a sound, Obadiah hurried up the portico stairs to join the royal delegation, leaving the second priest to search his heart. Could Yahweh overcome the decline Jehoiada had seen during his years at the Temple? If He had the power to stop evil, why didn't He?

Jehoiada heard little of the Levite choir's praise and barely noticed when Amariah made the king's personal offering. The royal delegation marched down the stairs and past the few worshipers lined up to present their sacrifices. As other worshipers filed out, Jehoiada walked against the flow toward the sectioning tables behind the brazen altar. Since fewer priests had reported for duty, he helped section the daily offerings—sacrificing the prescribed portion on the pyre and separating the priests' portion for their meals. The day passed in a blur of torment, his mind consumed with the wickedness of the royal house.

When evening came, he was more than a little surprised when the king reappeared with all four royal princes. The four Baal priests stood defiantly at the King's Gate, halted by the Temple guards, who refused them entry. Boasting their white priestly garb, bare feet, and shaved heads, they didn't come with a sin sacrifice, as their abba had earlier this morning. Instead, they stood aloof, protected by the Carites at the threshold of Yahweh's Temple while King Jehoram again stood on the upper porch to watch Amariah's sacrifice. Their unrepentant presence was an affront to Yahweh, His Temple, and His servants.

Jehoiada claimed a dark corner of the inner court, brooding, watching the evening sacrifice from afar. How could God forgive a king who had sinned so grievously? What if Amariah's prediction came true—which, of course, it never would—and Jehoiada became Judah's high priest? On the Day of Atonement, he would be expected to act as intercessor for *all* of Judah, transferring the sins of the nation to a single, sacrificial animal—a scapegoat. Could he, in good conscience, ever ask Yahweh to forgive people as utterly unworthy as Jehoram—and even his sons?

Another reason I can never be high priest.

The evening service ended, and Jehoiada lingered in the shadows, watching the king rejoin his sons and file out of the main gate with the straggling worshipers. When faithful Eleazar locked the last Temple gate, Jehoiada wandered over to one of the ten bronze lavers and washed the blood from the day's slaughters from his arms. He would help refill the ten basins with fresh water before helping Amariah remove his priestly garments tonight. His old friend knew him too well and would sense the unrest in his soul. The less time they spent alone, the better. Jehoiada needed a quiet evening, a good night's sleep, and a new day. Hopefully, a day unmarred by so many unanswerable questions.

5

→ 2 Chronicles 15:16 ←

*King Asa also deposed his grandmother Maakah from
her position as queen mother, because she had made a
repulsive image for the worship of Asherah.*

Sheba was still shaking from the evil she'd glimpsed in
Ima Thaliah's eyes at Gideon's Pool of Trembling. The
imminent reunion with Gevirah Jizebaal had awakened
a darkness in Ima that surpassed her typical discipline. After
their so-called bath, Ima returned to the demanding yet loving
woman Sheba knew her to be—with one exception. She insisted
they both wear heavy cosmetics, painting their eyelids with thick
malachite, lining them with kohl, and using red ochre mixed
with fat to redden their lips and cheeks.

"We must look like Phoenician royalty to meet Phoenician
royalty," she said, which Sheba thought odd, since they were
meeting the king and Gevirah of *Israel*—not Phoenicia.

Trumpet blasts from Jezreel's city walls announced their arrival shortly before sunset—a little later than Abba predicted,
but he couldn't have foreseen Gideon's Pool. Sheba kept the curtains of her sedan open, eager to absorb every detail of Jizebaal's
spring palace. She noticed a balcony with direct access to the
eastern city wall. Strange. It didn't seem safe for that chamber's

occupant to sleep so near a wall. Gawking, she craned her neck as her camel passed under the gates but quickly righted herself when she glimpsed kohl-rimmed eyes staring back.

Their procession halted outside a spectacular, pink-hued structure much like the palaces built by the Phoenician King Hiram for David and Solomon. Jezreel's royal residence was smaller, of course, but boasted the same four-pillared entry and grand stairway leading to double-cedar doors. Fully armored Israelites waited to usher the Judean delegation into the audience hall, but Ima Thaliah halted them in the entry, determined to perfect their appearance before meeting Gevirah Jizebaal.

She fluffed her own fox-fur collar before straightening Hazi's jeweled crown. She untied and retied the sash on Sheba's linen gown, dyed a deep purple with the rare shellfish found only in Tyrian waters. Finally, Mattan's freshly shaved head drew special attention to his high priestly appearance, which was accented by his golden turban and an embroidered stole suspended from his left shoulder by a jeweled broach. After a last glance at her charges, Ima Thaliah offered an approving nod, signaling the guards to open the double doors.

Sheba felt as if she'd swallowed a hornet's nest, and the buzzing in Jezreel's grand audience hall didn't settle her nerves one bit. In a room large enough to hold four sailing ships, King Joram—or Ram, as Ima Thaliah called him—sat on a gilded throne, scepter in one hand, Gevirah Jizebaal's hand in the other. The great lady sat on a second throne of equal height and grandeur, her kohl-rimmed eyes fixed on Sheba.

A huge soldier stood behind the royal pair. Probably Jehu, the general of Israel's troops. Sheba was suddenly grateful Mattan had quizzed her mercilessly on the political and economic climate of bordering nations—including the names of top-ranking military officers of their nearest neighbors. From the stories she'd heard of Jehu, he was ruthless, having taken harsh but necessary measures of discipline on his own people during Samaria's siege. His metal-studded breastpiece and armor, the deep scars on his face, and his watchful eyes certainly made a frightening impression.

The Judean delegation waited at the doorway until a handsome steward announced their arrival. "May it please our mighty king and worthy Gevirah to receive Queen Athaliah of Judah; Prince Ahaziah and Princess Jehosheba, children of Jehoram; and Mattan, Judah's high priest of Baal Melkart." He bowed slightly. "They come as envoys of the house of David, bearing gifts that affirm Judah's ongoing treaty with the house of Ahab and Jizebaal."

The four honored Judeans began their slow procession up the red woolen carpet as servants pulled a four-wheeled cart of copper behind them. Ima Thaliah stopped at the edge, where the tile began, two camel lengths from the double thrones. "A gift from my husband, King Jehoram of Judah," she said, directing all attention to the cart. "It is the finest copper from the mines of Edom—a people who rebelled against Judah as Moab rebelled against Israel. We've come to discuss these weighty matters with King Ram and his honored Gevirah."

Those in the gallery gasped, but Ima offered a mischievous grin before she knelt and placed her nose where the carpet met marble tile. Sheba realized she was the only one standing and felt Hazi yank her down beside him. Mattan had fallen to his knees on the other side of Queen Athaliah. Feeling as awkward as a three-legged camel, she buried her nose in the worn woolen rug, waiting in uncomfortable silence.

Nothing. More silence.

If this was to be a political visit, why had Ima spoken instead of Hazi? Was the king offended? Whispers fluttered across the gallery, and then nervous chatter.

Sheba didn't dare look up but furtively scanned to her left and right. The palace furnishings were distinctly Phoenician, the inlaid metalwork and carvings exquisite. But on closer inspection, she noticed scuffed corners, chipped ivory, and worn tapestries. Even the spectators appeared somewhat worn-out. Thin and frail, the onlookers seemed as nervous as Sheba felt.

"You may rise, my daughter," a smooth female voice purred, "and those with you as well."

The Judeans stood in a row, Mattan on Ima Thaliah's left,

then Hazi and Sheba on his right. Gevirah Jizebaal remained the spokesperson in King Ram's court and kept her eyes firmly fixed on Sheba. "We accept the gracious gift and will address political concerns momentarily. First, let me make you more comfortable." Turning to the steward, she said, "Bring two couches, and dismiss everyone except the seventy princes of Ahab and their guardians."

The room burst into activity, servants scurrying, crowd stirring, some leaving, while members of Ahab's clan vied for the best view of their Judean cousins. Sheba looked to Ima Thaliah for etiquette and noted her hands folded in front, head in a reverent bow. Sheba followed her example, keeping a watchful eye should the occasion call for a quick revision.

The servants delivered the couches. Ima Thaliah took her place on the first, but as Hazi directed Sheba toward the second, Gevirah Jizebaal announced, "The couches are for Ahab's family only, young woman."

The audience chamber fell silent, and Sheba gasped, glancing first at Ima and then at the Gevirah. How could this woman publicly flaunt the fact that she wasn't Athaliah's blood? Humiliated, she moved behind the couch and offered the seat to Hazi. He furtively reached back, offering his hand for comfort. Mattan stood behind Ima.

Jizebaal seemed unwilling to let the matter die. "You're not *really* my Thali's daughter, are you? You're one of Jehoram's children from a Judean wife, and my Thali raised you as her own when your ima died. Isn't that correct . . . what is your name—Beersheba, is it?"

"No. I mean, yes. I mean . . ." Angry tears stung Sheba's eyes, and she turned to Ima Thaliah for help—direction of any kind. Ima glared over her shoulder, offering nothing but warning. Sheba must face Gevirah alone. *No tears. Ima Thaliah detests tears.*

Breathing deeply, she calmed herself and lifted her chin. "You are correct, Gevirah Jizebaal. I am the daughter of King Jehoram, adopted by Queen Athaliah." Her voice grew stronger as she spoke. "And my name is Princess Jehosheba."

A slight grin creased King Ram's lips. He leaned over and whispered something in the Gevirah's ear—who ignored him *and* Sheba. Jizebaal redirected her attention to Ima Thaliah. "Since only Ahab's princes remain in the gallery"—she motioned for the guards to close the doors, locking out any stragglers—"we will continue our political discussion. Go ahead, my son. As king of Israel, you should lead the discussion."

"Why, thank you, Ima." Clearly amused, King Ram left his throne, causing his bodyguard to scurry from the dais and Ima Thaliah and Hazi to spring off their couches in a respectful bow. The king grasped Ima Thaliah's shoulders, drawing her into an embrace. "Shalom, Thali. It's good to see you."

Ima lingered in her brother's hug, and a puddle of tears formed under her lashes. *Ima's crying?* Sheba tried to remember if she'd ever seen the queen shed real tears. A few contrived drops when manipulation called for it, but never real emotion.

Israel's king whispered in his sister's ear, and she nodded—secrets shared between siblings. He finally released her and said with a mocking tone, "You look awful! What have they done to you in Judah?"

Uneasy laughter fluttered in the gallery of princes. Those dressed in royal robes ranged from toddlers to late teens. Though called princes of Ahab, they had to be Ram's children—King Ahab had been dead for eleven years. But could all seventy belong to King Ram?

Ima shoved his shoulder, as she'd done with Hazi at the pool. "Just because you've doubled the size of Israel with your own sons doesn't mean you can insult the queen of Judah." Sheba suddenly saw Hazi's reflection in Uncle Ram and realized why Ima had always favored her youngest son. The king kissed Ima's forehead, and she removed a linen cloth from her belt, repairing the smeared kohl around her eyes.

King Ram returned to his throne, his bodyguard seemingly relieved to be finished with the nonsense. Ram clapped his hands, the sudden noise jostling the Gevirah's crown. "I've got an idea! Let's have the Gevirah, Thali, and Jehosheba retire to Ima Jizebaal's chamber while I get to know my nephew and introduce him to my sons." He met the Gevirah's threatening stare and leaned forward, addressing Hazi in a mock whisper. "Though I'm supposed to call them the seventy princes of Ahab since I'm Abba's only living heir. Ima thought we should honor him with *my* offspring."

"Ram!" the Gevirah huffed.

But he continued without pause. "And I'll confess to Mattan that I destroyed the Baal temple and stone in Samaria. It was a political move, really. Perhaps he can explain why Yahweh's prophets are winning the hearts of my people. Is it punishment from Baal or simply because Yahweh is more powerful?"

Jizebaal stared at him so intensely Sheba felt the heat. "Take care, my son, how you speak about almighty Baal Melkart."

Ignoring her, Ram tapped his cheek, feigning bewilderment. "Thali, didn't one of Judah's kings depose his Gevirah because she made an Asherah pole? I mean, she'll always be my ima, but she needn't have any official pow—"

Jizebaal slammed her hand on her armrest. "Come, Thali! And bring the girl." She stormed past Ram without a bow, turning her back on Israel's regent—a serious breach in decorum.

Ima Thaliah issued a silent reprimand to her brother as she hurried to catch up, and Sheba followed both women through an ivory-inlaid door, wishing she could stay and chat with the men.

6

*Joram son of Ahab became king of Israel. . . . He did evil
in the eyes of the LORD, but not as his father and mother
had done. He got rid of the sacred stone of Baal that his
father had made.*

Nearly running, Sheba rushed with Jizebaal and Ima
down a long corridor lined with heavy tapestries—a
sea of faded glory. Waves of heavy, woven rugs, drap-
eries, and wall hangings bespoke a waning elegance reflected
in the great Jizebaal herself. When Ahab died, the queen was
given the title *Gevirah*—ima of the king. It was a title of grace
and respect but implied her diminishing authority. Jizebaal had
accepted the relegation as clumsily as Sheba rode her camel.

The three women arrived at ornately carved cedar doors,
where two guards bowed to their mistress and opened without
so much as a nod. The soldiers' attire combined Israelite armor
and Phoenician-curled hair under leather helmets. Inside the
chamber were ten eunuchs who immediately dropped to their
knees, foreheads on the floor, hands extended forward.

The Gevirah stepped over them as if they were stones in her
path on her way to an open-door balcony. "Do you see how
Ram treats me, Thali? It's intolerable!"

Ima Thaliah followed her to an ivory-inlaid ebony couch on the balcony overlooking the city wall. "Ram loves to show off, Ima. I'll talk with him." Thaliah settled on the couch beside the Gevirah and with her eyes directed Sheba to a goatskin rug in front of them.

The eunuchs resumed their duties in the large divided chamber. Behind a partially drawn curtain, three eunuchs fluffed pillows and brushed furs that covered an enormous wool-stuffed mattress. In the larger chamber connected to the balcony, the remaining servants busied themselves straightening cosmetics, sewing garments, and weaving extraordinary patterns of Tyrian purple fabric. Sheba returned her attention to the women before her but kept her eyes averted. They seemed to be in a world of their own, and Sheba didn't wish to intrude.

"Thali, my darling, why can't Ram be as pliable as your husband? If kings would simply leave the gods to their queens, nations would function much more smoothly." Jizebaal's demeanor had calmed, and she seemed content with leisurely conversation about trivial matters. Perhaps they'd discuss hennaed nails or scented oils next. Sheba inhaled the crisp country air, finally relaxing a little after the events at Gideon's Pool.

"My lord Ahab always left the gods to me," Jizebaal was saying. "He only interfered when we named you children, insisting that I add *Yahweh* or *Jehovah* to your names: Athal*iah*, Ahaz*iah*, *Jo*ram. But I've never called you by those names, have I? You've been Thali, Hazi, and Ram all your lives." She brushed her daughter's cheek, a loving gesture Ima Thaliah had offered Sheba countless times. The Gevirah cradled Ima Thaliah's hand, patting it gently. "I'm glad you named your son after your brother Hazi. I know I complained about Hazi's ability to reign after your abba Ahab died, but Ram is even worse."

Ima Thaliah jerked her hand away, eyes flashing. "You will *not* rid the throne of Ram as you disposed of Hazi."

Sheba's mouth went dry. What was Ima Thaliah saying? Sheba had been only a little girl when King Hazi died after a year on Israel's throne. She remembered reports that he'd fallen through his lattice-covered bedchamber window from the second story. Surely no ima would have . . .

The Gevirah locked eyes with Ima Thaliah. "I only do what's necessary to maintain a lasting legacy, Thali—as will you." Softening her features, she reached for Ima's hand again, this time with a crushing grip. "And, of course, I would never hurt any of my children. But Ram's unpredictable behavior *is* part of the reason I've changed our plan for your little Jehosheba."

Sheba swallowed hard at the mention of her name. Ima Thaliah's tone remained calm, but Sheba saw her stiffen. "What about Sheba's years of training to become the first presiding high priestess? She's only weeks from her initiation at the Awakening Festival." Crimson rose on Ima's neck.

Sheba's heart raced at the familiar warning. Instinctively, she pulled her knees up, hugging her legs close as a barrier.

"Sit like a queen, Sheba!" Ima slapped her, quick as lightning. "Or you will stand like a pauper until you can stand no longer."

"Forgive me, Ima." Sheba quickly knelt and delicately centered herself on folded legs, rearranging her fine linen robe. Chin lifted. Eyes forward. Pleasant smile. Cheek on fire. The queens resumed their discussion.

"As I was saying," the Gevirah nearly purred, deepening the creases around her lips, "Sheba, as you call her, will fulfill a new role in the plan my father, the great King Eth-Baal, passed on to me. We will continue to expand inland the Phoenician heritage and the worship of Baal Melkart." For the first time she turned her black eyes on Sheba. "Has Thali taught you of our Phoenician heritage?"

Sheba shot a panicked glance at Ima Thaliah. Of course Ima and Mattan had instructed her on Phoenicia . . . and Aram, Assyria, Egypt, Philistia, Cush, Edom, and every other nation of political or economic importance to Judah. A slight nod from Ima gave Sheba permission to speak.

"Phoenicia's cities have been assaulted by greedy nations for centuries, all eager to steal seafaring secrets and tactical ports. Your marriage to King Ahab was different than other treaty marriages, however, by benefiting both nations equally. Israel gained access to Phoenicia's seaports, and Phoenicia traded freely for Israel's rich agricultural products—grain and livestock.

The treaty was unique in one other way—you, Gevirah, since you weren't the typical treaty bride, but rather Tyre's delegate on Israel's soil, educated as a Baal priestess."

The Gevirah clapped her hands and cackled like an old hen. "Thali, she *is* marvelous! Is she as capable in languages and ritual arts?"

Ima Thaliah offered Sheba an approving wink before answering. "She speaks Egyptian, Hebrew, and Phoenician fluently, and she writes all three equally well. Sheba has shown great promise in magical arts. Mattan reports that her ability at reading omens rivals his own."

The Gevirah's kohl-rimmed eyes narrowed to slits, studying Sheba as if she herself were an omen. She clapped again, summoning her chief eunuch. "Bring me a goblet of water and a flask of oil. We'll prove the girl's skill."

Sheba felt the tension ease from her shoulders. She excelled at readings. If this was the only test, she'd easily be found worthy.

The eunuch placed the goblet and flask before her, and the Gevirah poured a little oil into the water. Sheba inhaled deeply, closed her eyes, and exhaled. "Almighty Prince Baal, Rider of the Clouds, speak!"

When she opened her eyes, she noted both queens had joined her on the rug, their heads bent over the goblet with hers. "I see two nations, harassed on every side," Sheba said, interpreting two large globs of oil with smaller bubbles bumping against them. When the two larger drops of oil combined, the now-single dollop clung to the side of the goblet. A shiver worked its way up Sheba's spine as she slowly met the curious expressions of the queens.

"What is it, Sheba?" Ima asked. "I haven't done a reading in years. I've forgotten the art."

Jizebaal stirred, maneuvering her old bones back to the couch. When she was finally settled, Ima Thaliah beside her again, the Gevirah challenged Sheba. "I haven't forgotten the art, Sheba. I know what that reading tells us. Do you?"

Sheba swallowed her hesitation. "Two nations harassed on every side come together as one—but there will be disaster in the morning." She saw approval in both women's eyes—and dread.

"You've proven yourself, Sheba," Jizebaal said with a slight grin. "Now, let me explain your reading in more detail. King Ahab and King Jehoshaphat built both Israel and Judah into world powers, but their heirs are squandering the two nations. Neither Ram nor your abba Jehoram is strong enough to rule, so it is the destiny of queens to reunite Israel and Judah into one nation, to be ruled by one king—and its people will worship our almighty Baal Melkart."

Reunite Israel and Judah? One king? This was treason!

"What about the disaster in the morning?" Sheba voiced her only safe question.

Ima intervened. "With every exchange of power, there is bloodshed, Sheba. This is the destiny of queens I mentioned to you in the Pool of Trembling. Concentrate on the honor the Gevirah has bestowed on you, Daughter. Your name will be remembered with ours as women who influenced history, shaped nations, and ruled kingdoms."

Ruled kingdoms? These women were insane! They actually thought themselves rulers.

Ima's black eyes glinted like polished obsidian. "What do you say to such an honor, Jehosheba?"

Sheba stared back—two women, identical but for the deep wrinkles creasing the Gevirah's face. "How will you reunite the nations, and who will be the king?" From the dangerous squint of Ima's eyes, her response was less than pleasing.

But Gevirah's tone seemed rather cheerful. "Let's review the kings enthroned at present, little Sheba, and perhaps *you* can decide who we'll choose."

Ima Thaliah squeezed her eyes shut. Trouble.

Jizebaal prattled on. "Your abba Jehoram has done everything Thali has told him to do. He killed his brothers, made Thali's sons governors in their places, and holds his nephews captive to ensure no retribution from other relatives. He even made Baal worship mandatory on every high place in Judah. His only mistake was almost getting himself killed during Edom's rebellion."

She leveled her gaze, all playfulness gone, and a warning shofar sounded in Sheba's mind as the Gevirah ground out the words. "My son Ram, on the other hand, has lost Moab's tribute, and Samaria wallows in ruin after a yearlong siege. The Yahweh prophet Elisha increases in popularity and fancies himself a statesman, healing Aram's leprous commander—the very man who shot my lord Ahab." Without warning, she lunged off the couch and grabbed Sheba's throat, strangling, hovering over her with a rasping voice. "Who should be king of our new nation, little Sheba? Do you dare instruct—"

"Ima, enough!" Thaliah shoved the Gevirah away, and Sheba skittered backward from the lunatic woman.

Shaking violently, Sheba rubbed her neck and then looked down at her trembling fingers. Bloody. Her neck burned where the Gevirah's fingernails had left their marks. No wonder so many in Judah called her Jezebel, "pile of dung." Jizebaal had clearly earned her enemies.

"Hazi!" the Gevirah hissed. "Your brother Hazi will be king as soon as we clear the thrones, you stupid camel."

Sheba's heart nearly stopped, and she felt herself grow pale. "What do you mean, 'clear the thrones'?" She glanced over her shoulder at the eunuchs in the room. None of them seemed bothered by the treason being discussed.

Jizebaal must have noticed her concern. "Are you worried about the servants' discretion?" She clapped her hands and motioned over two eunuchs carrying trays—one with olives and cheese, the other with three wine goblets. Both knelt and placed their trays on the tiled floor. "Open your mouths," the Gevirah commanded.

They obeyed, staring aimlessly beyond Sheba's left shoulder. She gasped and looked away. No tongues.

Jizebaal pointed to the other servants in her chamber. "None of them can write or speak. I trust them completely because I control them completely. It's the only way to ensure unquestioning obedience."

Ima Thaliah's words echoed in the corners of Sheba's mind. *If you ever disobey me, you'll wish I had drowned you in Gideon's Pool of Trembling.* She shuddered at the memory.

"Are you cold, my dear?" Jizebaal purred. "You are farther

north than you're accustomed to." The Gevirah straightened her robe, seeming to have wholly regained her composure. "How long have you spent training to be a Baal priestess, Sheba?" She picked at a snag on her blue silk scarf, docile as a lamb.

Resettled on her knees, Sheba placed her trembling hands in her lap and tried to ignore her stinging neck. "Ima Thaliah began my training when I was five, and I've served Prince Baal in thirteen Awakening Festivals."

"Your training is a testimony to the patience instilled into Thali as a queen of destiny. Unlike kings, who lead armies into battle and kill thousands for a quick victory, queens of destiny shape nations with our wits, and we only sacrifice a few lives as it becomes necessary." The Gevirah turned a foreboding glare at her daughter. "If my son Ram changes, grows more respectful, he could reign in Israel for years." Returning her attention to Sheba, she leaned forward and whispered, "And if you perform your duties well, perhaps your abba Jehoram will keep his throne until we've prepared Hazi to unite our nations peacefully."

Sheba swallowed a lump the size of Mount Hermon. Abba's life depended on her success? "And what are *my* duties?"

Jizebaal shifted her attention to Athaliah. "How well has Sheba learned Astarte's seductive arts?"

Ima Thaliah's neck burst into a deep shade of crimson that undoubtedly matched Sheba's cheeks. "She was training as a high priestess, so Mattan and I didn't concentrate on perfecting those skills."

"Sheba need not be Astarte to become the wife of Yahweh's high priest. I believe she'll accomplish more with whispers in the dark than we could manage with daggers in the daylight."

Sheba's vision suddenly darkened—both queens sitting at the end of a long, black tunnel. A loud roar muted all other noise. *Am I dying? By the gods, I hope so.*

While she blinked and gasped for breath, Jizebaal detailed the plan. "It's my understanding that when Yahweh's priest Amariah dies, the remaining priests will choose a new leader—probably a younger man—to serve for a full generation. That's when Thali will convince Jehoram to arrange your marriage." She paused, leaned closer to Sheba, and inspected her. "Thali, she looks ill. Maybe you should explain how an influential marriage works. Perhaps she doesn't understand."

Something inside Sheba broke, snapped, and spewed anger without thought of consequence. "How am I going to *influence* a man I've never met, or worship a god I care nothing about? I have no intention of learning Yahweh's rituals and traditions. I've prepared my whole life to become Baal's high priestess! How can you ask me to—"

"We're not asking. Don't you understand?" Ima Thaliah was suddenly shaking her, fingers digging into her arms. "You must calm down. Don't make me hurt you. It will be your fault if I must hurt you."

The threat was familiar. She'd heard it since she was a little girl. Tears were prohibited. Fear was forbidden. Excitement was for the ill-mannered. And in that moment Sheba realized—Gideon's Pool wasn't any different from a thousand threats before it. She had simply grown old enough to realize what she could lose.

The Gevirah chuckled as she watched Sheba's control return. "Women have few choices in life, little Sheba. At least as a queen of destiny, you'll have more privileges than most."

Ima released her iron grip on Sheba and turned a cold stare on Jizebaal. "Just tell her what you expect of her. Explain to us *both* how Sheba's marriage to Yahweh's high priest will benefit our unified nations better than her service as high priestess." Sarcasm dripped from Ima's words, and Sheba felt some vindication when she remained beside her on the rug.

Gevirah Jezebel leaned forward, pinning Sheba with a stare, ignoring Ima Thaliah. "Years ago, good King Jehoshaphat thought he created a Judean court system that would protect the Yahweh faithful after he died. The narrow-minded Yahweh high priest makes all rulings regarding Solomon's Temple, and a high-ranking civil leader decides matters concerning the king. Understand?"

Sheba nodded.

"When you marry Yahweh's high priest, you'll influence him to be, shall we say, *tolerant* of new styles of worship in Judah. He need not turn his back on Yahweh to be useful. He need only invite other gods into Solomon's Temple. We'll also install Mattan as the civil leader in central court, and by these gentle changes we'll unite Israel and Judah in policy and in worship, preparing them to crown a single king when the time is right."

When the time is right? Sheba's thoughts raced. How much time would they give her to influence her new husband? Abba Jehoram was a relatively young man, but it might take years . . . She would rather dance on broken pottery than ask this question, but better to address her fear now than fail in Jerusalem and be responsible for an assassin in Abba's chamber. "What if . . . what if my attempts at Astarte's seductions fail to influence Yahweh's high priest? What if my skills are inadequate—since I wasn't trained specifically as an Astarte priestess?"

The Gevirah's gaze softened as if coaxing a stray dog to a crust of bread. "The Yahwists are an unbearably stifling lot—their worship allows no dancing, no role playing, and no sacred coupling. By learning Baal's daily rituals, you have the power to . . ." She exchanged a knowing grin with Ima Thaliah. "Let's just say that even the simplest pleasures of Astarte will expand the high priest's narrow mind-set, and he'll soon be touting the benefits of worshiping *all* the gods."

Sheba still had many questions, but one nagging concern remained. "The oil in the goblet foretold disaster in the morning. Do you think it's a general caution—as you said, bloodshed must occur—or could it be a specific warning for tomorrow morning?" Jizebaal's raised brow reflected interest, so Sheba played to her pride. "I would be honored to hear the Gevirah's interpretation."

"Disaster will come unexpectedly if King Ram continues his disrespect."

Sheba gasped, and Ima Thaliah settled a granite gaze on Jizebaal. "If you harm Ram, you are dead to me." Then Ima turned the same stony stare on Sheba. "Disaster will visit your abba Jehoram unless you do as you're told. Do you understand?"

Finding words impossible, Sheba nodded, her mind spinning. Two days ago, Sheba thought Athaliah's love for Abba knew no bounds, and her greatest worry was a ruby earring. She was almost afraid to wake up tomorrow.

7

Now the sons of that wicked woman Athaliah had broken into the temple of God and had used even its sacred objects for the Baals.

Jehoiada lay awake in his bed, listening to the rain patter on the limestone tiles and reviewing today's burnt sacrifices. Six. Two of the animals were offered during the morning and evening services for the whole assembly, the other four by individual worshipers as a sin sacrifice. Were there only four sinners in Judah today? Not likely. *Yahweh, how can Your priests restore vibrant worship and sacrifice to Your Temple?*

Commotion outside his door stole his attention. Strange sounds. Running, and then hushed groans. All of Yahweh's servants were barefoot, but he heard sandals slapping the limestone tile. He and Amariah shared an adjoining chamber built into the Temple wall dividing the inner and outer courts. Their only entrance opened into the priests' courtyard—sacred ground. No one would dare wear sandals in the priests' court.

He rolled off his bed and hurried to the door, pressing his ear against it. An explosion of chaos erupted on the other side. He swung open the heavy cedar panel and stood in stunned horror. Two bodies lay in the courtyard outside, and a young Temple guard met him in the doorway. "Stay in your chamber with the high priest! Protect the high priest!"

The guard tried to push him inside, but Jehoiada was too hulking to be shoved anywhere. "Wait!" He grabbed the guard's collar. "Tell me what's happening!"

"It's a raid on the Temple." He attempted another shove, but this time Jehoiada stepped aside, causing the guard to lose his balance.

"You guard the high priest!" Jehoiada said, pulling the young man inside and shoving him toward Amariah's adjoining door. "You have weapons to protect him, and I'm needed to defend the Holy Place and its furnishings."

The guard steadied himself, hand on sword hilt. "You seem quite capable of defending yourself *and* the high priest. But how will you defend the Holy Place without a weapon?"

"I would never shed blood in Yahweh's Temp—"

"What's going on out here?" Amariah's sleepy countenance fled when he saw the guard.

The young man bowed. "We heard it all began when King Jehoram told his sons about Elijah's letter and removed them from their positions as governors. He'd hoped to stave off God's wrath, but his attempt at restitution merely enraged his sons. They rallied their personal guards to pillage Yahweh's Temple."

"Jehoram's sons are behind this?" Jehoiada didn't wait for the answer. Propelled out the door by righteous rage, he heard Amariah's garbled shout but kept moving. Amariah's forgiving nature wasn't in Yahweh's best interests this time. Jehoram's sons must pay.

Weaving his way through the Temple's inner court, he nearly retched. It looked more like a battlefield than a place of worship. Moonlight and torches revealed the broken bodies of Temple guards and gatekeepers who had given their lives to protect Yahweh's presence. A heavy rain soaked through Jehoiada's robe and mixed with priests' and Levites' shed blood, reddening the tile. Fury built as Jehoiada approached the stairs, where the pillars Jachin and Boaz supported the roof of the Temple porch.

Barely had his foot hit the first step when he heard the sho-

fars—rams' horns blaring from every watchtower of the city.
Jerusalem was under attack.

Impossible! Confused, Jehoiada ascended to the porch—the
highest point in the city—where he could see over Jerusalem's
walls into the valleys on the east, south, and west sides. When he
reached the platform between Jachin and Boaz, his heart nearly
failed him. Baal priests inside Yahweh's Temple! Billowing, white
linen robes and cleanly shaven heads left no doubt of their pagan
allegiance. The wicked delight with which they defiled the sacred
golden objects confirmed they were Jehoram's sons.

Ignoring the shofars and the city, he ran screaming through
the doorway. "How dare you defile the Holy Place of Yahweh!
Get out! You will not—" A blow to his belly sent him to his
knees, gasping for air. An unfamiliar Judean soldier stood over
him, grinning, holding one of the sacred lampstands—a symbol
of God's presence used as a weapon against His priest.

Another blast of the shofars, and the folly inside the Temple
stilled. "What was that?" One of the arrogant princes looked at
Jehoiada and scoffed. "Do you use shofars to call in reinforcements? Our watchmen will just kill the next wave of priests too."

Still gasping, Jehoiada gathered enough breath for a single
threat. "Ask your *watchmen* what the shofars mean."

The other princes halted their celebration, noticing their
brother's concern. "What *do* they mean?"

By now, the watchmen had raced to the doors and stood silent.
They turned to their regents, their faces finally reflecting the
proper fear. "The city is under siege, my lords. It appears those
caravans we passed on our way into the city weren't harmless
Cushites after all."

In a panic, King Jehoram's sons gathered the golden utensils, stuffing anything valuable into the pockets of their priestly
robes. Jehoiada's fury reignited, and with a roar he tackled two
of the princes before their guards could defend them. He felt
the hard, swift blow of a sword hilt to his head and staggered
back, landing near the table of showbread. Through a fog, he
watched Jehoram's sons and their watchmen scurry from the
Holy Place like rats into the darkness.

Jehoiada stood on wobbly legs and made his way to the porch, watching archers on the city walls send fiery arrows into the onslaught of an enemy attacking from the south and west. Priests and Levites dotted the Temple's courtyard, ministering to those who'd been injured or killed.

Anger. Fear. Despair. Each emotion warred for dominion.

"Jehoiada! Jehoiada, help!" a familiar voice shouted from the courtyard below.

Scanning the figures in the rain and commotion, he noticed a contingent of men advancing toward the steps, swords extended from both sides and shields held aloft, hiding the identity of those inside the mini cocoon. Jehoiada hurried down the stairs to meet them, and as he drew near . . . *Obadiah? King Jehoram?* The two men were escorted by three hulking soldiers—Carites, the king's mercenary guards—one behind and one on each flank, creating an impenetrable shield around the nobleman and king.

"Jehoiada, it's an invasion!" Obadiah said, breathless. "Hurry, we must hide the king." Jehoram stood silently, shivering between his four saviors, his hair hanging in wet ringlets and dripping with each quake.

For a long moment, Jehoiada, too, was speechless, the irony overwhelming. "You're right, Obadiah. It is an invasion—but not of Jerusalem alone. Would you like to see what the king's sons did to the Holy Place, the lampstands, the table of showbread?"

Obadiah began shaking his head, waving off Jehoiada's protest before he'd finished. "We don't have time for that now. King Jehoram must be saved! Jerusalem is under attack!"

"Yahweh's Temple was under attack by *his sons*!" Jehoiada shouted, advancing toward Jehoram. The Carite guards stepped forward, swords drawn. "Why should I care about this worthless pagan king?"

"We must get the king to safety," one of the Carites said, shoving Jehoiada aside.

"No! Wait! He'll take us to the high priest." Obadiah grabbed Jehoiada's arm and leaned close, whispering, "If Jerusalem falls and King Jehoram dies, a descendant of David will no longer sit on the throne, and Yahweh's Temple will be lost. Do you want to be responsible for breaking the covenant Yahweh made with David? And if we don't save Jehoram, do you want one of Athaliah's pagan sons to reign?" The nobleman released him. "Now take us to Amariah."

Jehoiada glared at the king but surrendered to Obadiah's persistence. This was a decision for the high priest. He turned toward their chamber, leading unholy men on holy ground to let the high priest determine their path. He glanced behind him at the archers—fighting, falling, dying—on Jerusalem's walls. He could barely fathom it. Would the impenetrable city actually fall? No foreign invader had breached Jerusalem's walls since Pharaoh Shishak in the days of Solomon's son Rehoboam.

"Who is attacking us, and how did they invade so quickly?" He threw the question over his shoulder, not caring who answered it.

Obadiah seemed the only one capable of conversing. "First reports say it's the Arabs from Cush who joined with the Philistines, but no one knows for sure."

They reached Jehoiada's chamber and burst inside. The young Levite guard drew his sword and stood between the intruders and Amariah, looking as frightened as a lamb on the altar.

"What is going on?" Amariah aimed his question at Jehoiada while the young man sheathed his sword. Jehoiada's emotions were too frayed to speak rationally, so once again Obadiah answered.

Placing both hands on Amariah's shoulders, he spoke slowly and deliberately. "Listen to me, my friend. The city is under siege. We can hide the king if we act now, but can we also move the Ark of the Covenant?"

"What do you mean, 'move the Ark'?" Jehoiada interrupted. "And why must the *priests* hide the king?"

"Quiet!" the other two men shouted in unison, silencing every breath in the room.

Amariah's answer came quickly. "We must protect the Ark, Obadiah. It is the very presence of Yahweh in our midst."

"I know, my friend, but we believe the Philistines are leading the attack, and considering their past history with the Ark, it's unlikely they would dare touch it—even if they breach our walls." Obadiah's years of diplomacy were evident. "However, if our troops save Jerusalem or somehow recapture the city, we must have a descendant of David to reign and rebuild what we've lost." He stepped back, placing a protective arm around the king's shoulders. "King Jehoram is our first responsibility!"

The high priest massaged his neck, exhaled, then shook his head and looked at Jehoiada. "I'll remain in the Temple, and you accompany Obadiah to hide King Jehoram. You will protect the king with your life."

Jehoiada stared, dumbfounded. "How will *you* defend the Ark? You can barely walk up the stairs. And where will we hide a king?"

One of the Carites joined the argument. "King Jehoram goes nowhere without his bodyguard."

Amariah exchanged a decisive nod with Obadiah, as if the two answered to no one but each other. "Jehoiada, I am the high priest, and you will obey me. Obadiah knows how to hide the king and maintain the safety of the Ark. And as for the king's guard, only one of the Carites may accompany King Jehoram. The fewer people aware of his location, the better. Now go. All of you, go."

Amariah pushed his way through the delegation as if the matter was settled, but the lead Carite clearly had no intention of letting anyone leave until he gave the order. He grabbed the high priest's arm, and Jehoiada lunged at him, ready to fight anyone who threatened his friend and Yahweh's anointed.

The other Carites quickly subdued Jehoiada, and Amariah shouted, "That's enough! We have no time for this nonsense."

The Carite leader released Amariah, commanded Jehoiada's release, and then bowed respectfully. "Please accept my apologies. I merely ask that the high priest wait for my men to accompany him. Give them instruction to take the Ark wherever you like. They will guard it—and you—with their lives." He lifted his head slightly to await Amariah's answer.

"That's a brave offer, but no one may enter the Holy of Holies, let alone touch the Ark and carry it to safety." Amariah exchanged some unspoken message with Obadiah. "Only Yahweh's priests can pass through the pillars of Jachin and Boaz into the Holy Place. I'll stand watch inside, near the golden altar, and you brave Carites may stand between Yahweh's pillars."

"I'll join the Carites," the young Temple guard said, stepping forward to support Amariah's left arm. "But if the raiders breach the pillars, we will enter the Holy Place to defend you—and the Holy of Holies to defend the Ark. I'd rather be stricken for holy zeal than watch Yahweh's Temple or high priest desecrated."

Amariah's eyes shone with unshed tears. "We all walk on holy ground tonight, my sons. It will be Yahweh's will alone that preserves any of us until dawn."

8

The Lord aroused against Jehoram the hostility of the Philistines and of the Arabs who lived near the Cushites.

The Carites and young Temple guard surrounded Amariah and whisked him out the door. Jehoiada turned to Obadiah and kept his voice level, though anger still simmered. "Well? Where are we going?"

The lone Carite glared, equally impatient.

Obadiah ignored the question, grabbed an empty shoulder bag, and started filling it with bread, hard cheese, lamps, wicks, and a flask of oil. "We'll need hooded robes, one for each of us. And you'll need a sword, Jehoiada." He stopped packing and aimed a grin at the second priest. "Do you even know how to use a sword, my friend?"

"I've never been *trained* to use one, if that's what you mean." Jehoiada stormed into Amariah's room to gather the robes, offended that Obadiah would point out his limited experience. He wasn't a gatekeeper, he was second to the high priest.

From the adjoining room, he heard the Carite chuckle. "If we put a sword in that big priest's hand, only someone very foolish or very brave will cross him."

Jehoiada returned, tossing robes at the three waiting men.

The Carite's grin was friendly, not superior, putting Jehoiada at ease. "I suppose if we're going to risk our lives together, I should know your name."

"I'm Zev." The Carite bowed slightly.

Jehoiada returned the polite gesture. "My name is Jehoiada, and I'll get a sword from one of the Temple guards in the courtyard on our way to . . ." He raised his brow at Obadiah, who had already donned his robe and was helping King Jehoram with his.

"I don't have time to explain." The nobleman pulled his hood over his head, and the other men hurried to do the same. Jehoiada glimpsed King Jehoram's pale features and saw him wince as Obadiah cradled his shoulders, leading him like an old woman out the door. "Keep your swords hidden unless you need them," Obadiah whispered over his shoulder.

They hugged the wall along the rainy courtyard. From the shadows, Jehoiada recognized one of his Levite guards, who was understandably startled by the four shrouded figures approaching.

"It's me!" Jehoiada raised his hood slightly when the guard drew his weapon. "Don't ask any questions. Just give me your sword and continue helping the wounded. If the city falls, get as many of the sacred articles out of the Temple as you can." To his credit, the Levite silently offered up his sword, his expression mirroring Jehoiada's fear and confusion.

"This way!" Obadiah looped King Jehoram's right arm around his neck, led them through the Temple's Sur Gate, and nearly ran toward the northern city gate.

Suddenly realizing their destination, Jehoiada cast a questioning glance at Zev. "We can't exit the Sheep Gate in the middle of a siege!"

Obadiah ignored them, continuing his intrepid path.

A few cubits before they reached the gate, Zev leapt in front of the nobleman. "Stop! You're not taking the king out of the city!"

"The entrance to the quarry is along a narrow path outside the northern wall." Obadiah kept his voice low, motioning to the guards in the watchtower above. King Jehoram moaned, and

Obadiah alternated glances between the king and his stubborn escorts. "He's getting worse. Please! We must hurry."

Zev looked to Jehoiada as if testing the trust of an ally. Jehoiada wasn't sure why they'd formed this tenuous bond, but the Carite seemed genuine. Jehoiada measured the king's growing discomfort and pinned Obadiah with a stare. "First, tell us how you know about this quarry." When the nobleman drew breath to protest, the priest folded his arms and planted himself beside Zev. "We will have answers before taking one more step."

"All right! King Solomon used foreign slaves—corvée—to quarry the limestone beneath Mount Moriah and build the Temple. Yahweh warned Solomon that Israel's idolatry would someday force Him to punish His people and demolish the Temple. Solomon believed God, and by destroying all record of the quarry and sealing its entrances, he hoped to secure a hiding place for the Ark when God's judgment fell. The only ones to know of the quarry's existence from generation to generation have been Yahweh's high priests."

"Then how do *you* know?" Jehoiada asked the nobleman.

"And why couldn't the king know?" King Jehoram spoke his first slurred words, and Jehoiada readied a biting reply—until he realized the drops running down the king's face were perspiration, not rain. Jehoram was suffering severely.

"I know of the quarry," Obadiah confessed, "because Amariah asked me to hide the prophet Eliezer there after he issued the Lord's scathing message against King Jehoshaphat."

Jehoiada remembered Eliezer's prophecy—only one of two times Jehoshaphat had earned Yahweh's displeasure. "All right," he said, nodding to the Carite. "Let's find this secret quarry."

Zev returned the nod and then glanced over his shoulder at the southern slopes of Jerusalem. "The enemy is approaching from the west and southwest. I'll tell the watchmen at the gate that we're escaping with King Jehoram to a caravan I've arranged—that we're taking him to a northern fortified city."

Zev disappeared into the watchtower, leaving Jehoiada and Obadiah supporting the ailing king. Within moments, the heavy iron gate opened and Zev returned, helping Jehoiada shoulder

Jehoram's weight so Obadiah could lead them on a muddy path along the city wall.

"Please, I must stop," the king whispered.

"We can't stop," Zev said. "We're too close to the gate, and there's no cover to hide us if the marauders should circle north." Looking to Obadiah, he whispered, "How much farther to the quarry entrance?"

"Not far."

Jehoiada noticed a foul odor and scanned the area of mostly undeveloped hill country. But the smell was distinctly human. "We're too far north to smell the Dung Gate, and the northerly wind isn't strong enough to carry the odor. Where is that stench coming from?"

Obadiah stopped, turned, and offered the king a pitiful look. "Oh, my lord, I'm so sorry. I didn't know your condition had worsened so quickly."

Head bowed, King Jehoram hung limp between Zev and Jehoiada. "Just keep going, Obadiah. According to Elijah, my *condition* is going to do nothing but worsen."

Obadiah met Jehoiada's gaze, eyes glistening. "The entrance is just behind those rocks and brambles. There's a pool inside where we can clean him and refresh ourselves."

Jehoiada shared a glance with Zev. What did the Carite think of Judah's king and Yahweh's judgment? Obadiah wanted to protect King Jehoram from foreign invaders, and Amariah had commanded Jehoiada to do so. But who would protect the king from Yahweh's judgment? And did Jehoiada even wish to try?

Dread robbed Sheba's first night's sleep in Jezreel. Disaster in the morning, the oil and water foretold. What could it mean? When the moonlight streamed through her window nearly as bright as noonday, she gave up all attempts at slumber and knelt before the life-sized clay teraphim beside her bed. She'd forgotten to pack her own Asherah and was forced to bow before Jizebaal's ancestral god. Perhaps if Sheba divined the secrets of the underworld, she could prepare for whatever disaster lay ahead.

But the teraphim proved as cantankerous as the Gevirah. No divination proved conclusive. Blood did not congeal at any decisive location, nor was the anointing oil diverted by unseen cracks. The teraphim's only definitive effects were left in dark circles beneath Sheba's eyes that her maids had worked since dawn to mask with heavy cosmetics.

"Should I braid your hair today, my lady, or will you wear it loose under your head covering?" One of the maids brushed her hair while another worked scented oils into her feet. A third had almost finished applying the malachite and kohl to her eyes when a loud knock sounded on her door.

Sheba inhaled a strengthening breath, certain it was Ima Thaliah, uncertain she was ready for the battles to begin this early in the morning. "Open the door." She flicked her wrist at Jizebaal's eunuch, a gift from the Gevirah. This one still had his tongue—an indication of his purpose. *You two-faced spy.* She remained utterly still, hoping the maids would finish her cosmetics quicker. She mustn't keep the Gevirah waiting.

Her handmaids let out prim gasps, and Sheba sensed someone approaching. Ready to offer a casual greeting, she opened one eye. "Hazi!" She bolted off the couch and into his arms.

He grabbed her waist and swung her around as he'd done since they were children. Then, planting her feet on the floor, he burst into laughter.

"What?" Sheba stomped her foot, feigning a pout.

He signaled to one of the handmaids for the mirror and held it in front of her, revealing a random streak of kohl from her eyelid past her brow to the edge of her hairline. Evidence of her startled maid's hand. Sheba cast a blazing glare and every maid fell to her knees, face to the tiles, hands extended.

Hazi retrieved a cloth from one of their hands, spit on it, turned her chin, and wiped away the damage. "The Gevirah wears heavy kohl, but I think this might be a little much."

Sheba pounded his iron stomach, and he flinched, chuckling. "What are you doing here?" she asked. Then, realizing Jizebaal's eunuch was laid out on the floor beside her maids, she amended her question. "Why don't we go out to the balcony and enjoy a breath of morning air?" She slipped her hand inside Hazi's elbow, led him to the balcony, and started to pull the lattice door closed on the eunuch who had followed them. When he protested, she interrupted. "Would you please bring dates, goat cheese, and bread. My brother is always hungry." She shoved him back inside, closed the lattice door, and locked it.

Hazi still held the cloth in his hand and looked a little confused. "What was that about?"

The tears she'd held back since yesterday suddenly breached their dam, words rushing out on a torrent of sobs. "They won't let me be a high priestess, but I don't want to marry Yahweh's high priest. What if I can't influence him because I was never trained as an Astarte priestess? And why can't women make choices *plus* enjoy privileges?" She buried her head on his shoulder, emotions forming her pleas more than reason. Her big brother had always been her best friend, and she told him everything—but no more. Revealing the Gevirah's detailed plans could endanger him.

When her crying ebbed, she wiped her eyes and was startled to find Hazi staring at her, something undefinable in his gaze. "Don't let them take your heart, Sheba. They'll try, but don't let them."

Was it fear? Anger? Desperation? Whatever it was, his reaction frightened her more than anything the Gevirah had said. Instead of melting into his arms, she turned away. "What? What do you mean?" She would do anything to guard their relationship, so she forced a giggle. "No one will ever have my heart but you, Brother. You know that." She stood at the balcony railing, gripping it as though it were a lifeline.

Hazi spun her around to face him, digging his fingers into her flesh. "Don't treat me like an imbecile. I know Ima threatened you at Gideon's Pool. I don't know what she and the Gevirah told you in private chambers, but I know this, Sheba. Ima tries to own you. She'll steal everything that's precious—and destroy it—if you let her." He released her, and his tone softened with his gaze. "But she can't take away your ability to love, little sister. Don't let her take that—from *us*."

Her throat too tight to speak, Sheba fell into his arms, thanking the gods for someone who knew her struggle without explanation. "I love you, Hazi." As they held each other, silence spoke what their words couldn't.

Ferocious pounding rattled the balcony doors, and then a key in the outer lock. Sheba roared her frustration. "How dare you—"

Ima Thaliah stood like a sacred stone—immovable—inspecting Sheba's red-rimmed eyes, Hazi's sober countenance. "You must have heard already." Without waiting for an answer, she marched onto the balcony, returned the key to the chamber guard, and began shouting orders. "Close the door and stand watch." Turning to her children, she demanded, "Tell me how you two found out before I heard the news!"

Sheba shot a puzzled glance at Hazi, fear and confusion rendering her speechless.

"We don't know much, Ima," Hazi said, playing coy. "Tell us what you've heard."

"The only certainty right now is that the Philistines and Arabs have invaded Jerusalem, but the walls still stand. Ram is speaking with General Jehu, and they're considering sending Israelite troops to help."

Sheba hurried to the balcony railing, hiding her shock from Ima Thaliah.

"I should never have left Jerusalem." Hazi's voice sounded tortured. "I must ready the Carites to return home. You and Sheba can remain here—"

Sheba turned, ready to protest, and saw Ima frantically embrace her son. "You will stay here with us, Hazi! If your abba is dead, we'll send messengers to Judah's fortified cities and crown one of your older brothers as king." Awkward silence followed her outburst. Seeming almost embarrassed by her emotions, she released him, straightened her rumpled robe, and returned to her stony countenance.

"What do you mean, if Abba is dead?" Sheba tried to staunch her tears, but this terrifying possibility on top of yesterday's barbaric revelations . . .

"You are a princess of Judah, Sheba—and now a queen of destiny. Act like it." The utter disgust in Ima's reprimand slapped her as surely as a physical blow. Judah's queen turned her attention to Hazi. "Right now, our best strategy is to remain in Jezreel until we know Jerusalem's standing—and that's the end of the matter."

Hazi trembled with barely controlled rage.

Please, Hazi. Don't make trouble here. Sheba remembered the Gevirah's glowing report of Hazi's pliability. It was the only thing keeping him alive.

He rolled his shoulders back, straightened his spine, and then inhaled before offering Ima an exaggerated bow. "If I am dismissed, General Athaliah, I would like to confer with *King Ram* and his commander. Perhaps I can arrange the menu for our midday meal—unless you'd like to decide that too." Without waiting for a reply, he marched away and slammed the lattice door—and Sheba's chamber door beyond.

Ima Thaliah turned to Sheba, lifting a single eyebrow. "He needn't bother with the menu. We're having roast lamb with lentils and garlic."

Sheba's heart twisted. Could she really be so cold? "Would you stay with me for a while, Ima?" Perhaps a little time together would remind Ima Thaliah of their bond—who they were before they arrived in Jezreel, before the Gevirah issued threats and changed Sheba's future. Maybe time together would remind Ima Thaliah of the love she had for Abba Jehoram.

"Your maids are lazy and undisciplined, Sheba. If you'd commanded them as you should, they would never have allowed Hazi into your chamber before finishing your cosmetics. Now we'll likely be late for our meeting with the Gevirah." She lifted a carefully painted brow. "Take care of your servants, Daughter, or I'll discipline them—and you."

"Yes, Ima." Sheba bowed as Queen Athaliah left the balcony with the same slamming of doors as her son moments before. Tears threatened again, but this time Sheba refused them. She would not suffer weakness—nor would she let herself consider what might be happening in Jerusalem.

9

→ 1 KINGS 18:26, 36, 38–40 ←

Then [the prophets of Baal] called on the name of Baal from morning till noon. "Baal, answer us!" they shouted. But there was no response. . . . Elijah stepped forward and prayed: "O LORD . . . let it be known today that you are God in Israel." Then the fire of the LORD fell and burned up the sacrifice. . . . When all the people saw this, they fell prostrate and cried, "The LORD—he is God! The LORD—he is God!" Then Elijah commanded them, "Seize the prophets of Baal." . . . They seized them, and Elijah had them . . . slaughtered there.

Jehoiada hummed one of the Levite's psalms, trying to block out the incessant sound of water dripping down the quarry walls. They'd set up camp near a pool of crisp, clean water, but King Jehoram's declining condition made it difficult to keep their water clean.

"Obadiah?" King Jehoram stirred, waking after another nap.

"No, it's me, the priest Jehoiada." He picked up the only clay lamp burning and positioned the small circle of light to encompass the king. The quarry ceiling in this area was as lofty as the Temple, a vast chasm at the bottom of a system of divergent tunnels and narrow passageways. Without Obadiah's sharp memory and sense of direction, none of them would have found this quarry, nor would they find their way out.

King Jehoram lay on his side, propped on one elbow, using his now-filthy robe as the only padding between him and the limestone floor. Jehoiada sat down and placed the lamp between them. "Obadiah and Zev have returned to the entrance, checking the time of day and making sure we haven't been discovered."

"Has there been any report on the city? Have either of them tried to reenter through the Sheep Gate?"

"Not yet." Jehoiada bowed his head, praying for wisdom. He'd had two days to gather his thoughts and calm down. "King Jehoram, may I ask you about something you said on the night we escaped?"

The king released a beleaguered sigh. "I'd actually like to ask you a few things about that night as well." Jehoiada bowed his head, deferring to the king's questions first. "You said my sons invaded the Temple and attacked the Holy Place and its furnishings."

Jehoiada nodded.

"Why didn't Yahweh strike them dead that night? If He's so powerful and demands such exacting holiness, why not kill anyone who steps into His Temple the moment they trespass?"

"I don't know."

"Well, you see, here's how my wife and Jizebaal would explain it. They would say Yahweh is declining in strength and Baal Melkart is increasing. They would say *their* priests can outshine your sacrifices with divination and sorcery, and so far, Priest, I would have to agree with them."

Jehoiada tamped down his rising temper and kept his voice calm. "And what about Elijah's rousing victory over Jezebel's priests of Baal on Mount Carmel?"

Jehoram erupted with a full-bellied laugh. "Well, the queen of dung, as you call her, concedes that Elijah's three-year drought, the slaughter of Baal's priests on Mount Carmel, and the pillar of fire that consumed the offering were impressive displays of Yahweh's strength."

"But . . ." Jehoiada coaxed.

"But after Elijah incited the Israelites to kill the Baal prophets, he ran for Jezreel and didn't wait for the rest of the display. The Gevirah says immediately after hearing of her priests' slaughter, she began killing Yahweh's prophets, and only *then* did the storm god Baal send rain. Why do you think Baal worship rose again so quickly in Israel? Queen Jizebaal convinced the people that Baal Melkart sent the rain to end the drought after she killed Yahweh's prophets."

A wave of nausea washed over Jehoiada. He'd never heard such a blasphemous interpretation of Yahweh's victory at Mount Carmel.

"Which returns me to my original question," the king pressed. "If your God is so powerful, why didn't He strike down my sons for invading His Holy Place?"

Fighting the urge to pummel the king of Judah, Jehoiada kept his tone even. "Perhaps I can answer your question when you answer mine. On the night of our escape, someone mentioned a letter from Elijah. What did the letter foretell—if you don't mind me asking?"

Lamplight gleamed in the king's eyes. Was it indecision battling behind the windows of his soul? Fear? Anger? "I *do* mind you asking," Jehoram said finally. "But because you might provide some understanding, I'll tell you. Elijah said that because I had killed my brothers and walked in the ways of the house of Ahab, Yahweh would strike my people, my sons, my wives, and everything I own. Plus, He'd afflict me with a disease in my bowels." He lifted a single eyebrow. "I suppose we have to admit Elijah got that one right, but he said my bowels would eventually come out. Have you ever heard such lunacy?" He scoffed, waving his hand as if shooing a pesky gnat.

Jehoiada's anger surrendered to pity—and then shame. *Yahweh, how do You tolerate any of us? Our feeble little minds and bodies have no grasp of Your infinite plan.*

"Well, don't just sit there!" the king shouted. "Tell me what you think!"

"I think Yahweh will strike your people, your sons, your wives, and everything you own—and your bowels will fall out of your body."

Silence. Nothing but the trickling of water down the walls of the quarry.

"Yahweh had His chance to kill my sons in the Temple. Why didn't He do it the moment they trespassed?"

Ah, the king's original question made more sense in light of Elijah's letter. Timing. The king wanted to know *when* the events in the letter would take place. Jehoiada himself had often struggled with God's timing. "We don't get to decide when or how Yahweh acts, King Jehoram." Amariah had spoken those words countless times, but they sounded contrived on Jehoiada's lips.

"But if my sons and I die, hasn't your precious Yahweh broken His covenant to forever maintain a son of David on Judah's throne? Where's the justice in that?"

"Justice?" Jehoiada's pity fled, chased by quick fury. "You measure the Creator's justice? You, the pagan king, who killed his godly brothers and innocent Judean governors so you could steal the treasures your abba Jehoshaphat gave them before he died. You speak to Yahweh—to me, His priest—about justice?"

"I don't want to lose my sons! Can't you understand that? Don't you have sons?"

The question pierced Jehoiada's heart, silencing his fury.

The king masterfully interpreted the silence. "You don't! You don't have sons. Ha!" Rising up on his elbow, he goaded Jehoiada. "You're probably like Mattan—celibate, unmarried."

"I am not like your Baal priest in *any* way, I assure you. I was happily married for forty years to a beautiful woman whom I loved more than breath."

The king held his gaze, refusing to be cowed. Silent, blinking, measuring—the two stared. Jehoiada would have thrashed any other man, but he waited, refusing to be baited into more futile words.

Finally, King Jehoram spoke. "Have you lived on the Temple grounds all your life?"

Not sure why it mattered, but realizing he must answer the king, he offered a single word. "Yes."

"Even as a child?"

"Yes."

"Why?"

Jehoiada gritted his teeth, begrudging his obligation to explain. "The high priest and his second priest always live on Temple grounds with their families. I am Amariah's second, as my abba was the second to Amariah's predecessor."

"And why is it necessary for the high priest and his second to live on Temple groun—"

"Really, I don't see why—"

"I am still your king, and you will not interrupt me!"

The sound of gravel crunching underfoot drew their attention, and Jehoiada blew out their lamp. The quarry darkness engulfed them, so utterly black it weighted them like soldier's armor. A dim light shone in one of the passageways, brighter as it bounced closer.

Trying to steady his breathing, Jehoiada whispered, "Stay here. I'm going to wait at the tunnel entrance to surprise them."

Taking his sword, he rose and kept his hands outstretched to keep from running into the natural limestone pillars. He stepped carefully, stealthily, toward the ever-brightening tunnel.

"Shalom! We're back!" came Obadiah's strained whisper.

Both Jehoiada and the king sighed, but it was the priest who vented his frustration. "You've got to give us more warning. You almost met the business end of my sword."

Obadiah and Zev walked toward the sound of Jehoiada's voice, and the three of them followed the sound of the king's tapping in order to find him in the looming darkness.

"What did you see at the entrance?" King Jehoram asked before the men lit a second lamp.

The two explorers shared a disappointed glance, and Zev delivered the bad news. "We didn't dare return to the Sheep Gate, but the whole area north of the city is quiet as a tomb."

"How will we know when it's safe to leave the quarry?" Jehoram sounded more like a pleading child than a reigning king.

"Amariah will come," Jehoiada said with certainty. "Or he'll send someone he can trust. For now, waiting is best."

Obadiah offered a compassionate gaze to the uncomfortable king. "Jehoiada's right. We've got enough food for another day or two."

"We didn't see anyone coming in or out of the northern entrance, my lord. No one." Zev's grave tone insinuated some deeper meaning Jehoiada didn't understand.

"Why the concern?" he asked. "Perhaps travelers are entering through the other gates."

The other three men gawked at Jehoiada as if he'd grown a third eye. The king released a disgusted sigh and turned to Obadiah. "I was about to tell the priest why living on Temple grounds narrows his vision. Why don't you interpret the broader view of decreased traffic through Jerusalem's north gate?"

Obadiah's forbearing smile made Jehoiada feel like a child. "It means the Israelites haven't come to help us. It also means no merchants from the north, which cuts into our already diminished trade profits from those traveling between Damascus and Egypt."

"Had you considered those issues, Priest? Allies and trade? Small things, really," King Jehoram said, sarcasm dripping from each word.

Jehoiada wished he could wipe off the king's smug grin, but he returned his own cynical sneer. "Why should I worry about trifles when such a godly man sits on Judah's throne?"

Obadiah frowned at both priest and king. "Did Zev and I miss an important conversation while we were checking the time of day? It's just past midday—if anyone was wondering."

King Jehoram fixed a stony glare on Jehoiada while addressing Obadiah. "The priest and I were discussing the many ways he is different from Baal priests, including Mattan's willingness to be involved in the world around him, whereas the Yahweh high priest—and his second—lock themselves away in their gleaming Temple, refusing to face the challenges of the real world."

"The *real world*, as you call it, King Jehoram, is in Yahweh's capable hands. Amariah and I dedicate ourselves to His service and allow the Lord's prophets to deal with rebellious kings."

Jehoiada saw Jehoram's superiority crack. "My future may

be forfeited, it's true." He paused and then struggled for words. "What if I offer Yahweh a gift—or a treaty like the treaty between two nations? Will it save my life or the lives of my family?"

Jehoiada scoffed. "Don't be ridiculous. The Lord is not a man or king that He would condescend to a *treaty*."

"What about His covenant with Noah?" Obadiah's quiet words echoed in the cavern. "Every rainbow is a reminder of Yahweh's covenant. And what about the Lord's covenant with Abraham that gave us the land beneath our feet? And what about the covenant Yahweh made with King David—"

"That's different!" Jehoiada shouted. "Surely you can't compare Jehoram with any of those righteous men!"

Obadiah waited until the echo of shouting died. "But God's covenants with Noah, Abraham, and David weren't based on their righteousness. Those men offered nothing to secure God's promise."

"And I'm willing to offer Yahweh my most precious possession," Jehoram said, desperation lacing his tone. "What if I pledge my favorite daughter, Jehosheba, to marry Yahweh's high priest?"

Jehoiada's laughter echoed off the limestone walls. "Amariah is more than ninety years old. He would never marry your daughter. She's a child!" When he realized no one else was laughing, Jehoiada stared at Obadiah, pleading for a reasonable man to join his reasonable argument. "Yahweh has given the Law to His people, and it's the *only* way sins are forgiven, the *only* treaty available, King Jehoram!"

Like Obadiah, the king allowed a few moments of silence to punctuate Jehoiada's shouting and then continued his argument. "Surely you realize the benefit of joining David's royal house with Yahweh's high priest. Amariah could give his blessing to the *next* high priest, a younger man. He could then marry my Jehosheba and become a member of the royal house—privy to the political and business aspects of the kingdom."

Before Jehoiada could dismiss the king's proposal, Obadiah interrupted. "Jehoiada, I believe the king's plan is something the high priest himself should consider."

"What? Obadiah, it's ridiculous. Amariah will never—"

"You don't know the high priest's mind. Nor do you know Yahweh's mind until you consult the Urim and Thummim." Obadiah's matter-of-fact tone left little room for reply. "Now, let's eat. Zev and I found some berries near the entrance that will make a welcome addition to our bread and hard cheese." He and Zev began a quiet conversation with the king, leaving Jehoiada to ponder the ludicrous proposal before him.

While watching the others divide the meager portions, Jehoiada found little appeal in the fare. After hearing Jehoram's plan to use his daughter to gain Yahweh's favor, he had weightier matters to chew on.

10

Say to [Ahab], "This is what the LORD says: Have you not murdered a man and seized his property?" Then say to him, "This is what the LORD says: In the place where dogs licked up Naboth's blood, dogs will lick up your blood—yes, yours!"

Escorted by the weasel eunuch Gevirah had assigned, Ima Thaliah and Sheba hurried down the now familiar hallway toward Jizebaal's chamber. The faded purple tapestries that had captured Sheba's attention at first no longer held her interest. After two endless days of waiting for news of Jerusalem, her only concern was Abba.

Without warning, Ima Thaliah seized Sheba's arm, halting her progress, and then pressed a quieting finger to her lips. A mischievous grin awaited the eunuch's realization that they no longer followed. Two camel lengths ahead, he glanced over his shoulder and jumped as if bitten by a serpent. "Why have you stopped? We mustn't keep the Gevirah waiting!"

Sheba laughed outright while Ima Thaliah glared at the impudent servant. "Proceed to the Gevirah's chamber and announce our arrival. Princess Sheba and I will enter directly."

Only a moment's hesitation preceded the man's frustrated

bow. The chamber guards opened the double doors at his approach, and Ima Thaliah began whispering as the doors clicked shut. "Jerusalem's instability has hastened Ima Jizebaal's plan to unite Israel and Judah. She's eager to be rid of my brother Ram, and if Jehoram is dead, she intends to make Hazi king and begin unifying the nations immediately. We can't let that happen."

Every emotion inside Sheba screamed for release, but she'd honed her calm facade during the last two days' insanity. While Ima Thaliah and Jizebaal spoke openly in King Ram's presence about uniting Israel and Judah, Sheba watched Hazi's face remain a blank parchment. He was a master of deception—a fine skill to possess amid their life of intrigue. He'd revealed no emotion, none of his opinions—even when the Gevirah unveiled her plan to eventually crown him king.

Sheba maintained her placid expression, keeping her tone level. "I am pleased to do anything you ask of me, my queen."

"Good." Ima Thaliah looped her arm in Sheba's and began walking again toward the Gevirah's chamber. "We must convince Jizebaal that my oldest son is a better choice for Judah's immediate king. Otherwise, Ram will be dead before the new moon."

Perhaps Abba Jehoram is still alive! Sheba wanted to scream. Instead, she walked silently, arm in arm with Ima Thaliah, as Jizebaal's chamber guards opened the doors.

"There you are, Thali," Jizebaal said. "We've been waiting." Her icy stare could have turned rain to snow.

Sheba bowed, allowing Ima to precede her toward a low couch positioned near a circular ivory table. Judah's queen took her place beside King Ram, and the seating appeared to alternate male/female. Sheba sat on King Ram's left, sharing a couch with Hazi. The Gevirah was positioned on a couch of her own next to Hazi, and Mattan was flanked by both queens. He looked as stiff as the teraphim on the Gevirah's balcony. Sheba scooted closer to Hazi, his nearness serving as silent assurance. *Perhaps this morning won't be as terrible as I feared.*

Jizebaal clapped her hands, alerting her servants and startling everyone else. "Leave us." The servants exchanged puzzled glances, hesitating only a moment before hurrying from the room.

Sheba's eunuch dared to question the Gevirah. "Would you like one of us to stay in case you have need of—" The Gevirah's glare stopped him. He turned and fled with the rest.

Sheba gulped. What was Jizebaal about to say if even the mute servants were ordered out?

Surprisingly, King Ram spoke first. "We received word this morning from the prophet Elisha. Ben-Hadad, the king of Aram, is dead—murdered by his trusted officer, Hazael, who has stolen the throne."

Sheba glanced at the others, waiting for someone to explain why this turn of events mattered when Abba and all of Jerusalem hung in the balance. "Is this the same prophet who wrote the letter to Abba?"

"What letter?" Jizebaal's indignation reminded Sheba too late that the Gevirah didn't know about the letter Obadiah had delivered the night before they left Jerusalem.

Ima Thaliah squeezed her eyes shut and sighed before reporting the news like a market list. "Jehoram received a letter written by Elijah's hand, predicting disaster to the king's household and a wasting illness of his bowels."

Silence stretched into awkwardness, giving Sheba ample time to study the intricate carving on the table. Why had she spoken without thinking?

"The letter couldn't have been from Elijah," Jizebaal said finally. "He's been dead for more than ten years. His students tell some ridiculous story about his departure to the underworld in a fiery chariot, but I believe the stinking, hairy prophet returned to Mount Horeb and died in the wilderness." Waving her hand, she seemed to dismiss the rumors, the prophet, and the letter. "Now, get on with it, Ram."

Ram turned to Sheba, his eyes having lost some of the sparkle she'd admired in days past. "The prophet Elisha is Elijah's successor. He has helped us overcome the Arameans in recent battles, but—"

"Tell them how your prophet friend betrayed you, my son," Jizebaal goaded with wicked delight.

"He's. Not. My. Friend." Ram released a sigh and turned

to Hazi. "Someday, when you become king, remember that prophets and priests are never your friends. They are tools for gathering information and gaining power. Never trust them." Sheba noticed Mattan squirm on his couch and wondered if Ram had somehow heard rumors of Mattan's corruption. "Elisha predicts the new king of Aram will bring fire and sword to Israel in the coming years. I suppose that means Elisha's days of helping Israel are over."

The Gevirah made no attempt to hide her smug grin. "And so ends King Ram's momentary allegiance to Yahweh."

Ram returned no spiteful comments—only a woeful expression as he cradled his sister's hand. "I'm sorry, Thali, but it also means Israel's military remains on high alert and can't offer aid to Judah—no matter what Jerusalem's condition after this raid."

Ima Thaliah's countenance remained chiseled stone, a silent nod her only reply.

Jizebaal's overly cheery voice broke the tension. "Why don't we let my grandson review the contingencies if Jehoram has been killed and yet we somehow retain power in Judah."

Hazi, ever calm and controlled, cleared his throat. "Of course, we pray that almighty Baal Melkart has protected Abba Jehoram somehow, but if for any reason he becomes unable to rule Judah . . ." He paused and held Ima Thaliah's gaze. "The succession will proceed in order from my eldest brother down. I will continue to serve in the royal guard, ensuring the safe transition of the throne from abba to son to son and so on."

Ima Thaliah exhaled and then nodded at the Gevirah, her relief palpable. "My oldest son will make a fine king and will work to fill Judah's treasury, using Abba Ahab's more aggressive style of leadership."

"Ha!" Ram showcased the fading opulence around them. "Because Abba's style of leadership stuffed Israel's treasury full of wealth," he said, sarcasm as thick as his curly black hair.

Gevirah Jizebaal's head turned slowly, like a cobra coiled to strike. "Would you spit on your abba's grave and say King Ahab's government failed? *You* squander what your abba built."

"It was *your* interference that killed Abba and started this decline!"

The Gevirah ignored her son and turned to Hazi with the sweet smile Sheba dreaded most—it was the last warning before she lost control. "Ram thinks I interfered when I helped Ahab acquire the fenced plot of land you passed between the palace and Gideon's Pool. That herb garden used to be a vineyard owned by a stubborn man named Naboth, who thought he could refuse when King Ahab *asked* to buy it. A strong king doesn't ask—and will not be refused."

"Listen closely, Prince Hazi," Ram interjected, seething, "to your savta Jizebaal's lesson on murdering an innocent man." Ima Thaliah placed a quieting hand on her brother's arm, pleading.

The Gevirah's smile widened, her eyes like daggers. "When *you* become king, Hazi, remember it's impossible to worship Yahweh *and* Baal. The Yahwists will never allow it. Both your saba Ahab and Ram have tried it and failed. King Ahab finally realized Baal Melkart—lord king of the city—is stronger than other gods, so he began buying small farms and moving people into the cities."

"But how did farmers earn a living for their families if they sold their farms?" Hazi's seemingly logical question wiped the smile from Jizebaal's face. Instinctively, Sheba brushed the scab marks on her neck and prayed to the gods for Hazi's protection.

The Gevirah's harsh tone matched her stare. "The small farmers carelessly wasted their profits, which forced them into servitude. However, most of them found even slave labor failed to meet their debts. So King Ahab offered further provision by facilitating the sale of their daughters to serve in the temples of Baal and Astarte. He then combined the small farms into parcels, selling them at a profit to wealthy merchants who grew wealthier because they reaped harvests from large plots of land near growing cities." Her bright smile returned. "You see, my dear Hazi? A strong king acquires land, wealth, *and* the loyalty of key leaders in the land."

Before Hazi could respond, Ram leaned forward and whispered as if conspiring, "And when a king won't steal a man's inheritance—his family's vineyard—from its rightful owner, the meddling queen conspires to kill that owner and his family, bringing down Yahweh's wrath on the king and all his descendants."

"Ram, please! Let it go." Ima Thaliah's eyes glistened, and again Sheba was startled by her genuine emotion. Why didn't Ima show that kind of concern for Abba Jehoram?

Ram patted his sister's hand and spoke with aching tenderness. "Do you think Yahweh's prophets will let it go, Thali?" Then he turned on the Gevirah. "Tell Hazi about Elijah's prophecy when he heard of Naboth's death."

"Elijah or Elisha?" Sheba squeaked the question before she could restrain herself and received glaring disdain from everyone in the room—everyone except Mattan.

Sheba's relentless teacher, the most powerful priest in Judah, appeared almost sympathetic. "*Elijah* confronted Ahab after assassins killed Naboth and his sons, saying Yahweh would consume Ahab's descendants and cut off every last male in Israel—slave or free. He said dogs would devour Queen Jizebaal by the wall of Jezreel and eat those in Ahab's clan who die in the city."

The Gevirah chuckled—low and menacing. "Oh, Mattan, don't forget about the birds that will feed on Ahab's family who die in the country." She stared at Ima and Ram as if daring them to speak. "I think that about covers it, doesn't it, children?"

Ram and Ima Thaliah sat like Baal stones. Sober. Silent.

Sheba could hardly breathe. "So, we're all cursed?"

"Oh no, dear." The Gevirah leaned forward, whispering, taunting. "Just us. You don't have a drop of Ahab's blood in you."

Sheba reached for Hazi's hand and found him as white as Mattan's priestly robe.

A loud pounding on the door caused everyone to jump. The Gevirah shouted, "Come!"

General Jehu entered, dragging a beleaguered messenger beside him. Sheba recognized his uniform as Judean and held her breath. The commander spoke before permission was granted. "I beg pardon, but this messenger has just arrived from Jerusalem with grave news." Shoving the trembling man forward, Jehu fairly snarled, "Tell them. Everything."

The man fell to his knees, head bowed. "I beg mercy for the tragic news I have to report. Philistines and Arabs routed Jerusalem. The city and its walls still stand, but the king's household is . . ." He buried his face in his hands, mumbling.

"The king's household is what?" Hazi leapt from his couch, grabbing the man's collar, lifting him to his feet. "Is King Jehoram safe?"

"May Yahweh forgive me, we don't know. The Philistines raided the palace and the Temple, killed the king's sons, and hung their bodies on the palace walls, but there's been no sign of King Jehoram."

Ima Thaliah leapt from her couch as well. "What do you mean, 'the king's sons'? You mean the king's nephews or the other wives' children? The king's *royal* sons—the princes—are governors of their own fortified cities—"

Her words were cut short by the hopeless shaking of the messenger's head. "I'm sorry, my queen, but King Jehoram had summoned *your* sons to Jerusalem, and all four of them arrived the evening before the attack." He hesitated, casting pleading glances at the commander and Hazi before finishing. "All four princes are dead, and some of the other royals were killed or taken captive when the invaders retreated from the city—the king's other wives, his other children, and some advisors."

A low, guttural keening began in Ima Thaliah's throat, and Sheba left her couch to comfort her.

Hazi, still searching for answers, asked the man, "How could you know the others were killed or captured but know nothing of King Jehoram's whereabouts?"

"We have only the testimony of a guard at the Sheep Gate, who said Commander Zev escaped with King Jehoram and two escorts during the heaviest fighting. No one has seen any of them since."

Before Hazi could question him further, the Gevirah stepped forward. "Thank you, Commander Jehu, you may go."

The commander seemed startled and looked to King Ram for confirmation. Receiving it, he bowed and backed from the room.

As the door closed, Jizebaal bid the frightened messenger to stand. "Young man, you said both the palace and the Temple were raided. We've heard the report on the losses in the palace, but what damage was done in the Temple? It's Yahweh's Temple of which you speak, is it not?"

The messenger seemed hesitant, but after receiving a nod from Hazi, he met Jizebaal's gaze. "Yes, Queen Jezebe—" Utter horror washed over the man's face when he realized he'd nearly called Israel's Gevirah a pile of dung in her hearing. "Forgive me, my lady! I didn't mean—"

Jizebaal's expression lit with compassion. "Think nothing of it." She chuckled warmly. "I'm aware of my Judean neighbors' play with my name. Now, your answer, please. Was it indeed Yahweh's Temple that was raided, and what losses were incurred?"

The man seemed to relax and offered a wholehearted explanation. "Yahweh's holy Temple was stripped of its gold and furnishings, but the greatest loss was the life of Amariah, our beloved high priest. All of Jerusalem mourns his passing."

The Gevirah feigned concern. "Oh, I'm sure he was a great man, your high priest. Sheba, my girl, did you hear that? It sounds as if your marriage date has been moved up. You'll have a new husband and Jerusalem a new high priest sooner than we had planned."

Mattan jumped from his couch, sending it skidding across the tiled floor. "Sheba is to be initiated as Baal's high priestess at the Awakening!"

Sheba held her breath. Evidently no one had informed her teacher of *that* detail in Jizebaal's new plan.

The Gevirah's sweet smile met Mattan's angry outburst. "Would you like to join our Judean friend here, Priest? The guards are about to escort him downstairs."

"Downstairs?" The messenger's voice quaked at the word.

Mattan's fury drained as he watched King Ram lead the messenger toward the door. Sheba closed her eyes, trying to imagine anything but the eunuchs' empty mouths. Would Jizebaal take only his tongue, or had the Jezebel remark cost the messenger his life?

11

*They attacked Judah, invaded it and carried off all the
goods found in the king's palace, together with his sons
and wives. Not a son was left to him except Ahaziah, the
youngest.*

The full Judean contingent left Jezreel just before dawn,
forfeiting horses in favor of swift, one-humped dromedar-
ies. They would stop only twice on the journey and arrive
in Jerusalem by nightfall. King Ram apologized that he couldn't
send an Israelite escort, but tensions with Aram were too high.
Though their longtime treaty called for reciprocal aid in times
of war, Jerusalem sat like a chicken amid a circle of wolves, and
Israel dared not risk dashing into the henhouse.

The Judean procession traveled without incident, stopping
at Tirzah and Bethel to refresh their animals and riders. Sheba
rode third in the caravan. Almost as proficient as Ima Thaliah,
she glided in rhythm with the camel's loping strides. Her back
and shoulders testified to the long day's ride, but she hadn't
spouted a single complaint. A satisfied grin creased her lips, the
first on this somber day of travel, as they crested Jerusalem's
northern hill at sunset.

A scout returning from the city rode like a man chased by

underworld legions. "My lord Hazi, the city is secure." Though it was a positive report, his furrowed brow and skittish eyes betrayed more news.

Hazi, on the lead camel, raised his fist, signaling the procession to a halt. Ima Thaliah guided her camel forward to hear the report, and Sheba braced herself for the worst. In the stillness, the eerie sound of a city in mourning rose to greet them. Keening echoed through the northern hills, sending a shiver through Sheba's bones.

"Only a few royal advisors survived." The scout offered a respectful bow to Ima Thaliah. "I'm sorry, my lady, but the guards confirmed the royal princes were killed. Some other wives and their children were taken captive. The palace treasury has been stripped of everything King Jehoshaphat stockpiled—spices, gold, silver, weaponry. They ransacked the individual chambers and vandalized the Throne Hall, slashing tapestries and smearing blood on the walls."

Sheba saw Hazi glance in Ima's direction, but her expression betrayed nothing. She'd been strangely silent after hearing the news of her sons' deaths and Abba's disappearance.

Hazi took charge. "Is there any word yet on King Jehoram's location? Have they sent out search parties?"

"Yes, my lord. Ten pairs of guards left yesterday but haven't returned." His tone softened with his expression. "They're still hopeful that your abba escaped to a fortified city and remains hidden."

"Well, considering our neighbors are eager to pounce . . ." Ima Thaliah's chin trembled as her words sliced the evening air. "Edom nearly killed Jehoram in the uprising last year, and Libnah aided them in the revolt. Moab rebelled against both Israel and Judah, and now the Philistines and Arabs have shown the world they can amble through our gates and steal whatever pleases them." She swiped away uncharacteristic tears. "I'd say if Jehoram is alive, he *should* be hiding after such failures."

Sheba bristled at Ima's open disrespect—and not only because of her fierce love for Abba. Why would she criticize the king in the presence of a subordinate? There'd be no cutting out of tongues in Judah, and soldiers reveled in royal gossip. If Abba was found and returned to the throne, royal discord could slow the nation's recovery. For the first time in Sheba's memory, Ima's emotions had overshadowed her reason.

Hazi cleared his throat and redirected the soldier's attention. "Join the procession at the rear, and alert the other Carites that we'll wait until we've stabled the animals to assess how many of the king's royal guard survived. I'll settle my ima and sister in their chambers immediately and then convene the remaining advisors. Also, summon my royal cousins. They've just been appointed to the council. We'll need every drop of royal blood to rebuild Jerusalem."

To Sheba's surprise, Ima didn't insist on attending the council meeting. Her vacant eyes looked to the city atop Mount Zion. Jerusalem—King David's crowning achievement and Judah's heart and soul. Sheba dreaded what awaited them. The whole city would be in mourning, of course, but would her half brothers' bodies still hang on the palace wall? Had they been burned already, or would the funeral pyres await Mattan's return? Many of the Yahwists refused funerary burnings, carving out stone boxes—sarcophagi—for their dead. Would blood stain the streets, the palace, the royal bedchambers?

Sheba squeezed her eyes shut, trying to block out the gruesome images. *I must rely on my training for strength.* She was a high priestess of Baal, a princess of Judah, favorite daughter of Jehoram.

Hazi gave the order to resume the march toward the city, now slowly, respectfully. For the first time, the staggering realization that they'd been spared this tragedy dawned fully. Why had they been saved? What cruel game were the gods playing?

As they approached the Sheep Gate, two men hurried round the northern wall—one stooped and slow moving, the other in a filthy Carite's uniform, both waving at the procession.

"Surround the women and take your positions," Hazi shouted, drawing his sword. He shielded his eyes from the setting sun and leaned forward. "It's Zev!" Hazi sheathed his sword and tapped his camel's shoulder, jumping clear of the beast before it was on its knees. He nearly tackled his captain with an embrace.

Sheba watched their animated conversation but couldn't hear the words. She recognized the stooped man as Obadiah, the nobleman Ima Thaliah had banished the night Elijah's letter was read. Captain Zev invited the old man to whatever conversation he and Hazi were sharing.

Before Sheba could demand a servant's help to dismount, she heard rocks crunching underfoot. Ima walked beside her, past her camel, toward the men. Surprised the queen had dismounted so quickly, Sheba looked back and saw that Ima's camel was only now coming to its knees. *If Ima can jump, so can I!*

"Wait!" she called out, leaping to the ground behind Ima Thaliah.

Her plea stole the attention of the three men and won a dazzling smile from Hazi. "Abba's alive!" he said, opening his arms. Sheba rushed to him, and he swung her around in their traditional childlike twirl. "Abba's alive, Sheba!"

"You forget yourself, both of you!" Ima Thaliah stood with arms folded, a disapproving frown on her face. Aiming her question at Zev, she asked, "Where have you been, and why didn't anyone know the king was alive?"

Obadiah interjected before the guard could draw a breath. "We're sorry to have frightened you, but King Jehoram felt his location must remain secret to ensure the unbroken lineage of King David on Judah's throne. But I assure you he is most eager to see his family."

A shadow of grief nearly doused Ima Thaliah's fury—nearly. "You may tell King Jehoram—wherever he is—that he no longer has a family." She turned abruptly and marched back to her camel, shocking Sheba and the men, who stood with their mouths gaping.

Hazi was the first to gather his wits. "Is Abba nearby? Can you take me to him?"

"I'm going with you." Sheba folded her arms and planted herself beside her brother.

Zev looked at Obadiah, deferring to the old nobleman, who

bowed humbly. "Our first glimpse of safety has been your return. Your abba has been stricken with a sickness that's left him weak and somewhat . . . disheveled. Please, let us bring King Jehoram into the palace after sunset so that we might wash him before he's seen."

Hazi's brow furrowed. "Captain Zev is my superior in the royal guard, but as a prince of Judah, I could order you to take me to Abba immediately."

"Indeed you could, my lord." Obadiah's tone remained kind and humble. "And I would obey if that is your command. However, I would hope that you'd consider your abba's condition and the ordeal he's survived the past three days." Meeting Hazi's gaze, he added, "I believe King Jehoram would be relieved if he could greet his family and advisors with his dignity intact."

Zev stepped forward and placed a hand on Hazi's shoulder. "Your abba would not want you to see him like this."

Sheba's heart was in her throat. "What's wrong with him? Was he injured in the raid?"

The approach of several camels interrupted their conversation. Ima Thaliah had regained her mount and commanded a small contingent to escort her. "I'm returning to the palace. Anyone coming with me?" she asked as she ambled by.

Hazi seemed torn, like a man tied between two horses pulling him in opposite directions. He turned to Sheba. "What do you think?"

"I want to see Abba now, and if Ima is as angry as she appears, he'll need to know he has our unwavering support."

Raking a hand through his desert-brown hair, he sighed. "Stay here," he said to the other three. Marching back to the waiting guards and servants, he shouted, "Follow Queen Athaliah and her escort into the city. Princess Sheba and I must accompany Captain Zev and the king's advisor on a short diplomatic journey." He captured the attention of his second-in-command and added, "Tell Queen Athaliah that I'll return Sheba safely to her chambers by nightfall. She can visit King Jehoram in the morning." The soldier affirmed with a nod, and Hazi returned to those waiting by the road.

Obadiah glanced at Zev and then at the prince, his discomfort seeming to increase. "I'm sorry, my lord, but may I speak freely?" Hazi's raised brow opened a floodgate for the nobleman's words. "I cannot reveal the hiding place of the king without the approval of Yahweh's high priest. Until this invasion, only Amariah and I—and one prophet in Judah—were aware of its existence, and—"

"Yahweh's high priest is dead, Obadiah."

Obadiah's instant tears testified to his friendship with the old priest. Zev placed a comforting hand on his back. "I'm sorry, Obadiah. He seemed like a good man."

"He was a good man." Overcome by emotion, he asked Hazi in a whisper, "Do you know how Amariah died?"

Sheba's heart broke. The two old men had probably been friends for years, worshiping the same archaic god. She thought of the pain Ima Thaliah suffered in hearing of her sons' deaths, and wondered which hurt more—losing the young or the old. She'd barely known Hazi's brothers, her half brothers. Abba Jehoram had over sixty children, and all of Ima Thaliah's sons except Hazi had tormented her mercilessly, so though she mourned Ima's losses, Sheba's personal grief had been averted when she heard Abba was safe.

Hazi braced Obadiah's shoulder. "We know very little, I'm afraid. I've heard only that the Philistines and Arabs invaded, killing all four of my brothers and—"

"Oh, son." Obadiah reached for Hazi's hand, patting it with sincere sympathy. "I'm so sorry, and your abba will be devastated."

"I believe Ima blames him. Do you know why he summoned them to Jerusalem? It seems odd."

As if measuring his answer, the old man pursed his lips. "Perhaps it's best if he explains it to you personally. I'll take you to him." Then, studying Sheba, he asked, "Are you sure you want to see your abba in such a weakened state, my dear? This will not be easy."

Sheba gathered her courage and straightened her spine. "I am a priestess of Baal Melkart and princess of Judah. I am not afraid."

Obadiah offered a kind smile and then his hand to escort her. "I admire your courage, Princess. Perhaps I'll lean on you if I grow weary."

The four of them began their trek around the city, the sounds of the mourners persisting like the whine of a loose wheel on a long journey. When finally they arrived at a small clearing, wildflowers budded amid the spring grasses, and Sheba watched with wonder as Zev lifted away a circular wall of thorns, well hidden among a pile of rocks.

Obadiah pointed toward the dark hole and then offered Hazi two flint stones and an oil lamp. "Light this, and hand it to me after your sister and I step inside."

Sheba thought it would have been wiser to light the lamp *before* they stepped into a yawning black cavern, but she followed the kindly nobleman into the hole. *High priestess of Melkart. Princess of Judah*, she reminded herself while waiting on the others to light the low-ceilinged blackness.

Obadiah led them, Hazi next. Sheba followed. Zev trailed the group after replacing the thorn cover from within. Sheba's heart quickened as they walked farther and farther into the depths of the earth, the sounds above them completely muted. Some parts of the tunnel were barely wide enough to squeeze through. How did the hulking Captain Zev fit?

After what seemed like ages, the sound of trickling water captured her attention, and Obadiah called out in a cheerful voice, "We've returned with visitors!"

Sheba heard no response, but the narrow tunnel soon opened into a large cavern, the stench so overpowering she nearly retched. Covering her nose and mouth with her wide sleeve, she followed Obadiah, letting her eyes adjust to the small circle of light near what appeared to be a pond. Two men looked back, stunned— one seated, one reclining.

The seated man leapt to his feet, and Sheba immediately recognized the linen robe of a Yahweh priest. He began railing at Obadiah. "How dare you bring them here! Amariah will be furious that you've disclosed—"

"Amariah is dead, Jehoiada."

Sheba heard little of the irate priest's response. Her whole being was focused on the form that lay beside the cavern's pool. "Abba? Is that you?"

The man staring back was a mere shadow of the king she'd left a few days ago, his eyes dark-circled, cheeks sunken. Sheba approached slowly, but Hazi ran past her and fell to his knees beside Abba. "What's happened to you?" Turning to the angry priest, he demanded, "What have you done to him?"

Obadiah spoke quietly with the priest now, probably explaining about Amariah and the city, while Captain Zev offered Hazi answers. "Your abba began showing symptoms the night of the attack. We've kept him as comfortable as possible in the quarry, but I'm sure the palace physicians will be able to help him."

"I wish you hadn't seen me like this." Abba Jehoram hid his face from his children, but Sheba lifted his hand and kissed it.

"We love you, Abba, and we're here to help."

"Where's Thali?" he asked through strained emotions. "Where's my Thaliah?"

Hazi and Sheba exchanged a mournful glance, and the prince sighed, preparing himself to issue the hard news. "Ima is grieving, Abba. My brothers were killed in the raid."

Grief. Fury. Terror. A swirl of emotions twisted the king's face and elicited a groan from the depths of his being. "Nooooo! Yahweh, no!" Suddenly he tried to sit, grasping for Hazi and Sheba to help. "Jehoiada! Jehoiada, come here!"

Hazi cradled his weakened abba and motioned to the other men in the cavern. They came running, summoned by the king's frantic grief. All of them knelt, but it was Obadiah who spoke. "What? What is it, my lord?"

"Jehoiada, this is my daughter Sheba. She's the one."

Sheba felt her heart racing, confused by Abba's desperation and then his strange introduction. She turned to the priest for some sort of clarification but saw only disgust.

"No," Jehoiada said simply.

"Please! I must find a way to stop Yahweh's judgment! He's taken my sons. Did you hear? My sons are dead. I'll give Sheba to the high priest. I am king, and I command—"

"You cannot make a treaty with Yahweh or command Him!" Jehoiada's anger echoed off the limestone walls. "Amariah is dead, but Yahweh's judgment lives on. Only the Lord gives life and takes it."

With all the intimidation a desperately ill man could muster, Abba rose up on one elbow. "Your high priest is dead, Jehoiada, but another will be chosen by Aaron's descendants, and the *new* high priest can let Yahweh decide through the Urim and Thummim if my daughter will become his bride."

Sheba began to tremble. She'd never heard Abba speak of Yahweh or the traditions he must have learned from King Jehoshaphat. And how had Abba decided she should marry Yahweh's high priest—the same decision Ima and the Gevirah had reached in Jezreel? Unseen forces were undeniably at work, forces as real as Sheba's magical arts. What if Baal Melkart wasn't stronger than Yahweh? What if . . .

She stared at the Yahweh priest, his whole being trembling with faith and conviction. He reminded her of King Jehoshaphat. Though she'd only met him a few times, Saba Jehoshaphat had spoken with the same zeal for Yahweh. Mattan had never spoken so passionately about Baal Melkart. Was it the gods who differed or the men who served them?

Her next thought stole her breath. *Why me?* Why had *she* been chosen to enter the conflict? Suddenly it seemed more than petty struggles between queens, priests, and kings. Sheba had entered an unseen war. Yahweh and Baal battled for control of nations, rulers, and individual hearts. Was she to be the weapon or the prize?

12

⋯⟶ 2 Chronicles 21:18 ⟵⋯

After all this, the LORD afflicted Jehoram with an incurable disease of the bowels.

Sheba slipped out of Abba Jehoram's chamber unnoticed. He hadn't acted very kingly tonight, wailing in pain, begging to die as they'd settled him into bed. *It's a good thing Ima Thaliah didn't see him.* Sheba descended the guards' circular stairway and pulled open the heavy cedar door leading to the second-floor women's chambers, where she was greeted by two Carite guards. Familiar faces, though she didn't know their names.

Ima Thaliah had ordered the city's wailing to cease at sunset, but the silence shrouded Jerusalem like a tomb. Enemy bodies smoldered in the Valley of Hinnom, smothering the city with death ash. Yahweh's followers buried their dead in sarcophagi west of the city, while Baal's faithful lit funeral pyres in shifts at the new temple. Mattan had gone to oversee the preparation of the princes' bodies for a special ceremony that would take place tomorrow.

Sheba focused on her bedchamber door. *Just a few more steps and I'll sleep in my own bed, wake up in my own world.* The ridiculous thought paused her hand on the door latch. Her world was gone forever. Merchants' stalls lay in ruins, with trade goods—grain, spices, pottery, silk—strewn along the streets. Even the palace had been marred by death. Bloodstains tainted the royal men's hallway, and Sheba stared down at her feet, where a tapestry lay in pieces—slashed by an enemy sword.

Weary to the bone, she turned the latch, noticing the door slightly ajar. Invading Philistines on her mind, she considered signaling one of the Carites but dismissed her caution as paranoia. If she were to embrace Jizebaal's destiny of queens, she should have the courage to walk into a dark chamber. Sheba closed the door behind her.

"How sick is he?"

Sheba screamed, startled nearly to death. A single flickering oil lamp revealed Ima Thaliah's shadowy silhouette leaning against Sheba's balcony.

Carites pounded on her door, but she opened it only a crack. "I'm sorry to alarm you. I thought I saw a mouse." She offered her most beguiling smile and changed their barely hidden frustration to poorly veiled desire. After closing the door, she sighed and melted against it. "Ima, what are you doing in my chamber?"

"I want to know how sick your abba is."

"How do you even know he's ill? You left before Obadiah and Zev told us he'd been stricken." Sheba coaxed her to sit on a couch near the balcony. "He's in a great deal of pain."

Ima's black eyes held no emotion. "Tell me the truth. Is Jehoram dying, or must we deal with more of his incompetence?"

"I thought you loved Abba! You're acting like Gevirah *Jezebel*!"

Without warning, Thaliah slapped her, and the silence grew more profound—no mourning, no crickets, no footsteps. Only her heart pounding in her ears.

"Don't ever call the Gevirah that name. Do you hear me?"

Sheba covered her stinging cheek and nodded, staring into the granite countenance of a woman she once thought loved her.

"And don't *ever* accuse me of being like her. She's never loved anyone except her precious abba, Eth-Baal. The Gevirah will kill anyone who stands in her way—including her children. But I love my sons, Sheba. Now that only Hazi remains, I will do anything to see him made king of Judah. Do you understand me?" The muscles in her jaw danced, her teeth grinding. "Anything."

"I love Hazi too," Sheba said, desperate to please. "And he's so much like King Ram. I can see why you want to protect your brother as well."

A shadow of sadness passed over Ima's features before the stony mask returned. "I can't worry about Ram now. Hazi must be my only concern. Tell me about your abba Jehoram. Where did they hide him all this time?"

"Zev and Obadiah hid him in some abandoned quarry beneath the city."

"And you said he was in pain?"

Sheba slowed her breathing, choosing her words carefully. "He's quite emaciated after only three days. His pain is bearable while reclining, but the moment he moves, he becomes inconsolable, and he . . ."

Sheba's hesitation fueled Ima Thaliah's frustration. "He what? Really, Sheba. Now is not the time for decorum. What's wrong with your abba?"

"The disease of the bowels . . . it's come upon him as the letter predicted. Obadiah called for the palace physician."

Ima's features brightened. "And Hazi witnessed his abba's suffering?"

Sheba nodded, horrified.

"Splendid!" Ima clapped her hands, seeming delighted. "Did Hazi meet with the royal advisors tonight as he said he would?"

"He's meeting with them right now." Sheba grew more perplexed as Ima's excitement mounted. "Ima, forgive me, but why aren't you meeting with them? If you and the Gevirah plan to unite Judah and Israel, shouldn't you begin by meeting with Abba's advisors and at least hint at the idea?"

"Ah, youth, they're always in such a hurry." Ima Thaliah spoke to no one in particular and then turned to Sheba as if she were a child again. "Gevirah and I *will* unite Judah and Israel, but we always allow men to think it's their idea. This is an important lesson to use with your new high priest husband, dear."

A knock on the door interrupted them. "Come!" Sheba said. Her maids entered, carrying warm honeyed wine and pitchers with washbasins. "Leave the wine, but I'm not ready for bed yet. I'll ring the bell when I wish you to return."

A maid began pouring wine in wooden cups. "What's this?" Sheba asked, slapping the cup from the girl's hand.

The maid mopped the spilled wine with a cloth while explaining. "I'm sorry, mistress, but all the gold and silver was lost in the raid." After refilling Sheba's cup with trembling hands, the girl bowed and hurried from the chamber.

Sheba sipped the sweet nectar and glimpsed Ima's approving smile over the rough-hewn rim. "What? Did I do something right for once?"

"You do a great many things right, Daughter, but I'm afraid the past three days might have shaken your confidence." Ima brushed her cheek, summoning warm feelings nearly snuffed out by all Sheba had learned of this duplicitous woman. "I had five sons by the time I was twenty-one years old. I wanted a daughter, and you were the one I chose. I've never been sorry."

A sudden chill crept up Sheba's spine. *The one she chose?* "You mean you chose to raise me when my ima died."

"I mean the nursemaids said you were the most beautiful and clever of all Jehoram's daughters, and I was determined to have you." Her eyes sparked with unspoken meaning, and Sheba began to tremble.

What was she implying? Had Queen Athaliah just confessed to murdering Sheba's ima?

A loud knock startled her, and she jumped to her feet. "I told those maids I'd ring when I was ready for bed." Ima Thaliah would undoubtedly chastise her for answering her own door, but she needed to put some distance between her and this stranger she called Ima. Sheba began shouting while reaching for the latch. "How dare you return before I call—"

Hazi stood there alone, his face a shroud of concern. "I came to see if you were all right."

Sheba embraced him like an anchor in a storm, relief summoning forbidden tears. He lifted her off the ground, carried her into the chamber, and planted her feet on the tiled floor. His expression changed the moment he glimpsed Ima Thaliah, and Sheba quickly released him. "Look who came to check on Abba," she said a little too brightly.

He knelt before Ima, bowing his head on her knees. "I thought you'd gone to bed. If I'd known you were awake, I would have included you in the advisors' meeting."

Sheba wondered what expression was hiding on Hazi's down-turned face.

Ima cupped his chin, drawing his gaze to meet hers. "You're more than capable to speak to your abba's advisors." She seemed utterly genuine, pleased with and proud of her only remaining son.

"Did Sheba tell you about Abba?" He was measuring her reaction. The last time they'd seen her, she was angry—but he had no idea she was Leviathan in human form.

"Yes, Sheba told me, but she wasn't sure how serious the illness. Did you get a report from the physician?"

Hazi wiped his weary face and appeared to age before their eyes. "Yes, I'm afraid Abba won't leave his chamber for the foreseeable future. The physician has no cure, and the best he can offer is something for the pain."

Ima Thaliah dissolved into a swaying mound of grief, be-moaning the unbearable loss of her sons and then babbling some nonsense about her undying love for Abba.

Hazi gathered Ima in his strong embrace, consoling the heart-less queen, while Sheba sat on the bed, aloof, sickened by the scene.

When Athaliah's uncharacteristic tears had ebbed, Hazi listened with rapt attention as she sniffed and spoke in broken phrases. "My son, you must relinquish your position on the royal guard and prepare to become Judah's king."

"No, Ima. I can't. I won't." His voice was kind but firm. "I've given it much thought, and we both know I'm not ready to be king. You've seen how the Gevirah treats Ram. I don't want our relationship to become so hostile—and it would, you know, be-cause you would try to rule me while I tried to rule the nation."

Thaliah ducked her head, pretending coyness. "Well, we mustn't let it come to that, Hazi, because Judah needs you as king. You and your abba are the only living descendants of King David. Have you considered that?"

Hazi raked a hand through his hair, defenses weakening. "But Abba remains king. He's not dead yet, Ima. I refuse to steal his throne."

"You wouldn't be stealing his throne, dear. I simply ask that you *prepare* to rule if this illness should take your abba from us."

Hazi stared at the floor for several heartbeats. Sheba considered praying that the gods would give him wisdom, but at this point she wasn't sure which god was on her side—or if the gods were on anyone's side. She assessed the ivory and stone images that filled the corners and wall niches. Baals, Asherahs, and teraphims to whom she prayed for life, health, protection, blessing, even cursing of her enemies. To which god could she confide her fears about Ima and the Gevirah? Which gods were on her side?

Hazi interrupted her brooding. "What do you think, Sheba? Is this one of the Gevirah's conspiracies, or does Ima Thaliah really need me to prepare to become king?"

With all her heart, Sheba wanted to say, *Ima's plan is as bizarre and dangerous as one of the Gevirah's conspiracies! Don't listen to her!* But Jizebaal had no inkling of Abba Jehoram's illness or knowledge that Ima Thaliah's other sons were dead. Whatever Queen Athaliah planned for Hazi came from her dark heart alone. "The Gevirah has nothing to do with *Ima's* plan for you, Brother."

Hazi nodded and kissed her cheek, accepting Sheba's honesty as approval. She stared at her hands as Hazi offered his full attention to the queen. "All right, Ima. I'll listen, but I don't promise to comply with your every wish."

"When have you *ever* complied with my every wish?" A spark of real frustration seeped into Ima's performance. "My plan is this: I'll remain in Jerusalem to facilitate your abba's day-to-day decisions. You, my son, must follow the example of your saba Jehoshaphat and travel to all the cities of Judah, building strong relationships with the people of your nation."

Hazi's brows arched. "So far, I approve. But how do you suggest I strengthen these relationships?"

"First, you'll encourage our people to be more open-minded, worship any god of their choosing, and make the temples of Baal and Astarte more, shall we say, *pleasing* to the common Judean." Ima motioned for Sheba to kneel beside Hazi and cupped both their chins, adoration in her eyes. "By the time your tours are arranged, Sheba will have married the new high priest, so it will appear that the royal house of David is still quite devoted to Yahweh." She brushed their cheeks with her hands and waited, appearing every bit the proud ima.

Hazi sighed and glanced at Sheba. "What do you think, little sister?"

Sheba glimpsed a threatening stare from Ima and gave an approving nod. "The people of Judah will love you, Hazi."

Ima interrupted. "Of course, dear. I have only your best interests and Judah's future at heart. And that's why you must also marry the daughter of a nobleman in every city you visit."

"What?" both Hazi and Sheba asked in concert.

"Don't act so shocked. By the time I was Hazi's age, I had four children."

"I enjoy my concubines, thank you, Ima. I see no need—"

"Then open your eyes, Son, because the need to build a royal household has never been greater!" Ima jumped to her feet and stood over Hazi, hands fisted on her hips. "You can't tell me that it's a burden to find the most beautiful daughter of a nobleman in every Judean city and take her to bed."

Hazi stood, towering over her by a cubit. "You, more than any woman, should understand that sentencing a woman to a king's harem is worse than death. I won't do it, Ima. I won't!"

"Being remembered as a failure is worse than death." Ima Thaliah whispered the words, and Sheba saw by the pain on Hazi's face that they'd hit their mark. "And if you don't build King David's house, death will be too good for you." She stormed out of the chamber without a backward glance.

Ima Thaliah cared nothing about King David or Judah, but she knew Hazi did. Hadn't she said she'd do *anything* to make him king? She might not be willing to kill her son, but she had no inhibitions about breaking his heart.

Sheba reached for Hazi's hand, but he pulled away. "We all need rest. Let's talk in the morning."

He slammed the door behind him, and Sheba stood in the silence. Alone. Again. The gods of her childhood surrounded her, but they felt like strangers, their carved faces devoid of life, their empty eyes unable to see her pain. She crawled into her bed and curled into a tight ball, releasing the torrent of emotions that warred within. She had no one. No home. No gods. Soon she'd have a husband—but how could she ever trust a priest of Yahweh?

13

Then the LORD said to Moses, "Tell the Israelites: 'When any of you or your descendants are unclean because of a dead body or are away on a journey, they are still to celebrate the LORD's Passover, but they are to do it on the fourteenth day of the second month at twilight.'"

Jehoiada parted with Obadiah and the royals at the King's Gate of the Temple, overwhelmed by the death and destruction plaguing Yahweh's city. The Sabbath moon shone into his small chamber, imprinting on his memory the disheveled furnishings exactly as they'd left them. The small kitchen in disarray from Obadiah's hurried packing. Amariah's chamber door ajar. Why hadn't he sent the high priest to the quarry and guarded the Ark himself? *Would I have been strong enough to ward off the heathen raiders?*

Obadiah had said the Philistines wouldn't want the Ark of the Covenant. He'd been correct, but the Arabs arrived at the Holy of Holies first. The Carite guards fought valiantly, losing their lives as the Arabs advanced toward the Most Holy Place, where Yahweh's presence dwelt. Amariah warned them, but they silenced him with their swords, keeping the young Temple guard alive to educate them on the contents of the spectacular golden Ark. The moment they touched the sacred box, Yahweh struck them dead, and the Temple guard dragged their corpses to the porch, proclaiming Yahweh's judgment on others who dared enter.

"My lord?" A heavy hand fell on Jehoiada's shoulder, startling him. The young guard stood behind him, eyes red-rimmed and swollen. "I offer my resignation. Again." He inhaled an unsteady breath, looking to the ceiling, fighting back emotions that seemed to be drowning him. "I'm not worthy to serve Yahweh. I failed Him. I failed Amariah. I've failed my family. Everyone."

He turned to flee, but Jehoiada captured his arm and pulled him into a fierce embrace. "You have failed no one." Choking on his own emotions, Jehoiada let silence minister to their broken hearts. When both men regained a measure of control, Jehoiada patted the guard's shoulder. "I'm sorry, but I don't even know your name."

"I'm Zabad."

"Well, Zabad, your resignation is not accepted." Jehoiada noted his Kohathite leather breastpiece. "What clan of Kohathites is your family?"

"My abba's name is Seth, but no one remembers him. It's my ima's name by which I'm known." His gaze dropped to his sandals, his neck and ears instantly crimson. "I'm the son of Shimeath, an Ammonite woman, and you know the old saying: 'Abbas eat sour grapes and the children's teeth are set on edge.'"

"Look at me, Zabad." Jehoiada's commanding tone brought the young guard's head to attention. "I don't know your abba, but you have nothing of which to be ashamed. Your bravery while protecting the high priest shows leadership. And the way you rallied the remaining priests and Levites to clear the carnage from Temple grounds and prepare our dead brothers for burial . . . We need strong leaders, commanders of hundreds, to replace the men we've lost. I was told almost half of the priests and Levites serving that night were slain. I suppose it was a blessing we had so few report for duty."

"But I let the invaders kill the high priest." Zabad spoke as if in a daze, seeming immune to encouragement or reason.

Jehoiada grabbed his shoulders, steadying him. "You displayed the dead bodies of the raiders struck down by Yahweh. When word of it spread through the Philistine and Arab troops, they took their treasure and fled. You're a hero, Zabad, not a failure."

"I don't feel like a hero. I keep seeing Amariah's face when that sword pierced his heart, and I want to know—why? Why does Yahweh allow good men to die violent, senseless deaths?"

Jehoiada swallowed the lump in his throat. Would it shake the guard's faith to know that the high priest's second was plagued by the same questions? "We cannot know the mind of God," he said instead. "For now, we must wait on the Lord to reveal His next step."

Immediately he recalled Amariah's similar counsel on the night they'd quarreled about Jehoram. His old friend and high priest had patted the sacred breastpiece, confident that the Urim and Thummim would give them direction—if they would wait. But some decisions couldn't wait. They must decide tonight if priests could mourn Amariah for the traditional thirty days and still provide priests to maintain Temple sacrifices. Should Jehoiada broach the subjects of choosing the new high priest or Jehoram's marriage request on the same night they discussed grieving? *Yahweh, give me wisdom.*

With a deep sigh, he wrapped his arm around Zabad's shoulders, directing him out the door and down the hall toward the rear gallery. "On almost every Sabbath of my life, I've gathered with brother priests to seek Yahweh's will through the Urim and Thummim. Tonight is no different."

Zabad looked somewhat daunted but followed Jehoiada across the inner court, into the separate place, and past the bronze lavers. They slowed as they approached the gallery, unable to pass through the crowd.

"What's going on?" Jehoiada asked one of the Levites waiting outside. "Why aren't you going in?"

"There's no room." The Levite motioned toward the door several chambers ahead. "It seems every son of Aaron has turned out to see who of Zadok's clan will be chosen as high priest."

Jehoiada fought a testy reply. *Where were all the sons of Aaron when it was time for weekly service?* He remained silent, however, realizing how very different tonight was.

After shouldering through the crowd, Jehoiada reached the central table, where a priest's assistant waited for the event to begin. The rumbling of priests stilled, and Jehoiada motioned toward the breastpiece of decision lying on the table. "I've come tonight to seek Yahweh's guidance on weighty matters—the first of which is the length of our high priest's grieving period."

"Brother Jehoiada." One of the older priests stepped forward. "How can we observe the traditional mourning customs when so many of our number have been killed and Passover is barely two Sabbaths hence? If we as Yahweh's priests are to maintain an unbroken pathway between Him and His people, we must ordain a new high priest and young priests to replace those who have fallen."

Widespread agreement filtered through the gathering, and Jehoiada waited until a natural lull stilled them. "Are you ready for me to ask for Yahweh's will through the Urim and Thummim? The white Thummim will signify Yahweh's approval to choose a new high priest and ordain young priests immediately. The black Urim signifies we mourn the traditional thirty days and delay Passover according to the law of defilement."

Again, the consensus of the priests was overwhelmingly positive, so Jehoiada turned to the center table where the breastpiece of decision waited. Within the high priest's breastpiece was a pocket containing the sacred Urim and Thummim—the instruments of God's judgment and decision.

Reaching inside, he removed the white Thummim and held it high above his head. A reverent stillness rested over them. "Yahweh has spoken. We will move forward with the selection of a new high priest tonight, and we'll ordain all of Aaron's male descendants thirty years or older as soon as a census can be taken." Jehoiada's heart began to pound as the import of the moment settled on him. "Those of you who have touched a dead body, please step to the left and register your seventh day, when you'll become clean again, with one of the assistants.

To all of you, whether you helped prepare bodies for burial or remained clean to continue the sacrifices, thank you. But now we must remain clean at all costs in order to serve Yahweh in both ordaining new priests and celebrating the Passover Feast."

A holy reverence filled the gallery as Jehoiada returned his attention to the center table and noticed two baskets. "Good work, Elan." The priest's assistant bowed humbly. He'd prepared well for the possibility of the high priest's choosing.

The first basket contained distinctly marked lots for each of the families within the clan of Zadok. Jehoiada, as second priest, would draw one lot from the first basket, giving the firstborns from that family the chance to mark a blank white stone from the second basket with their individual names. Jehoiada would then draw the name of the chosen firstborn from the second basket—the lot for high priest.

But the final decision would be Yahweh's. Jehoiada reverently traced his finger over the bloodstained breastpiece worn over Amariah's heart the night he died. Fighting back tears, he tried to tamp down the already rising resentment. How could anyone take Amariah's place? Squeezing his eyes shut, he reminded himself that Yahweh had spoken through these two stones for generations. The Thummim sealed Yahweh's approval. The Urim meant they removed the chosen name from the basket and began the process again.

With a determined sigh, he opened his eyes, ready to hear Yahweh speak. He lifted his hands, stifling the low hum of conversation. "Are there any questions before we begin?"

An old priest from Beersheba stepped forward and met Jehoiada's gaze, speaking to the group with disarming personal warmth. "Brother Jehoiada, we know Amariah was more than your high priest. He was your dear friend. We're sorry for your personal loss, and we'll do whatever we can to help."

Overcome by the unexpected sympathy, Jehoiada cleared his throat, trying to maintain his dignity. "You can help most by serving Yahweh with all your hearts. It's what would have pleased Amariah, and it's what will save Judah." With their hearts united, Jehoiada felt encouraged to continue. "We will choose the high priest tonight, and tomorrow we'll gather the family heads of Aaron's descendants, gaining an accurate count of all males over age thirty. We'll begin the seven-day ordination ceremony as soon as our unclean priests have met their requirements and all the new candidates arrive on Temple grounds." He scanned the expectant faces before him. "Does this sound agreeable?"

Nods spread among the crowd, and Jehoiada felt an intense brotherhood—a bond strong enough for him to trust them with the matter heaviest on his heart. "Before we begin, I must bring to your attention a matter from King Jehoram. The king received a mysterious letter from Elijah the night before the raid, predicting he'd lose his wives, sons, and earthly treasure, as well as foretelling the wasting illness that has attacked his bowels." Wonder rippled through the priests, and Jehoiada inhaled a strengthening breath for the most difficult part of his speech. "King Jehoram has asked to give his daughter Jehosheba in marriage to the new high priest as a sort of treaty agreement with Yahweh in hopes of forestalling further judgment."

Silence.

The uproarious protest he'd expected came instead as a timidly raised hand of a young priest. "Do you think it will help?"

Startled by the seeming ignorance, Jehoiada was first inclined to ask if the boy slept through his classes on the Law. Instead, he forced patience into his tone. "A marriage relationship is a sacred covenant between a man and a woman, established by God to represent His unyielding love for His people. A marriage cannot establish a treaty between God and man. Yahweh's covenants have already been made with Noah, Abraham, Moses, and David—some on condition of obedience, some through the Lord's mercy alone. But none of Yahweh's covenants have been made with a pagan king seeking to manipulate God's favor."

The timid priest hung his head, but another priest spoke up. "Perhaps this marriage would open the king's heart to Yahweh. Shouldn't we at least employ the Urim and Thummim to ask Yahweh's opinion on the matter?" The crowd began to nod in consensus. "It's a yes or no question that can be determined by the breastpiece of decision, Jehoiada."

"Wait, wait." Jehoiada raised his hands to quiet them. "What if the new high priest is already married?"

More shouting and debate erupted, creating division and disunity in a gathering that moments ago had enjoyed complete harmony. One man's voice rose above the din. "Let's choose the high priest, and if he's not married, we put the question directly to Yahweh."

Jehoiada scanned the room and saw general agreement, encouraging him to begin the process of choosing their high priest. The assistant Elan lifted the first basket, and Jehoiada closed his eyes in silent prayer. *Yahweh, guide my hand.* Lifting out the first stone, he recognized the family symbol as devout men from Beersheba. "Remiel. All firstborns of Remiel's family, step forward and make your personal mark on a smooth stone in the second basket."

Nervous chatter filled the room as fifteen men made their way to the table, each marking a stone with his unique symbol. Jehoiada guessed three generations in Remiel's clan: the patriarch Remiel, his firstborn, and the firstborns of all other males in his clan. After all the men had cast their lots, silence fell over the crowd, and the assistant held the second basket above Jehoiada's head.

"Nathanael," Jehoiada nearly shouted, announcing with joy one of Remiel's grandsons. He didn't know young Nathanael personally, but Remiel's was a prominent family of strong character and faithful service.

Oohs and aahs rippled among them as Nathanael's family jostled him with congratulatory hugs and shoves. The man's face turned as white as the stone when Jehoiada approached. "Are you married, Nathanael?"

"No." He swallowed hard. "I'm not."

Jehoiada tried to hide a grin. Perhaps Yahweh would sanction this marriage after all. Nathanael was young, handsome, strong, and healthy. Perhaps he could lead Jehoram's daughter—and maybe the whole royal household—back to Yahweh.

"I'll proceed to the breastpiece of decision to hear Yahweh's final word on Nathanael as high priest." Jehoiada stepped toward the breastpiece, and once again the room became reverently still.

He reached into the pocket and drew out the black Urim. Jehoiada's heart plummeted, and the whole room exhaled a disappointed "Oh no." Nathanael laid his stone on the table, removing it from the baskets, and the whole family of Remiel melted back into the sons of Aaron.

Inhaling a deep breath, Jehoiada approached the first basket once more and addressed his brother priests. "We need not be disheartened when Yahweh is specific in His choosing. We have seen the Urim and Thummim prove faultless in communicating the Lord's perfect will." He reached into the first basket and stirred the lots before withdrawing a second family stone.

His heart fell. His mouth went dry. "Jehoiada." Eyes stinging, he could barely breathe, let alone speak. How could *he* be Yahweh's choice? And how could he bear the shame of stating there'd be no need for a second basket to write his family names?

He cleared his throat and forced his gaze up from his sandals, but found his brother priests staring intently at their own. "I have no sons or grandsons."

Awkward silence ushered him toward the breastpiece of decision, where Elan had already replaced the Urim and jostled the two stones. Jehoiada need only reach in and hear the Lord speak. His hand trembled, hovering over the pouch. *Yahweh, please. I cannot be Your high priest. I am not worthy.*

He reached in and drew out the white Thummim.

The room erupted in celebration, but Jehoiada heard it as if in a dream. Leaning against the table for support, he gasped for air, suddenly wondering if he might die on the spot and be the shortest-tenured high priest ever.

The celebration died into silence, and Remiel approached the table. "Jehoiada, since you're no longer married, we need only consult the Urim and Thummim to determine Yahweh's decision on King Jehoram's request that you marry his daughter."

Beads of sweat gathered on Jehoiada's brow. A nod was his only reply as he offered the white Thummim back to the assistant and turned to face Remiel as the stones jostled within the breastpiece. The air hummed with anticipation, but for Jehoiada the scene felt as if he were in another place.

"The breastpiece is ready, my lord," Elan said, giving Jehoiada the encouragement he needed.

The new high priest reached into the breastpiece. His fingers slid around one stone—then released it and drew out the other.

The white Thummim. *Yahweh said yes.*

A cheer arose, so loud the Temple rafters shook, and Jehoiada braced himself against the table while well-wishers slapped his back and offered premature congratulations. Had they forgotten the circumstance of this bizarre marriage? Had they and the king lost their senses? But the question uppermost in his mind, the issue that stole his breath: *What kind of marriage can I have with the child I met in the quarry?*

14

Saul replied, "Say to David, 'The king wants no other price for the bride than a hundred Philistine foreskins, to take revenge on his enemies.'"

Well after dawn, Sheba awoke, curled in a ball atop her fur-covered bed, wearing the filthy robe she'd traveled in all day from Jezreel. The Asherah she'd forgotten to pack for Jezreel sat on the bedside table. "Perhaps if you'd been there to protect me, I wouldn't be promised to a priest of Yahweh." Jizebaal's teraphim had certainly betrayed her.

Sheba's mouth tasted like a camel smelled, and her stomach noisily protested missing last night's meal. She had just reached for the servant's bell when a knock sounded on her door. Perfect timing. "Come!" she said, her voice as rough as she felt.

A maid entered and assumed a deep bow. "You've been summoned to the king's chamber—immediately."

Sheba dropped the bell, hearing it clatter to the tile floor as she dashed out the door, down the hall, and up the grand staircase. Nearly slipping in front of Hazi's chamber, where a servant knelt scrubbing bloodstained tiles, she righted herself and leaned against the wall, mind racing. Had Abba died in

122

the night? *God, oh god, whichever god is listening, please don't take Abba so soon.*

Hurrying to the king's private suite at the end of the hallway, she slowed her pace when she saw the Carites standing like pillars on each side of the entry. No torn clothing or ashes in their hair or beards. A measure of relief crept into her frantically beating heart.

Sheba bowed to the guards, and they opened the doors without hesitation. The fumes of incense and human waste nearly overwhelmed her. Clay incense bowls surrounded Abba in his bed, now the centerpiece of what used to be the king's private meeting chamber. Abba Jehoram appeared pale as the white linen beneath him. Hazi sat on a couch to his left and Ima on a couch to his right, dabbing her nose with a purple sachet holding aromatic spices. Mattan stood like a gold-turbaned soldier behind Ima Thaliah, stone-faced. He'd barely acknowledged Sheba since the Gevirah announced her marriage to the Yahweh priest.

"You look as bad as your abba." Ima's disapproving gaze roamed the length of Sheba's morning appearance. "How dare you come into the king's presence like a beggar?"

"Thaliah." Abba's one-word rebuke quieted his wife and warmed Sheba's heart. Though only days had passed since he'd been her champion, it seemed a lifetime since anyone had challenged Ima Thaliah.

"Please forgive me. I meant no disrespect." Sheba bowed, holding back tears. "I'm afraid sleep was a miser and made me a beggar. I awoke to your summons and responded without preparing myself."

"Come, sit between us, Sheba." Ima Thaliah's voice softened, and she patted a place on the couch beside her.

Sheba glanced at Hazi, trying to guess what was coming. He looked grim, and her heart plummeted. Servants hustled about the room, tearing sheets into bandages and rinsing soiled cloths. The palace physician consulted with three other Baal priests, no doubt preparing to plead for supernatural healing since a physical one seemed hopeless. For a fleeting moment, she wondered if she'd be called on to assist the other priestesses, stitching the priests' wounds after their frantic chanting, dancing, and cutting.

"We'll attend your brothers' funeral pyre this evening at twilight." The warmth in Ima's voice sent a shock of warning, and her smile resembled Jizebaal's.

Mattan leaned over her shoulder, his beady eyes suddenly devouring her. "After your maids have done what they can to make you more appealing, you'll serve as chief priestess for tonight's ceremony—since it will most likely be your last offering to Baal Melkart." He smiled, his pointed nose resembling an eagle's hooked beak. Sheba felt like prey. "Since you'll never be initiated as a high priestess, I believe your ima will appreciate the special role I have planned for you in tonight's festivities."

Dread strangled her voice, and she reached for Abba's hand like a lifeline. He squeezed her fingers, and she found him smiling through a pained expression. "They've chosen a new Yahweh high priest, my lamb."

"Already?" she said, turning to Ima Thaliah.

"Yes, and he's coming here to discuss the arrangements."

"Here? When?"

"Soon." Abba ventured another smile, but the effort seemed to cost him dearly. A low moan escaped, and beads of perspiration gathered on his brow. Sheba released his hand, snatched a wet cloth from a servant, and began dabbing Abba's forehead herself.

Hazi stilled her hand and tilted her chin to meet his gaze. "Sheba, he's coming here now to talk about your marriage. Perhaps you'd like to . . ." A sweet smile creased his lips. "I don't know. Maybe smudge a little dirt on your other cheek so they match?"

"Now?" She used the cloth to scrub both cheeks, hoping to redden them. She bit her lips, tasting blood, and then smeared them together. A knock on the door stilled her. Back stiff. Eyes wide. "What do I do now, Ima?"

Athaliah rolled her eyes and commanded the servant at the door. "Escort the priest."

Sheba laced her fingers together on her lap, waiting for the first glimpse of her new husband. Would he be short, tall, fat, thin? He must be handsome. She couldn't bear to stare at an ugly man for the rest of her days . . .

"You?" Sheba gasped at the sight of him—the angry old priest from the quarry. There must be some mistake. She glanced at Ima, Abba—both stared at their guest. She looked at Hazi for reprieve, but his compassionate gaze told her there was no mistake.

Jehoiada had sent a Levite to the palace this morning as a simple courtesy to inform them of Yahweh's choice of high priest. He'd thought, *Surely the king will wait to speak of wedding plans until Jerusalem is rebuilt.* But no! Jehoram summoned Jehoiada to his chambers immediately, despite the mounds of restoration yet to be done.

Frustration at its peak, Jehoiada determined to engage the king in *real* bridal negotiations. He'd negotiate as fiercely as any other suitor, demanding the bride's fidelity—to him and to Yahweh—and requiring her to leave her abba's household, as would any other bride.

Escorted by two Temple guards, Jehoiada ignored the Carites at the king's chamber and pounded on the door himself. After an inexcusable delay, the double cedar doors opened, and the smell of illness assaulted him. The beleaguered faces of the king, the queen, and their two children startled him into the painful world of Jehoram's illness and the adjustments this family was enduring.

"You?" he heard the young woman gasp, and for the first time he considered her broken dreams. From the moment this marriage was mentioned, Jehoiada had considered only the high priest's interests. *But what of this young woman's first love? What of the children she'd hoped for?* His heart nearly stopped at the thought. Did the princess know of Jehoiada's previous marriage, of his childlessness?

Her cheeks were flushed. So young, so beautiful—she looked terrified. *Yahweh, did You really consecrate this marriage with the Thummim?*

"Come, Jehoiada," Jehoram said, his voice weak. "Surely I haven't grown more repulsive than I was yesterday."

Jehoiada realized he'd stopped at the threshold. Regaining his senses, he proceeded into the chamber, thanking the servant who placed an extra couch near Prince Ahaziah. Jehoiada took his place between the prince and the king's bed. "You are not repulsive, and I'm sure you feel better under your physician's care."

King Jehoram attempted a smile but winced instead.

Prince Ahaziah offered his hand in greeting. "I'd like to thank you properly for protecting Abba during the raid." His expression, his whole countenance, seemed genuine. "I'll be speaking for King Jehoram today since his illness makes it difficult to converse."

Jehoiada nodded, agreeing. He glanced at Athaliah and the princess—the queen cool and distant, the young woman trembling, unwilling to meet his gaze. He squeezed his eyes shut, inhaled, shook his head. "Perhaps we should reconsider this marriage, Prince Ahaziah. Isn't it plain that your sister deserves a younger—"

"No!" Jehoram rallied his strength.

"No!" Queen Athaliah's eyes blazed, and she placed a quieting hand on the king's shoulder. "My husband and I have discussed the matter and both agree that offering our daughter to Yahweh's high priest is a worthy match—whether it averts His judgment or not. We seek to make a covenant with the god of Jehoshaphat."

Jehoiada considered the queen's argument, realizing Jehoram must have shared the details of their conversation in the quarry since Athaliah's words so closely matched the king's pleas. "We do not make covenants with Yahweh," Jehoiada replied. "The sons of Abraham, Isaac, and Jacob are already in covenant with Him, and the best course of action for everyone would be to abide by the covenant He gave to Moses at Sinai, which is the *Law*. Now, if you'll let me explain—"

"The king of Judah needs no explanation of his own heritage," the Baal high priest sneered. "You take the term *covenant* too literally, Priest. It's a simple treaty marriage to unite the king's house with Yahweh's priests."

"A treaty marriage," Jehoiada repeated as understanding began to dawn. This was as much—or more—a political maneuver as a spiritual act. "And why do you wish to join the house of David with Yahweh's high priest?"

Prince Ahaziah tapped his shoulder, wresting his attention from the stone-faced queen. "You see, Jehoiada, as high priest you judge matters concerning the Temple in central court at the palace only once a week. On all other days, you remain sequestered on Temple grounds. Abba Jehoram feels that through the treaty marriage with my sister, you'll become more attuned to the overall political matters of the entire nation."

Jehoiada studied the prince's eager expression. He'd obviously been briefed on all that Jehoiada and King Jehoram had spoken about in the quarry. If he knew Jehoiada had lived in the Temple all his life, he undoubtedly knew of Jehoiada's previous marriage and inability to produce children. If that presented no problem for the royal household, Jehoiada would leave the issue unspoken. However, some things must be declared.

"If I am to marry Princess Jehosheba, *she* must agree to my terms."

The princess sat stoically perched beside Athaliah, still refusing to look at him.

Ahaziah scooted to the edge of his couch, apparently prepared to negotiate. "We waive the mohar, understanding that you as a priest of Yahweh have no personal wealth to offer as payment for a bride." He chuckled, nerves seeming to get the better of him. "I suppose you're a little like the young David, who paid the bride-price for King Saul's daughter in Philistine foreskins."

Jehoiada was not amused. "I'm not young, nor am I *asking* for the king's daughter."

Ahaziah cleared his throat and continued. "Well, Sheba will still receive a shiluhim from Abba Jehoram on her wedding day. The dowry will be reduced due to the recent raid but will probably contain greater wealth than you've seen in your life." The prince's features registered regret as soon as the words escaped.

"Have you forgotten that I minister in the splendor of

Yahweh's Temple every day—that is, every day of my pauper priestly life?"

"I'm sorry, Jehoiada. I—"

"How could you know what my life is like, Prince Ahaziah?" He clasped the young man's shoulder, casting a penetrating gaze in the queen's direction. "I don't believe your ima or any of her children have attended a single sacrifice at Yahweh's Temple."

Queen Athaliah offered a slow, sinister smile. "How flattering that you've noticed our absence, Priest. But I assure you that my children and I are extremely devout." She patted the princess as if stroking a pet. "Sheba has been well trained in ritual arts and will continue to serve Judah well as a confidante in political matters."

Jehoiada felt as if his chest were on fire. *Ritual arts? Confidante in political matters?* Containing his initial spark of fury, he issued a condescending smile equal to the one given. "I will gladly marry your daughter, Queen Athaliah, after our ordination ceremonies and after our Feasts of Passover and Unleavened Bread."

The queen shared a triumphant glance with the Baal priest behind her, making Jehoiada's next words to Prince Ahaziah all the more satisfying. "And I have two more conditions. First, she must renounce any claim to Baal Melkart and worship Yahweh alone." He heard gasps all round but continued undaunted. "Second, she will leave the palace and live on Temple grounds as a common priest's wife, not as a pampered princess or *partner* in whatever you have planned for Judah. These are my terms."

He stood amid a flurry of Jehoram's pained cries and Athaliah's outraged shrieks. Prince Ahaziah met him eye to eye and extended his hand. "I will speak with my sister and send word of her decision by sunset tonight."

"Good. Our seven-day ordination begins in four days, and I don't want anything to distract from our worship of Yahweh."

The prince nodded his agreement. Jehoiada turned and walked out of the room, his back to the raging royals.

15

➤ 1 Chronicles 9:19 ◄

*The son of Korah . . . and his fellow gatekeepers from
his family (the Korahites) were responsible for guarding
the thresholds of the tent just as their ancestors had been
responsible for guarding the entrance to the dwelling of
the LORD.*

Sheba watched the priest walk out of her abba's chamber,
stunned by his rudeness, amazed at his boldness. No one
had ever treated Ima Thaliah that way—not even Abba.

"He'll regret the day he crossed swords with me." Ima threw
herself back onto the couch beside Sheba, directing her comment at Abba, whose face twisted in pain.

Sheba cast a woeful glance at Hazi, and emotion closed her
throat. She'd held her tongue and her tears in check during the
priest's visit, but she was at her limit. Shoulders back, head
held high, she wrapped herself in tattered dignity and walked
toward Abba's chamber door.

"Where do you think you're going?" Ima shouted behind her.

"Let her go, Ima." Hazi's quiet words nearly released the
floodgates of Sheba's tears, but she held on.

She glided down the grand stairway and through the hall
of women, then opened her chamber door with exaggerated

control. Startling her maids, she kept her voice level. "Get out. Now. All of you." Her trembling began before the last maid hurried past her. Sheba slammed the door and flung herself across her fur-covered bed, releasing her screams into an embroidered pillow.

Muffled and completely unsatisfying, her tantrum spent what little energy she had left. She lay on her bed, numb. How had her life come to this? A few days ago, she had skipped into an evening meal, her only care the ruby earring a clumsy maid had dropped under her couch.

Now she faced the yawning emptiness of a lonely existence among poor priests in the Temple of a god she wasn't sure existed—scheduled after some ceremony and two feasts.

A timid knock interrupted her pity fest. She grabbed a clay lamp and hurled it against the door. "Stay out!" The latch clicked, and she looked for another lamp to ready her aim.

Hazi peeked around the edge of the door. "Is it safe?" Her wellspring of tears gushed again, and he hurried to her side. "Oh, Sheba." He gathered her in his arms and rested his chin on her head. "I suppose your first meeting didn't go as well as we'd hoped."

She shoved him away. "As well as *we'd* hoped? How long had you known I was to marry Methuselah?"

"Ha!" Hazi's belly laugh lightened the mood. "He's not *that* old, is he? I thought he was quite good-looking for an ancient priest."

Sheba wouldn't be distracted. "How long have you known, Hazi? And did you realize I would be reduced to a maid?"

His eyes softened, and he smoothed the curls off her forehead. "Ima summoned me to Abba's chambers only a few moments before you arrived. That's when I was told of Yahweh's new high priest. They prepared me with a list of demands for bride negotiations that Jehoiada never gave me the chance to stipulate." He winked and issued a tentative smile. "But I like him, Sheba."

"Then you marry him!" Sheba thrashed him with her pillow. "How old is he anyway?"

"I don't know exactly, but Abba said he served with the high priest Amariah during Saba Jehoshaphat's reign."

Sheba gasped, doing some quick figuring in her mind. "He's got to be at least . . ."

"But he doesn't look any older than Abba," Hazi added before she could hazard her guess.

Her brother was pressing too hard in this priest's favor. Her eyes narrowed, measuring his all-too-perky expression. "Ima sent you in here, didn't she?"

Pursing his lips, he hesitated before answering. "We've always been honest with each other, haven't we, Sheba?"

Her heart twisted. She ignored the question and said, "Tell me, Hazi. What is it?"

"You're right, Abba and Ima sent me to convince you to marry Jehoiada, but the truth is—I'm afraid for you to stay here alone after I'm gone." She couldn't meet his gaze, didn't deserve his love and loyalty, but he tilted her chin up and studied her. "I don't know what happened in Jezreel with Gevirah Jezebel"—they both chuckled at his daring use of the slanderous name—"but I know whatever they planned is tearing you apart, and I believe Jehoiada will protect you. It may not be the life you hoped for, but it's life. Marry him, Sheba." He tapped the end of her nose and grinned. "It will put my mind at ease while I marry every pretty girl in Judah."

She wanted to smile and pretend it was okay—but it wasn't. "What about a bride's betrothal year? What about a bridegroom preparing for his bride and coming with attendants to collect her? Am I to be robbed of every happiness in this life?" The last words were garbled by a sob, but Hazi didn't need to understand what she said to know her heart.

He gathered her in his arms again. "I don't know exactly how your wedding celebration will proceed, but I know everyone in the city is adjusting to death and destruction. Perhaps your wedding will give Jerusalem something to celebrate while we're trying to rebuild. I know it's not perfect, but . . ."

"I hate her. I hate both of them." Sheba spoke the hard words softly into Hazi's shoulder. He knew who she meant.

"I know." He held her. Silently. Patiently. Without judgment. When her muscles began to cramp, he helped her stretch out on the bed. "I'll get your maids. You need some sleep, and I'll return before the evening meal to hear your answer for Jehoiada."

The thought of giving an answer made her nauseous, but she let him send the maids. Sleep. She needed sleep. Perhaps the gods would reveal what she should do in a dream. *And if Hazi likes this old man, perhaps he's not all bad.*

She was too weary to wrestle with her thoughts and gave herself to the ministrations of her maids.

Jehoiada returned through the King's Gate to a multitude of curious priests awaiting word of the bride negotiations.

"Will you pay a mohar out of the Temple treasury?"

"When's the wedding ceremony?"

"Is she beautiful?"

A string of questions and a line of priests followed Jehoiada all the way into the rear gallery, where more priests anxiously awaited his return. Before they could add their inquiries, Jehoiada lifted his hands—as much in surrender as pleading for silence. "Please, brothers. We have much to accomplish and little daylight to do it." An eruption of more questions confirmed that the marriage topic wouldn't be put off so easily.

"All right. All right!" He slammed his hand on the center table, startling them into silence. "I presented King Jehoram with two conditions, and the royal household has promised an answer by tonight's sacrifice. As for your other questions: No, the date has not officially been decided. No, Temple funds will not be used for a bride-price. And *if* the marriage occurs—as Yahweh directed through the Thummim—the princess will live on Temple grounds as the high priest's wife and nothing more."

Shock. Disbelief. Utter horror stared back at him. What had they expected? That the couple would share a palace on the western ridge?

"We have much to accomplish today," he continued without addressing their obvious concern. "The first task being the appointment of my second priest. The Law gives no specific requirements, leaving it to the high priest's discretion and Yahweh's approval by Urim and Thummim. I have chosen Nathanael ben Jotham, of Remiel's family. After drawing the family's lot from the first basket last night, and Nathanael's stone from the second basket, I believe the Lord's hand of favor is on the young man."

An excited buzz worked through the room, and like the Red Sea the crowd of priests parted, allowing Nathanael to join Jehoiada.

Nathanael bowed slightly, whispering, "Me? Are you sure? I have no idea what a second priest's responsibilities entail."

Jehoiada chuckled and matched his quiet tone. "Neither did I when Amariah chose me." Again lifting his voice above the excitement, Jehoiada questioned Nathanael publicly before drawing from the breastpiece. "Nathanael ben Jotham, of the family Remiel, I have chosen you to serve as second priest for all the days I, Jehoiada ben Jonah, serve as Yahweh's high priest. You will be required to live in community, with whatever wife and children Yahweh blesses you with, in the chambers of Yahweh's Temple for as long as you serve Him. Can you commit to such a calling?"

The young priest blinked several times before answering, and Jehoiada wondered if fear of another Urim rejection might deter him. "Yes, Brother Jehoiada. If Yahweh accepts my service, I will commit my life to Him."

Jehoiada placed both hands on Nathanael's shoulders, steadying him, and then reached for the breastpiece of decision lying on the table behind them. Jehoiada lifted his brow at the priest's assistant, silently asking if the stones were ready. A confirming nod, and Jehoiada reached inside. He closed his eyes and drew out the stone, holding it aloft without looking—so certain was he of Yahweh's approval.

The room erupted into cheers, and Nathanael covered his face and wept.

Jehoiada engulfed him in a hug, surrounded by others joining their celebration. The high priest stepped aside, allowing those who knew Nathanael best to encourage him most. To feel rejected by Yahweh as he might have last night would embitter some, but this young man was willing to lay his heart bare before the Creator again. Jehoiada wiped a tear and called the group to order once more.

"Another task lies before us, and then we must resume our many duties." The priests quieted as Jehoiada continued. "Eleazar, the chief keeper of the threshold, was killed in the Temple attack. I'm appointing a new chief gatekeeper." He scanned the sea of faces but saw only priests, no Levites. Addressing the priests nearest the doorway, he said, "Send for the Kohathite guard Zabad." A low hum rumbled through the gathering. "Many of you won't know this young man, but he's largely responsible for saving Jerusalem, and I believe him to be courageous and strong of heart."

Zabad appeared at the doorway, confusion etched on his features. "You called for me?" He glanced around the room of priests, clearly intimidated, but stepped inside, fixing his gaze on the new high priest. "How may I serve you?"

Jehoiada smiled, accepting the young man's question as unwitting compliance. He extended his hand, summoning the Levite to the center table. He whispered for Zabad's hearing alone, "Remember last night when I told you we'd need leaders to replace those we've lost?"

Zabad's brow furrowed, but he stood courageously as Jehoiada began his public questions. "Zabad *ben Seth*." He paused, emphasizing Zabad as the son of a Levite, not simply the son of an Ammonite woman. The guard nodded furtive thanks. "I choose you as chief keeper of the threshold to oversee the Temple gates, treasury, and chambers, and to open Yahweh's gates for His worshipers every day for the rest of your life. You will be required to live in community, with whatever wife and children Yahweh blesses you with, in the chambers of Yahweh's Temple for as long as you serve Him. Can you commit to such a calling?"

Zabad glanced around the room and back toward the doorway, where a few curious Levites had gathered. "May I ask a question before giving my answer, Brother Jehoiada?"

"Of course."

"Why? Why would you make me *chief* gatekeeper? Why not honor one more worthy or experienced?"

Jehoiada lifted his voice, addressing the growing crowd. "I have chosen Zabad because I have seen him defend Yahweh's Temple and its high priest without prejudice or favoritism—against the king's Carites, against heathen Philistines and Arabs—and I believe he would defend this Temple against even Yahweh's priests, should any of us transgress His laws." He placed a hand on Zabad's shoulder. "This is why you are my choice. Shall we ask Yahweh for His decision?"

Zabad gulped audibly, his eyes as round as the king's incense saucers. A nod was his only reply, but it was enough to send Jehoiada's hand into the breastpiece of decision once more.

He held up the white Thummim in front of Zabad's eyes before checking its color. "This, Zabad, is Yahweh's approval of you. Don't let any man say you are less than worthy of Yahweh's best."

A reserved applause rippled through the priests, quite subdued compared to the festive response Nathanael had received. But Zabad didn't notice. His eyes were full of Yahweh's approval, which flowed in tears down his cheeks.

Jehoiada watched the celebration surrounding him and was suddenly awed at Yahweh's grace and mercy. Though he still mourned Amariah's loss, the blossoming ministries of these young men provided hope, where yesterday there was only discouragement. And Jehoiada's marriage to the young princess was beyond unconventional, but perhaps Obadiah had been right when he reported Elijah's letter to Jehoram and said Yahweh was at work in Judah.

Jostled back to the present as the priests exited, Jehoiada shouted above the commotion, "You've each been given your tasks for this day. We'll meet back here shortly before the twilight sacrifice."

Nathanael and Zabad lingered beside him, and Jehoiada opened his hand, realizing he still clutched the white Thummim.

"Were you as amazed as me when the Thummim was drawn to approve your high priesthood?" Nathanael stood gazing at the white stone.

"I daresay I was every bit as amazed as you." Jehoiada placed the stone into the pocket of the breastpiece. "Come, you two. Nathanael, I'll show you to your chamber. You can sleep in my bed, and I get Amariah's wool-stuffed mattress."

The new second priest chuckled. "As it should be."

Jehoiada stopped, a terrifying thought striking him like a blow to the head. "Zabad, now that you're in charge of assigning priests' chambers, we should talk about preparing a bridal chamber—if the princess actually agrees to my terms." He felt his cheeks flush and noted the young men elbowing each other. "And Nathanael will need to live in the chamber next door."

Zabad grinned and squeezed Nathanael's cheeks. "Wouldn't you rather wake up to a princess instead of this ugly mug?"

Jehoiada lifted a single brow, stopping their antics with a scowl. "I will awaken to the cleansing of the Molten Sea and the high priest's garments." He walked away, knowing they'd follow, hoping his blush would disappear by the time they needed to discuss tonight's sacrifice. The thought of waking up to a beautiful princess was entirely too much to bear.

16

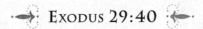

EXODUS 29:40

With the first lamb offer a tenth of an ephah of the finest flour mixed with a quarter of a hin of oil from pressed olives, and a quarter of a hin of wine as a drink offering.

Sheba woke to afternoon sunlight streaming through her balcony with the eerie feeling of doom. She opened one eye and then the other, waking from sleep as deep as death, trying to remember what day it was, what year. Her eyes felt as if someone had poured sand in them—swollen and scratchy. With utter despair, life came rushing in. *I'm to marry an old man and live as a common priest's wife.*

"Ooh!" she groaned, pressing her fists into her eyes.

"So you're finally awake."

She screamed, nearly falling off the bed at Ima Thaliah's greeting. Irritation overcame decorum. "Haven't you already ruined my life? What more can you do to me?"

Ima sat like an Asherah on the couch by the balcony. She raised a single kohl-defined brow, addressing the maids. "Leave us."

Heat rose in Sheba's cheeks. Fear. Regret. Shame. She should never have spoken so disrespectfully—especially in front of witnesses. "I'm sorry," she said before the last maid hurried out the door. "I didn't mean it. I'm tired, confused."

137

Ima remained unmoved. Waiting. Sheba tried to tamp down her rising panic, unnerved by the extended silence, her heart beating like a drum. Could Ima hear it across the room?

"You seem to have assumed that our plan for your future has taken some unexpected turn." Ima's voice was cool, distant. "When I chose you as my daughter, I sent word to the Gevirah that we had our next queen of destiny. You were lively and quick-witted, accepting of change, and eager to learn—even as a young child. I believed you could be a queen."

Sheba's nerves gave way to confusion. "But how can I be a queen if I'm to live in squalor as a priest's wife?"

Ima Thaliah sighed, shaking her head. "You are a queen of destiny because you will influence Yahweh's high priest as an honorary daughter of Jizebaal. Your name will be remembered throughout history as a woman who saved the house of David by your sacrificial marriage." At the mention of the house of David, a sudden warmth enfolded Sheba—not the familiar flush of fear, but a balm of peace unlike any she'd known. And just as quickly it was gone, replaced by a shiver and Ima's piercing stare.

"I hope your tremor is a sign of excitement at the days ahead." Thaliah tugged at a leather necklace, lifting a stone seal from beneath her robe. She produced a similar bauble from her pocket. "Do you recognize these?"

Sheba scooted off the bed and joined Ima on the couch. The spring breeze from the open balcony was cool, making her shiver again. "They're seals like Abba uses to imprint his official mark on parchment scrolls."

Ima Thaliah smoothed her hair, an affectionate gesture done a thousand times, but this time it felt contrived. "Yes, Daughter, but these seals are almost identical to Gevirah Jizebaal's, different by only one letter. Mine adds the first letter of my name." She pointed to the seal hanging from her neck. "And this one adds the first letter of your name."

Sheba gasped, accepting the precious gift from Ima's hands. "You had it carved for me?" Ima Thaliah nodded, her eyes misting as if genuinely moved by the enduring heirloom. Perhaps Sheba had been too hard on her. The visit with the Gevirah had

138

placed them both under enormous strain, and maybe, now that they had returned home, their relationship could regain the tenderness she craved.

"Here, let me fasten it securely." Ima nudged her to face the balcony, and Sheba lifted her hair so she could tie the leather knot. "You must never take off your seal, Daughter. It's like a second skin to you, and it will be the only way we'll have to communicate when you live on the Temple grounds with the priest." The words pierced Sheba's freshly exposed heart. "Since he's insisting you live like a common priest's wife, we won't be able to send a maid with you, so you'll have to write any urgent correspondence and use your seal on the scroll to ensure its privacy. I'll make sure you can trust at least one of the Temple guards, and we'll exchange our messages through him."

She fluffed Sheba's hair around her shoulders and turned her around. "And do you see why your priestess training in several languages is so crucial? Find out which language your new husband does *not* understand, and use that one in our communications."

Sheba maintained even breaths, refusing to grieve over leaving this woman who obviously cared nothing about her. "It seems you and the Gevirah have everything well thought out."

Ima fiddled with the new seal dangling around Sheba's neck. "Hide it beneath your clothes, and when your priest demands you remove it, refuse him. It's good for a wife to refuse her husband *something* now and then." She winked as if they were old gossips sharing a secret and then patted her knees, a nervous tick signaling she was ready to leave. "Well, it's time I sent your decision to the priest. We don't want to keep the old curmudgeon waiting." Her forced cheerfulness was so sickeningly sweet, Sheba almost asked for bitter herbs to offset the charade. Instead, she remained silent, letting Ima brush her cheek. "Would you like me to send a personal message to your new bridegroom?"

Mischief crept into Sheba's tone. "Tell him I'll bring balm of Gilead for his creaking joints."

Thaliah's eyes lit with fury. "You will make Jehoiada believe he is the love of your life because that's the way a woman gains power over a man. If you haven't learned that by now, Jehosheba, perhaps the Gevirah and I were wrong about you." She sat there fuming, staring.

Sheba's heart pounded again. This was her chance. If she was ever to refuse the marriage, now was the time. But what then? After all she'd learned about Ima Thaliah, the Gevirah, kings on thrones, and the destiny of queens . . . The world was a grinding stone, and she could choose to be the hand that turned the wheel or the kernel that was crushed.

She stood, and Ima Thaliah quickly matched her stance. "I'll convince Yahweh's priest he's a god," Sheba said. The approval in Ima's eyes pressed her to the next level of dread. "And tell Mattan I'll be ready to assist him with your sons' burial service after our evening meal."

Shortly before last night's twilight service, a palace messenger brought word to Jehoiada that Jehosheba had accepted his terms. He'd nearly sliced off his thumb during the evening sacrifice—his concentration was lacking, to say the least.

This morning, Jehoiada stood on the elevated porch of the Temple with over three hundred priest candidates—robed, barefoot, and as nervous as he'd been while awaiting his consecration years ago. The weeklong ordination would begin in three days. Jehoiada would lead this morning's regular sacrifice and then have a senior priest announce both the consecration and the wedding planned after the feasts. At least Jehoiada could concentrate on the Feasts of Passover and Unleavened Bread before his new wife demanded his attention.

Yahweh, help me focus on serving You. It would be a miracle, considering he recalled Jehosheba's face with every breath.

Lifting his hands, Jehoiada began the familiar Hebrew prayer, inviting the congregation to recite with him. "Hear, O Israel: Yahweh is our God, Yahweh alone. Love Yahweh with all your heart and with all your soul and with all your strength." The crisp spring air rang with the melody of the faithful, the courtyard full to bursting. The Levite choir began their sacred psalms, and Jehoiada folded his hands at his chest, content to scan the faces of those he would serve for the rest of his days.

And then he saw them.

Prince Ahaziah, Princess Jehosheba, Obadiah, and Zev the Carite captain stood discreetly near the Guards' Gate in the inner court—the entrance normally used by palace and Temple staff. Why hadn't they entered through the King's Gate as was customary for royalty? What business had Obadiah with the princess? Had the king's condition worsened? They would surely send for Mattan if he'd died—considering the royal sons' burial last night at Baal's temple.

He stole another glance at the princess standing between the Carite and her brother. She was stunning, lithe, and graceful—more beautiful than he'd remembered. Her dark, round eyes beckoned him, though her uplifted chin screamed nobility. He shook his head, trying to rid himself of the distraction.

The Levite hymns were ending, and Jehoiada was expected to offer the sacrifice. Preoccupied yet dutiful, he descended the porch stairs, gathered the wriggling year-old lamb in his arms, and heard the crowd gasp when he reached the platform surrounding the brazen altar. Only after the fleeting memory of Amariah's painful struggle up the altar steps did Jehoiada realize why the worshipers had grown utterly silent. Toting the stout, yearling lamb up the steps was effortless for Jehoiada. In all his years as a priest, he'd wrestled dozens of rams and bulls to the slaughtering tables in the courtyard. But no one except other priests had seen it.

As if sensing his discomfort, the lamb stilled and looked up with its mournful black eyes. "I know you don't deserve it," he whispered to the innocent lamb, "but that's the point."

The two priests waiting exchanged worried glances, no doubt wondering if the new high priest had lost his mind—talking to sacrifices.

Jehoiada placed the animal on the platform, held its neck over the drainage trough, and raised his voice. "May the blood of the lamb atone for the sins of God's people." With a swift, clean slice, Jehoiada offered the atoning blood into the channel surrounding the altar. He knelt there until the light of life left the lamb's eyes. *Thank You for forgiving Your people, Yahweh.*

While the other priests went about the work of sectioning the lamb for burning, the prayers of Yahweh's faithful created a reverent hum. Jehoiada received the sacred grain offering from a third priest, who had baked the flatbread this morning using fine flour and the purest olive oil—always seasoned with salt.

Jehoiada lifted the grain offering before the crowd with his right hand and held a quarter hin of fermented wine in a pitcher with his left. "May these offerings made by fire be a pleasing aroma before the Lord—even as the prayers of His people ascend to His holy throne." He tossed the unleavened bread into the fire and poured out the wine, mingling it with the blood of the lamb.

The Levite choir began their closing hymns, and Jehoiada descended the altar stairs, his heart and mind consumed with the realization of his high and holy calling. This would be the last sacrifice he'd make as an ordinary priest. After his ordination, he would appear before the people wearing the golden garments of the high priest—the ephod, the breastpiece, and the diadem affixed to his turban. In the past, he'd performed the morning and twilight services when Amariah had been unable to serve due to illness, but care for God's people had never before rested squarely on his own shoulders.

"Brother Jehoiada." Zabad approached, jarring him from his contemplation as he reached the porch steps. "Prince Hazi and Obadiah have come with the princess to see you. Captain Zev has asked to escort them to your private chambers for a brief meeting."

Everything within Jehoiada screamed, *No! I'm distracted enough! We must begin our preparations immediately!* But he remembered the four troubled faces and sensed something out of the ordinary. "Ask them to wait in my chamber. I'll explain my delay to Nathanael so the assistants can continue their work."

Zabad bowed and hurried to deliver his message. Jehoiada glimpsed Zev and the prince ushering the princess through the inner court, noting her wince when they supported her arms. Obadiah shook his head and followed like a fretting ima. Dread crept up Jehoiada's spine. This visit had nothing to do with King Jehoram.

Jehoiada quickly explained the circumstance to Nathanael while the senior priest announced suspended public worship during the seven-day ordination service. Faithful worshipers began grousing but were soothed by the promise of ordination sacrifices on the community's behalf.

"And a bit of happy news," the senior priest added. "Our new high priest will marry Princess Jehosheba, daughter of King Jehoram, in a private wedding ceremony!" A resounding cheer rose, and Jehoiada ducked his head, fairly running toward his chamber to escape well-wishers.

Whispering a prayer as he hurried across the inner court, he stopped outside his door and inhaled a calming breath. Why was his heart beating like the hooves of a horse in a chariot race?

He opened the door and began talking at once. "How may I help—"

The sight of her took his breath. Princess Jehosheba stood like one of the Temple pillars—as white as limestone from the quarry. They'd removed her outer cloak and pushed up the sleeves of her robe. Bloodied bandages lined her forearms, and her left hand bore a stitched wound.

Jehoiada stumbled back against the door frame. "Yahweh, help her." The whispered prayer escaped before he realized he'd spoken, and the young woman winced as if she'd been slapped.

Prince Ahaziah stepped forward, his eyes red-rimmed, his face chiseled granite. "Actually, I was hoping *you* would help her."

Confused, Jehoiada regained his footing and crossed his outer chamber in three steps. The young woman recoiled as if frightened—of him. "What happened to her?" He posed the question to any of them but directed his increasing anger at the men. "Who did this?" he shouted.

Obadiah drew a breath to answer, but the prince intervened. "A priest!" He matched Jehoiada's fury. "A priest did this!"

Obadiah stepped between them, placing a calming hand on both their chests. "Jehoiada is not like Mattan. Tell him what happened to your sister. He will listen."

Ahaziah lifted his trembling chin, grasping at nobility, struggling against tears. "Ima Thaliah and I attended the burial ceremony for my older brothers last night at Baal's temple. Mattan asked Sheba to serve as chief priestess, bestowing that honor since her marriage disqualifies her from the role of high priestess." He stepped aside, showcasing the violence. "Mattan said four dead princes required a great deal of virgin's blood to gain entrance into Mot's underworld."

Jehoiada's whole world tilted precariously on the edge of a single question. "How could your sister—my newly betrothed—serve as a Baal priestess?" His tone betrayed his threat. Yahweh's high priest could never marry a pagan priestess.

Prince Ahaziah appeared suddenly confused, then panicked. "You knew she was a priestess! When she demanded to see Abba in the quarry, she told you—"

Obadiah turned slowly toward the prince. "No. Princess Sheba told *me* she was a priestess—on the road to Jerusalem before we entered the quarry. If you didn't disclose that to Jehoiada in negotiations, he didn't know and can't be bound by the betrothal."

Every eye turned to Jehosheba as the legal ramifications settled like dust after a windstorm. She squared her shoulders and lifted her chin—but couldn't staunch her tears. "I am a princess of Judah, trained as a Baal high priestess. I did not intend to hide either fact. To me, they are one and the same—it is who I am."

Jehoiada's heart broke at her hopeless tone. He stepped toward her, but she flinched like a frightened animal and stepped behind her brother. All breath left him. "I won't hurt you."

She trembled violently, clutching the prince's sleeve with her good hand, peering around his broad shoulder.

Jehoiada backed away, unwilling to cause added distress. "Jehosheba, you are more than priestess and princess. Those are simply roles you play, like Astarte in the Festival of Awakening. It's not who you *are*." He paused, his throat tight with emotion, and then whispered, "I will marry the princess. I pray you destroy the priestess before the priestess destroys you."

17

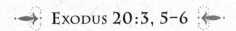

Exodus 20:3, 5–6

You shall have no other gods before me. . . . For I, the LORD your God, am a jealous God, punishing the children for the sin of the parents to the third and fourth generation of those who hate me, but showing love to a thousand generations of those who love me and keep my commandments.

Sheba hid behind Hazi, regretting this visit to Yahweh's Temple and its high priest. Jehoiada's presence filled the tiny chamber—a man of power, conviction, zeal. The cuts on her arms, back, and legs burned like a thousand hornet stings, and the only image in her mind was Jehoiada hoisting the lamb on the altar as if it weighed no more than a feather. She'd seen many sacrifices but never a man so large, so strong—with such a passion for his god. His whisper was so tender now, but what would he do when he discovered their marriage was a ploy to destroy his god? Would he turn his flint knife on her as Mattan had done last night?

"Stay away!" She hid her face in Hazi's back, startling the three men in the room.

The priest's voice was a mingling of emotions she couldn't decipher. "I won't hurt you, Jehosheba. I promise. Sit down here at my table."

Sheba peeked over Hazi's shoulder and found the big priest's hand outstretched, inviting. *Those are simply roles you play,* he'd said when she declared herself priestess and princess. "Were you playing a *role* when you cut the lamb's throat?" She tried to sound formidable, but hiding behind Hazi undoubtedly spoiled the effect.

The high priest's hand dropped to his side, and the remaining anger drained from his features. "No, I was obeying Yahweh's command to atone for our people's sin. He chose me as His high priest, and I must sacrifice innocent animals to save the people God loves."

The people God loves? Sheba was speechless. The gods might lust for each other and for beautiful women, but they didn't feel *love* for humans. Who was this Yahweh, and who was this priest? She swallowed the lump in her throat. And why would he agree to marry *her*?

"Come, Sheba. Sit down." Hazi cradled her elbow and she cried out. It seemed everywhere he touched her bore a wound from last night's ceremony. He waited, coaxing her with his eyes. "Let's at least listen to what Jehoiada has to say."

The priest backed away, keeping Hazi between them. Trembling, she moved to a cushion beside the low table. Hazi sat beside her, letting her rest against him. Closing her eyes forced a stream of tears down her cheeks. Ima Thaliah would be appalled at her behavior—not at all like a queen of destiny.

"Okay?" Hazi whispered. She nodded and peeked beneath her lashes. Hazi addressed the priest, who waited patiently by the door. "All right, Jehoiada. Please sit with us."

The priest crossed the distance in two steps, nimbly folded his legs beneath him, and cleared his throat. "I wish to make myself clear, Prince Ahaziah. I stand by my agreement to marry Princess Jehosheba under the conditions of our original negotiation. I ask that Jehosheba worship Yahweh alone and live with me as a common priest's wife. If she still agrees to those terms, then she is *not* a Baal priestess—correct?" He lifted his brow, awaiting Hazi's answer.

Sheba sat up, studying the big man. "But I *am* a priestess," she said stubbornly. "And don't talk about me as if I'm not in the room. Why are you now arguing reasons you *should* marry me?"

The priest grinned and folded his hands on the table. "I apologize, Princess Jehosheba."

Sheba's breath caught at the sight of dried lamb's blood on his hands. Following her gaze, he noticed it too and rose from the table to wash his hands in the basin. When he returned to his cushion, he wore an impish grin. "I've never met a priestess so afraid of blood."

Hazi snorted—almost a chuckle. She shot him a glare and refocused on the priest. "I doubt you've met many priestesses." Obadiah and Zev tried to stifle their grins. "And I've never seen a priest lift a lamb like it was a toy or wield a knife with such skill." Her voice caught, emotions still as raw as her wounds. All the mirth in the room evaporated.

Jehoiada's eyes welled with tears. "Yahweh's priests never use knives to sacrifice a human being—man or woman, adult or child." He spread his hands flat on the table—thumb to thumb, they nearly spanned the small, round top. "These hands will never harm you, Jehosheba. If you become my wife, these hands will protect you and show you kindness every day of my life. Remember what I said about marriage being a covenant, representing Yahweh's love?"

She nodded, not sure if she wanted to hear more of his ridiculous views on marriage.

"When we become husband and wife, we will be united before Yahweh with an unbreakable bond. Marriage is a covenant, an oath founded on the character of those pledging their lives. It's not a treaty maintained by fear or manipulation." He laced his fingers together, causing her to look into his eyes once more. "I must have your word that your hands, your lips, and your heart will never worship Baal Melkart again. I need to know that you will enter into this marriage as a covenant."

She locked eyes with him, refusing to blink, refusing to confess all the deceit she had planned for this so-called marriage. How could he ask her to enter a covenant? Ridiculous! This was political strategy, sheer survival, nothing more.

"Sheba, he's a good man." Hazi's whisper sounded like a shout in the silence. "Jehoiada can give you life. If you return to serve Mattan . . ."

She closed her eyes. *Death*. She knew what awaited her with Mattan. Something in him had snapped when he discovered she no longer belonged to the priesthood. He'd stopped his lusty stares and seemed to be plotting her ruin.

"I give you my word," Sheba said, wiping stubborn tears, avoiding the priest's gaze. "I will not worship Baal Melkart." Her words hung in silence. Why wasn't he answering? Did he expect an argument, more discussion? She met his gaze and displayed her carefully honed facade, emptying herself of all emotion. Ima would have been proud.

Jehoiada seemed at a loss, confusion warring with disbelief on his chiseled, masculine face.

Hazi broke the awkward silence. "I fear for her safety after Mattan's aggression last night. How quickly can you marry her?"

"Oh, by the gods!" She hung her head, humiliated beyond repair. "Am I a broodmare or a king's daughter?"

More silence met her coarse question. She lifted her eyes to the high priest's hard stare. "There is only one *true* God, Jehosheba, and that will be the last time you call on any other." He turned to Hazi. "The seven-day consecration ceremony begins in three days. Afterward, there are two days before the feasts begin. Your family may decide whether I will marry the princess before or after ordination." He rose from the table and offered a curt bow. "Now if you'll excuse me, I must help with preparations for ordination and Passover. Please send a messenger when you've decided the wedding date."

18

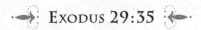

Exodus 29:35

Do for Aaron and his sons everything I have commanded you, taking seven days to ordain them.

I demand to see my abba!" Sheba shouted at the two Carites guarding the king's chamber. She was desperate to discover if he'd approved tomorrow's wedding ceremony. Hazi had taken Sheba to her chamber yesterday after meeting with Jehoiada, ordering a physician to tend her wounds. He then conspired with Ima Thaliah to set the wedding date and notified Yahweh's high priest without Sheba's knowledge, giving her only one day for bridal preparations. Tonight was her last night in the palace.

"Please, Princess, go back to your chamber." The biggest guard, whom she met eye to armpit, broke protocol and spoke to her. "We've been given strict orders that no one is to see King Jehoram except the queen—not even you."

"And who gave those orders?"

"I did." The door opened a crack, and Ima Thaliah slipped through.

Sheba nearly swallowed the clove she'd been sucking on to freshen her breath for the wedding. Choking, gasping, she bent over, and Ima pounded her back and whispered, "If you continue to make a fuss, I'll send in Mattan with a priest of his choosing to sharpen your Astarte skills."

Terror gripped her anew, so she allowed Ima to guide her to a private corner. "Why can't I see Abba?"

"We've discussed this, Sheba—"

"But how can I leave the palace—leave my family—without even *speaking* to Abba?"

Sheba noticed a commotion at Abba Jehoram's door and saw Hazi slip out of the chamber. "Why does Hazi get to see him and not me?" Without waiting for an answer, she shoved past Ima and began flogging the brother who'd betrayed her.

Hazi caught her around the waist and pinned her arms down, tearing open her freshly scabbed wounds. "Stop it, Sheba," he whispered against her ear. "Abba doesn't want you to see him like this. Stop. Fighting. Me."

His strong arms held her immobile, and she dissolved into dejected sobs. "Why, Hazi? Why won't Abba see me?"

Hazi loosened his grip and tilted her chin. "Abba is dying. He can't eat. He can only lie in his filth and misery. I can hardly bear to see him myself. Abba is protecting you, little sister. Trust me."

Could she trust him? She wasn't sure after hearing his explanation when Ima asked why he'd shown Jehoiada Sheba's wounds: "I realized the old priest could've nullified the betrothal on grounds that we didn't disclose Sheba's priestess standing." Ima had congratulated him on his shrewdness, but Sheba marveled at his glib deception. What were his *true* motives for their visit to Jehoiada—concern for her well-being or political positioning? The uncertainty broke her heart.

Ima wrapped her arm around her son's broad shoulders. "Come now, both of you. Tomorrow's wedding will be a celebration, an anchor of joy in this sea of sorrow. Let's go to Sheba's chamber and finalize the details, hmm?"

Defeated, Sheba followed them down the guards' stairway. They often traversed the circular steps to avoid gawking servants and Judean watchmen on the grand stairway. A Carite guard greeted them as they entered the women's hall by Ima Thaliah's private suite. They continued halfway down the corridor to

Sheba's chamber, past the empty rooms where Abba's wives once lived. The royal children had lived in separate quarters, closer to the courtyard so their nursemaids could play with them after daily lessons. Now everything in the palace felt empty, hollow, lifeless.

Yahweh's Temple couldn't be any worse. It was Sheba's only consolation.

She pushed open her heavy cedar door and found two maids preparing henna stain for her hands and feet—at least this was one bridal tradition she needn't forgo on her wedding day. "Out!" The maids bowed and left the henna behind.

Ima Thaliah waited to speak until the door clicked shut. "We've negotiated wedding events with the high priest." She glanced at Hazi, who sat on the couch near the balcony, stoic and silent, and then she assumed an instructional tone with Sheba. "After tomorrow's ceremony and feast, you'll go immediately with your new husband to live at the Temple. Unfortunately, because their ordination and Feasts of Passover and Unleavened Bread come in such quick succession, he has refused the traditional week of yihud after the wedding."

Hazi closed his eyes, as if anticipating Sheba's pain.

"He refuses me the union week?" she whispered, bracing herself against the bed. Loneliness choked her. Rejection robbed her of breath. Was she to be deprived of every joy of a young girl's dreams? Where were the privileges the Gevirah had promised? Sheba saw only lost choices, a ruined life.

"Sheba!" Hazi nearly shouted, evidently not the first time he'd spoken her name. "I tried to argue that even the patriarch Jacob spent a union week with a bride given to him in deception, but Jehoiada wouldn't budge. He said ordination must occur before Passover, and Passover is only delayed if he's defiled by a dead body within seven days of celebrating it."

"It's all right," she whispered, staring at the blood seeping through her bandages. "Perhaps he's afraid of being defiled by a Baal priestess."

Hazi left the couch and nudged Ima aside, which earned him a scowl. He ignored her, knelt before Sheba, and cradled her hands. "He said marrying a beautiful princess wouldn't make him unclean—simply distracted. He has promised to honor your yihud week immediately following Passover and the Feast of Unleavened Bread—because he wants to be completely focused on you."

Sheba slammed the iron doors of her heart closed. "Don't, Hazi. Nothing about this match resembles a real wedding. No betrothal contract. Abba won't be there. No foreign ministers will celebrate with a king's daughter. We're either at war with their country or their ambassador can't arrive in such haste. I don't suppose it matters that I relinquish yihud with an old priest—perhaps he'll die before I have to bed him." She lifted a cynical eyebrow in Ima's direction and then turned her stare on the wall, snubbing both family members. *Let them fume.*

Ima sat down beside Sheba, her voice surprisingly soft. "I know this isn't a typical royal wedding, Daughter, but we'll make it a wedding famed in Judah's history. We'll incorporate some of Tyre's traditions, and since your bridegroom refused Mattan's offer to officiate the service, Baal's high priest will stand as proxy for your abba and escort you and me to the chuppah."

Sheba glared at her. "How can you let Mattan near me after what he did?" She lifted her sleeves, baring her bandaged arms.

Ima lifted the sleeve of her own robe, revealing two tiny scars. "Mattan honored you with the initiation of a high priestess though the Gevirah robbed you of that role. My virgin blood was spilled—just like yours." She lifted a single eyebrow, daring Sheba to argue.

How could Ima compare her forearms to the gashes on Sheba's arms, legs, back, and hand? If Hazi hadn't wrested the knife from Mattan during the attack, she'd be dead.

Hazi tugged her chin toward him. "I'll officiate the ceremony as the crown prince of Judah, which means I'll be waiting for you under the wedding canopy. Keep your eyes on me, Sheba, just like you're doing right now." He winked, trying to lighten the mood. "I need to practice standing under a chuppah—since I'll marry a maiden in every city on my tour."

Sheba tried to smile but found herself studying her brother

instead. Was he really resigned to his future of nameless, faceless wives? Or was this another convincing bluff for Ima Thaliah?

"What happens at the feast?" she asked him, hoping he'd have kinder answers than Ima. "How long can we celebrate before I must leave the palace?"

"That's the best part, my darling." Ima shoved Hazi aside this time and nestled beside Sheba on the bed. "You are to tease him. Use what you've been taught as a priestess of Baal to entice your new husband. And while you're making him ache for your days of yihud after Passover, Hazi and I will spoil him with the pleasures and privileges Prince Baal offers *his* priests. By the time the abbreviated wedding feast is done, your Yahweh priest won't want to leave the luxurious life of Baal's pleasures."

The thought of tempting an old man nearly sent Sheba running for the basin, but she stared into the expectant faces of her ima and brother and knew she had no choice. "Send in my maids on your way out."

After a sympathetic smile, Hazi started toward the door, but Ima hesitated. "Would you like me to stay and direct your maids on proper wedding preparations?"

A few days ago, Sheba would have been thrilled—honored, even—that Ima Thaliah wished to spend time with her. "No. I'll direct my maids. Thank you, Ima."

Jehoiada's knees nearly buckled when he first glimpsed the tall and slender silhouette of his new bride in the archway of the Throne Hall. She waited, veiled and radiant between Queen Athaliah and Mattan, until the palace musicians began King David's wedding Psalm, her virgin attendants in two lines behind her. In the pre-wedding negotiations, Jehoiada had asked to maintain the tradition of bedeken.

Hebrew brides were typically covered head to toe on their wedding day with a heavy veil woven with golden thread. After the patriarch Jacob was fooled by the heavily veiled Leah, every Hebrew husband had the right to visit his bride's chamber and peek under her veil before the ceremony. It had become a joyous part of the wedding day, meant to give the couple a few private moments before the service. Jehoiada had hoped to speak with Jehosheba alone—even for a moment—to determine if she came to the chuppah willingly or under compulsion.

But Jehoiada's request was denied, the rejection written on a scroll of Tyrian parchment and closed with a seal bearing Jezebel's name and Jehosheba's first initial. The scroll read, "If the high priest refuses the tradition of yihud, the bride refuses bedeken. I will dress as a daughter of Tyre."

The whole thing was ludicrous. Yahweh's high priest stood in Solomon's palace, waiting under a wedding chuppah with the crown prince of Judah, to marry a king's daughter—a pagan priestess. He winced. He'd promised to forget her past—but had she?

The musicians' stringed instruments strummed King David's familiar song, and the Levitical choir continued their verses:

> Listen, daughter, and pay careful attention:
>> Forget your people and your father's house.
> Let the king be enthralled by your beauty;
>> honor him, for he is your lord.
> The city of Tyre will come with a gift,
>> people of wealth will seek your favor.
> All glorious is the princess within her chamber;
>> her gown is interwoven with gold.

Jehoiada felt a lump form in his throat. Was Jehosheba listening to the prophetic mystery of King David's psalm written almost four generations past? He watched his willowy bride in her Tyrian gown interwoven with gold. An embroidered purple belt cinched her tiny waist, glimmering with rare jewels matching the crown of gold that held in place a sheer veil—through which large, kohl-rimmed eyes stared at him defiantly.

No. She wasn't listening to the song. Her eyes burned with the same fire he'd seen the first night they'd met in the quarry. Only one thing was different now. He knew the fire would consume her if Yahweh didn't intervene.

Jehosheba arrived at his side, the breeze of her approach carrying with it the sweet scent of acacia and lavender. She let her gaze linger on Jehoiada, offering a seductive pout, and then turned toward her brother. The veil danced as she trembled. His bride was a study in conflict, driven by too many masters.

Prince Ahaziah raised his voice to the gathering. "Honored guests, priests of Baal, servants of Yahweh." He nodded at each contingent huddled with their kind. "King Jehoram has asked me to welcome you on his behalf. The king is beset with a most inconvenient ailment and hopes to return to his throne shortly, but until then he's asked Queen Athaliah and myself to satisfy the responsibilities of his office."

Jehoiada's respect for the young prince plummeted. He knew from Obadiah's reports that the king would not recover and, in fact, grew worse each day. The prince lied well. Wondering how much he could ever trust Hazi, Jehoiada was caught off guard when he heard the prince repeat his name.

"Jehoiada?" he coaxed while the Throne Hall waited in silence.

Yahweh's high priest glanced at the quizzical stares of those around him. Athaliah, with her usual vengeful expression, joined Mattan's sinister smirk. He turned to Nathanael, who had agreed to serve as friend of the bridegroom, and the kind young man whispered clarification. "Prince Hazi explained the ceremony as a bit unorthodox, including both Hebrew and Tyrian traditions, and he awaits your permission to proceed."

Jehoiada's heart raced, and he thought perhaps this was the miraculous release he'd hoped for. He glanced at Jehosheba's soulful, pleading eyes. Her lips, the color of the deepest red rose, trembled slightly.

Do you trust the Word of Yahweh through the Urim and Thummim?

Startled, Jehoiada turned to search out the questioner. Only Obadiah would speak to him so boldly—but he was perched on his cushion in the back row.

Do you trust the Word of Yahweh through the Urim and Thummim?

Again Jehoiada glanced about, but slowly he realized the voice emanated from deep within. Understanding dawned. *Yahweh! Yes, I trust You.*

He returned his attention to his bride, who had gone pale waiting for his answer. "I am ready to proceed!" he nearly shouted, startling everyone.

Prince Ahaziah chuckled and winked at Jehosheba. "Then as the representative of the king of Judah, I now join Yahweh's high priest to the house of David. Jehoiada ben Jonah, do you vow to provide for Jehosheba, daughter of King Jehoram . . ."

The words flowed through Jehoiada's mind and over his heart. They were mere ceremony now. His vow had been made when he remembered the Thummim, the covenant made upon his promise to care for Jehosheba all his days.

19

If a man or woman living among you . . . has worshiped
other gods . . . take the man or woman who has done this
evil deed to your city gate and stone that person to death.
On the testimony of two or three witnesses a person is to
be put to death, but no one is to be put to death on the
testimony of only one witness.

After the ceremony Sheba and Jehoiada were escorted by a detachment of Carite guards to their feasting table in the grand courtyard—a low rectangular table perched on an elevated platform. Ima Thaliah sat at Sheba's right hand, and Hazi, Mattan, and handsome Nathanael sat on Jehoiada's left. Seating women *with* men publicly was quite unconventional, but as Ima promised, nothing about the wedding had been common.

Sheba peered down the long row of honored guests, furtively inspecting the second priest. *Why didn't the Yahwists choose Nathanael as high priest?*

Jehoiada leaned forward, raised his eyebrow, and blocked her view.

Mortified, her cheeks burning, she needed a quick distraction. She wrapped her veils tighter, accentuating her curves, and

157

then began serving Jehoiada wine and tasty morsels with sultry glances and an occasional brush of skin. As the feast wore on, Yahweh's high priest seemed more annoyed by her coy games than tempted, and Sheba's confidence waned with each of his disapproving sighs.

Trumpets announced the last round of speeches and jokes just before twilight. Panic threatened to choke her. In moments, Sheba would walk away from the only life she'd known.

No longer a princess. Now, a priest's wife.

Hazi stood, bowing grandly, and the courtyard erupted in applause. He'd already won many hearts in Jerusalem. "Have you heard about the high priest who wandered into the Temple of Astarte?" Men began jeering as Hazi continued the coarse joke.

Sheba glanced at her bridegroom, who appeared utterly miserable. Ima's plan to win him with wealth and pleasure had gone awry. For the extravagant gifts of a golden waistband and an ivory-inlaid collar, he'd offered obligatory thanks before whispering to Nathanael that they'd sell the items to feed the poor in the City of David. He then dismissed the remaining Yahweh priests to make preparations for the evening Temple sacrifice. The man's piety was infuriating.

Ima Thaliah gripped her arm, pulling her close. "Why are you just sitting there? Charm your high priest."

Sheba donned her practiced smile and pressed against Jehoiada's right arm while reaching for a pitcher. "How may I serve you, my husband?" she asked in a sultry voice, refilling his wine but refusing to meet his gaze.

He placed his hand on hers, steadying her hold on the pitcher, and leaned close, his whisper warm on her cheek. "You may continue this pretense a little longer, but when you walk out with me at twilight, you will never again live a lie." He tightened his hand on hers. "Do you understand, *Wife*?"

She dropped the pitcher, shattering the Egyptian amphora and spilling wine on his priestly garments. Gasping, she leapt to her feet, covering her mouth with trembling hands and staring in horror at the crowd who stared back. Hundreds of eyes focused on her awkwardness.

What will Ima's punishment be this time?

A shadow hovered over her, and a hand brushed her face—light as a feather. "It seems I'm to be anointed twice in two days." She felt Jehoiada's breath against her cheek again, his nearness suddenly a relief, not a threat. "Today anointed with wine as your husband, and tomorrow with sacred oil as high priest. I consider both Yahweh's calling." He coaxed her hands away from her mouth, kissed her palms, and cradled them gently to his chest.

Hazi leapt to his feet and raised his goblet. "Lift your glasses to celebrate the union of Yahweh's high priest with the house of David."

Sheba pulled her hands from Jehoiada's grasp, struggling to steady her ragged breaths. How dare he pretend kindness after his harshness had caused her blunder? He appeared confused—even hurt—that she pulled away.

Distracted, she noticed Mattan whisper something to Hazi, causing her brother to relinquish his role as host. Baal's high priest motioned for the audience to be seated, and Jehoiada cast a questioning glance at Sheba. She answered with a shrug.

Mattan swept his hand over the crowd. "King Jehoram has asked that I not allow you, his honored guests, to leave this grand occasion without sharing his hope for the nation of Judah. Princess Sheba's marriage celebrates the joining of Yahweh's high priest to the house of David, but let it also mark the blending of old traditions and new expressions." He paused, allowing approval to spread. "Let this marriage inaugurate a new day in Judah—a day in which the beloved King Jehoshaphat's traditions are revered, and the auspicious Prince Ahaziah's reforms are explored!" He seized Hazi's hand, lifting his arm like a champion charioteer, and the room burst into applause.

Sheba stood with the rest, clapping wildly, but noticed her husband and his second priest sat awkwardly without so much as a smile. She felt her cheeks flame, embarrassed at the open disrespect Jehoiada showed. The applause died as others, too, noticed his rebuff and resumed their seats. Hazi sat beside his new brother-in-law and cast a questioning glance at Jehoiada, who met Hazi's gaze with a pitiable expression. Yahweh's high priest placed a hand on Hazi's shoulder as if comforting him. The crowd grew still, the moment tense.

Mattan shattered the silence. "Our good Prince Ahaziah plans to follow in his saba Jehoshaphat's wise footsteps and tour the cities of Judah, assuring them of his commitment to their safety and exploring necessary national reforms. If we are to survive in this ever-changing world of trade, we must embrace the cultures around us and learn to respect all people and all gods."

The crowd cheered once more, but Sheba kept a watchful eye on a dancing muscle in Jehoiada's clenched jaw. Sheba still envisioned him toting the lamb up those altar stairs and slicing its neck. She scooted closer to Ima Thaliah, choosing a known threat to her unknown fear, while Mattan prattled on.

"Though we've decided to forgo Baal's Festival of Awakening—out of respect for those killed by the Philistines and Arabs—the Yahwists have chosen to proceed with their annual festivals of Passover and Unleavened Bread. As a show of solidarity, Prince Ahaziah has agreed to participate in their festivals this year." A flutter of approval worked through the crowd, and Hazi nodded, receiving the hushed praise.

Sheba saw Mattan glance at Jehoiada, a silent challenge of sorts. "In lieu of our festival, Queen Athaliah has asked that we enact Baal's Awakening as the final event of our wedding feast. What could be more appropriate than a true royal wedding to celebrate the sacred marriage of Prince Baal and Lady Astarte? Let the new life of Jehoiada and Jehosheba produce fruit in keeping with the new life of our crops and livestock. My assistant priest, Gattam, will become Prince Baal in the sacred act, and our lovely bride, Sheba, will play the part of Astarte."

Wild applause met Mattan's introduction, but Sheba couldn't breathe, couldn't think. She kept her eyes downcast, humiliated. How could she enter a marriage tent with a priest during her wedding feast—before she lay with her husband? Ima and Mattan had placed her in an impossible situation. If she played the part, she betrayed her husband. If she didn't play the part, she betrayed her nation.

Sheba felt Ima Thaliah's hand nudge her leg. Cheeks aflame, Sheba turned to meet the queen's cheerful applause and granite stare. *Today I die.* Sheba knew Jehoiada would kill her if she became Astarte, just as Ima would kill her if she didn't. She stood, willing her legs to hold her. *Let death come swiftly.*

A meaty hand clamped down on her forearm like a vice. "You will *never again* serve Baal." Jehoiada rose with surprising agility, his face a terrifying mix of emotions. He faced the wedding guests, drew Sheba protectively under his arm, and lifted his hand to silence the applause. "How many of you are native Judeans, born of the tribe of Judah?"

Silence met his question, averted glances.

"Perhaps some of you recall your parents' stories about Moses and the wandering Israelites in the wilderness. At that time, Yahweh made a covenant with Israel promising we could live in this land—on the very dirt upon which your homes are built. In order to maintain that covenant, his Law must be kept."

A disgruntled rumble spread over the gathering, but Jehoiada seemed unaffected. "One of those laws is this: 'If a man or woman living among you has worshiped other gods, take the man or woman who has done this evil deed to your city gate and stone that person to death. On the testimony of two or three witnesses a person is to be put to death, but no one is to be put to death on the testimony of only one witness.'" The crowd gasped, frantic jeers and dissents rising, but Jehoiada quieted them with an uplifted hand. "Now, if my second priest and I witnessed my new bride worshiping a pagan god, we would be bound by this law to stone her at the city gate."

Sheba whimpered, knees buckling, but Jehoiada held her close, his strong arms both protecting and threatening.

Hazi leapt to his feet, trying to shove Jehoiada away, but the big priest held him at arm's length and ground out between clenched teeth, "You heard Jehosheba's vow in my chamber, Prince Ahaziah. She promised to never again worship a false god. Now she is my wife, and I will teach her the truth about Yahweh, about your saba Jehoshaphat, and about Judah. I hope you can learn the truth about them someday as well."

Hazi stood, gaping, as Jehoiada swept Sheba into his arms and carried her down the center aisle of the courtyard, Nathanael trailing behind them. Guests on both sides sat in awkward silence. Sheba hid her face against Jehoiada's shoulder, too humiliated to protest her inglorious palace departure.

Jehoiada kicked himself all the way out of the palace courtyard, past the Horse Gate, and through the Temple courts. Why had he allowed the farce to continue? Yahweh had approved the marriage with the Thummim, but He had never condoned a vulgar feast.

"Are you going to put me down, or am I doomed to be carried like a slaughtered lamb for the rest of my days?" Jehosheba lifted red-rimmed eyes and a defiant chin. She was still trembling violently, and he didn't want to upset her further.

He stopped near his chamber—their chamber now—and planted her feet gently on the limestone courtyard. "I'll only carry you when necessary." He smiled, trying to soften their harsh beginning, and then leaned down to unbuckle her sandals. "You won't need these anymore. Everyone who lives on Temple grounds is barefoot."

When he handed them to her, their eyes met for a moment before she pointed at Nathanael. "Will *he* be joining us in the bridal chamber?"

"Oh no! I, uh—no!" Nathanael's stammering wrenched a begrudging grin from both bride and groom.

Jehoiada rescued him. "No, Nathanael is my second priest. He lives in the chamber beside us and will arrive each morning before dawn to dress me in our outer chamber."

"Aren't you old enough to dress yourself?"

Lord God, give me patience! "If his presence in our chamber offends you, I can go to Nathanael's room to don the golden garments." Silence—finally. He reached for the latch, shoved open the door, and allowed her to enter first.

Nathanael waited respectfully outside, clearing his throat. "Shall I wake you at dawn?" He was crimson from the neck up.

Jehoiada chuckled. "I doubt I'll oversleep on the day we begin ordinations, but yes, Nathanael. A knock at my chamber would be much appreciated."

He closed the door and turned to find Jehosheba's back pressed against the far wall, her eyes wide. Henna-stained toes peeked from beneath her gold-trimmed bridal gown, the wine she'd spilled still a damp streak down her left side. Trembling, she held her chin high. Defiant. Vulnerable. So beautiful that his heart ached within him. *How can she stir this feeling inside me, Lord? She's infuriating!* But somehow she was Yahweh's gift to him.

"Will you sit with me at the table?" He reached for two wooden cups and the water skin. "We have a few things to discuss before the seven-day ordination begins tomorrow." She approached tentatively while Jehoiada filled the cups.

After settling on a cushion beside the table, she reached for a cup, her hand still shaking. Deep brown eyes peered over the rim while she drank her fill and then set it down, silently demanding more. He hid a grin and indulged her. After she had drained that cup too, her trembling eased. "What do we have to discuss?"

Jehoiada felt a flush on his cheeks. "Tomorrow begins my ordination as high priest, and during the next seven days, I must not lie with—"

"I know!" she nearly shouted, startling Jehoiada. Noticing her cheeks shade crimson too, Jehoiada watched her knees bend to her chest, hands locked around them. "Ima told me there would be no yihud until after your Feasts of Passover and Unleavened Bread. I understand our marriage is an arrangement, Priest. You need not feel obligated to me."

"Our *wedding* may have been arranged, but our *marriage* is not an obligation. You are a gift to me from Yahweh. And please call me Jehoiada. It means 'God knows.' Has anyone told you what *Jehosheba* means?"

Indignation replaced her reticence. "My name is Sheba."

"Your name is Jehosheba, and it means 'God's oath.' Your saba Jehoshaphat suggested the name to your abba Jehoram to remind him of Yahweh's enduring promises."

The revelation quieted her, and Jehoiada wished he knew what thoughts raged behind those liquid brown eyes. He reached out to take her hand, but she skittered backward like a frightened fawn.

Frustration welled up before he could tamp it down. "What have I done to frighten you so, woman?"

"You mean besides threatening to stone me? Or maybe grabbing my hand while I was pouring your wine and bullying me when I was simply being *kind* to you?"

"That wasn't kindness. That was a game Queen Athaliah instructed you to play with my heart." He watched his words hit their mark. Her reply seemed to dissolve in whatever conscience she had left. "I will never harm you. Do you hear me? I squeezed your hand while you poured my wine as a solemn promise that you will never have to live a lie again. Not a threat, a promise."

"I'm tired." She stood abruptly. "Will I be sleeping on this couch?" The cushioned bench under the small window was the only piece of furniture besides the table in the outer chamber.

"No, Jehosheba. You'll sleep in the bedchamber and I'll sleep out here on the floor. But I have one more thing to discuss before we retire for the evening."

She crossed her arms and plopped down on the cushion. "What?"

He stifled a grin. Her emotions were a ball of tangled yarn, but indignation seemed her favorite.

"The seventh day of ordination ceremonies falls on the tenth day of the month. It's the day all faithful Judean families choose lambs to care for in their homes until Passover begins at twilight on the fourteenth day."

Her eyes brightened. "You actually bring a lamb into your chamber and care for it?"

He chuckled at her delight. "This year, *you* will choose the lamb since I'll be busy with the ordination, and then we'll care for it together until Passover begins."

Wonder showed briefly, but her trembling returned as some dark thought shadowed her features. And then panic set in. "I can't choose your lamb. You'll be the high priest. What if I choose the wrong lamb?" She shuffled to her feet, eyeing the bedchamber door for escape.

Jehoiada leapt to his feet and caught her arm. She winced, and he released her, remembering her wounds. And then she stood utterly still—obedient, beaten, resigned to whatever he was about to say or do. The same resignation he'd seen when Mattan announced her role as Astarte at their wedding feast.

In that moment he realized—Mattan's blade hadn't inflicted the deepest wounds. Jehosheba's inner wounds, though invisible, were far more destructive. He must allow those wounds to heal also. Like a scapegoat, his wife had borne the sins of others all her life. How much violence had been poured out on this young woman?

He laid his hand at the small of her back and kissed her cheek. "Good night, Jehosheba."

She fled to the bedroom and shut the door behind her. Jehoiada heard distinct sounds of furniture being moved, table legs scraping the floor, rattling against the door. He chuckled to himself. She was barricading herself in the bedroom.

Another sigh—and then a wave of wonder. *Thank You, Yahweh, for speaking to Your servant.* Jehoiada fell to his knees, the frustration, the anger, the unanswered questions swept away by that holy *knowing* during their wedding ceremony. Without the certainty that Yahweh had approved this marriage, Jehoiada might have given up before it began.

PART 2

20

In the third year of [Jehoshaphat's] reign he sent his officials . . . to teach in the towns of Judah. With them were certain Levites . . . and the priests. . . . They taught throughout Judah, taking with them the Book of the Law of the Lord; they went around to all the towns of Judah and taught the people. The fear of the Lord fell on all the kingdoms of the lands surrounding Judah, so that they did not go to war against Jehoshaphat. Some Philistines brought Jehoshaphat gifts and silver as tribute, and the Arabs brought him flocks. . . . Jehoshaphat became more and more powerful.

Sheba sat on the new stool Jehoiada had placed in their outer chamber, grinding barley into the fine flour the priests would use for tomorrow's bread. The sun had set long ago, and she waited—rather impatiently—for her husband to return home after the crowds dispersed on this last night of the Unleavened Bread Feast. Tonight began their weeklong yihud, and she felt both terrified and anxious to know her husband more fully.

Over two weeks had passed since their wedding, and Sheba had spent most days sequestered in Jehoiada's chamber, unable to return to the palace and refusing to observe Jehoiada's violent sacrifices. She'd enjoyed the days they cared for the Passover lamb together—Methuselah, she'd named him. The little beast had become so tame, they'd taken it outside the city for an afternoon hike through the Kidron Valley—making it all the more heartbreaking when Jehoiada wrenched the bleating ram from Sheba's arms at twilight when Passover began. She'd refused to speak to him for two days, but he didn't seem angry—not even when she stubbornly refused to participate in either feast. He said he'd rather she learn of Yahweh before worshiping Him. He wanted her to live in truth rather than living a lie.

His integrity was exasperating.

She'd slept alone in his bed every night, having barricaded the door only once. Why didn't he kiss her again? For that matter, why hadn't he even touched her? She knew he desired her when she noticed his eyes roam the length of her one evening. His neck turned four shades of crimson when he realized she'd discerned his interest, and he fairly shoved her into the bedroom, closing the door behind her. She half expected *him* to barricade the door.

A knock interrupted her musing. Odd. Jehoiada had set a Temple guard outside so she wouldn't be disturbed, and her husband would certainly never knock.

"Just a minute." She set aside the grinding wheel, thankful for something to keep her hands busy during the long days alone. After wiping the grain dust from her hands, she reached for the latch. "Hazi!" She leapt into his arms, nearly knocking him over. "What are you doing here?" Joyful tears anointed his fox-fur collar.

He walked through the door with Sheba hanging on him like a necklace. "I've come to see how my sister is faring as a priest's wife." The Carite guard Zev waited outside, nodding his greeting before the door closed behind Hazi. "I've just attended the last day of the interminable Feast of Unleavened Bread." He rolled his eyes. "What a lot of rules with absolutely no entertainment. I could only stand four days of their ridiculous crackers before sneaking over to the palace for some *real* bread, and they don't even have any priestesses involved in the ceremonies. How do

170

they expect to attract a crowd if they don't appeal to their sense of adventure and excitement—and need for pleasure?"

She, of course, had no idea what he was talking about, since she hadn't attended the ceremonies, but she felt a stab of resentment at his criticism. "Did you hear any of Jehoiada's teaching on the rituals? Did you learn anything that will help you relate to all the people you'll meet on your Judean tour?"

Hazi had become distracted and ignored her question. Having found her grinding wheel, he pinched some flour between his fingers, letting the fine dust fall back into the trough. "So they've got you grinding grain like a servant girl, eh?"

"Stop your teasing." She shoved his shoulder, eliciting the expected chuckle. "I'm quite good at it, if you must know."

He cupped her cheek. "You're good at everything you do, little sister. You were a good Baal priestess, and Ima was furious when Jehoiada announced your vow to turn from Baal." He searched her eyes, concern lacing his tone. "Are you unhappy here? Has Jehoiada been unkind to you?"

"No, Hazi!" She tore her chin from his grasp. "Jehoiada has been very kind."

He grabbed her hands and inspected the blisters. "You call this kindness?" Anger tinged his tone. "Why must you work so hard?"

"Because I choose to." She let her gaze settle the words into his soul. "Jehoiada has forced me to do nothing, Hazi. He's given me a freedom I've never known."

Her words seemed to have the opposite of her intended effect. "Freedom? You call being locked in a guarded chamber *freedom*?"

"The guard is to ensure no one bothers me."

"Or is it to keep away anyone from the palace who would wish to communicate with you?" Hazi's eyes sparked with fury.

"Hazi, I don't understand. Why are you so upse—"

"He's upset because the Temple guard he tried to bribe came to me and ruined Queen Athaliah's plan to pass messages to you with her secret seal." Jehoiada's large frame filled the door as it swung open.

Sheba's heart was in her throat. "Jehoiada, I didn't. I haven't."

"I know you didn't." His gaze softened. "But you would have."

Shame silenced her like a shroud. The pain in her husband's eyes tore down a few bricks in the wall around her heart. He was right. She would have betrayed him if a guard brought a scroll.

"You cannot keep my sister locked away like a prisoner," Hazi challenged, but after an excruciating pause, he exhaled and tried a calmer approach. "I'm leaving tomorrow on my tour of Judah's cities, and I need to know she's safe, Jehoiada. You promised to protect her."

The high priest stepped closer, nose to nose with Judah's prince. "Why do you think I've cut off her communication with Athaliah?"

"You don't know Ima Thaliah like Sheba and I know her. She thinks Sheba betrayed her when she turned her back on Baal." Hazi thumped the big priest's chest. "And if you turn this into a war with Sheba as the prize . . . I assure you, Ima Thaliah will kill Sheba rather than lose the battle."

"Every guard on Temple grounds would give his life for us!" Jehoiada thundered.

"And how long could a few hundred Temple guards stand against all of Jerusalem's watchmen?" His question silenced Jehoiada, and Hazi returned his attention to Sheba. "I leave the decision to you, Sister. Ima's last scroll summoned you to the palace for a meeting in her chamber. You can either stay in this limestone prison until one of Ima's assassins slips past a Temple guard, or spend an afternoon with Ima Thaliah. Your choice."

Sheba's vision clouded with spots, and a growing roar dulled her hearing. Breathless, she tried to speak but was unable. Jehoiada seemed just out of reach . . . and then darkness . . .

She awakened lying in her bed, Hazi seated on one side, Jehoiada on the other. The dim glow of lamplight revealed concern on both faces. "What happened?" she asked.

Jehoiada lifted a single wiry eyebrow in Hazi's direction, and her brother seemed abundantly contrite. "You fainted, Sheba. I shouldn't have spoken so roughly." He stroked the back of her hand, his eyes sincere, a single dark curl fallen onto his creased forehead. She hadn't seen him look so grave since they'd found Abba in the quarry. "We've discussed a plan for you to communicate with Ima Thaliah."

"No!" Panic rose in her chest, quickening her breathing. "It's peaceful here with Jehoiada. I can't leave. I won't."

Jehoiada gathered her into his arms, the sensation both comforting and . . . strange. He'd never held her before. Did he simply feel obligated to protect her, or did he really care? "Your brother and I discussed a plan, but nothing is settled until *you* decide," he whispered against her ear, stroking her back. "Will you listen to Hazi and then make your decision?" He loosened his embrace, but she clung to him. "Shh, I've got you," he said, his arms tightening around her again. As the three sat in silence, her heartbeat slowed, and she felt herself relax.

Jehoiada laid her gently on the lamb's wool pillow, and Hazi cradled her hand. "I'll tell Ima Thaliah you're struggling to adjust to life as a priest's wife. Grinding grain, weaving cloth . . ." He glanced at Jehoiada. "You could find some cloth for her to weave, couldn't you?"

The high priest raised an eyebrow. "Tell the queen that Jehosheba is very busy *adapting* to her new life."

"Right." Hazi bounced his eyebrows at Sheba, making her smile, and then brushed her cheek. "Ima must believe she has unrestricted access to you, or your life will be in danger. If you won't go to the palace, you must at least accept her secret scrolls."

"The scrolls that aren't secret anymore." Jehoiada leaned down, tilting her chin toward him.

Sheba's tears began again, and she covered her face, ashamed.

"What? What is it?" Jehoiada stroked her hands, coaxing them away so she could speak.

She tugged at the leather cord around her neck, drawing out the personal seal Ima Thaliah had given her.

Hazi reached out to inspect it. "Even I don't have my own

seal yet. Where did you get this?" He inspected the design and dropped it like a hot ember when he recognized the pattern. "This is Jizebaal's seal, adding your first initial. Did the Gevirah give this to you in Jezreel?"

"No, Ima gave it to me soon after we returned. The Gevirah planned for me to marry Yahweh's high priest before any of us knew of Jerusalem's raid."

"Jezebel wanted you to marry Amariah?" Jehoiada asked.

Sheba squeezed her eyes closed. Her answer would alienate the only person who had shown her honest concern. But he deserved the truth. "The Gevirah's plan was to wait until Amariah died—of natural causes—and then arrange my marriage. I was then to use my influence with the new high priest to incorporate idolatry with Yahweh worship, and thereby sway his decisions in central court." She buried her face in the pillow, guilt chewing her insides.

Silence. She waited for Jehoiada's shocked disdain, his command that she return to the palace with Hazi. Rejected, she'd be sentenced to execution, or worse—to service as one of Mattan's priestesses. Unable to bear the silence, she peeked from beneath her pillow and found the two men staring back, wonder on their faces.

Jehoiada recovered first. "So, you're saying Queen Jezebel had already commissioned you to marry Amariah's successor *before* King Jehoram made the same decision in Jerusalem?"

Hazi's mouth still gaped, so Sheba confirmed. "Yes. When Abba told me *his* plan in the quarry, I realized the gods must have been conspiring—" Sheba clamped her hands over her mouth, hoping the mention of other gods hadn't ruined her husband's apparent good humor.

Jehoiada again drew his wife's hands away from her face and cradled them gently. "There are no other gods involved in this plan, Jehosheba. Only Yahweh. And on the night we left the quarry with your abba Jehoram, I was certain the king's decision to wed his daughter to the high priest's successor was a mistake." He smiled sheepishly and kissed her hand, sending the most exquisite fire up her arm. "On that same night,

Yahweh chose me to be your husband and you to be my bride, and I'm so glad He did."

Sheba stared into her husband's eyes, her breath growing ragged. Tonight was to be the beginning of their yihud. She'd dreaded their seven days of uninterrupted solitude—until now.

Hazi cleared his throat, interrupting their intimate moment. "I must have a decision, Sheba. Will you exchange scrolls with Ima until you feel well enough for a meeting?"

Sheba's fluttering heart suddenly turned to stone.

Hazi leaned forward, closer to the light so she could read his eyes. "Your scrolls can still report the truth. Tell Ima Thaliah that your husband is a stubborn man—no offense, Jehoiada—"

"None taken."

"And that his age makes him less responsive to your seduction." Again Hazi raised an eyebrow, looking distinctly uncomfortable before continuing. "I'll explain my long visit with you tonight by saying Jehoiada showed some curiosity when I spoke to him of Baal and Astarte."

"What?" Jehoiada and Sheba asked in unison.

The prince grinned. "We must convince Ima that Sheba's efforts are still promising, but that my help will also be beneficial. Plus, it gives me an excuse to visit you more often when I return from my city tour."

"But it's not the truth, Hazi." Jehoiada was respectful but firm.

Sheba watched her brother squirm, saw the thoughts spinning behind his eyes. "It's not the *whole* truth, but it's not a lie. Aren't you curious about Baal and Astarte, Jehoiada—why so many Judeans are drawn to Mattan's new temple?"

Jehoiada shook his head, released a sigh, and returned his attention to Sheba. "The decision is yours, Wife. *If* you write scrolls to your ima Thaliah, we'll write them together, and we'll be wise without lies."

Hazi grew agitated. "I'm not sure Jehoiada should be involved in writing them. Ima must believe they remain a secret. If Sheba writes them in Hebrew—"

"What language would you prefer?" Jehoiada asked. "I'm fluent in Egyptian, Phoenician, and Assyrian."

Sheba gasped. "Will you teach me Assyrian? I had no idea Yahweh priests were educated in—"

"Sheba!" Hazi gripped her shoulder, refocusing her attention. "Write the scrolls in Phoenician, and then you *must* prepare to meet with Ima. She won't wait forever."

Jehoiada shoved his arm away, standing over Sheba protectively. "The only thing my wife *must* do now, Prince Ahaziah, is remember she is loved. Jehosheba will meet with the queen when—and if—she's ready."

Hazi stood, meeting the challenge. "Being loved won't save her from Jerusalem's watchmen."

"Enough!" Sheba said, scooting off the bed toward her brother. "Hazi, go on your tour tomorrow. Marry lots of beautiful women, make adorable babies, and learn how to be a king." She shoved him into the outer chamber toward the door amid both men's chuckles.

Before he reached for the latch, he turned and hugged her, resting his cheek atop her head. "I love you too, Sheba. Don't ever forget that."

She nodded, her throat too tight to speak.

"Good night, Jehoiada." Releasing his sister, Hazi embraced the high priest, kissing first one cheek and then the other. "Take care of her."

"I plan to."

Jehoiada followed the young prince out the door and greeted the Carite captain, who stood with the chief gatekeeper. "I'd like to speak with Prince Ahaziah alone for a moment," he said to both guards. He guided Hazi about five camel lengths away, lowering his voice to ensure their privacy. "I want to be sure you know certain things about your saba Jehoshaphat before you tour Judah's cities."

"To what *certain things* are you referring?" The prince offered a quizzical grin. "Did you know my saba?"

"I wouldn't say I knew him well. He was quite close with my friend and high priest, Amariah, but King Jehoshaphat and I spoke occasionally." He paused, trying to think of a tactful way to broach the subject.

"Out with it, brother-in-law." The prince's charm was undeniable and would take him far.

"How much do you know about Jehoshaphat's tours of Judah?"

He chuckled. "Obviously not as much as I'm about to learn. And I'd appreciate it if you'd call me Hazi. Only my abba calls me Prince Ahaziah, and then only when he's angry."

"Well, that breaks my heart." Jehoiada's remark sobered the prince. "I'll call you Hazi if you can tell me the true meaning of your full name, Ahaziah." He waited, noting grief shadow the young man's face before he replaced his carefully sculpted mask.

"*Ahaziah* means 'held by Yahweh.'" He swallowed hard. "And, as I said, I'd appreciate it if you'd call me Hazi."

Jehoiada nodded, realizing the topic was closed. "I'm sure I don't need to tell you that your saba Jehoshaphat was the most successful king in Jerusalem since Solomon." The compliment refreshed Hazi's smile. "But do you know *why* your saba toured every city in Judah?"

"Yes. On his first tour, he built fortresses and trained a professional army in each city rather than relying on volunteer farmer corps. He also provided each city with storehouses to withstand independent sieges. And on his second tour, he instituted a judicial system in the cities, incorporating the central court here in Jerusalem . . ." He smiled through his final words. "And you know all that, but there's something else you want to tell me."

Jehoiada chuckled. "Indeed. In the third year of your saba's reign, he visited every city in Judah, taking with him the Book of the Law of Moses, enlisting Levites and priests to help him teach its precepts to the people. The fear of the Lord fell on surrounding nations, and the same Philistines and Arabs who invaded Jerusalem a few weeks ago bowed at Jehoshaphat's feet, bringing him gifts and tribute and flocks."

Hazi stood expressionless. "I've never heard that part of the story."

It was just as Jehoiada expected. The prince had been given

only the portions of truth that served Athaliah's purposes. "You can build armies and storehouses—or loyalty through marriages—but only Yahweh protects Judah from its enemies, *Hazi*." He paused, measuring Hazi's reaction, but the prince was a blank slate. "Would you like to hear more about Jehoshaphat, or should we say good-bye for now?"

Hazi's answer came with a practiced smile and a curt bow. "I leave at dawn, and my company breaks its fast in Bethlehem with the nobleman Ozem. If all goes as planned, I'll have married his daughter by midday and move to the next town after I enjoy a week of yihud with my new bride." Sadness shadowed his expression, erasing all folly. "Your week of yihud begins tonight, doesn't it?" Jehoiada nodded, measuring the young man's intent. "Treat her kindly, my friend. She deserves to be loved."

The high priest drew him into a fierce hug. "Be well, Hazi. May you realize Yahweh holds you." The prince hurried away and Captain Zev ran to catch up.

Jehoiada turned toward his chamber and nearly ran headlong into Zabad, who stood beaming on this moonlit night, silly grin fixed in place. "All preparations have been made for your week of yihud. Meals and fresh water will be delivered to your door three times a day, but I've left strict instructions that you're not to be disturbed." He lingered, brows forming twin peaks.

"Well?" Jehoiada asked.

"Well what?" The gatekeeper's grin faded.

"Exactly." Jehoiada took some delight in the deep crimson that flooded Zabad's cheeks just before he scurried away.

Chuckling, Jehoiada opened his door and peered inside. The outer chamber was empty. His heart sank. Perhaps his wife had grown tired of waiting and had gone to bed alone. He knew how hard waiting could be.

During the two short weeks since their wedding, Jehosheba had been so fearful and fragile that Jehoiada avoided any physical temptation. He'd diligently resisted even the slightest show of affection, and with such a beautiful wife, it had been torture! He might be old, but he wasn't dead.

"Jehoiada?" There, standing in the bedroom doorway, Jehosheba wore a sheer tunic. "I wondered if you'd be willing to comb my hair. My maids always did it for me, and I've tried—but now it's a tangled mess." She held out an ivory comb, her breath coming in quick gasps.

Oh, Yahweh, can it be? Last night he'd tossed and turned, wondering how he could show a husband's love without demanding the rights of yihud. On the other hand, she was so young and beautiful. How could he ever believe she came to his bed willingly—without hidden motives? They'd both entered this relationship out of obligation, but at some point it had become . . . more. *Yahweh, help me to love her well—to show her true and lasting love.*

"You don't have to," she said, her cheeks shading a lovely crimson. "I'm sure you're tired." She turned to close the door.

"Jehosheba, wait!"

She froze, her back still toward him. He covered the distance in three large steps and gently lifted the comb from her hand. His heart began to race at the sight of the ebony tresses cascading down her back. He grazed the bend of her neck as he lifted a section of curls. She gasped, shivering at his touch, and he paused, afraid he'd frightened her. *Yahweh, give her strength.* He continued working the comb, easing the tangles to the end. Noticing her breath had become ragged, he issued another silent prayer and kissed the alabaster neck that beckoned him. She groaned softly, leaning into his kiss.

And then he knew. Yahweh had answered his prayers—spoken and unspoken. Jehoiada had been given a wife with whom he could share the rest of his days.

21

On the day of firstfruits, when you present to the LORD
an offering of new grain during the Festival of Weeks,
hold a sacred assembly and do no regular work. Present
a burnt offering of two young bulls, one ram and seven
male lambs a year old as an aroma pleasing to the LORD.

Sheba broke Ima Thaliah's seal on another scroll, hoping—even praying—this one included an update on Abba Jehoram's condition. Ima's scrolls arrived faithfully each week on the day before Jehoiada's appearance in central court. Full of news on Hazi's progress, Judah's political woes, and Israel's suffering at Aram's hands, they never revealed Abba's condition. Jehoiada helped craft Sheba's carefully worded replies, making sure each message was true, always writing them in the Phoenician script to infer Jehoiada's ignorance of their content. His counsel was consistent before they sealed each scroll: *Live the truth; be wise without lies.*

Tomorrow would mark six weeks since their yihud had begun—the sweetest, most precious days of her life. On the last night of the Feast of Unleavened Bread, her mighty high priest held her tenderly and taught her of real love—and of Yahweh. To her husband, love and Yahweh were the same les-

180

sons. When their weeklong isolation ended, a new education began—that of living as the high priest's wife in a community with hundreds of men.

Only one other woman—a paid servant—visited Temple grounds daily, preparing the side dishes to accompany the priests' offering portions. But the fussy maid banned Sheba from her kitchen. So Sheba attempted spinning and dyeing the special threads of wool and flax for the priestly robes. She'd worked with the Levites for only a day when Jehoiada explained that several of the men found it too tempting to work so close to her.

A tear splashed on Ima Thaliah's scroll, bringing Sheba back to the moment. Why was she crying? Loneliness was nothing new, and at least here Jehoiada loved her. But she missed . . . people. She hadn't been friendly with her maids, but their incessant chatter and activity was a melody of life she'd taken for granted. With a sigh, she wiped her eyes, unrolled the parchment, and began reading.

From Athaliah, Queen of Judah.
To Jehosheba, Daughter of Jehoram, King of Judah.

I send greetings with blessings from almighty Baal Melkart and Mattan, his high priest.

May the Rider of the Clouds make your womb as fertile as the pastures of Hebron. Nearly eight weeks have passed since your wedding, and we have not yet received word of a child. Is there yet hope, or does your husband's age disqualify him for sons?

Your brother has returned his tenth bride to Jerusalem, having persuaded two noblemen each week to offer their daughters as royal wives. Mattan has divined signs of a child in the first four. We rejoice that the house of David may soon be replenished. Hazi returns next week to celebrate his tour of Judah.

I must speak with you on another matter too sensitive for written correspondence. Arrange for a guard to bring you to my chamber when your husband reports to the Throne Hall for his central court duties tomorrow.

Written by my own hand.

Shaken, Sheba rolled up the scroll and set it aside. Hazi had warned her that Ima Thaliah would eventually demand a personal meeting. Fear clawed at her chest. *Maybe I could bribe one of the Carites to sneak me into Abba's chamber.* The thought comforted her a bit.

"Jehosheba?" Her husband's deep voice startled her. He'd slipped into the chamber and stood over her like a mighty oak, his concern warming her to the depths.

Sheba rushed into his arms. "Ima still hasn't revealed anything about Abba, and now she wants me to come to her chamber tomorrow—alone—while you serve your regular duty at central court—"

"No! You're not going to the palace." His arms tightened around her.

She grew quiet, trying to decide if she felt relieved or angry at his commanding tone. In the space of a few heartbeats, anger won out, and she shoved him away. "Did you rescue me from Ima and Hazi so you could become my new master?" He winced as if she'd slapped him. "We don't even know *why* she wants me to meet her."

"I don't have to know why you've been summoned because I know *who* summoned you! She hates all that Yahweh holds sacred, and I won't allow her to destroy anyone else I love!" His serene mask had slipped, and Sheba suddenly saw the roaring lion beneath. Had he been pretending kindness all these weeks?

"How dare you yell at me when I'm the one who's upset!" Sheba glared at him, relying on anger to quell other emotions.

He stepped toward her, and she recoiled, the image of a slain lamb forming unbidden.

"How can you still be afraid of me?" The thunder drained from his voice, but she couldn't let her guard down. He raked his fingers through that handsome silver hair. "I'm sorry I shouted. I'm not angry with you. I simply don't trust Athaliah."

She lifted her chin. "You don't trust Athaliah, or you don't trust *me*?"

His penetrating gaze nearly dismantled her defenses. "I trust you, Jehosheba, but I'm not sure why you don't trust me."

His challenge unleashed the tears she'd so expertly denied. "You've been nothing but kind to me for eight weeks, but people I thought loved me all my life betrayed and threatened to kill me." She released a frustrated sigh, wiping the despised tears from her cheeks. "Who am I *not* afraid of, Jehoiada?"

He offered both hands, approaching her slowly as if she were a skittish pony, then cradled her face. He leaned down, brushing her lips with a gentle kiss. She melted into his protective arms, lingering in the safety.

"You never have to fear me, my wife," he whispered against her ear. "Why did Athaliah summon you? Maybe Zabad can escort you with a detachment of Temple guards."

In the protection of his arms, she could nod her agreement, but when tomorrow came, could she really walk into Athaliah's chamber?

"Sheba, my dear!" Ima Thaliah opened her arms but remained rooted to the floor near her couch. "I've missed you. Come, give your ima a hug."

Zabad took one step through the door with Sheba, and two Carites caught his arms. He started to fight, but Sheba placed a calming hand on his forearm. "I'm fine," she whispered, holding his gaze. "Wait for me outside." She sounded more confident than she felt.

He wrested his arms from the gloating Carites. Sheba issued malevolent glares and they sobered. She'd almost forgotten the power of a princess.

The queen had dropped her welcoming arms and was now standing, hands balled on her hips. "Really, Sheba, must you cause a scene wherever you go?" With a huff, she resumed her seat on the finely embroidered couch facing the balcony. An early summer breeze beckoned Sheba to join her.

The enormous chamber seemed even bigger after living in Jehoiada's modest rooms. With every step across the lush red carpets, she silently repeated Jehoiada's oft-spoken advice. *Live the truth; be wise without lies.* She sat on the couch beside Ima, clasping her hands in her lap to keep from fidgeting.

The queen began her perusal immediately, her kohl-sculpted eyebrows rising in disdain. "Why do you greet me without cosmetics or lotions? Honestly, Sheba, you smell like you sleep in a sheep pen."

"On the contrary, Ima, I sleep with Yahweh's high priest." The comment earned a half grin from the queen. Though Ima's criticism threatened a familiar stab of shame, Sheba remembered Jehoiada's love and was strengthened. The taste of his kiss, his gentle touch—these convinced her she was desirable to the only one who mattered. "The wives of Yahweh's priests are forbidden to wear lotions or perfumes."

"By the gods, why? Do they like their women smelling like sheep?"

Sheba chuckled. "The priests keep only one type of scent on Temple grounds, the sacred incense burned before Yahweh. In order to avoid any temptation for priests' wives to steal the precious scent, they've asked all wives on Temple grounds to forgo the luxury." Ima didn't need to know she was the only wife on-site at the moment.

"You seem quite knowledgeable about life on Temple grounds, my dear," Mattan said, emerging from behind the heavy tapestry separating Ima's sleeping chamber from her meeting area. "Your knowledge will help with our plan." A sickening grin creased his lips when he saw Sheba measure the distance to the door. "Don't worry, *Priestess*. I won't ask you to do anything that might force your husband to stone you." Mattan and Ima shared a laugh.

Sheba remained silent and straightened her spine, trying to stifle her fear and regain her dignity. "What is it you wish from me, Ima? I'd like to see Abba before I return to Yahweh's

Temple." Narrowing her eyes, she held Thaliah's gaze, making her point clear. "I'm sure you'll find a way for me to see Abba Jehoram, since you obviously need my help."

"I'd like nothing more than to reunite you with your abba *after* our little chat." She signaled Mattan to commence what Sheba assumed was the real reason for their meeting.

The priest tented his fingers, tapping them together while staring at her with his dead gray eyes. "We'd like to know all you can tell us about Yahweh's Feast of Weeks."

The request seemed utterly harmless, which frightened Sheba more than a blatant threat. "Why?" she asked Ima, refusing to converse with the weasel high priest.

Ima turned her attention to Mattan, deferring to his answer. "We plan to institute in Judah a long-standing Phoenician festival called Marzeh. And we will celebrate Marzeh on the same day as Yahweh's Feast of Weeks."

"Shavuot. Yahwists call it the Feast of Shavuot," Sheba corrected him, feeling her defenses rise.

Mattan and Athaliah exchanged satisfied grins. "Excuse me." Mattan bowed. "I can see you will be most helpful in our quest to understand *Yahwists*."

Sheba stood abruptly, startling them both. "I really don't see how I can be of any help. Why don't you ask Jehoiada? He knows much more—"

Ima Thaliah grabbed her wrist and twisted. "Sit down, Sheba—or have you decided not to visit your abba?" Her voice was tender and sweet, her message so vicious and clear.

Sheba resumed her seat, focusing on a lamp in the wall niche across the room. "The Feast of Shavuot occurs fifty days after Passover, celebrating the first harvest of wheat. It is the second pilgrimage festival of three . . ." She offered a condescending waggle of her head at Mattan. "That means the second time all families of Judah are required to appear before the Lord at the Temple."

He returned her favor with prayerful hands and an exaggerated bow.

She rolled her eyes and continued. "Between prescribed sacrifices by the high priest, each family brings a freewill offering according to the blessings they've received from Yahweh during the past year. It's a time of celebrating and sharing with orphans, widows, and foreigners—you know, those less fortunate—"

"And that, my dear, is why Baal grows in power and Yahweh's power wanes." Ima Thaliah placed her hand on Sheba's knee, patting her gently as if explaining the stars to a grasshopper. "While Yahwists are celebrating their pathetic little kernels of wheat, servants of Baal will offer him gold and silver, fine jewelry, flocks and herds."

"I don't understand." Sheba felt like a grasshopper learning about the stars.

"On the day Jehoiada coaxes poor farm families to share their meager produce with beggars, Hazi will return with his wives and their wealthy families. Mattan and I will invite all the wealthy noblemen from Judah to Baal's temple, offering memorial gifts and sacrifices to the spirits that still hover near the tombs. Beloved King Jehoshaphat's spirit will miraculously show his approval through sheep's entrails—won't he, Mattan?"

"I'm sure he will." The feigned innocence on the priest's face made Sheba nauseous.

Ima laughed, raising gooseflesh on Sheba's arms. "And *every* nobleman will attend—a few more may even offer Hazi their daughters as wives." She leveled her gaze, daring Sheba to disagree. "The nobles will attend because no one would risk the disfavor of Judah's queen—and future king—by refusing an invitation to the first Marzeh."

All the blood drained from Sheba's face. She wished Jehoiada were here to defend her—to defend himself. Had she betrayed him by divulging too much? She'd spoken the truth as he'd told her to do, but in the process she may have harmed him and Yahweh severely.

"Come, Sheba. You look like you could use a visit with your abba to cheer you up." Ima Thaliah's eagerness seemed suspicious.

"Really? You'll take me to him?"

"Of course. I've been trying to get him out of his chamber for weeks, but he's become lazy, locked in his chamber with his concubines. Drinking too much wine, chewing qat from

186

Arabia. He's not even in his right mind most of the time. I've sent messengers to Hazi for him to make the major decisions of the kingdom."

Ima offered a hand of assistance, but Sheba stared at it, as confused by Ima's civility as she was by Abba's recklessness. "Abba hardly ever drinks too much, and the only time he tried qat was to soothe tooth pain a few years ago. I remember because he became sick from it. He'd never choose to—"

"No one knows about his reaction to qat except you, me, and Hazi. The doctor who pulled the tooth is . . ." She smiled in Mattan's direction. "Well, he's no longer able to testify to any treatment he prescribed for your abba." She grabbed Sheba's arm, squeezing as if she might break it. "At Baal's Festival of Marzeh, all of Judah will realize that King Jehoram blames himself for our sons' deaths and guilt has driven him to unrestrained decadence. His absence at the festival will be viewed as an offense against King Jehoshaphat and his sons—the spirits we've gathered to memorialize. Hazi's strong presence will dispel any doubts of his leadership ability, and the kingdom will be his."

Sheba stared, stunned. "Hazi won't do it. He loves Abba and won't steal his throne. How could you pretend to love Abba all those years?"

Ima motioned Mattan toward the door with a nod and then lowered her voice for Sheba alone. "I love those who submit to my will, and I love the children issued from my womb." Her eyes grew sharp as daggers. "Your abba broke faith when he summoned our sons without my knowledge or approval. My sons were slaughtered while he hid like a rat in a hole." A single tear leapt over her bottom lash, but she swiped it away, seeming offended at its intrusion. "Hazi is now my only child—and you are my queen of destiny. You will *both* do as I command." Linking her arm with Sheba's, she added, "Let's go visit this great man you long to see."

22

Celebrate the Festival of Weeks to the LORD your God by giving a freewill offering in proportion to the blessings the LORD your God has given you. And rejoice before the LORD your God at the place he will choose as a dwelling for his Name—you, your sons and daughters, your male and female servants, the Levites in your towns, and the foreigners, the fatherless and the widows living among you.

Jehoiada held his brokenhearted wife on the small couch in their outer chamber. "Abba didn't even recognize me. He's out of his mind with pain, writhing on a straw pallet in his chamber. Only one doctor is allowed to treat him, and that man looks like death." Overcome, she sobbed the broken words into the sleeve of Jehoiada's priestly robe.

"I should never have let you go," he whispered—as much to himself as to her.

She lifted her head, pausing her tears. "I may never see Abba alive again. As difficult as it was to see him, I needed to go."

He wrapped her in the cocoon of his priestly robe, wishing he could protect her from life's pain. She'd already seen too much. *Yahweh, how can she endure more?* One of the Levites' psalms came to mind, and Jehoiada laid his cheek on top of his wife's head. "When King Saul's jealousy caused him to pursue David in the wilderness, David prayed to the Lord, 'Hide me in the shadow of Your wings from the wicked who assail me, from my mortal enemies who surround me.' Just like my arms enfold you now, beloved, Yahweh surrounded David with protection, saving him from the whole Israelite army." Jehoiada tilted Jehosheba's chin up, peering into her eyes. "We must both remember that *Yahweh* is the one who protects you, Jehosheba. Hide in the shadow of *His* wings, my love." Did she realize he spoke those words as much for his own comfort as for hers?

She snuggled closer, pulling his arms around her tighter. "I must remember that Yahweh is big enough."

The absolute innocence of her faith squeezed Jehoiada's heart. "Indeed Yahweh is more than big enough, and though I cannot fathom how, He loves you even more than I." She didn't respond, and Jehoiada sensed the telltale sniffing of fresh tears. He sat her upright to search her expression. "What? What is it?"

"I'm not sure *you'll* love me when I tell you what I've done." She averted her eyes. "Mattan was waiting in Ima Thaliah's chamber when I arrived. They plan to ruin Shavuot with a competing Baal festival called Marzeh, luring wealthy noblemen of Judah to believe lies about Abba Jehoram."

Jehoiada tucked a stray curl under his wife's headpiece, touched by her zeal for the Lord. "We can't prevent people from believing lies, but we'll continue to worship Yahweh and welcome whoever comes for Shavuot—"

"But you don't understand," she shouted, her eyes suddenly wild. "I betrayed you! I betrayed Yahweh! I revealed the rituals of Shavuot, and now they'll make sure Marzeh attracts the elite of Jerusalem to Baal's temple." She leapt to her feet and began pacing. "Perhaps you could find out how Elijah made fire descend on Mount Carmel, or maybe somehow trick people into thinking—"

"Jehosheba!" Indignation erupted, startling his wife, leaving her frozen where she stood. "Elijah didn't command the fire on Mount Carmel—Yahweh did. And Yahweh's servants don't use tricks to attract worshipers."

She wiped away all expression, and he sensed the door of her heart slam shut. "I understand," she said, rolling her shoulders back, straightening her spine. "May I be excused to the bedchamber? I'm tired."

Jehoiada closed the distance between them in two steps, but she stood like a statue, her focus on his chest. "Jehosheba, please. I'm sorry I shouted again, but you must realize Athaliah didn't summon you to discover answers about Shavuot."

Curiosity seemed to force her to meet his gaze, and he wiped a lingering tear—and then held it out for her inspection. "*This* is what Athaliah and Mattan wanted—turmoil. They want to divide *us*."

"Arrr," she growled, squeezing her eyes closed. "Why do I let her manipulate me?"

Jehoiada tilted her chin and she opened her eyes. "You've lived in Athaliah's shadow all your life—as she lived in the shadow of Jezebel. Fear, distrust, and deceit were daily bread, and it takes time to break the chains binding your heart and mind. But Yahweh is faithful, Jehosheba." He brushed her cheek tenderly. "And I get to demonstrate His love to you for the rest of my life."

She hugged him fiercely. "I love you, Jehoiada."

His heart nearly melted—it was the first time she'd spoken those words. "And I love you, my wife." *Thank You, Yahweh, for comforting us both in the shadow of Your wings.*

Priests and Levites stood reverently at dawn in the inner court while Jehoiada carried another year-old lamb to the pyre atop the brazen altar. Sheba stood at the north court gate, separate from others who lived at the Temple. Though Jehoiada had helped her make the proper sin offering—a male goat without defect—she still felt unclean, when beneath her robe she bore the scars of a Baal priestess.

The sight of her husband's sacrifice no longer frightened her now that he'd taught her the enormous value of each offering. The daily services provided ongoing worship and atonement for the community's unintentional sins. Each Sabbath heaped more worship on a God who had blessed abundantly the previous six days, and each New Moon served as yet another opportunity to remember, worship, and sacrifice. Today the outer courts were already filling with faithful Judeans who'd come to celebrate Shavuot.

Gooseflesh rose on her arms as sunrise cast its glow on Jehoiada's high priestly garments. Nathanael had arrived to dress him well before the cock crowed, as was their daily routine. This morning, however, Sheba asked if she could watch the process in their outer chamber. Nathanael seemed a bit unnerved by her presence, but Jehoiada used the opportunity to continue his wife's education of Yahweh's symbolic ways.

Each piece of Jehoiada's daily golden garment was applied in order. He slept in his linen undergarment, so Nathanael helped him don the white tunic first. Then came the sky-blue robe with wool pomegranates and bells woven into the hem, cinched at the waist with a belt of embroidered wool and twisted linen. The high priestly ephod fit like an apron, held in place by two sardonyx stones at the shoulders. The breastpiece of decision hung around Jehoiada's neck, set with twelve precious stones— three across in four rows, one for each of Israel's original twelve tribes. Jehoiada then lowered his head, allowing Nathanael to settle the high priest's turban in place. When he lifted his head, the golden crown with the inscription "Holy to the Lord" shone in the lamplight. Sheba had gasped at the sight, finally realizing why the priests' garments were considered too holy to launder. When they became soiled, they were cut and twisted into wicks for the golden lampstands in the Holy Place.

"Hear, O Israel: Yahweh is our God, Yahweh alone." Jehoiada's declaration over the morning offering brought her back to the moment.

"Why me?" she whispered to no one, watching her husband lift his hands to heaven and then signal the Levite choir to begin their psalms. She was afraid to even whisper the real truth. *Yahweh, why did You give me a husband so handsome, faithful, strong, and gentle? One who loves me enough to teach me of You? Finally, someone I can trust.*

Tears coursed down her cheeks as she remembered the young priests teasing Jehoiada about marrying a beautiful young princess. *It's I who married above my equal.* She wiped her tears and grinned, amused that her self-assessment might conflict with Ima Thaliah's destiny of queens.

Sheba noticed a group of older women entering the Sur Gate. Huddled together, they were followed—actually, more like herded—by a younger woman with a baby in a sling. "Shh, keep your voices down," the young woman said. "Stay together, and don't take food or wine from anyone except a Levite or priest. I'll find a place near a Temple guard so that no one harasses us."

Fascinated, Sheba listened as one of the older women tugged at the younger's robe. "Keilah, tell us again why we can't accept food or wine from anyone except the priests?"

"Because the beggars said Baal's temple servants plan to offer tainted bread and wine in the Shavuot crowd, hoping to frighten future worshipers."

Sheba's heart was in her throat. If the rumor was true, she must warn Jehoiada. She rushed to the woman named Keilah and grabbed her arm, startling her horribly and waking the babe in the sling.

Keilah's face paled to match the Temple limestone. "My lady?" She bowed at once, as did the women with her, and Sheba was left standing in a sea of tattered brown robes, a squalling babe the only sound.

"No, please stand. I heard what you said about the tainted bread and wine."

Keilah stood, her shoulders slumped, head still bowed. "I spoke without knowledge. It was a rumor. I meant no disrespect against the queen or any of your family. I—"

"No! No, I don't care about that. If you believe what you've heard, we must warn the high priest."

The young woman glanced up, eyeing Sheba with suspicion. "Please, Keilah."

"How do you know my name?"

"I heard one of the old women—your friends say it." Sheba

192

smiled at the curious faces gathered around them. "Are they your relatives?"

"Oh no, dear." One of the toothless women grinned, pink gums shining. "Keilah is a widow like us. She shares her food with us now that she's found work as a nursemaid—"

"Hobah, the princess isn't interested in our woes." Keilah herded her flock of widows toward the outer wall, settling the oldest ones on camel-hair blankets she'd brought. "Wait here while I go with the princess." She glanced over her shoulder, and Sheba noticed her nervousness. "If I don't return by the end of tonight's service, you must find your way back to our safe place in the city. Know that I love you, and Yahweh will protect you." She hurried away amid promises of prayer and comforted the babe in the sling around her waist.

As if walking to her execution, Keilah arrived at Sheba's side and bowed. Confused, Sheba wondered why the woman was so certain the truth would bring disaster. Perhaps she was afraid to disturb Jehoiada, but the morning service had ended, meaning they had a few moments before Shavuot sacrifices began. "Do you need to care for the baby before we speak to my husband?"

"A fussy baby will give me a reason to speak quickly to the high priest and go." She lowered her head. "I will leave the child with the widows if you command it."

Sheba's heart twisted in her chest. As a princess, she might have commanded it. As the wife of Judah's high priest, she'd rather sit with this woman and hear her story. How had she become a widow so young? Whose baby was she tending?

But Keilah saw only the princess before her, or the wife of Judah's high priest—someone she felt could hurt her; in fact, someone she seemed almost certain would. "Keilah." She placed her hand on the young widow's forearm, trying to put the woman at ease. "I was once a princess, but now I'm merely a priest's wife. I live here on the Temple grounds with my husband." She lifted her eyebrows, shaking her head. "Surrounded by hundreds of men and no women—it's awful!"

The young widow gasped and then covered a giggle, her first sign of ease.

Sheba peeked at the baby and stroked his black curls, thankful for a distraction. She wasn't especially fond of asking a favor or having to trust so quickly. "My husband needs to know of the Baal priests' treacherous plan. You would serve both Yahweh and Judah with your courage—and I would be grateful if you would speak freely to Jehoiada."

A tentative grin edged away Keilah's fear. "I'll try, my lady."

"Come, I'll introduce you, and please—call me Sheba."

Keilah nodded and followed her through the growing swell of worshipers. Zabad stopped them at the gate separating the outer court of worshipers from the inner court of priests. "I'm sorry, Lady Jehosheba, but your friend can't come any farther." His expression was kind but unyielding. "Surely Jehoiada explained the inner courts are reserved only for royalty and consecrated priests and Levites."

Keilah turned back like a frightened dove taking flight, but Sheba grabbed her arm and addressed the chief gatekeeper. "This woman must speak with Jehoiada immediately, or hundreds of Yahweh's faithful will become ill."

Eyes wide with surprise, Zabad hesitated only a moment before rushing toward Jehoiada, who was descending from the great altar. Sheba wrapped her arm around Keilah's shoulders—partly to comfort, partly to ensure she didn't flee—as they watched the two men confer.

Jehoiada hurried across the priests' court, confusion and concern evident before he spoke. "What is it? Are you all right, Jehosheba?"

"I'm all right, but others may not be if Mattan and Ima have their way."

"What now?" he demanded, looking utterly ferocious, brow furrowed, eyes aflame. He would have frightened Judah's fiercest warrior.

Keilah stood silent, mouth agape, shivering. Sheba leaned close to her new friend and whispered loud enough for Jehoiada to overhear, "You see all that handsome silver hair, Keilah? He bawls like a baby when I comb out a tangle."

"Jehosheba!" Jehoiada glanced around sheepishly to see

194

who might have heard, and Keilah giggled, breaking her terror-stricken trance.

Sheba calmed her husband, who had already figured out her motive. "I needed her to know you weren't going to eat her alive."

Keilah's cheeks pinked. "Your wife has been most kind and cares deeply for Yahweh's worshipers. Baal's priests plan to disperse tainted bread and wine to the orphans, widows, and foreigners, since they're the ones who benefit most during the Shavuot celebration."

Jehoiada exchanged a glance with Zabad. "What do you suggest?"

"I'll alert our guards," Zabad said. "They'll require anyone sharing food or wine to taste a portion themselves before sharing it with others. That should take care of the ploy." He was away before any of them could thank him.

Jehoiada bowed slightly to Keilah. "Thank you for protecting Yahweh's worshipers. You were brave to come forward."

Keilah stood a little taller, and the babe in her sling began a full-throated howl. "I'm sorry, but I must feed the baby."

Sheba watched sadness shadow her husband's face. "How old is your little one?"

"Oh, he's not my son. My husband and son were killed by Philistines in the recent raid. I'm a nursemaid for a nobleman's family so this sweet boy's ima can regain her figure and begin bearing children again." Keilah forced a smile. "The nobleman wants to build his family quickly."

"I'm sorry, Keilah," Sheba said, her heart breaking. She'd never considered the lives of the nursemaids hired at the palace. The noble families cared only about sufficient milk to feed their royal babes.

Keilah wiped her tears and bounced the fussing child. "Don't be sorry, my lady. It's how Yahweh provides food for me and the widows. We're here at Shavuot to give Him thanks." She bowed to Jehoiada and hurried back to her flock.

The high priest grabbed his wife in a fierce hug. "Thank you, my love." His voice was choked with emotion. "I'm sorry I can't spend much time with you today. I'll be very busy with various duties." He released her but wouldn't meet her eyes.

"It's all right. I think I've found my first friend."

Jehoiada nodded, looking distracted, and walked away. Something had affected her husband deeply. Keilah's circumstance? The Baal priests' scheming? Or was it the baby boy who broke his heart? She'd never asked him about his life before their marriage. Had he ever been married before? Did he already have a family? The words from Ima's last scroll echoed in her memory. *Does your husband's age disqualify him for sons?* What if Jehoiada couldn't give her children? Refusing to let the thought ruin this day of celebration, she turned toward the outer courts to join Keilah and her widows.

23

2 CHRONICLES 21:8, 10

In the time of Jehoram, Edom rebelled against Judah and set up its own king. . . . To this day Edom has been in rebellion against Judah.

Jehoiada stood at the threshold of the palace courtyard, Jehosheba at his right, waiting to be announced as part of the honored royal household. His stomach rolled at the thought. Or perhaps he was still reeling from yesterday's encounter with the young widow and baby—a painful reminder of his lifelong failure. It had been years since he'd been so near an infant, since Amariah's children had lived on Temple grounds. His life at the Temple usually shielded him from his most torturous thought: *Yahweh believes I'm unfit to be an abba.*

Jehosheba seemed to sense his sullenness but had respected his privacy and didn't press. They'd never discussed his first wife, Anna, or their childlessness, but she probably felt as uncomfortable about the topic as he did. Perhaps he'd ask Hazi how Jehosheba had responded to the news when she was informed about their match. During their bridal negotiation, the prince had seemed aware of every detail of Jehoiada and Jehoram's quarry discussion. Surely Hazi would know how Jehosheba felt about Jehoiada's childlessness.

197

Jehoiada glanced at his beautiful wife and ached for what they would never have. Since he couldn't give her children, he loved to offer her gifts—like the new robe she was wearing, woven of linen using the priestly dyes of blue, purple, and crimson. He'd commissioned a weaver in the City of David three weeks ago, but Jehosheba's joy at discovering the package this morning had been worth the wait. Her eyes had grown round as Solomon's gold shields.

Startled at the thought, Jehoiada inspected the walls of the courtyard where the king's shields once hung. Gone, all gone. The first time Jerusalem had been invaded, generations ago, Egypt's king stole Solomon's gold shields, and a humbled King Rehoboam replaced them with bronze shields.

Jehoiada leaned over, whispering for his wife's hearing alone, "Were the bronze shields gone during *our* wedding feast?"

She lifted a half smile and matched his tone. "Yes. They were stolen in the raid with most of the other gold, silver, and bronze furnishings in the palace. Should I be flattered or concerned that you were so unobservant at our wedding feast?"

The high steward began his announcement before Jehoiada mustered an answer. "Jehoiada, Yahweh's high priest, and Lady Jehosheba rejoice with the returning crown prince."

Trumpets blared, and they marched forward, down a long aisle between fifty low tables. Most guests were already reclining, waiting for royalty to be seated. They passed Obadiah's table, but Jehoiada knew very few of the other Judean aristocracy and even fewer of the Baal priests seated at the six tables near the front. Two head tables perched on the elevated dais, bearing pitchers of wine and platters of olives and cheese. The first table was reserved for Queen Athaliah, the crown prince, and his special guests, while the second waited to be filled with Hazi's burgeoning harem. Jehoiada and Jehosheba arrived at the queen's table and took their places on opposite ends, leaving room for the other royals and guests to fill the spaces between them.

"Athaliah, queen of Judah, and Mattan, Baal's high priest, offer their blessing on the marriages of Prince Ahaziah with the

preeminent families of Judah." The high steward's introduction
initiated Mattan's march as he led the queen on his arm. "All
praise to mighty Prince Baal who has blessed the land of Judah."

Jehoiada raged inwardly at the credit Baal received for blessing Judah. Would the whole day be one jab after another aimed
at Yahweh—and His high priest? He glanced at his wife, who
lifted her hand to her heart and mouthed, "I love you." His
heart leapt in his chest, captured anew by this woman Yahweh
had given him.

Athaliah sat on the center cushion, blocking their view of
each other. Mattan occupied the cushion beside Jehoiada. *Yahweh, help me.* A whole day of dining beside the pompous Baal
high priest. Jehoiada tossed an olive in his mouth to keep from
gritting his teeth.

A hush fell over the waiting crowd. When Prince Ahaziah
appeared at the archway, the whole courtyard gasped in unison.
His purple robe, gold-braided belt, and leopard-skin cape were
almost as dazzling as the bride who appeared beside him. She
seemed hesitant, timid, but stunning—as radiant in her natural
beauty as Hazi was in his grandeur.

The girl's hair fell in dark ringlets around her face. She wore
a simple gold crown, from which a sheer veil mingled with more
dark ringlets, golden thread, and precious stones, all cascading
down her back. Her eyes, round and black, appeared kohl-rimmed
because of thick lashes, somehow having escaped Athaliah's cosmetics. The effect distinguished her from Hazi's other women.
The rest of the new wives tittered and whispered behind the couple, then were hushed by a solemn stare from their husband and
lord. Hazi nodded to the steward when his women were quiet.

Trumpets sounded and the herald crowed, "Welcome, Crown
Prince Ahaziah and Lady Zibiah with the favored wives of Judah.
May the mighty Cloud Rider make your wives' wombs fertile,
your sons plentiful, and your life a testimony to Baal's power."

The six tables of Baal's priests led the audience in celebration,
but it was the utter joy on Hazi's face that intrigued Jehoiada.
He'd seen the prince's deceptive charm, but his rakish demeanor
was lost in the depth of emotion he bestowed on Zibiah.

Mattan leaned over, lifting his hand to shield a whisper. "Our young prince can't take his eyes off Zibiah. If there were a boulder in the aisle, Hazi would trip over it."

"I believe he might float over it. He appears to be walking on air." Jehoiada had no intention of becoming close-knit brethren with Baal's high priest, but he should at least be civil.

The royal couple ascended the dais, and the brood of wives dispersed to the smaller table. Hazi placed Zibiah between Jehosheba and his ima Thaliah before taking his place on a center cushion between the queen and Mattan. He glanced around Baal's priest and grinned at Jehoiada. "Hello, Brother."

Jehoiada's heart warmed toward the young man. "Your Zibiah is almost as beautiful as my bride."

Hazi laughed. "Indeed, the two are very much alike. I believe they will be fast friends."

Queen Athaliah stood, interrupting their conversation, and lifted her wine-filled golden chalice—the only gold in the courtyard. The guests drank spiced wine from wooden goblets but seemed no less ready to celebrate. "Today begins a new era in Judah's history." She waved her glass over the two head tables. "My son has completed his first tour of Judah, emphasizing our strong traditions and honoring the memory of King Jehoshaphat, while at the same time embracing the reforms that will keep our nation great. As a sign that we're embracing the evolving cultures of Phoenicia, Egypt, and the land between the rivers, both men and women of Judah share the same feasting table. And because of King Jehoram's current *condition*, I, as his queen, am forced to take on roles never before assumed by a first wife." She turned and lifted her goblet to Hazi. "But we embrace the new roles and new challenges before us!"

Hazi stood and faced the audience. "Indeed we do. Let the feasting begin!"

His enthusiasm elicited a cheer from the audience and released couplets of servants—young men carrying trays of roasted game and young women serving vegetables, dates, and fruit from heavily laden platters. A scantily clad Egyptian pair was sent to the queen's table, the girl wearing little more than scarves knotted at her neck and back, the young man dressed in a loincloth exposing his sinewy long legs. They served the prince and queen first, and the audience eased into an indiscriminate hum.

Mattan drained his first goblet of wine and offered his cup to be refilled by a waiting servant. "So, how was the attendance at your Feast of Shavuot yesterday, Jehoiada? I heard your guards averted an incident with some tainted bread and wine."

Jehoiada tamped down his revulsion for this serpent in priest's clothing. "Baal's priests are not welcome in Yahweh's Temple courts unless they bring a sin offering. Those who came yesterday, dressed as ordinary citizens sharing moldy bread and soured wine, were given the choices afforded in Moses's Law. Depart or die. On last report, Baal's priests wisely retreated." He held Mattan's gaze and watched his practiced smile fade. Seeming to have lost his appetite for games, Mattan turned away, seeking a safer conversation with the crown prince.

Jehoiada was thankful for the reprieve and offered his plate when the Egyptian servants arrived to serve his portion of fattened calf. The girl used glimmering gold tongs to reach for a thick slice of roast.

Jehoiada seized her wrist. "Where did you find the sacred tongs from Yahweh's Temple?" He ripped them from her grasp and leapt to his feet, shaking the golden tongs at Athaliah. "Your sons stole these from Yahweh's Temple!"

The courtyard fell silent. Hazi and Mattan kept their gazes forward while Queen Athaliah stood and met Jehoiada face-to-face. Carites hurried to surround their queen. "Obviously you're mistaken, Priest. If you had attended Baal's Festival of Marzeh yesterday, you would have witnessed the miracle, as we all did." She swept her hand over the crowd. "Baal Melkart gifted us with these tongs and several other golden items in the belly of our sacrificial bull. When Mattan faithfully led us to honor the noble Jehoshaphat and my poor murdered sons, the almighty Rider of the Clouds revealed his miraculous power and visited us with profound generosity." With a dangerous gleam in her eye, she added, "I believe King Jehoram, you, and Princess Jehosheba were the only Judeans of any significance who missed the display."

Jehoiada drew a breath to unleash his fury but noticed a scuffle at his left.

Mattan stirred, but Hazi leaned on his shoulder, seating him securely while the prince rose instead. "I'm prepared to give my report on Judah's fortified cities while our guests enjoy their meal, Ima, but I need to speak with my brother-in-law alone first." He grabbed Jehoiada's arm with an iron grip.

Queen Athaliah shooed away the Carite guards as Hazi nudged Yahweh's high priest to the back corner of the dais.

Finally at his limit, Jehoiada shoved the prince away, earning another gasp from the audience and the return of the Carites. Hazi waved off his guards, keeping his voice low. "Don't be a fool, Jehoiada. Think about those watching. You're Yahweh's high priest, the only example of Yahweh they may ever see. Ima Thaliah wanted you to react. Why do you think *our* servants had the golden objects? You're in Ima's world today, and you must play by her rules."

Jehoiada ground out his reply between clenched teeth. "I will *never* play by your ima's rules."

"Then Yahweh will be defeated by the Phoenician *Jezebel* and her scheming daughter." Hazi's use of the disrespectful title shocked Jehoiada into silence. "Just because I *seem* to be Ima's dumb sheep doesn't mean I'm ignorant of her sordid schemes or the lives at stake." The prince glanced over his shoulder, keeping his back to the head table and the crowd. "You won't get back your sacred Temple objects. Mattan literally found them hidden in one of the sacrificial animals when we returned from Jezreel—no doubt put there by my worthless brothers during the raid. But Ima will kill you or anyone else who tries to take them from her. So we must let her have them, and—"

"No!" Jehoiada shouted.

"Listen, and hold your temper!" he said with equal passion, clutching Jehoiada's sleeves. "Zibiah serves Yahweh and wants me to learn more about Saba Jehoshaphat." Again Jehoiada was stunned into silence. "So, as I said, let Ima keep the sacred objects—which she will do anyway—but use your acquiescence as leverage to get something you want in return."

"Leverage? What could I possibly want from your ima Thaliah?" The thought of asking anything of the queen reeked like King Jehoram's sickbed.

"Ask if Zibiah can come every day to visit Sheba at the Temple." Hazi folded his arms, looking entirely too pleased with himself. "Sheba and Zibiah will enjoy a new friendship, and I'll fetch my wife from the Temple each day, which gives you and me the opportunity to discuss Saba Jehoshaphat's faith in Yahweh."

Jehoiada glanced over Hazi's shoulder, studying the host of people who would judge Yahweh by His high priest's actions. The thought sobered him. Thankfully the guests and Hazi's harem had returned to idle chatter, enjoying their meals, but Sheba and Zibiah still cast concerned glances at their arguing husbands.

"I feel as though I'm selling Yahweh's sacred objects to buy a friend for my wife and the crown prince's faith."

Hazi chuckled and placed a comforting hand on Jehoiada's shoulder. "You aren't selling them. They've already been stolen, and you're finding a way to benefit from the loss—without getting anyone else killed."

Sheba continued her subtle watch while chewing another bite of garlic-and-onion-sautéed lamb. Zibiah hadn't eaten anything. The girl's first taste of lamb fell off her fork at Jehoiada's outburst, and she'd nearly climbed into Sheba's lap when Ima Thaliah began her taunting.

"Do your husband and the queen always fight like that?" she'd whispered.

"Only when they're in the same room." Sheba had laid a comforting hand on the girl's shoulder during the foray, and when Hazi rose to join in, she gave the girl a quick lesson in palace living. "When Ima returns to the table, we cannot whisper or mention the confrontation. We must smile and continue to eat delicately, as if nothing unpleasant is happening."

Zibiah nodded, eyes wide with fright.

Ima returned to her cushion, perfect smile in place. "Zibiah, dear, you haven't tasted your lamb. I had the cook prepare it with spices from Beersheba so you'd feel at home."

Zibiah clutched Sheba's knee and smiled. She began shoving her food around the wooden plate, pretending to eat.

Hazi and Jehoiada seemed more settled into conversation, and Sheba slipped her hand beneath the table, working to dislodge the girl's iron grasp. She lifted her fork, eyed Zibiah, and waited for her to do the same. The girl finally lifted her fork as well and began nibbling at the lamb on her plate.

"So tell me, Zibiah, why has my son chosen you as his favorite?" Ima asked. Zibiah choked on her third bite of lamb, and Ima slapped her back. "There, there, dear. You shouldn't gobble such large bites."

Tears pooled in Zibiah's eyes, and Sheba knew they weren't from choking. "I think it's quite obvious why she's Hazi's favorite, Ima." Smiling brightly, she noticed a fuss just beyond the queen's shoulder and motioned toward Hazi with her wineglass. "It appears Hazi is changing the seating order."

The queen spun around like a child's toy top, and Sheba tried desperately to mask her delight as the servants moved Mattan's cushion to the end of the table, placing Jehoiada at Hazi's left.

Zibiah's large, black eyes looked as if they might fall out of her head. "What will Mattan do?" Baal's high priest had turned a deep shade of crimson on every visible surface.

Before Sheba could shush her, Hazi's voice rang out over the buzzing crowd. "I've returned from visiting our brethren in Judah's fortified cities with news of lingering hostility from nations on our borders." At the mention of neighboring nations, the courtyard hushed.

"I'll begin first with the reports from my uncle, King Joram of Israel," Hazi used their uncle's full name, making Ima Thaliah wince. "Israel is harassed on every side. Moab continues its rebellion, fighting among their own tribes while refusing to pay tribute in wool or lambs to Israel. Aram has increased raids on Israel's north and northeastern borders since Hazael usurped Ben-Hadad's throne, and Israel has once again lost control of Ramoth Gilead."

"Oh no . . ." Dismay fluttered over the audience, and Hazi paused to let the impact of Israel's weakening defenses settle in.

"Farther north, Assyria's relentless King Shalmaneser has emerged from his land between the rivers, seeking to extend his domination westward, demanding tribute from the coastal nations of Tyre and Sidon. The mandatory tribute is so daunting that Phoenicia's king—the Gevirah Jizebaal's own brother—refused Israel's request for military and economic aid."

Sheba noted Ima Thaliah's silent seething, but Hazi seemed undaunted, empowered by his recent tour of independence. "Amid all this grave news of our northern brethren, imagine my relief at traveling through the lovely hills of Judah and finding twelve loyal households with whom we could join the house of David, strengthening *our* nation." He paused, seeming overwhelmed. "My brother Judeans, in the seven weeks since my departure, Jerusalem has been rebuilt into a capital that would make our forefathers proud. Let us pray that Prince Baal Melkart blesses your daughters to provide many fine sons." He swept his hand over the lovely brides at the second table.

Resounding cheers began at the Baal priests' table and spread through the gathering, quieting only when Hazi raised his goblet again. "And let us praise Yahweh for His gift of my beloved wife Zibiah, and pray His blessing on her womb."

Obadiah stood and applauded, prompting obligatory praise throughout. Sheba's heart lodged in her throat when she saw Ima Thaliah turn a dark smile on Zibiah. "I hadn't realized you worshiped Yahweh, my dear."

Zibiah clutched Sheba's knee again but didn't reply. Ima Thaliah turned away, seeming suddenly eager to hear more of Hazi's report.

"During my travels, I discovered information every bit as troubling as the murderous invasion of Jerusalem." Hazi paused, letting silence build the anticipation. "After Edom rebelled against Abba Jehoram last year, the cliff rats of Seir crawled back to their holes and planned more evil deeds. It appears they knew of the impending Philistine raid and did nothing to warn us! They watched from a distance while our gates were breached and then stole the booty from our attackers. And they put to the sword any Judeans who sought refuge in Edom's mountains."

Outrage filled the courtyard. Noblemen leapt to their feet, raising their fists and shouting obscenities. The rage became a roar, building, rolling, growing into a living thing until . . .

Obadiah walked up the center aisle toward the head table. Hazi met him, but over the noise, Sheba understood only that Obadiah wanted to address the guests. She held her breath. She hoped his court experience proved effective. From the look on Ima Thaliah's face, his life depended on it.

24

Obadiah was a devout believer in the LORD. While Jezebel was killing off the LORD's prophets, Obadiah had taken a hundred prophets and hidden them in two caves, fifty in each, and had supplied them with food and water.

I am neither a prophet nor the son of a prophet," Obadiah began, "but I have been given a revelation from Yahweh, the one true God of Jacob."

Jehoiada was as stunned as everyone else. Obadiah, his friend and a nobleman, had spent his life hiding prophets in Israel and occasionally doing the same in Judah. But he had vehemently denied any role as a seer of God's direct wisdom.

"This is what the Sovereign Lord says about Edom," the old man began.

Shock. Silence. Awe. The guests at the feast watched this unassuming nobleman speak with power and authority born from above. Even the Baal priests sat in rapt attention. Jehoiada was almost as fascinated by the faces of those who listened as by the words of Obadiah's prophecy.

"Because of the violence against your brother Jacob, you, Edom, will be covered with shame; you will be destroyed forever. On the day you stood aloof while strangers carried off his wealth and foreigners entered his gates and cast lots for Jerusalem, you were like one of them. You should not gloat over your brother in the day of his misfortune, nor rejoice over the people of Judah in the day of their destruction. You should not wait at the crossroads to cut down their fugitives, nor hand over their survivors in the day of their trouble. The day of the Lord is near for all nations. As you have done, it will be done to you."

The air throbbed with silence in the wake of Obadiah's declaration. Jehoiada, realizing his mouth was agape, closed it. He observed Queen Athaliah and Mattan recovering their facades, replacing wonder with indifference.

Hazi stepped from the dais, embraced the old nobleman, and then addressed the crowd. "I'm not sure what qualifies a man to be called *prophet*, but with all my heart, I pray Obadiah's words are a promise from Yahweh."

A resounding cheer brought most guests to their feet, including Jehoiada. The Baal priests sulked where they sat.

Hazi invited Obadiah to dine at the head table, moving Jehoiada's cushion down and placing Obadiah between them. Mattan sat moping on the end closest to his flock of priests below.

Obadiah kept his voice low, waiting until the queen's attention was focused on Hazi's new bride. "How is King Jehoram, my prince? I haven't spoken with the palace physician since he was permanently moved into the king's chambers."

Hazi cast a furtive glance at Mattan before answering, but Baal's high priest had begun drinking barley beer between glasses of wine and seemed thoroughly content to talk to the slab of fattened calf on his plate. "He worsens each day," Hazi whispered. "When Zev and I returned from the tour, we were appalled at his condition—and the conditions in which he must live. Zev even asked me if I wanted him to end Abba's suffering with the sword."

Jehoiada's heart nearly broke, and then Hazi leaned in, addressing him. "Are there laws against such a thing, Jehoiada? I know murder is forbidden by Yahweh, but have you seen my abba? It wouldn't be murder. It would be mercy to end his suffering."

Jehoiada noticed Athaliah's attention still drawn toward the women's side of the table, so he ventured a cautious question. "Have Mattan and your ima counseled you on the decision?"

"Yes. Ima believes it's the only merciful thing to do, and Mattan says that Mot would gently guide Abba Jehoram to the underworld . . ." Hazi's whisper died, and his features grew somber. "I am asking *you*, Jehoiada. Are there *laws* against such a thing?"

Jehoiada noticed poor Obadiah shifting uncomfortably between them. "There are indeed laws against it, but more suitable to your circumstance is the story of your ancestor David, who faced a similar dilemma. He waited years to be named king and then punished a man for killing King Saul when he'd been mortally wounded. King David believed—as I do—that it's never right to take the life of the Lord's anointed king."

At the mention of *king*, Queen Athaliah interrupted their conversation. "Did someone speak of the king?"

Jehoiada straightened, tight-lipped, and Obadiah looked like he might relinquish his few bites of fattened calf. Hazi, however, equaled his ima's pretense with a blinding smile. "Your intuition is astounding as always, Ima! Indeed, Jehoiada was telling me David was a man of integrity who waited for King Saul's death before assuming his throne. David waited *years* to become king."

Athaliah's eyes narrowed, aiming daggers at Jehoiada. "Unfortunately for King Jehoram, I'm sure his overindulgence and diseased body will demand his life much sooner. I doubt years will pass before Hazi becomes Judah's king."

Jehoiada met her stare, refusing to be cowed.

Hazi lifted his goblet and leaned forward between them, effectively breaking the battle glare. He took a long draw of wine before he spoke. "Jehoiada regrets his outburst over the golden tongs and asks to make amends by offering hospitality to Zibiah."

Hazi's awkward change of topic clashed like a tone-deaf Levite. Even the young brides cast questioning glances at him.

The high priest recounted Hazi's carefully chosen words. *Jehoiada regrets his outburst . . . asks to make amends by offering hospitality to Zibiah.* None of it was untrue. The standard of "wise without lies" reached a new level in this world of kings and queens. Hazi tiptoed on high and narrow walls, and Jehoiada must be sure they didn't fall off the edge.

Queen Athaliah seemed perplexed by Hazi's tactless transition. She laid her fork aside and kept her eyes focused on Jehoiada while addressing her son. "You're saying that Yahweh's high priest will admit the golden tongs were part of a miraculous gift from Baal?"

Jehoiada flushed. "I will nev—"

"I said . . ." Hazi leaned into Athaliah's line of sight, blocking her view of Jehoiada again. "My brother-in-law regrets his outburst. And that is enough." Taking another swig of wine, he focused on the courtyard. "Jehoiada has also confided that Sheba is bored and needs a friend. I think Sheba and Zibiah will get along famously. I plan to have guards escort Zibiah to Sheba's quarters for a visit each day."

"Out of the question." Athaliah slammed her hand on the table, causing Zibiah and Sheba to jump and the whole courtyard to still. Realizing her lapse in etiquette, the queen lowered her voice. "Sheba can come to the palace daily, but I see no reason for Zibiah to visit the Temple."

"Of course there is reason, Ima," Hazi said, raising his wine for another sip. "The reason is simple. Zibiah is my wife, and I wish her to visit Yahweh's Temple." Setting his goblet on the table, he spoke in a voice barely perceptible. "I have always been—and continue to be—a willing lamb in service to you and the Gevirah, but if you so much as touch a curl on Zibiah's head . . . I. Will. Destroy. You."

Before she could respond, Hazi stood, shouting above the din. "Begin the music and dancing!"

Queen Athaliah resumed her practiced smile and toasted the approving crowd, offering a seemingly improved countenance to her daughter-in-law. Jehoiada toasted Obadiah, a silent celebration of hope sparked by Prince Hazi's zeal. He could hardly wait to return home to gain Jehosheba's insights.

Sheba sat on the couch in their outer chamber, watching as Nathanael helped Jehoiada remove the high priestly golden garments. After a long day of feasting, they were both tired, but Jehoiada's routine of disrobing was as sacred as his predawn procedure. Careful to reverse the exact order, the second priest removed the golden diadem from the turban before unwrapping the long strip of linen from Jehoiada's full head of silver hair. When Nathanael lifted the jeweled breastpiece from her husband's neck, she mustered her courage. "Could I look more closely at the breastpiece?"

Even in the dim lamplight, she noted Nathanael's eyes bulge. Jehoiada patted his shoulder, easing the man's obvious trepidation. "You may *look* at it, but take care not to touch it. It's a sacred object, consecrated to Yahweh for the use of His high priest alone, my love."

She reconsidered after hearing his caution, and besides, Jehoiada's explanation reminded her of another topic. "How did Hazi convince you to let Ima Thaliah keep the consecrated Temple objects? They used the gold tongs to serve meat today, and Ima said they used the wick trimmers and other utensils in the Marzeh service last night. How can that be all right?"

"Yahweh's sacred objects in Baal's temple?" Nathanael's face paled, and his pained expression revealed more sorrow than anger.

Jehoiada squeezed the bridge of his nose, sighed, and placed both hands on Nathanael's shoulders. "Athaliah's sons stole the sacred objects during the raid and hid them in Baal's temple. Mattan discovered them, and the queen is determined to keep them. Hazi believes if I fight Athaliah on this, I'll lose the Temple items *and* get loved ones hurt in the process. The consecrated objects had already been defiled in Baal's temple, so I traded golden objects for priceless lives." He searched his second priest's eyes. "Do you understand, my friend?"

Nathanael remained silent, seeming deep in thought. When he answered, his words were heartfelt, not contrived. "I do understand. Consecrated objects are replaceable." With an affirming nod, he resumed the disrobing process, lifting the ephod over Jehoiada's head.

Sheba watched silently, her stomach twisting as she considered Hazi's influence on her husband. By the time Nathanael completed his task and bid them good night, Sheba's question fairly spewed out. "So, if Hazi convinced you to think like we do in the palace, does that mean I must now measure your every word—as I do his?"

Jehoiada stood in his simple white tunic, looking completely vulnerable. "No, my love. No." He joined her on the couch, removed her head covering, and twirled a lock of her hair around his finger. "I'll admit, it felt wrong at first, but Hazi explained that I must lose some battles to win the war. I believe it's the right thing to do."

She remained unmoved, searching his eyes for any sign of corruption. Had his time with Hazi tarnished her husband's integrity? In the unshuttered windows of his soul, she saw nothing but pure surrender, complete honesty.

He bounced his wiry eyebrows. "Zibiah worships Yahweh."

"Zibiah worships Yahweh!" Sheba giggled and squealed— very unlike a queen of destiny.

He kissed her gently and then hoisted her into his arms. "Let's talk about this in the other room." A roguish grin creased his handsome face.

She enjoyed the weightless journey to their bedchamber and let her head rest against his chest. "Maybe Hazi will begin to worship Him too."

He placed her gently on the bed and lay beside her. "Hazi has already devised a plan to visit me and hear stories of Jehoshaphat's faithfulness while you and Zibiah get to know each other."

"So that's why he fought Ima Thaliah so hard to let Zibiah visit the Temple each day?"

"You'll finally have another woman to talk to."

The idea pierced her. How could she tell him friendship terrified her? She scooted into the bend of his arm, listening to the heart that had loved and accepted her unconditionally. Women had never been kind to Sheba. Athaliah used her. The handmaids feared her. What did Sheba know of being a friend?

He kissed the top of her head. "Did I say something wrong?"

"You said nothing wrong, but I might have." She sat up and tried to quiet her racing heart. "Do you remember Keilah, the young widow from Shavuot?" A barely perceptible nod. "Well, she already attends every morning service, so I invited her to stay awhile longer and spend time with me each day. You know, so we could—"

"Is she bringing the child?" He sat abruptly on the edge of the bed, his back to her.

Sheba remained silent, startled by his reaction. Did he despise children? The station of wet nurse?

"I said is she bringing the child?" He kept his back turned, but his voice rose.

"Yes, I suppose she is."

"I have duties that will keep me away from our chambers each morning. Make sure she's gone when you come to the kitchen for our midday meal." He walked to their outer chamber.

Sheba sat, completely baffled, crushed. The longer she sat there, the angrier she became. She heard dishes rattle, and finally a cup shattered. "This is ridiculous," she whispered as she leapt off the bed. Rounding the corner, she began shouting before her shadow fell in the outer chamber. "What is so terrible about a baby in our chambers?"

She stopped the moment she saw Jehoiada slumped over, kneeling, sobbing. "What is it?" She ran to him, but he waved her away, his head shaking violently. "Jehoiada, talk to me."

His strong arm pointed her toward their bedroom, commanding her to go. Still no words.

She turned but glimpsed him clutching his head with both hands, rocking now, silently keening. He wasn't in physical pain. She was certain of it. This was a rending of his soul, something too deep to speak aloud. She lingered at the door between their two rooms, torn. What does a wife do when her husband cannot—will not—share his inner war?

Pray. The answer came like a gentle voice on the evening breeze. Without thinking how she might sound, she whispered into the stillness, "Hear, O Israel, Yahweh is God, Yahweh alone. May the Lord look down on you, His servant and high priest, and give you strength to bear whatever burden seems too heavy to share with your wife. May Yahweh give you wisdom and understanding to know the measure of my love for you."

She walked into their bedroom as her husband's silent mourning turned to racking sobs. She left the door between the rooms open, hoping Jehoiada would sense her need to help and open his heart.

Sometime after the moon passed its zenith, she woke to silence—and an empty bed. Perhaps the dawn would shine some light on her husband's pain.

25

When Jehoram established himself firmly over his father's kingdom, he put all his brothers to the sword along with some of the officials of Israel.

Sheba stood in the Temple courtyard at sunrise between two women, letting the psalms of the Levitical choir strengthen her. Her lonely night had extended into a solitary morning, adding to her disquiet. Jehoiada and his golden garments were gone when she emerged from their bedroom—undoubtedly both had made their appearance in Nathanael's chamber before the second priest had expected them. Sheba wondered if anyone else in the sparse crowd noticed their high priest's somber mood. He'd delegated this morning's altar sacrifice to Eliab—not a blatant indication of a troubled high priest, but certainly a signal to those who knew him that Jehoiada was not himself.

Zibiah leaned close, whispering, "I hope Jehoiada didn't feel compelled to invite Hazi to stand in the priests' court. Hazi came early this morning—before the Temple gates were opened—to bring his sin offering so he could stand with Jehoiada."

Perhaps that's why Jehoiada left our chamber so early. A little relief nudged away the dread Sheba had felt since last night.

215

"Jehoiada isn't easily compelled," she said, working at a smile. "I'm sure if Hazi's sacrifice was sincere, Jehoiada gladly made atonement to the Lord on his behalf."

Keilah tugged on Sheba's other sleeve. "My lady, the baby is beginning to fuss. Perhaps I should go and let you and the princess enjoy some time alone—"

Sheba's chastising glare stopped further excuses. "I want to spend time with both of you. I think you and Zibiah will become fast friends too." She reached into the sling and brushed the baby's rosy cheek. "No more talk about princesses. We're all simply friends while here on Temple grounds."

Keilah offered an unconvincing smile and quieted the babe as the last notes of the choir faded. The faithful Yahwists began to disperse, and Sheba led her fledgling friends through the gate of the inner court. Zabad watched with an eagle's eye as Keilah and Zibiah removed their shoes. Sheba had secured special permission for Keilah to enter the court of priests. Zibiah qualified as Hazi's wife, but no one could walk the sacred ground with sandals on their feet.

Sheba hurried them toward her chamber, hoping to avoid any contact with Jehoiada.

"Wait!" Zibiah tugged in the opposite direction. "Aren't we going to speak to our husbands first?"

Sheba's stomach knotted, but Keilah lightened the mood, rolling her eyes in feigned frustration. "Uhh, newlyweds." All three chuckled, and Sheba breathed a sigh of relief as they nudged Zibiah toward the high priest's chamber.

Upon reaching her door, Sheba was suddenly nervous, thinking of all the things their living space was not. "I've never entertained guests here. It's not very big, and since we eat with the priests, we don't have a real kitch—"

Zibiah placed a quieting hand on her shoulder. "We've come to visit you, not to inspect your home."

Sheba swallowed hard and opened the door.

"Oh, Sheba, it's lovely!" Zibiah was the first inside, walking four steps and sliding her hand over the embroidered couch under the single window. "And you don't need a kitchen." She pointed toward the small, stone-ringed fire pit and washbasin, where cups and supply baskets hung from the walls. "You've got everything you and Jehoiada need right here."

"It's a palace to me." Keilah's words revealed a heart longing for a brighter future. "And I'm so grateful you invited me to see it. Thank you, my lady."

Sheba wanted to hug her but refrained, afraid she might squeeze the baby in his sling or overstep social boundaries. Zibiah had no such qualms, however, and gathered both women in a tight embrace—sending the squished infant into a full-throated squall.

"All right, all right." Keilah nudged her new friends aside and freed the boy from his sling. "Why don't you come out here and meet my new friends? Samson, this is Lady Zibiah and Lady Jehosheba."

Amid a flurry of oohs and aahs, baby Samson's mood seemed to improve. Zibiah sat on the embroidered couch, and Sheba offered Keilah the spot beside her.

"If you don't mind, my lady, I'd rather sit on a cushion beside the table. It'll be easier to nurse Samson when the time comes."

"Oh, of course." Sheba sat on the couch beside Zibiah while Keilah propped her elbow on the table and sat the baby in her lap.

"How old is your son?" Zibiah asked. Sheba felt her cheeks grow warm and wished she'd explained Keilah's circumstances to Zibiah privately.

Keilah seemed unfazed. "Samson was born six full moons ago, but he's the son of a wealthy Jerusalem family. I'm only his daytime wet nurse. I return to the City of David each night to care for other widows who can't earn a wage like I can."

"I'm sorry, Keilah." Zibiah reached out, brushing the woman's shoulder. "You're so young to be a widow. How did your husband die?"

Sheba watched the two women in amazed silence. Their ease and depth of sharing seemed so natural. Was this how friends spoke?

"He was a watchman on Jerusalem's wall during the Philistine raid," Keilah was saying. "I had just delivered his evening meal when a small contingent of raiders took my husband's watch by surprise. They entered the city disguised as caravaners, sneaked up the western wall, and killed our guards. Then they posed as Jerusalem watchmen while their comrades scaled the same wall from the other side."

Sheba gasped. "Oh, Keilah, how did you find out the details of the attack?"

She paused as if weighing her words. Sheba was ready to apologize and withdraw her question, thinking she'd ruined her first attempt at conversation.

The nursemaid answered in a voice barely over a whisper. "My baby and I were still on the wall delivering my husband's meal when the raiders attacked and killed the first of our watchmen. The Philistines held me hostage while they . . ." Keilah's mouth twisted with emotion, making more words impossible. She buried her face in Samson's neck, and as if sensing her grief, Samson began to cry too.

Zibiah scooted off the couch, reaching for the boy. "Here, give him to me. I'm sorry, Keilah. You don't have to tell me any more."

Sheba was mortified, heat racing up her neck and cheeks. "Keilah, please forgive me. I should nev—"

"No!" She beat her fists against her legs. "I haven't been able to tell anyone. There's no one left to listen!"

Sheba joined the widow on the floor, cradling her balled fists. "We're listening."

The young widow squeezed her eyes shut as if reliving the scene. "They killed my husband first—mercifully, as I was to realize later—with a single sword through his heart. I cradled our newborn son in my arms. He had lived only two full moons. When they hurled him off the western wall, I thought it was the worst they could do to me." She shook her head, seeming consumed by the memory while Sheba and Zibiah listened in horror. "The Philistines took their turns with me, and I prayed . . . oh, how I prayed . . . that they would hurl *me* off the wall. They didn't." She bowed her head, taking a deep breath, regaining composure. "When they tired of me, I was left for dead and found the next day by Judean soldiers. They took me to Samson's family, who said they would pay for my healing herbs as long as I wasn't carrying a Philistine child."

"Yahweh, help us." Sheba's sorrow turned to indignation. "How could anyone be so cruel?"

Keilah slowly turned to meet her gaze. "Yahweh did help me. I did not become pregnant, and the family not only paid for my recovery but hired me as Samson's wet nurse." She attempted a quivering smile. "Life is cruel, but Yahweh is good, my lady."

"You are right on both counts, Keilah." Zibiah's strong affirmation startled the baby, and he wailed in earnest. His nurse offered her arms, and Zibiah set him in the familiar resting place.

"Tell me, Lady Zibiah, how has life been cruel to you?" Keilah placed the babe in his sling, opened her robe, and began feeding to comfort him. She met the new bride's gaze and pressed, "A woman who has married the crown prince doesn't spend time with a beggar woman unless she's known adversity."

"But she didn't know you were a beggar," Sheba said without thinking.

Keilah exchanged a knowing glance with Zibiah. "The princess may not have known my *exact* circumstances, but my appearance told her I am a woman well below her station." New tears formed on her lashes. "Such humility gave me courage to share my heart." Swiping away the tears, she ventured a half smile. "Can you share your heart, Lady Zibiah?"

Sheba watched a moment of indecision shadow the new bride's face. She'd seemed so confident, so adept at the social graces. "I think I can trust you both. My ima told me, 'Don't trust anyone in Jerusalem, especially from the palace.'" She laid her hand on Sheba's arm. "But I don't suppose you qualify for that anymore, do you?"

The girl's transparency lightened the moment for Sheba to tease. "Well, Keilah thinks my chamber is a palace."

All three chuckled, Zibiah's winding down with a faraway stare. "I guess my adversity began when King Jehoram killed the governor of Beersheba, his brother Jehiel." She met Sheba's eyes without condemnation or apology. "Your abba Jehoram ordered the executions of any other wealthy landowners faithful to Yahweh and placed his son, a Baal priest, as the new governor over Beersheba. My abba understood the king's message and converted to Baal worship in order to save our lives and his wealth—though our family had been devout Yahwists for generations. My brother refused to convert and was found murdered in a ditch outside the city."

Sheba felt the blood drain from her face, horrified. She remembered Abba's brothers' deaths, the royal cousins who lived at the palace under guard, and the Gevirah's revelation that Abba Jehoram had murdered his brothers at Ima Thaliah's command. Nameless stories—until a young woman she knew lost a brother and called evil by its real name. "Zibiah, I'm so sorry. I had no idea—"

"Of course, you couldn't have known," she said. "What do women have to do with politics?"

Sheba's mouth suddenly went dry. She would avoid that topic like a hot ember. "How have you maintained your devotion to Yahweh when your abba worships Baal?"

"My ima and I remained true to the one God without Abba's knowledge. When Abba heard the crown prince was coming to Beersheba for a bride, he arranged with the Baal priest for me to marry Hazi. Ima told me not to confess my true faith to the prince, but I couldn't allow our marriage to be built on a lie, so I told him while we were alone during the bedeken ceremony."

Keilah gasped. "What did the prince say when you told him?"

"Hazi laughed and said his sister would be pleased." She squeezed Sheba's hand. "And then he told me you were married to Yahweh's high priest, which pleased my ima immeasurably."

Sheba's heart swelled at the joy in her sister-in-law's eyes. "What an amazing testimony of Yahweh's goodness. Hazi was right. I am pleased."

An awkward silence settled between them as the obvious moment for Sheba's story arose. Keilah settled Samson on her other breast, a fascinating process to the young brides, and then she turned to Sheba. "I've been wondering, Lady Jehosheba, how did your marriage to the high priest come about?"

Sheba tried to maintain a smile but felt it fade. "I . . . um . . .

well, we . . ." How much should she disclose? Where did she begin?

Zibiah and Keilah exchanged a quizzical look, and Keilah spoke up again. "It can't be worse than rape and murder."

Sheba stared into the expectant faces of two women who had laid bare their hearts. How could she lie to them—but how could she tell the truth? Who would believe Jezebel ruled both kingdoms with the destiny of queens? She didn't dare confess to exchanging secret scrolls with the queen—documents written in Phoenician to appear hidden from her husband. And how could she betray her husband, confiding that he'd knelt in this very spot last night, sobbing for reasons unknown to her?

Live the truth; be wise without lies. Jehoiada's advice breathed into her heart, and she began her story.

"My abba Jehoram is enduring Yahweh's judgment for following the ways of Ahab's household and for the sins against his brothers and other faithful men." She squeezed Zibiah's hand, comforting the girl, while still hating her abba's suffering. "During an evening meal, on the night before the Philistine raid, Abba Jehoram received a mysterious letter from the prophet Elijah."

"You mean Elisha," Keilah corrected her, seeming to have lost all inhibitions during their morning visit.

"No, I mean Eli*jah*."

"Ooooh!" both women crooned, duly impressed.

Sheba grinned, amazed and strengthened by their transparency. "The letter predicted judgment on Abba's entire household as retribution and a wasting disease of the bowels that would eventually claim his life. He called his governor sons from their cities the next morning with the intention of rescinding their positions, but the Philistines and Arabs stormed the city, killing the royal sons. Jehoiada and Obadiah, with the help of a single Carite guard, hid my abba until the danger passed, and Abba promised to offer me in marriage to the high priest in hopes of diverting Yahweh's further judgment."

Zibiah's eyes softened with compassion. "But your abba assumed Yahweh's priests would choose a younger high priest when Amariah was killed."

Avoiding her pity and her question, Sheba gave a precise answer rather than a complete one. "The priests only *suggest* the new high priest, but ultimately Yahweh reveals His choice through the Urim and Thummim." Her tears began before the last word was spoken, and she hated herself for it. "I don't know why I'm crying. I love Jehoiada. I do."

Keilah's eyes pooled with tears. "I see the way you look at him, Lady Jehosheba. It's obvious you care for him deeply, but . . ."

Zibiah alternated glances between the two, and Sheba was equally confused. "But what?"

"When I went back to the City of David with my widows after Shavuot, they told me Jehoiada had been married before and his first wife never had children."

"Jehoiada was married?" Sheba's whole world tilted. How had she not known Jehoiada had been married—and had no children?

Keilah's expression reflected the same panic Sheba felt. "I thought you knew. I didn't mean to—"

Sheba looked at Zibiah. "Did you know?"

"No! I never knew the high priest until I met you both at the wedding feast."

As she stared hard at Zibiah, the next question lodged in her throat. *Did Hazi know?* She tried to steady her breathing, but it came in quick, uneven bursts. Did Keilah tell her to intentionally hurt her? Ima Thaliah would have. Women always had an agenda. How could Sheba have trusted these two so freely?

Sheba bolted to her feet and hurried to the door. "I'm sorry to be abrupt, but Jehoiada asked that our visit end before the midday meal. I'm needed in the kitchen to . . ." Her brain was too addled to think of a lie. Thankfully the women rushed toward the door without need of one.

"Forgive me, my lady. I didn't mean to upset you." Keilah had swaddled Samson, her eyes filling with tears as she walked out the door.

Sheba couldn't speak but nodded, confused. Was there malice in Keilah's words? No. The widow hadn't lied to her.

Jehoiada had lied.

The one person she thought she could trust—he'd lied. She'd been utterly gullible to trust him.

"Should I stay or go?" Zibiah lingered at the door.

"Zabad!" Sheba screeched at the chief gatekeeper as he ambled through the priests' hallway. "The princess needs an escort."

Zibiah waited in awkward silence until Zabad arrived at the door. "I won't say anything to Hazi. May I come back tomorrow?"

Sheba nodded, avoiding the woman's gaze. Was Zibiah as skilled a liar as Hazi? Had she been sent by Ima Thaliah?

Zabad led her away, and Sheba closed the door, then leaned back and banged her head against it—harder and harder. She had no one. No one. *Don't cry. Don't cry.* If she let a single tear fall, could she stop the flood? She must keep her wits or all was lost.

I'm already lost. Finally, releasing a low moan, she slid into a heap on the stone floor, tearing out handfuls of hair. "He lied. Jehoiada lied. The only person I trusted betrayed me." Another thought pierced her soul and paused her lament. "Yahweh, are You a lie as well?"

Silence answered. Nothing. How could she trust an invisible God? No list of omens. No entrails or oil or arrows to interpret.

Wailing low and deep, she laid her cheek on the cold tiles, wishing Mot would swallow her into the utter darkness of his well-defined doom.

At least she could trust death.

26

⇢ 2 Chronicles 17:3, 5–6 ⇠

*The Lord was with Jehoshaphat because he followed the
ways of his father David before him. . . . The Lord established the kingdom under his control; and all Judah
brought gifts to Jehoshaphat, so that he had great wealth
and honor. His heart was devoted to the ways of the Lord;
furthermore, he removed the high places and the Asherah
poles from Judah.*

Jehoiada enjoyed his morning with Hazi, discussing King
Jehoshaphat's long and faithful reign. The young prince
seemed genuinely interested in hearing not only the stories
of his ancestor but also the real truth of what made Jehoshaphat
strong.

"Your saba was a great man first, and then he was a great
king. The annals of kings said he walked with Yahweh in the
ways of David."

"But what does that mean?" Hazi asked, and Jehoiada delighted in telling the stories of David as shepherd boy, warrior,
and persecuted king-to-be.

Disappointed when Nathanael knocked to announce the
priests' midday meal, he asked, "Have I frightened you away,
Hazi, or will you return tomorrow?"

"I'll be back, my friend, but I'm ready for a break. I'm starving! Let's see if our wives have finished their gossip so I can take Zibiah back to the palace." Jehoiada hesitated too long, and Hazi's cheerfulness died. "What is it? Are you and my sister quarreling?"

Jehoiada issued a "that's none of your business" glare, and Hazi lifted his hands in surrender. "Okay, but will you at least walk me to your chamber? I get lost in this Temple's maze of hallways and galleries."

How could Jehoiada explain that he was afraid to return to his rooms because he didn't want to see a wet nurse or hear a baby cry? "Of course, but I don't know what's so difficult about the side chambers. They were constructed in a horseshoe shape around the Temple . . ."

Hazi regained his jovial demeanor as Jehoiada explained Solomon's floor plan. They reached his chamber and he lifted the latch, but something blocked the door. Hearing scuffling on the other side, Jehoiada opened the door slowly and glimpsed a flash of Jehosheba's sky-blue robe as she dashed into the bedroom. The two men stood in the outer room, puzzled.

"Jehosheba?" the priest called out, lifting both eyebrows at Hazi.

The prince shrugged as a weak voice echoed from the bedroom. "Zibiah already returned to the palace. I sent Zabad to escort her."

Jehoiada shared a concerned glance with Hazi, who patted his shoulder and whispered, "I'll get one of the Temple guards to escort me to the Horse Gate. It sounds like your wife needs you. I'd better get back to the palace to see if my wife is in the same shape." Hazi slipped out the door, closing it silently, and Jehoiada considered following him.

Coward, he inwardly chided. He'd dreaded facing Jehosheba after the way he'd acted last night. The strength evident in her prayer had wrenched his heart. Why hadn't he allowed her—the person he loved most—to help carry his burden? Pride. He didn't want to admit that Yahweh's high priest needed help. He must apologize, but now it seemed something had upset her during the visit with Zibiah and the young widow. He took a deep breath, prayed for courage, and walked into their bedchamber.

Sunlight through a single, narrow window revealed his wife's form curled into a ball on their bed. "Jehosheba? Are you all right?" That was a foolish question. He stepped closer but couldn't see her face. He picked up two flint stones and struck them together, then lit a lamp in the wall niche over the bed.

Her face was splotchy as if she'd been crying, but her eyes were dry, fixed in a distant stare. Blinking.

He sat on the bed and rested his hand on her shoulder. "Jehosheba, my love?" Nothing. He waited, rubbing her arm gently.

"My name is Sheba, and I am not your *love*. Yahweh is a lie." She turned over, pulling her knees tightly to her chest. "Get your hand off me."

Jehoiada lifted his hand away. He sat stunned, trying to process the heartrending, life-changing statements she'd made. Where did he even begin to address her pain?

He leaned over her, whispering, "I . . . I don't understand . . . What—"

"Get out." Emotionless. Resigned. Empty.

He stared at her fetal form. This was not the wife he knew. Something—someone—had hurt her deeply. "No!" he said, sliding his arms beneath her, dragging her into his lap like a child. "I will not leave until you talk to me. Tell me what's happened."

She continued a vacant stare, barely breathing. He grasped her chin, forcing her to meet his gaze, but the silent rage in her eyes terrified him. His wife was gone. The woman before him burned with hate.

He released her chin, and she turned away.

Shaken, he laid her gently on the bed and snuffed out the lamp. "I'll return after tonight's sacrifice." No answer, and he sensed no remorse or tears. Fear coiled around his heart. If his wife wouldn't tell him what upset her, perhaps Zibiah would.

Jehoiada marched past his Temple guards at the southern gate without so much as a nod. He'd never visited the palace without an invitation, but he remembered ascending the grand stairway to the third floor when he visited King Jehoram's chamber for bridal negotiations. Surely, if no one stopped him before he arrived at the king's chamber, the Carites there would be happy to direct him to Hazi—or to the palace prison. He passed through the Horse Gate without any problem, but second thoughts assailed him as he walked through the bustling courtyard. Perhaps he should have told someone at the Temple where he was going.

"Jehoiada?" a voice called from behind him.

"Captain Zev! I'm thankful for a familiar face."

"What are you doing here?" The Carite glanced all around. "Unattended? This isn't the entrance you use to serve in the Throne Hall—and central court isn't in session today."

Suddenly feeling rather silly, Jehoiada cleared his throat before trying to explain. "I'm here to see Prince Hazi."

"Weren't you with him all morning?" Zev raised an eyebrow. "If you weren't, he and I need to have a serious talk. I can't be held responsible to protect him if I don't know where—"

"No—I mean yes. Hazi was with me all morning, but I need to see him again." Jehoiada refused to say, "Because my wife won't speak to me, and Hazi's new bride is the only one who can tell me why." Evidently, Jehoiada's pitiable expression convinced the battle-hardened warrior of his desperation.

"Follow me." The captain led him to a secluded corner staircase circling upward to a third-floor entry beside the king's private chamber. At the opposite end of the long, tiled hall, Zev approached a second set of double doors, where two of his men saluted and stood at strict attention. A single nod from their captain directed one of the guards to strike the door twice with his spearhead, then return to attention.

Jehoiada heard a female giggle and Hazi's frustrated growl. The prince began his rebuke as he flung open the door. "This had better be important—" His mouth gaped when he saw Jehoiada. "What's wrong? Is Sheba all right?" Zibiah appeared behind him, concern on her features too.

"I'm sorry to interrupt," Jehoiada began.

Zev cleared his throat. "If you don't mind, my lord, I'll wait here until the high priest is ready for an escort back to the Temple."

Hazi motioned Jehoiada inside. "Yes, yes, Zev. Thank you. Jehoiada, what's happened?" He pulled the high priest into the chamber, closing the door behind him. Four male servants kept their heads lowered, two kneeling close to a food-laden table and two flanking a bronze washbasin and pitcher. Hazi must have noticed Jehoiada studying them. "Out, all of you!" They disappeared behind a heavy tapestry into a second chamber.

Zibiah placed her hand on his arm. "Please, Jehoiada, tell us how Sheba's doing."

Hazi looked at his wife askance. "I thought you said you enjoyed this morning's visit with Sheba and Keilah."

"I did."

"Then how did you know Sheba was upset?"

Zibiah cradled her husband's cheeks and kissed him gently. "Women can enjoy a friendship and still cry." She paused and cast a furtive glance at Jehoiada. "Plus I told Sheba I wouldn't tell you until we had a chance to talk tomorrow."

"But do you know what's wrong with her?" Jehoiada's desperation built with each word.

Zibiah looked first at Hazi and then at the high priest. "Yes, but I won't break Sheba's confidence. I won't say anything until after I talk to her again."

Jehoiada felt his temper rising, but what could he do? Zibiah was keeping her word, and he couldn't fault her for that. But he needed answers. "Would you both return to the Temple with me to speak with Jehosheba?" Emotion tightened his throat, and he feared losing control. "Hazi, I haven't seen her like this since you first brought her to my chamber after Mattan cut her. She's desperate. I don't know what else to d—" His voice broke, and he rushed to the door. "I'll wait outside for your answer."

Wiping his eyes, he fairly ran into the hallway, where Zev was waiting as promised. "I'll escort you to the Horse Gate, Jehoiada."

Shoulders slumped, the high priest heard hushed voices inside the chamber and realized how foolish he'd been. He and Anna

228

had been married for forty years and never once needed family help in a quarrel. Ready to turn and leave, he was startled when the chamber door opened and both Hazi and Zibiah appeared. Gratitude strangled his voice.

Hazi placed a hand on his shoulder. "Zev, we're going back to the Temple."

The captain led them down the guards' circular stairway as discreetly as possible. Queen Athaliah had nearly toppled the head table yesterday when she heard of Zibiah's daily visits. She didn't need to know of two visits in a single day.

Sheba lay in her bed, dozing in and out of desolation. She was alone in this world, completely alone. The one person she thought she could trust—a betrayer. The one she thought loved her—a liar. Awake, she yearned for the abyss. Asleep, she dreamed of death. *Yahweh, if You are real, release me from this meaningless life. Mot, if you exist, swallow me whole.* Her tears reclaimed her, confirming her fear. She'd lost control and would almost certainly lose her mind. Would she become like Jezebel and Athaliah? Maniacal? Destructive? No. She would take her own life before she ruined so many others.

Jehoiada's face taunted her memory. Why had she so easily given her heart? How could she have been so foolish? *Never again. Never again.*

"Sheba?" A woman's voice.

It couldn't be. Sheba lifted her face out of the pillow she was using to muffle her cries. "Zibiah?" Her brother's wife stood in the doorway. Beautiful. Innocent. "What are you doing here?" And then Hazi and Jehoiada appeared behind her, and she knew—Zibiah had betrayed her too. "Get out, all of you!" She threw the pillow at them, then a wooden cup from the bedside table, then her comb. "Out! Get out!" She clutched at the blankets, the air, her robe, seeking something else to throw.

Before she could grab the lamp, strong hands pinned her arms to her sides. The scent of her husband—sacred incense, burnt offerings, Yahweh's high priest. "Nooooo!" She raged against his strength, kicked and flailed, clawed at his face. "Liars! All of you, liars!"

"Hazi, take Zibiah out!" Jehoiada pressed Sheba beneath him, wrapping his legs around her.

"Jehoiada, don't hurt her!" Hazi's voice. "I'll take Zibiah home and come back."

Leaving! My brother is leaving me! Another betrayal fueled her hysteria. "Let me go!" she screamed. "Kill me! Give me to Mot! Where is your knife? Use it! Use it!" The words came from somewhere deep inside, frightening her as much as Jehoiada's strength terrified her.

He was crying, "Please, Jehosheba, please," tightening his grip, pressing his full weight against her.

The precious stones of the sacred breastpiece scraped her face. She felt the sting, tasted blood. Perhaps her blood would satisfy the gods. Digging her face against the sharp stones, she chanted, "Blood for Baal. Blood for Yahweh. Blood for Baal. Blood for Yah—" She glimpsed the red stains on the sacred ephod and realized her sacrifice had soiled the precious garment. Panic reclaimed her. "Have mercy, Jehoiada! Kill me now before Yahweh's wrath devours me like it has Abba!" Completely trapped beneath his weight, she could do nothing but squirm and shriek wildly.

Jehoiada locked her head between his hands. "Stop this!" he screamed, startling her into silence. His face twisted in agony. "I love you, Jehosheba. Can you hear me?" He shook her. "Can you hear me? I. Love. You."

Suddenly she felt like a filthy rag, used up and wrung out—no more strength, not even enough to argue. She closed her eyes. Wilting.

"No, Jehosheba, don't leave me." He shook her again. "Say something. I'd rather you yell at me! Kick, shout, cry. Say something. Don't leave me!" He broke into sobs, cradling her head gently now.

Sheba opened her eyes, saw a kernel of hope in his expression, and determined to crush it. "Did your first wife kick and shout and cry when you couldn't give her children?" The horror on his face almost made her falter, but one more question burned on her tongue. "How long did you lie to her before she realized you'd betrayed her—*Priest?*"

Sheba stared defiantly, ready for Jehoiada's fist to land its first blow. Instead, gasping for breath, he released her and scooted away. Unable to watch another person walk out that door, she buried her face in the wool-stuffed mattress and let quiet tears escape. She felt wretched, certain she'd finally become Athaliah's spawn—as heartless and insane as a true queen of destiny. *But I cannot betray as I've been betrayed.* She would rather die than inflict this kind of pain on another.

"Jehosheba." A hand rested on her shoulder.

She shrieked, startling Jehoiada, who still sat beside her. "Why are you still here?" she snapped.

"Where else would I go?" His voice was infuriatingly calm, challenging her expectations, forcing her to reason.

She glanced at the small bedside table, the neatly stacked baskets of clothing and linens in the corner. "Of course, the high priest must live on Temple grounds. I'm the intruder here." Her heart beat wildly, but her reasoning powers were returning. She scooted off the bed, wondering where she might go. The palace? No, she couldn't face Ima. Maybe she could find Keilah and her widows in the City of David. Living with one wicked woman was no different than living with another.

Jehoiada grabbed her arm, sitting her back on the bed. "I didn't betray you. I thought you knew."

She jerked her arm away, thoughts racing. He was trying to trick her. How could she have known? She'd been a Baal priestess who knew nothing of Yahweh's Temple or its priests. But Abba Jehoram . . . She squeezed her eyes shut and covered her face, the wounds on her cheeks stinging at the touch. "Abba knew, didn't he?"

"Yes."

"Did Hazi know?"

"I'm not certain." She glared at him, and he studied his hands. "I think so."

She left him sitting there and began packing a few items in

a small shoulder bag. *What will I need to live with widows on the streets? Will people recognize me immediately?* Perhaps she could trade one of her linen tunics for a plain woolen robe.

Sheba sensed Jehoiada's approach but kept her back turned, hoping he'd pass by and walk out the door. She bent over to pick up her ivory comb and placed it in her bag. Perhaps she could sell it and buy bread for the widows.

Jehoiada's hand slid around her waist until his strong arm pulled her against him. Her breath caught, heart still pounding. He pressed his lips to her ear. "I was wrong to shut you out last night, Jehosheba. When I saw Keilah with the baby at Shavuot, my lifelong failure to produce a child haunted me in the hopeful face of my beautiful young wife." His voice broke. "I'm sorry I was too proud to share my pain. If I had, you would have discovered last night that I didn't intend to keep my past from you."

Jehosheba stood like a crumbling pillar, terrified of this man's power over her. Did he truly love her, or was he a gifted liar like Hazi and the rest of them? She couldn't give him her heart again—for if he broke it once more, it would end her.

The trembling began in her shoulders—and grew to quaking as Jehoiada waited for her to respond. She dropped the bag and grabbed fistfuls of her hair, her breathing ragged, her mind becoming muddled. What should she do? Where could she go? A low whine started deep in her throat. As she clawed at the wounds on her face, the pain distracted her from the here and now.

"Jehosheba, no! Shh, my love." Jehoiada seized her wrists and then led her toward the bed. "Shh. Come here."

She thought he meant to bed her, and panic nearly blinded her. "No, please! I can't give myself to you now."

"I only want you to lie down," he whispered. "I won't ask anything of you." He cradled her elbow, guided her to the bed, and eased her head onto the lamb's-wool pillow. Still shaking, she let him cover her with a linen sheet.

He sat beside her, brushing sweaty hair from her forehead. "I've never lied to you, Jehosheba. Our marriage happened quickly, but we both agreed it was ordained by Yahweh. Remember? I heard Yahweh speak through the Thummim, and you realized He was at work when both Athaliah and Jehoram independently contrived our marriage."

She closed her eyes slowly, then opened them. Almost a nod.

It was enough to invite more words from her husband. "Though I'm not perfect, I've never betrayed you, and I never will. Baal is a lie, Jehosheba. In the palace, people lie. But Yahweh is truth—perfectly dependable—and He has sealed a covenant of love with us that He'll never break. Don't let lies from your past tarnish the hope of our future. Trust Yahweh first, and then trust me."

The gentleness of his voice eased her shaking, but so many emotions and questions chased in circles around her mind.

"Do you want to talk?" The mere question sent her into renewed trembling and tears. "Okay, no talking," he amended quickly. "May I lie down beside you while you rest?"

She nodded. More tears, less trembling.

Jehoiada lay facing her. He closed his eyes too, and she fell into a fitful sleep.

27

Take the finest flour and bake twelve loaves of bread. . . .
Arrange them in two stacks, six in each stack, on the table
of pure gold before the LORD. . . . This bread is to be set
out before the LORD regularly. . . . It belongs to Aaron and
his sons, who are to eat it in the sanctuary area, because
it is a most holy part of their perpetual share of the food
offerings.

Jehoiada edged slowly onto the bed, trying not to jostle his
sleeping wife. She'd been resting all afternoon, giving him
time to think, to pray. *Lord, please don't let my sin and the*
sins of others destroy this precious lamb. He glanced around
their bedchamber, making sure everything was ready for when
she awoke—clean linens, a fresh robe, pitchers of fresh water.

Tears clouded his vision as he lay next to Jehosheba, studying this gift from Yahweh. He'd rehearsed her hysterical words
again and again, trying to make the irrational, rational. *I am*
not your love . . . Yahweh is a lie . . . Give me to Mot . . . Kill
me now before Yahweh's wrath devours me like it has Abba . . .
Then her piercing words about his first wife, meant to destroy
him. Jehoiada thought Jehosheba had overcome the ravages of

Athaliah's abuses, but he was wrong. The inner wounds were still healing, torn open with devastating consequences.

Hazi had seen enough of Jehosheba's collapse to frighten him. He'd returned shortly after she fell asleep, quietly knocking on the outer chamber, escorted by Zev and Zabad.

"Did you know about my first wife and our childlessness?" Jehoiada had asked.

The guilt written on Hazi's face answered for him. "Who told her?"

"The point is—*you* didn't tell her. I thought she knew, so she found out from someone else and feels betrayed." Jehoiada spoke in a whisper at the doorway, not wishing to wake his wife. When Hazi studied his bare feet like a scolded student, Jehoiada instructed Zabad to fetch Nathanael, requesting the extra linens, water pitchers, and basins. The chief gatekeeper eagerly obeyed and hurried down the hall, knocking on side chambers to find the second priest.

When Zabad left, Hazi finally spoke. "Zibiah is very upset that Sheba called her a liar."

Jehoiada stared at his brother-in-law, incredulous. "I suppose Jehosheba thought Zibiah broke her promise about keeping silent." Indignation rose up, causing the overdue question to be asked. "Explain to me how you could sentence your sister to a life of barrenness without even gaining her consent. The Law gives all Jewish maidens the right of refusal before they enter into a betrothal . . ." He stopped, realizing how foolish he sounded. Why would Jehoram and Athaliah care about the Law of Moses?

"Jehoiada, you're making too much of this." Hazi broke into his charming smile, bracing the high priest's shoulder like an old friend. "Sheba is a strong woman. She'll overcome this, and she'll have lots of nieces and nephews to bounce on her knee—"

"Don't you dare." Jehoiada ground out the words as Zabad arrived with Nathanael.

The second priest toted fresh linens over his arm. "Jehoiada, you're bleeding!" Nathanael wiped blood from the sacred breast-piece and pointed to a smear on the ephod.

Hazi's face drained of color. "What did you do to her? I want to see my sister!"

He tried to push past the chamber door, but Jehoiada stopped him, tears choking his voice. "She cut her face on my breastpiece, offering her own blood to Baal *or* Yahweh. Her mind is confused, and she's frightened. She *will* have peace in this chamber." He released Hazi, who stumbled backward into Zev's arms, dazed, speechless.

In the awkward silence, Nathanael took charge. "May I suggest Eliab perform the high priest's duties tonight and tomorrow while you tend to your wife's needs?" Jehoiada nodded, and Nathanael turned to Hazi. "My lord prince, might I ask if you would send something from the palace that might refresh Lady Jehosheba? Perhaps her favorite food or some luxury we don't have here?" The capable second priest continued his detailed planning at the door, and Jehoiada slipped inside and melted onto the embroidered couch.

Finally, Nathanael entered and closed the door, leaving the two men alone. The second priest helped Jehoiada stand and then began removing the priestly garments—crown first, then he unwound the turban. Nathanael had just removed the breastpiece and ephod when they heard another slight knock. Zabad let himself in, followed by three priests, each carrying a fresh pitcher of water, a basin, and a towel. Nathanael waited until the others left before removing the high priest's tunic, giving Jehoiada a chance to wash the scratches on his face before donning a fresh woolen robe.

"Thank you," Jehoiada said as his second took away the golden garments and dirty water. "I don't know how I can ever repay your kindness."

"There are no debts in Yahweh's service. It is my privilege to serve you—and Him." He bowed, maneuvered the door open with his elbow and foot, and then turned. "I'll leave a tray of bread and cheese outside your chamber for this evening's meal." And he was gone.

Jehoiada's stomach rumbled at the thought. A dusky amber glow lit the bedchamber now. The evening service would soon be starting.

Jehoiada found the food tray outside the door as Nathanael promised but didn't want to eat without Jehosheba. So he lay beside her, watching her sleep, aching to touch her.

Dried blood from the breastpiece cuts had pasted clusters of hair to her cheeks and forehead. Long, black lashes lay in clumps, dried together with tears. The front collar of her gown was bloodstained—but all this could be washed away. *Yahweh, how do I heal what's broken inside her?* What lasting scars caused her to yearn for Mot and doubt Yahweh? What emotional cruelty had created the need to pack a bag and flee at the first sign of conflict?

His stomach rumbled again, and this time he blamed anxiety. The sound roused his wife, her face so peaceful—until she glimpsed him lying beside her. Her eyes filled with tears, and the trembling began instantaneously.

"What are you doing here?" She bolted upright, looking at the dusky glow from the window. "Why aren't you at the sacrifice? Where is your breastpiece? Your ephod?" Her breathing grew ragged. "You're heaping more of Yahweh's wrath on me."

Jehoiada lay still, speaking quietly. "Did you know that your ancestor King David once ate the holy showbread?"

Her only response—blinking streams of tears down her cheeks. At least she was looking at him, holding his gaze, listening.

"When Saul was still king of Judah, David fled his murderous attempts and was hungry when passing through Nob. Ahimelek the priest had just replaced the sacred showbread with fresh loaves at the Tabernacle. David and his men ate the old showbread—though the Law said it should only be eaten by priests." He raised his eyebrows, waiting for her response.

She turned her back to him, curling into a ball. "I don't care about showbread."

She might not care, but her trembling had eased and her crying abated. Perhaps apathy was better than panic—for now. Jehoiada scooted off the bed, retrieving a pitcher of water and washbasin with a clean cloth. He walked to the other side of the bed, placed the basin on the table, and poured fresh water over the cloth. He wrung it out and began dabbing her face. She didn't resist.

It was a start.

After a few more damp cloths, her hair began to loosen from the wounds on her cheeks and forehead. He gently pulled it away and began explaining again. "I am consecrated showbread, my love. Sometimes I am present in the Holy Place before Yahweh, but on other occasions—like tonight—I am given over for a special purpose." He wiped her fresh tears with the cloth. "I am showbread to nourish a daughter of King David."

She turned away and shook her head, shame as visible as the blood that stained her robe. "I am a priestess of Baal, not a daughter of David. I am Athaliah's daughter—not by blood but by careful training. We were pretending I could become something else."

He leaned down to kiss her. She turned away. So he brushed his lips against her ear. "We were not pretending. You *are* becoming something else, with Yahweh's help and my love. All your life, you've been abused by those who should have protected you. But it wasn't your fault, Jehosheba. It's something that happened to you, not who you *are*."

Her eyes grew distant. She'd withdrawn again, the shutters closed on the windows of her soul. Gone, and he didn't know how to bring her back.

Serve her. The words blew over his heart like a warm breath, giving direction.

Remembering the servants he'd observed at the palace, thinking of Nathanael's humble spirit, Jehoiada busied himself around the chamber. He carried the embroidered couch from the outer room, lifted his wife's empty shell, and laid her on the couch. Her head rested on its edge. He placed an empty basin on the floor and released her long, black mane over the armrest. He knelt beside her, one hand pouring water from a pitcher while the other massaged the blood and sweat from her hair. The aroma of acacia and lavender filled the chamber, scented oils Hazi had brought from the palace that Jehoiada worked into the taut muscles in her neck and shoulders.

Eyes closed, she began sobbing quietly. He kissed her forehead, her cheeks, her lips, continually rinsing her hair, massaging the oils into her silky skin, cherishing the precious gift Yahweh had given him. Words would only betray the moment. Fine arguments, deception, and broken promises had driven her to this brokenness. It was time for action—time to live the truth he'd touted so long.

He reached for one of the wool towels to wrap around her wet hair, but Jehosheba clutched his neck, deep, racking sobs shaking her. He laid everything aside and drew her into his lap on the floor, rocking her as she poured out her pain. Time held no purpose. Love had no bounds. The chamber was completely dark by the time she grew quiet, and Jehoiada's legs had progressed beyond cramping to utterly numb. He laid her on the goatskin rug and stood, stretching in the moonlight.

"I'm sorry." Jehosheba's small voice was barely audible even in the black stillness.

Jehoiada rushed to lift her to the bed. She weighed no more than a yearling ram. "No, my love. No," he said, wishing he could see her face. "There's no need for apologies." He waited, but the silence stretched into loneliness. He lay beside her again.

"I'm afraid."

He found her hand in the darkness, cradling it in his own. "Whatever comes, we'll face it together. Yahweh will never leave us."

Yahweh, give me understanding to speak when You've given wisdom and listen when she's ready to share.

Sheba woke to the sound of hushed voices in the outer room. "Jehoiada?" Trembling, she saw his face at the bedroom door almost immediately. He looked exhausted.

Keilah appeared behind him, and Sheba's heart stopped beating. She heard herself gasp.

Jehoiada hurried to the bed and sat beside Sheba, his huge frame moving side to side, keeping her from seeing the wet nurse. "Keilah was worried when she didn't see either of us at the sacrifice this morning. She was just leaving."

Sheba's mind reeled. "Do you want her to leave? Are you angry that she came?" In the new light of dawn, she wondered if she might trust Keilah. Had she been silly to think the nursemaid might have intentionally hurt her?

Jehoiada looked perplexed. "No, no. I thought *you* would want her to leave. She came to me crying, confessing that she was to blame for your pain—the one who told you about Anna."

"Anna?" The name escaped on a sob, piercing Sheba's heart. "Was that your wife's name?"

A shroud of shame swept over Jehoiada's face, and he seemed to struggle with control before leaning forward to kiss her forehead. "Yes, my love, her name was Anna. There is much we need to discuss."

Sheba glimpsed the back of Keilah's robe and heard the outer door click. "Wait! Don't let her leave!" she shouted, startling her husband. He looked hurt, but she had to explain to Keilah. "This wasn't her fault," she said through tears. "She can't believe this was her fault, Jehoiada. Please."

He nodded somewhat reluctantly and left their bedchamber about the time Sheba heard more voices.

"Keilah! I'm so glad to find you here." It was Zibiah's voice, and then Hazi chimed in, chattering at Jehoiada. Sheba wanted to find a hole and crawl in it. She couldn't face everyone at once.

"Sheba?" Zibiah appeared at the door, hope and trepidation sketched in equal parts across her face. She gathered Keilah under her wing, and the two stepped together across the threshold into Sheba's sanctuary.

"Please, don't," she said, choked by tears. They stopped, waiting for her to say more. "I can't talk now, but please don't give up on me." She turned over, sobbing into her pillow, emotions completely out of control again. Would she ever be able to speak without crying? Were fear and darkness her permanent prison?

"Ladies." She heard Jehoiada's strong voice. "Thank you for checking on Jehosheba. Neither of you were at fault for her sorrow, and she'll need good friends when she's regained her strength. May I send for you both when my wife feels ready for a visit?"

Sheba kept her head buried in her pillow but heard both women's kind assurance of their love and friendship. She didn't deserve such goodness.

"And Keilah." Jehoiada lowered his voice as if Zibiah had already gone. "I owe you an apology. I treated you coolly because of my own pain. I hope you can forgive me."

"Of course, my lord, think nothing of it."

"Thank you, my dear."

Sheba wanted to see their faces, but she dared not risk more pity by emerging from hiding too soon. Feet shuffled to the outer chamber, and the door clicked. She sensed Jehoiada's return and peered out from beneath her pillow. "Thank you." Tears started again, and she growled her frustration.

He sat on the bed, pulling her close. "We must talk about many difficult things in the days to come, my love. If I promise not to be ashamed of my tears, can you promise to abide with yours?"

Such sweetness melted what little restraint she had left. How could anyone be this good, this loving? Surely he would disappoint her again or grow tired of her weakness. Dare she open her heart to him once more?

"Let me tell you about my life," he said, laying her on a pillow and crawling into bed beside her. "Make yourself comfortable, because it's a long one." His dark eyes sparkled, and she almost grinned. Almost.

Sheba yearned to nestle under his wing, but her eyes fell on the partially packed shoulder bag from last night. Jehoiada, Hazi, Zibiah, and Keilah—could she trust any of them? All of them? None of them? Perhaps if she preserved a relationship with Keilah, she'd have a way out if Jehoiada proved as good a liar as Hazi.

28

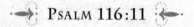

In my alarm I said, "Everyone is a liar."

"No, Hazi." Jehoiada paced the small Temple side chamber. "I don't care if Queen Athaliah sends the whole Judean army after her. Jehosheba is *not* going to the palace for a private meeting with your ima. Only a few weeks have passed since Sheba's collapse, and she's just begun eating regularly again. She's in no condition—emotionally or physically—to face the queen."

"But Zibiah says she's improving, that she's talking to both her and Keilah now."

"She's talking, but she's not ready to play war with Athaliah!" Jehoiada ceased his pacing and sat in the chair opposite Hazi. "Why don't *you* stand up to Athaliah and tell her to visit Jehosheba at the Temple?"

"Because I enjoy breathing."

Jehoiada lifted a brow. "We've been talking about your saba Jehoshaphat for weeks now, but perhaps you don't know the story of his abba Asa. When Asa became king, he deposed his ima—the Gevirah Maakah—because she made an Asherah pole. Perhaps we should learn more about King Asa."

242

"I know about King Asa. Uncle Ram threatens Jezebel with the story regularly."

"You have to make a choice, Hazi. You can't serve Yahweh *and* Baal."

"You sound like the Gevirah." Hazi leaned back in his chair and then gawked as if seeing it for the first time. "Why isn't this table and chair set in your living chamber? I sent it as a gift for Sheba."

The two ebony chairs and ivory-inlaid table had been delivered from the palace the day after Jehosheba's collapse, but the sight of them sent her into a trembling panic. "We don't really have room in our chamber, Hazi, and I thought we could use them while studying the records of the kings of Judah."

"Sheba hated them, didn't she?"

Jehoiada sighed, nodded. "But what I said is also true. We don't have room in our chamber." He tried to sound encouraging. Hazi had been especially concerned for his little sister.

"She hated them because they reminded her of Jezebel—because everything at the Jezreel palace was ebony and ivory."

Jehoiada eyed his brother-in-law, utterly bewildered. "If you knew that, why did you send them?"

"Has Sheba told you everything that happened in Jezreel?" Hazi's chin rose defiantly, making his point.

"No . . . I don't know. But I don't want *you* to tell me!"

"Why? What if I think you need to know?"

Jehoiada slammed his hand on the table. "Don't you understand? Jehosheba feels betrayed by *everyone* who loves her. If you confide something about Jezreel that she hasn't told me, then you've betrayed her again."

"Aaaggghh!" Hazi removed his crown and raked his fingers through his hair. "How do we help her then?"

"We love her with integrity while Yahweh heals her from the inside out. It's taken years for Athaliah to tear her down, Hazi. We've got to give ourselves time—and trust the Creator—to build her back up." He placed his elbow on the table, hand in the air. "Whoever loses has to tell Athaliah that her daughter is feeling ill and is unable to answer her summons."

Hazi rolled his eyes and thumped his elbow on the table. "It's hardly fair. You're an old man." They locked hands, and the arm wrestling began.

Jehoiada had conquered many unsuspecting younger priests—usually winning their portion of vegetables or escaping waste pot duty. Hazi's face reddened and his neck veins bulged.

"Impressive strength for a prince." Jehoiada's compliment completely deflated his opponent, as intended.

Hazi's arm bent back, his hand pinned to the table. "Not fair, old man!"

Jehoiada laughed, accustomed to similar reactions from over-confident young priests. "Give the queen my regards." He stood, moving toward the door.

Hazi remained seated. "Ima Thaliah commands Sheba's presence."

Jehoiada halted where he stood, his back toward the crown prince. "Give me the truth, Hazi. No pretty arguments."

"Ima heard from one of her Temple spies that Sheba's mind is gone. She fears the information she and the Gevirah divulged in Jezreel is at risk and might fall into Yahwist hands—namely, yours."

Jehoiada stormed back to Hazi, sweeping the chair and table aside like toys. "Your ima has *Temple* spies?" Hazi nodded, eyes round as sacred censers. "And you expect me to deliver my wife to her executioner?"

"I'll stay with Sheba for the meeting. I wouldn't let anyone hurt her."

Jehoiada grabbed the prince's robe, lifting him to his feet. Hazi winced, but the high priest merely drew him near enough to whisper, "You will remove the queen's spies from Temple grounds. And let me assure you—if your ima hurts Jehosheba, I will hurt you." Jehoiada released his robe and led Hazi out the door. "*You* will explain to your sister that she must face Queen Athaliah. I refuse to inflict this pain."

The two marched through the side gallery, down the steps, and across the inner court, and arrived at Jehoiada's door. Hearing the women's voices inside, Jehoiada paused, having learned that any sudden movements sent his wife into a panic. He issued a final glare at Hazi and opened the door slowly. Someone should have prepared *them* for the sight.

The three women stood in a circle, drafts of wool wound round each shoulder, every one of them dangling a weighted spindle near the floor.

Hazi was first to ask the obvious. "What are you doing?"

Zibiah giggled. "We're spinning wool. What does it look like?"

Jehoiada's heart nearly burst when he saw the smile on Jehosheba's face. Forgetting his anger at Hazi, he hurried to his wife, who chewed her bottom lip, concentrating.

"This was Keilah's idea when she heard that Zibiah lived in Beersheba—sheep country."

Zibiah chimed in. "I sent one of the guards to the palace to gather the wool and spindles."

Jehoiada's heart twisted in his chest. *Yahweh, thank You for giving Jehosheba this joy—before the grief.* He met Hazi's gaze, lifted an eyebrow, and spoke. "Jehosheba, your brother has something to say."

Her hands dropped to her sides, knotting the hard-earned yarn. Fear stole the pleasure from her features. The other women stilled too and then gathered around her. Hazi stood alone, and Jehoiada almost pitied him. Almost.

Sheba stared at the ivory comb on her bedside table and willed herself to stop shaking. "I want a mirror to see how my cheeks are healing before I meet with Ima."

Jehoiada had removed every mirror from Temple grounds when he'd discovered Sheba crying at her reflection. He'd promised that her self-inflicted cuts from the breastpiece would heal completely, but the rough, peeling scabs told her she could expect Ima's disdain.

"Look at me, Jehosheba." He tilted her chin, and she obeyed. "You don't need a mirror. See your reflection in *my* eyes. You're the most beautiful woman in the world, and I love you more than life. And Yahweh Himself loves you with an everlasting love."

She cradled her husband's gray beard and peered into the deep-set, dark eyes that searched her heart. "In your arms, I can believe all those things."

In the weeks since she'd discovered Jehoiada's first marriage, her tears had become less frequent. She still startled easily and felt a constant trembling within, but Yahweh somehow seemed more real, felt more present in her solitude. Jehoiada's staggering transparency had taught her much about the invisible God they must both trust.

Jehoiada kissed her gently, but his passion grew—seeming almost desperate—as he clutched her finest robe like a lifeline. She pressed his shoulders, a gentle reminder that a roomful of guests lingered in their outer chamber. "I must go."

"If you're not back before the twilight sacrifice, I'll put a sword in every Levite's hand and search the palace."

She laid her head on his chest, listening to his heart thunder. "If I'm not back before the twilight sacrifice, you should search the Valley of Hinnom for my bones."

"Jehosheba!" He grabbed her shoulders. "Don't say that."

She pecked his cheek with another kiss. "For the first time since Hazi's feast, I'm calmer than you are." The thought comforted her.

The two emerged from their bedchamber and met four sullen expressions—Hazi's, Zibiah's, Keilah's, and Nathanael's. Each looked as if they'd already carved her sarcophagus and chosen the tomb.

"Are Zabad and Zev waiting to escort us to the executioner?" Sheba's offhanded remark earned rebukes from everyone but Hazi.

He chuckled, offered his arm, and bowed. "It won't be so bad. We'll prepare some of your answers on our short walk, and when we get to Ima's chamber, I'll do most of the talking."

"You always do most of the talking." Sheba grinned, heart pounding, and stepped away from her husband to link arms with Hazi.

She glanced over her shoulder, fighting tears, for one more look at Jehoiada as they walked out the door. Nathanael pressed against Jehoiada's chest, holding him back, whispering something as determination knit her husband's brow. Zabad closed the door behind them, providing rear guard, as Captain Zev led them toward the Guards' Gate.

Hazi tightened his grip on her arm and squeezed her hand. "Relax, you're with me, Sheba. I'm still your Hazi." He leaned over and kissed her forehead. As promised, he began coaching her on their journey between the Temple and palace. "Ima will use her usual tactics with you, attacking immediately. She'll put you on the defensive somehow—criticize your appearance, insult Jehoiada, challenge your loyalty. Something to throw you off balance right away. She'll undoubtedly say something about the marks on your face, so be ready."

Sheba stopped abruptly, nearly causing Zabad to trample her. "I never realized her comments followed a pattern. She always does this to me, doesn't she?"

Hazi's belly laugh captured the attention of several guards milling about. "Yes, little sister. She always does this." He gathered her under his arm and began walking again.

"Why didn't you tell me before?" She was still contemplating when they passed the Horse Gate and neared the servants' entrance.

Hazi tapped Zev's shoulder, halting his captain, and then turned to the Temple guard behind them. "Zabad, I'd like you and Zev to stand guard while I meet privately with my sister in the captain's chamber. I'll return with Sheba in a few moments." Zev blocked Zabad from the royals, hand ominously placed on his sword.

Zabad reached for Sheba with one hand and his sword with the other. "Jehoiada won't approve—"

"I am Judah's crown prince!" With the speed of lightning, Hazi—trained by the king's Carites—wrenched the Temple guard's arm and rendered him helpless, his dagger at Zabad's throat. "I don't take orders from Yahweh's high priest. Is that clear?"

Zev grabbed Sheba's arm, pulling her clear of the fracas.

Zabad's face was crimson fury. Fearing he'd do something

heroic—and utterly unnecessary—to protect her, Sheba jerked free from Zev's grip. "Hazi, put your dagger away." She marched toward Zabad, grabbed Hazi's wrist, and pushed it away from the guard's jugular as she reassured Jehoiada's dear friend. "My brother will not harm me, Zabad. We both get a little tense before meeting Ima Thaliah."

She turned and shoved her brother toward the servants' quarters, casting a glance over her shoulder. Zev and Zabad stood awkwardly side by side. She hoped they didn't kill each other by the time she and Hazi returned.

Hazi sheathed the blade as they walked down the long, smelly corridor. She assumed it was the guards' barracks, though she'd never seen their accommodations until now. Hazi opened the last chamber door on the right, and she followed him in, closing the door behind them.

He stood in the center of the room, a superior smirk on his face. She walked to within a handbreadth and slapped him. "That was stupid and uncalled-for."

A slow, sinister smile creased his lips. "And that's how I hoped you'd respond."

"What?" She tilted her head, releasing a frustrated snort. "You're insane."

"And you must prove to Ima you're not." He stepped forward, backing her up. He kept walking toward her, stalking like a lion cornering his prey. "No! Don't retreat!" he shouted. "Sheba, you've been meek as a lamb for weeks. You must remember how to fight or Ima will destroy you."

She felt the heavy cedar door behind her. *Yahweh, help me! There's no way out.* She glanced at Hazi's dagger and back at his eyes.

He smiled. "Sure, go for my dagger. Try it." She flattened herself against the door, turning her face away, wincing as he drew near. He slammed both hands against the door beside her face, shouting, "If you show weakness, Ima will kill you and everyone you hold dear! You've got to prepare for the fight."

Without thinking, she drove her knee into a man's most vulnerable spot. Was it Ima Thaliah's priestess training that prepared her to disarm a man, or was it in answer to her prayer that she remembered the tactic? Regardless, it worked. Hazi staggered, bent over, groaning.

She stood there, rattled, but felt a measure of satisfaction. "I think I'm prepared to fight now, Brother. Would you still like to do the talking, or should I plan to carry the conversation?"

29

Speak to the Israelites and say to them: "When anyone among you brings an offering to the LORD, bring as your offering an animal from either the herd or the flock. . . . When anyone brings a grain offering . . . their offering is to be of the finest flour. They are to pour olive oil on it, put incense on it and take it to Aaron's sons the priests . . . and burn this as a memorial portion on the altar, a food offering, an aroma pleasing to the LORD."

Zev nodded to one of the two Carites at Queen Athaliah's chamber door. The soldier rapped on the double doors with his spearhead, and Zabad leaned forward to whisper in Sheba's ear, "Are you all right, my lady?"

She barely had time to pat his forearm and nod, assuring him for the third time since returning from Zev's chamber. His worried expression was the last thing she glimpsed before Zev and the two Carite guards nudged her and Hazi into Ima's chamber and closed the door.

"Sheba, you look like walking death! And your face—how awful!" Athaliah gasped. Mattan stood like a sentry beside Ima's couch, his bald head gleaming in the afternoon sunlight. Ima cradled Sheba's elbow, leading her on the narrow red carpet, while Hazi followed close behind. "What has that Yahweh priest done to you?"

"Jehoiada is very kind to me, Ima." Sheba nodded at Mattan before taking her seat at the opposite end of the couch. "I haven't been myself since Hazi's banquet."

Ima joined her, sitting too close, and Hazi pulled up a stool at Sheba's right. "Perhaps you're with child." Ima grasped her hand, patting it, massaging it. "Or was it the old priest's fault that he and his first wife never had children?"

Sheba's heart twisted inside her. "I suppose we'll know in time." For a fleeting moment, she'd hoped Ima hadn't known. She shouldn't have been surprised.

"Jehoram said the priest confessed he and his first wife never had children, but there's always a chance that *she* was the barren one." Ima glanced at Hazi. "Tell your sister there's always hope, dear."

"Sheba knows where to place her hope, Ima." Hazi's tenderness washed over Sheba, his eyes, his smile, his gentle voice. He winked and took her other hand. She felt like a toy being tugged between warring children—Hazi's compassion on one side, Ima's scheming on the other.

Sheba closed her eyes, remembering Hazi's advice on their short journey from the Temple. Ima Thaliah had done everything he had warned—criticized Sheba, condemned Jehoiada, and planted doubts. His methods had certainly been deplorable, but perhaps his heart could be trusted. She opened her eyes, strengthened, ready for whatever came next.

"I summoned you both to emphasize the importance of your roles in our success." She snapped her fingers, signaling Mattan to retrieve the scroll lying on the table beside her. He placed it in her palm and gave a cursory bow, his dead gray eyes never leaving Sheba.

"I received this urgent message from Gevirah Jizebaal." Ima Thaliah unrolled the rather large scroll and began reading.

From Jizebaal, Gevirah of Ram, the Reigning King of Israel.

To My Revered Daughter, Thali, Queen of Judah.

We send greetings with blessings from almighty Baal Melkart, Rider of the Clouds. May he bless the fruit of your womb—our beloved crown prince, Hazi. And may the gods grant special favor to the lovely Sheba as she casts the spell of Astarte on Yahweh's high priest.

The words sent a shiver through Sheba, and Ima Thaliah looked up. "Are you cold, dear? Would you like Mattan to fetch a blanket from my bed?"

Fighting for control, Sheba cursed her weakness. "No, Ima. Thank you. I'm still battling what remains of my illness. Please continue." She bowed her head, hoping to hide her fear but knowing Ima saw everything.

Aram continues their border attacks, and the usurper King Hazael threatens another siege on Samaria. Baal Melkart continues his faithful protection of cities, but small farms and Israelites on our eastern borders are savagely attacked. Your brother Ram refuses to restore mandatory worship of Baal Melkart, and Elisha continues to gain support of the rural areas with three prophets' schools near Jericho, Bethel, and Gilgal.

Ram refuses to mandate Judean military aid, but I'm sure you will guide Hazi in the proper course of action. The time is drawing near for our nations to unite under one god.

Written by my own hand.

Sheba kept her head bowed, refusing to acknowledge the pressure the Gevirah's letter placed on their shoulders. Silence stretched the tension like a bowstring.

Finally, Hazi sighed. "Ima, I know you feel obligated to do as the Gevirah *suggests*, but Judah cannot offer military aid when our own army was decimated so recently. Our general

252

was killed in Edom's rebellion, and hundreds of watchmen died in the Philistine raid. During my tour of Judah, I reestablished leadership of garrisons in the fortified cities, which created some stability, but the watchmen my brothers installed when they became governors were given free access to the temple prostitutes. It will take time for the new commanders to drill real discipline into these soldiers."

"Your abba was a fool. I told him our sons weren't ready to appoint leaders."

Sheba's head shot up, anger shoving aside every other emotion.

The queen smiled wickedly. "Finally, a glimpse of the old Sheba."

Her neck and cheeks burned, but before Sheba could release her venom, Hazi laid a quieting hand on her arm. "We're not going to discuss past decisions, Ima. We're going to talk about *now*. Judah has no army to help defend Israel. Uncle Ram and General Jehu know it. That's why they refuse to ask for Judah's help. The Gevirah—and you—would be wise to listen to your sons."

Ima Thaliah's glare screamed into the interminable silence. Sheba wanted to speak her mind, yearned to defend Abba, but knew she dare not enter the fray with emotions as fragile as Persian glass. She noticed her hands fidgeting and laced her fingers together, but Hazi didn't flinch.

"Well, Ima? Are you going to answer me, or shall we have Mattan divine your reply from a goat's liver?"

Ima Thaliah smiled, calm and cool. Instead of answering, she turned to Sheba. "Perhaps Sheba would like to divine the answer." She lifted a single eyebrow in challenge.

Sheba's heart was in her throat. How could she call on the pagan gods when she'd promised Jehoiada she wouldn't? More importantly, she'd be betraying Yahweh, and suddenly that thought repulsed her. *Yahweh, give me wisdom to answer—*

"Your brother seems empowered by his recent independence," Ima began before Sheba could speak, "and I fear both of my children have become distracted by marital bliss, forgetting their *true* responsibilities." She glanced over her shoulder at Mattan and nodded toward her bedchamber.

He disappeared behind the curtain and emerged with the golden tongs stolen from the Temple. He placed them in Sheba's hands. "You may return these to your husband as a sign of goodwill from Baal's high priest." His cold, dead eyes raked over her.

Sheba's heart raced, fear and confusion tying her tongue. She looked at Hazi for direction, but his furrowed brow reflected her surprise. "Why would you give them back?" she asked finally, but Hazi squeezed her arm, reminding her to weigh every word. "I mean . . . is there a message I should deliver with the tongs?"

Mattan's lips curved into an insolent smile. "My priests and I have cursed this instrument, and when your husband takes it into His temple, Baal Melkart will begin his destruction from the inside out." He cast a disparaging look at Hazi. "We have indeed divined through a *bull's* entrails that some kind of destruction will originate from within Yahweh's Temple."

Sheba concentrated on keeping her breathing steady, praying silently to the one God she knew could save her, while speaking to those who sought her destruction. "I will deliver your gift to my husband, but as you know, he is a stubborn man. I can't promise his response."

"Sheba, my dear, I'm disappointed. I thought by now your Astarte training would be wielding greater power over your husband." Without waiting for a response, she turned her attention on Hazi. "However, I anticipated Sheba's slow start, and I'm depending on you, my son, to change the opinion of both Yahweh's high priest and our nation as a whole."

"I'm doing all I can, Ima," Hazi said dismissively, cradling Sheba's hand.

Ima's dark smile cast its shadow over them. "No, Hazi. You're about to do more—much more. You will annex small Judean farms to build the royal treasury. You will bribe Yahweh's priests to overthrow Jehoiada's leadership. And in your spare time, you'll marry more wives and give me granddaughters to add to my queens of destiny. Any questions? Hmm?"

"I won't do it, Ima." He raised his chin. "When I sit on Judah's throne, I will lead with integrity—as my saba Jehoshaphat did."

Sheba held her breath, waiting for Ima's fury. Instead, the queen giggled. Quietly at first, and then she exploded to full-throated laughter—her gaiety more frightening than her anger. Ima tugged on Mattan's sleeve. "Tell the guards we're ready."

The high priest strolled toward the chamber door, his smug satisfaction adding to Sheba's dread.

"What guards?" Panic swept Hazi's features. "My Carites or the watchmen? What have you done, Ima?"

"Nooooo!" A bloodcurdling scream from the hallway pierced the air. The doors burst open, and two Judean watchmen dragged in one of Hazi's wives, her face bruised and swollen.

Hazi leapt from his stool and it clattered across the tiles. He pounded a watchman's jaw, sending him to the floor, while the other guard held Hazi's wife like a shield in front of him. The girl stood sobbing, clutching her belly.

"You see, my son," Ima Thaliah said with icy calm, "when you spend all your time with Zibiah, your other wives go unprotected and come to harm."

"How could you do this, Ima?" Hazi screamed. "She is with child!"

Thaliah nodded to the guard holding the girl, and he released her to the comfort of Hazi's arms. "I chose your least favorite wife, Hazi, and no harm came to your child." She motioned for both watchmen to leave and continued her explanation when the door clicked shut. "You have thirteen wives, and you've spent every night with Zibiah since your return to Jerusalem. Only six of your wives have proven to be with child, so you still have work to do, my son. You will spend equal time with each wife until they are *all* with child—and then you will acquire more wives."

Hazi was whispering to his young wife, kissing her bruised cheeks, caressing her hair. Ima's cool facade began to crack. "How much farther must I go to gain your attention, Prince Hazi?" she screamed, rousing terrified stares from the newlyweds.

Sheba couldn't bear to watch. She bowed her head, tears dripping onto her folded hands.

"Pay attention, Sheba," Ima said, regaining her calm. "This is your brother's Pool of Trembling, the moment I demand his full obedience—and show him the consequences of rebellion."

Hazi placed his bride behind him and faced Ima. "May I summon Zev to escort my wife to her chamber while we finish our discussion?" His face was chiseled stone as he waited for Ima's barely perceptible nod.

Ima Thaliah watched the interchange intently as Hazi delivered his bride into Zev's care. The two men whispered, the captain nodded, and Zev cradled the woman's elbow as they left. Without warning, Ima clutched Sheba's hands to stop her mindless fidgeting.

Hazi watched Zev escort his wife to her chamber before he closed Ima's door. He returned to the couch, righted his stool, and sat beside Sheba. His wicked determination resembled his ima's. "Tell me exactly what you expect from me, *Queen Athaliah*."

"We will appear together every day in the Throne Hall, acting on behalf of your abba Jehoram. You will summon the garrison commanders from all fortified cities, and *we* will issue orders from King Jehoram to take possession of all small farms in the surrounding countryside. It's the way Abba Ahab built Israel into a strong nation."

"Ima, we can't command Judah's army to break the Law of Moses. The Law specifically protects the inheritance of land by tribe, clan, and family." He paused, his eyes sparking with real passion, true leadership. "If we dispose of our standards, our foundation, we weaken the threads that weave the fabric of our nation."

Sheba's heart nearly burst with pride. Oh, how she wished Jehoiada could hear him.

Ima seemed more amused than impressed. "I hear the ramblings of the high priest from my son's lips. When we dispose of Yahweh and His Temple, we'll have no more need for the Law of Moses. Baal Melkart—the king of *cities*—will be our lawgiver. And that's where your system of bribery comes into play." Her eyes glinted with an unnerving flame. "Of Judah's three standing armies—the king's Carite bodyguards, the Judean watchmen, and Yahweh's Temple guards—the watchmen, of course, far outnumber the other two contingents, but the Carites and Temple guards are far more skilled and fiercely loyal to their respective masters."

She turned to Sheba, brushing her cheek. "I want to thank you, Daughter, for your recent . . . what should we call it—illness?" Sheba pulled away. "Your high priest husband has been so absorbed in caring for his bride that he's neglected his duties, stirring resentment among his followers. We've found it much easier to purchase their loyalty."

Emotion tightened Sheba's throat, cutting off any defense. But what could she say? Her weakness had made her husband vulnerable and could destroy Judah if Ima Thaliah gained control of the Temple.

Hazi placed his hand on her back, the warmth of it bringing her comfort as he spoke. "Surely you don't think the people of Judah will lie down and let you replace the Yahwist heritage they've held for hundreds of years with a Phoenician god—no matter how seductive."

"I won't replace Yahweh, Hazi. You will."

He ripped off his crown and raked his fingers through his hair. "Ima, it can't be done!"

"It *will* be done," she said, "and this is how you will do it. You'll appear in the Throne Hall whenever central court is held, winning the respect and affection of the Judean people. On the days Jehoiada presides over Temple matters, you'll show your support for the Yahwists. On Mattan's days, you'll show your allegiance to Baal. And at *every* opportunity, you will speak ill of your abba, the once great King Jehoram, who chooses to abdicate his responsibility rather than rule your saba Jehoshaphat's mighty kingdom."

"I will not betray Abba Jehoram!" Hazi shouted.

"Guards!" Her single cry brought six Carites from behind her bedchamber curtain. Sheba saw recognition on Hazi's features. "These men who were your comrades needed to hear that your loyalty to King Jehoram remains strong. The royal guard swears to protect Judah's ruler, and I've hand-selected these men to protect you, Hazi—from yourself."

"But I'm not Judah's ruler," he said, pleading with Ima and with the men he once called friends.

"*We* are Judah's rulers now, my son."

Sheba gasped, and Hazi's head snapped toward Ima Thaliah. "No. Abba Jehoram remains king until he draws his last breath . . ." Hazi's words died, and Sheba's heart nearly stopped.

"Ima, did you kill . . . ?"

Ima patted Sheba's hand. "No, my dear. It suits me to keep your abba alive, writhing in his own filth until Hazi gains the people's favor." She jerked her head toward Sheba, and the Carites advanced on her like crows on carrion.

Sheba screamed and Hazi fought them, but his skills were no match for the men who had trained him in combat. Four of the guards restrained the prince while Sheba flailed and kicked at the other two. Ima Thaliah whispered quietly to Mattan until her children were subdued.

"Ima, you can't do this," Hazi screamed. "I won't let you!"

The queen nodded, and one of the Carites backhanded Sheba, sending her to the floor. White-hot pain burst into her left cheek. Heart pounding, tears flowing, she made no sound as she covered her throbbing cheekbone.

Hazi broke free from the Carites and fell at the queen's feet. "I'll do it!" he said, sobbing. "I'll do whatever you say, but stop this. Stop hurting the women I love."

Ima Thaliah caught the leading Carite's eye and signaled all six to leave the chamber. Sheba sat where she'd fallen, remaining on the floor in hopes of averting further violence. Mattan leered at her with a carnivorous grin while Ima combed Hazi's hair with her fingernails, soothing, calming.

The queen's eyes—and her words—were aimed at Sheba. "Obedience is all I ask. Those you love will be safe—as long as you remain loyal, completing the tasks for which you were chosen."

Sheba swallowed hard, refusing to answer with the phrase she'd learned as a child: *I am pleased to do anything you ask*

of me, my queen. Her silence wrapped her in a thick darkness.
Heavy. Binding. Stifling. She could hardly breathe. This oppression
was life in the palace—life devoted to Baal.

Yahweh, help me! She closed her eyes again, this time remembering
her husband, his love, and the God he'd revealed.
How different her life had become in Yahweh's Temple—the
light and life she felt there. Both Baal and Yahweh required
blood sacrifice, it was true, but Baal was fickle and scheming,
requiring human blood and pain. Yahweh offered atonement
through the blood of perfect animals and fine harvests—gifts
from His own hands lovingly returned to Him, purposefully
sacrificed. Obedience to the one true God was a response to His
worth. Baal's rituals—and obedience to his leaders—were base
attempts to manipulate through deceit and torture.

"Well, Sheba?" Ima interrupted her contemplation, and Sheba's
eyes were truly opened. "Do you see that obedience must
be unswerving and without question?"

Overwhelmed by peace, she felt warmth radiate from within
her. "Yes, Ima, I will be more obedient than you can imagine."
Ima need not know that Sheba intended her obedience for Yahweh
alone.

Ima grabbed a handful of Hazi's hair and tilted his head back
to hold his gaze. "Did you hear your sister? You will do well to
imitate her obedience, my son. Learn from her."

She released his hair, letting his head fall forward. "Yes, Ima.
I am pleased to do anything you ask of me."

Sheba's heart twisted—her brother was broken. She stood,
pulled Hazi to his feet, and retrieved the golden tongs from the
couch. "I must return to the Temple before my husband becomes
suspicious. I'll have Hazi escort me to my chamber."

Ima Thaliah undoubtedly saw that it was Sheba leading Hazi
out the door, but she didn't try to stop them. She was evidently
finished with her threats—for now.

30

But you, LORD, do not be far from me. You are my strength;
come quickly to help me. Deliver me from the sword, my
precious life from the power of the dogs. Rescue me from
the mouth of the lions.

While Hazi and Jehosheba were at the palace, Jehoiada retired to the second priest's chamber to dress for tonight's service. It would be his first public sacrifice in almost a full moon cycle, and he was eager to add a personal offering afterward, a thank offering for Yahweh's faithfulness during these difficult days. Nathanael secured the ephod at his shoulders with two sardonyx remembrance stones and attached the breastpiece with its golden chains and rings.

Jehoiada released a satisfied sigh, welcoming the weight of the high priest's garments. "Thank you, my friend."

The second priest stood. "It's a privilege." His eyes shone with a peculiar light, drawing Jehoiada from his own circumstances.

"Why are you so happy these days?" He appraised the young priest, provoking a full-blown blush.

"I don't know what you mean." Nathanael busied himself tidying his small chamber, and Jehoiada settled onto a cushion at the low-lying table, pretending to study a scroll. He'd given his own chamber to Zibiah and Keilah for their spinning while they waited on Hazi's and Sheba's return. In truth, he was glad for an opportunity to uncover the mystery of Nathanael's almost bubbly behavior.

Then, the clue he needed. Nathanael began whistling.

Jehoiada grinned. Men only whistled when there was a woman. He began rehearsing his second priest's schedule. The change had occurred during Sheba's recovery, but who could Nathanael have met? He never left the Temple. Thinking through his second's schedule, Jehoiada started at sunrise: cleansing at the Molten Sea, gates open, sunrise sacrifice. He could have met a woman at one of the sacrifices while greeting the crowds in Jehoiada's absence. After the morning service, Nathanael delegated duties to other priests. Midday, he brought a meal for Jehoiada and Jehosheba to enjoy in their chamber. Most days he stayed to eat, as did Hazi, Zibiah, and—

"Keilah!" Jehoiada said aloud, startling himself and his second priest.

Nathanael's whistling stopped, face paling to match the limestone walls. "What about her?"

Jehoiada felt his own color drain. What could he say? Jehosheba had told him Keilah's story, but did Nathanael know? "She seems like a nice woman."

Nathanael returned to his tasks, and Jehoiada chided himself. *What if Nathanael interprets my response as approval? Do I approve?* He wasn't sure. He had hoped Nathanael's abba would find a nice girl and arrange a marriage for the young man.

"My lord, are you all right?"

Jehoiada looked up, startled. "I'm fine. Why do you ask?"

"Well, you keep sighing as if deeply troubled. Is it something I said? Something I've . . . done?"

The two men stared at each other in silence for an interminable moment. Jehoiada caught himself sighing again. "Oh, this is ridiculous!" he said, standing abruptly, startling the poor young priest. "I'm concerned about your marriage, Nathanael."

"I wasn't aware I had a marriage to be concerned about."

"Yes, well . . ." Jehoiada grinned, squeezing the back of his neck. He'd started gutting this fish. Now he had to fry it. "I've noticed you seem to enjoy Keilah's company, but I wonder if there might be another young maiden—perhaps a girl from your hometown—who might be more . . . well, a girl your abba might be more comfortable welcoming into your family."

Nathanael's jovial air disappeared. "You mean, because I'm a priest, I should marry a virgin." The edge in his voice was unmistakable. "I've only spoken with Keilah a few times. I haven't asked her to *marry* me."

"I simply think you should speak with your abba before you set your heart on any woman."

"I know my abba's opinion on the matter," he said. "I rejected his choice, and he's left me to my own stubborn heart." Nathanael raised both eyebrows, uncharacteristically defiant. "Those were his exact words."

Jehoiada knew to tread lightly. What did he know of giving advice to a son? "May I ask why you rejected your abba's choice?"

"Because I didn't love her." He paused, glancing at his feet. "And she loved another."

Jehoiada nodded, realizing he'd wandered into painful territory. "I'm not one to give romantic counsel, my friend, but hear me out. Sometimes obedience comes first—and love comes later."

Nathanael shook his head and gave a mirthless laugh. "That's easy for you to say."

"Easy? You of all people know my marriage hasn't been easy."

Nathanael's features softened. "Easy, no. But you had Yahweh's undeniable direction from the Thummim."

Jehoiada pondered the words, remembering how the Thummim had silenced his doubts on his way to the negotiations. "It's true that the Urim and Thummim made the initial decision less confusing, but both Jehosheba and I made a choice to believe Yahweh ordained our marriage. We choose every day to see each other as a gift from the Lord."

"How can I know if Yahweh has given Keilah to me? Do I have your permission to at least pursue a friendship? To speak with her freely as I enjoy speaking with Lady Jehosheba, Lady Zibiah, and Prince Hazi?"

"Surely you understand that it's not the same, Nathanael. Keilah is a widow, and you are unmarried. Decorum dictates certain precautions be taken—"

"And I would never place Keilah or myself in a compromising position." His jaw was set, his gaze determined.

Jehoiada returned his stare, testing the man's mettle. His usually compliant second priest didn't budge. Unable to hide a grin, Jehoiada held up his hands in surrender. "Yes, my friend. You have my permission to pursue a *friendship* with Keilah, but please be careful. I'd hate to see you or Keilah get hurt by any misunderstandings."

Nathanael's relieved smile was stolen by heavy pounding on his door. Before he could answer, Zabad burst in. "Hurry, we have news." He was gone as quickly as he'd come.

Jehoiada's heart fell at the despair he'd glimpsed on Zabad's face. He turned to Nathanael, finding concern etched on his features too. Without a word, both men hurried toward Jehoiada's chamber next door.

Sheba waited for Jehoiada outside their chamber door, knowing he might blame Hazi for her bruised face. Her brother hadn't spoken a word all the way back to the high priest's chamber, where he waited now, surrounded by his wife and friends.

Zabad emerged from Nathanael's chamber. "They're coming out."

Sheba braced herself for Jehoiada's reaction as Zabad hurried past and entered the neighboring chamber. The moment Jehoiada saw her, he gasped and stopped walking.

Clearly struggling for control, he approached slowly and cupped her face. "Are you all right? Who did this?" Before she could answer, his anger rose. "I'll kill him! Where's Hazi? He was supposed to pro—"

"Hazi was beaten more severely than me, Jehoiada." She watched her words hit their mark, compassion softening his angry features. "Not physically beaten, Jehoiada, but Ima made terrible threats, and watchmen had beaten one of his pregnant wives."

His fury ebbed with a deep sigh. "Where is he? How can we help him?"

This was the man she loved. Protective, yes. But compassionate and caring to the core. "He's inside our chamber. He hasn't spoken since we left Ima's chamber. Perhaps you can reassure him of Yahweh's power and presence. I believe all he can see right now is Ima's brutality and the prison of his birthright."

Jehoiada pulled her into a fierce embrace. "I'll talk to Hazi, but I must know what happened to you."

Absorbing her husband's strength, she let her first tear fall. "Zev and Zabad were separated from us at the door. Hazi resisted Ima's demands and threats, but Ima had bribed Carites to overpower Hazi and strike me." She swallowed the panic that rose at the memory. "I'm afraid she's broken him, Jehoiada."

After a final squeeze, he kissed her forehead and released her. "Come, let's talk to your brother." He opened their door, letting her enter first.

Keilah stood in the far corner, holding Samson in the sling around her waist. Nathanael moved away from her when they entered, joining Zabad and Zev, who stood like sentinels in the center of the room. Tucked behind the guards were Zibiah and Hazi, seated on the embroidered couch. Hazi looked twelve years old, his hair mussed, his cheeks wet with tears. Sheba's heart shattered at the sight.

Jehoiada nudged past her and the guards, kneeling before the prince but remaining silent.

Hazi lifted his head slowly to address Yahweh's high priest. "I cannot return to your Temple, Jehoiada—ever. Too many lives are at risk."

"Hazi, please." Sheba rushed to Jehoiada's side, cradling her brother's hands. "Yahweh is the only way to fight Ima and Jezebel."

Jehoiada laid his hands on top of Sheba's, quieting his wife. "Your sister is right, my friend. Only by Yahweh's strength can we defeat this darkness."

Hazi gently removed his hands and stood, bringing everyone else to their feet as well. "I learned today that no one can defeat

Ima and the Gevirah." He offered a sad smile to Sheba and then turned to Jehoiada. "Zibiah may attend morning sacrifices and continue her visits with Sheba, but I'll send Zev to retrieve her. I can't risk the lives of my other wives and children for a god who refuses to display his power." He gently but firmly placed his hand on Zibiah's back. "Come, Wife. We're expected at the palace."

"Wait . . . Brother." Jehoiada grabbed his arm, halting the prince. "Choose Yahweh. You're a strong leader, and you have the loyalty of the people. Walk in the ways of David and your saba Jehoshaphat. Yahweh will deliver you if you choose Him."

He pointed at Sheba's purple cheek. "Where was Yahweh when the Carite hit your wife? When they beat my Tekoan wife who bears my child? I won't risk those I love for an invisible god."

He turned to go, and Jehoiada tried to stop him again, but Zev blocked his attempt. "No, my friend. The prince has given you his decision. You must obey."

Hazi hesitated, head bowed. "I know it's difficult—and dangerous—for Sheba to continue communication with Ima Thaliah, but if Yahweh worship is to survive in Judah, Sheba must court Ima's favor. But I can't help." He grabbed Zibiah's elbow and fairly dragged her out of the chamber.

Nathanael rushed to Keilah and Samson, who remained safely tucked in the corner. After a few private whispers, he turned to Jehoiada. "I'll escort Keilah to the Sur Gate and return to discuss tonight's twilight service." Keilah kissed Sheba's cheek as they left, and Nathanael said over his shoulder, "You're a brave woman, Sheba. I'm proud to call you my friend."

As the door clicked shut, Zabad lingered in the chamber awkwardly. Jehoiada ignored him.

Thoroughly focused on his wife, the high priest escorted her to the couch and kissed her bruised cheek. "I can't bear the thought of someone hurting you, and I don't care what Hazi says. I can't willingly send my wife back into the lions' den." He squeezed his eyes shut, shaking his head.

Zabad now stood looming over them. Why was he still here? Sheba wasn't sure whom she could trust after discovering Ima had bribed Temple guards. Even if Zabad was as trustworthy as an old pair of sandals, she wasn't comfortable with the chief gatekeeper delving into personal matters.

Surprising the couple, Zabad knelt beside Jehoiada. "If you don't mind, my lord, I believe I must speak freely as chief keeper of the threshold. I need to know exactly what your wife discussed with the queen." He lifted an eyebrow at Sheba. "And perhaps Lady Jehosheba should tell *you* what happened on our way to the palace."

She'd hoped Zabad would forget about her private meeting with Hazi in Zev's chambers. "It was nothing, really." Those words elicited a raised eyebrow from her husband as well, and when she recounted the story—including the part about rendering Hazi breathless, speechless, and possibly childless—both men chuckled, lightening the mood considerably.

Jehoiada brushed her cheek. "All right, my love, are you ready to tell us about your visit with the queen?"

Sheba breathed deeply, bracing herself for the memories and the emotions the account would likely stir, but her husband quieted her with his finger on her lips.

"May I first say that I'm very proud of you? You seem almost stronger after a grueling meeting with the queen of Judah than you've been in weeks." He leaned in and kissed her—right in front of Zabad! "Now tell us how Yahweh made you stronger in the midst of battle."

Cheeks burning, she wasn't sure where to start. "Well . . ." The golden tongs lay on the table behind Jehoiada, unseen as yet by Yahweh's high priest. She reached for them, and his eyes rounded like saucers.

"Did you smuggle those out of the palace?" He cradled them like a precious jewel.

"No, they're a 'gift' from Mattan." She acknowledged her husband's raised brow. "I know. The message I was supposed to deliver was something about Baal's high priest showing goodwill, but he actually cursed the tongs and divined some sort of catastrophe originating from within the Temple. Isn't that ridiculous?"

But Jehoiada didn't show the skepticism she'd expected. Angst, dread—maybe even fear—crossed his handsome face. He exchanged a glance with Zabad. "I want more guards atop the walls around the inner and outer courts. And double the guards near the entrance to the Holy Place. Obviously these tongs will never again be a sacred instrument before the Lord, but I don't want to take a chance that—"

"And Ima's been bribing Temple guards." Sheba blurted the awful truth. There was no easy way to say it.

Zabad's face flushed crimson. "I don't believe it. Did she give you names?" Without waiting for her answer, he turned to Jehoiada. "I'll kill them myself if I find out who they are."

Jehoiada steadied his breathing, noticeably working to control his temper. "Hazi told me there were spies in the Temple, but he was supposed to remove them. We can't rely on help from him regardless. Athaliah tried to bribe a guard before, but the loyalty on Temple grounds prevailed. How did she succeed this time?" His voice grew louder, demanding.

"It's my fault her bribery succeeded this time." Her throat nearly closed, her voice a whisper, and her inner trembling had returned. "Because I'm weak, you had to care for me and neglect your duties. Your absence caused resentment among the priests and Levites, making them more willing to betray you."

"They're not betraying me, they're betraying *Yahweh*!" He bolted to his feet, neck veins bulging, face crimson as he paced the tiny chamber. "Zabad, you will find the traitors and strip them of their duties. Do you hear me?"

Sheba hugged her knees to her chest, rocking on the couch, shaking uncontrollably. "I'm sorry, Jehoiada. I'm so sorry. So sorry." Though it was barely a whisper, her husband heard and the chief gatekeeper bowed his head. Was even Zabad angry with her?

Jehoiada glanced at her and fell to his knees again. He tried to cradle her cheeks, but she turned away, ashamed. "It's my fault, Jehoiada. You have every right to be angry with me."

"I'm not angry with *you*, Jehosheba." He tilted her chin to meet his gaze.

When she glimpsed his expression, she saw only love. How? "How can you love me?" The words escaped without permission.

"My love for you is unshakable, and you have nothing for which to be sorry. *You* didn't offer bribes. *You* didn't make the guards accept them." He buried his head in her waist and drew her into a ferocious embrace. "I owe *you* an apology. My anger has always been my downfall."

Zabad knelt beside them, his head bowed, lips moving without sound. Praying.

The thought comforted Sheba, though she still yearned to hide from the whole world. She was exhausted. Tired of fighting Ima Thaliah, defending Hazi, befriending Zibiah and Keilah. Why couldn't she simply hide in her bedchamber all day and see only Jehoiada?

Because you're called to a greater purpose. My purpose.

The unspoken words accosted her. "What did you say?" Her question, spoken aloud, seemed to rouse both Zabad and Jehoiada.

"I said my anger has always been—"

"No, I heard that part. I mean . . ." Sheba glanced from one man to the other, both of whom now shared a puzzled glance. Would they think her insane if she confessed to hearing a voice?

"Are you all right?" Jehoiada sat back on his heels, studying her expression. "Did you hear something?"

Her heart hammered in her chest. Dare she admit it?

Before she could answer, a sweet smile creased her husband's lips. "Let me tell you a story about the days before Israel had a king. Yahweh spoke in the middle of the night to a little boy named Samuel. The boy thought Eli, the high priest, was calling his name, but after Eli had sent him back to his room several times, he realized that Samuel must have been hearing Yahweh call his name." Jehoiada reached up to touch her cheek. "I'll ask you again, Jehosheba. Did you hear something?"

Her heart still thundered, now with wonder rather than fear. "I was feeling overwhelmed and thinking I wanted only to hide in our bedchamber, but I heard a voice say I am called to a greater purpose."

Jehoiada chuckled, happy tears welling on his lashes. "Indeed, I believe Yahweh has spoken to you." He kissed her palm and laid it against his cheek, sadness dimming his smile. "We must believe Yahweh's purpose will prevail—even if you must return to the lions' den."

Part 3

31

→ LEVITICUS 16:1-2 ←

*The LORD spoke to Moses after the death of the two sons
of Aaron who died when they approached the LORD. . . .
"Tell your brother Aaron that he is not to come whenever he chooses into the Most Holy Place behind the curtain in front of the atonement cover on the ark, or else he
will die. For I will appear in the cloud over the atonement
cover."*

Jehoiada left the northwest courtyard of the priests, satisfied that the laws for boiling this morning's offerings were
being followed to the letter.

"My lord!" Zabad's voice rose over the rumble of the inner
court, where priests tried to look busy even though sacrifices
to Yahweh continued to decline. "It's past midday, nearly time
for central court. I'll escort you to the palace if you're ready."

The chief gatekeeper had proven not only a loyal guardian
but also a faithful friend, wise beyond his years. In the two
Sabbaths since the meeting with Queen Athaliah, Jehosheba
had received only one scroll from her ima, its contents inconse-
quential. Jehoiada was torn between relief and angst, the royal
silence piquing his need for an emergency plan. What if Athaliah
attacked the Temple compound? Jehosheba's insight into palace

intrigue was invaluable, but eyes and ears *inside* the palace were essential to ensure a timely escape if a Temple attack occurred.

"I'm going to kiss my bride, and then we can go." Jehoiada kept his tone light but communicated more with a raised brow.

Zabad fell in step and kept his voice low. "Does Jehosheba know we've tried to contact Obadiah and had no response?"

"Yes, and she still thinks Hazi might change his mind and help us." Jehoiada's heart ached. "How do I tell her we can no longer trust the one person who's always been her champion?"

Zabad offered a reassuring smile. "Princess Jehosheba is learning to recognize a true champion."

Jehoiada nodded, considering his wife's growing faith. Yahweh had indeed become her champion, more real to her since her collapse.

"I meant me, of course. I'm the champion." Zabad puffed his chest and flexed his biceps—then dissolved into laughter. Jehoiada couldn't help but join him.

The two hurried across the inner court. The summer sun filled the air with the sweet scent of acacia and warmed the white limestone. They stopped outside Jehoiada's chamber, listening to the happy voices of women's chatter.

"Seems a shame to interrupt." Jehoiada winked at his friend.

"Whatever else Prince Hazi proves to be," Zabad said, "I'm thankful he allowed Princess Zibiah's continued visits. She and Keilah have been good for Jehosheba."

Jehoiada nodded his agreement, but he knew the deeper truth. Though his wife spoke fondly of Zibiah and Keilah, she still held back, finding trust elusive. "Why do they want to be my friends?" she'd asked him last night.

Yahweh, let Jehosheba see Your love through the lives of these good friends.

He knocked as he entered. "Shalom, ladies." The now familiar sight of three women deftly working wool and spindle was made more precious by Jehosheba's concentrated expression.

Her tongue peeked out the corner of her mouth, and her focus never left the spindle. "Shalom, Husband. I thought you'd be at the palace by now." She pinched the yarn and coiled it around her extended fingers like Jehoiada had seen the Levites wind flax and wool yarn for their sacred garments.

"You're becoming quite good at that."

She giggled—music to his ears. "You sound surprised." She finally looked up, one eyebrow raised.

Zibiah and Keilah continued their work, chatting quietly, while Zabad stood watching. Jehoiada crossed the small chamber in two steps, snagged his wife's waist, and pulled her toward a corner. "You surprise me every day, Princess Jehosheba." After making sure the others were distracted, he stole a quick kiss. Surely the high priest should strive for some decorum.

Her cheeks flushed a lovely pink, and she whispered for only him, "Have you heard from Obadiah yet?"

"Not yet, but I hope to find him at the palace after I finish my duties at court. Have you thought of anything else I should tell him?"

She laid her head on his chest and hugged his waist. "I just wish we knew more about Ima Thaliah's plans for him. She said nothing in the scroll, and she hasn't invited me back to her chamber. Are you sure we shouldn't ask in my next reply to her?"

"We'll only respond to *her* questions. I fear if we ask questions of our own, we might inadvertently offer information, giving new arrows for her quiver." Jehoiada kissed the top of her head. "I need to speak with Obadiah. If he's in the palace today, Zabad and I will find him."

Her eyes filled with tears. "Please be careful. Ima wants to destroy Yahweh's power and presence in Judah. What would keep her from destroying you?"

"Yahweh, my love." Jehoiada kissed away her salty tears. "Yahweh is the only one who can defeat Athaliah."

She nodded, shame shadowing her beautiful features. "I know. I'm sorry. I—"

"No apologies. We are one flesh, you and I. When I'm afraid or angry, you remind me that Yahweh is the answer—and I do the same for you." He cupped her cheeks, wiping her tears with his thumbs. "No blame. No guilt or shame. We live and fight with Yahweh's strength, not our own. Now, pray that Yahweh will help me find Obadiah, for I believe he's the only one with knowledge of that quarry—and I believe that quarry is Yahweh's provision for our future."

Zabad escorted Jehoiada across the Temple courts and out the Guards' Gate, hurrying down the garden path to the palace's Horse Gate. Jehoiada much preferred this entrance—especially when he was late for court like today—to avoid the crowds waiting in the main hall.

His weekly duties at central court provided reason to explore the ground floor of Solomon's palace, a building six times the size of Yahweh's Temple. Hurrying through a dimly lit hallway on the northern wall of the stables, Jehoiada and his guard emerged through a side door of the courtroom with only a smear of their stable journey clinging to his bare foot.

"Ah, I see Yahweh's high priest decided to join us after all." Hazi lifted a golden goblet, toasting his brother-in-law's presence. He looked all too smug on his abba's throne, surrounded by fawning noblemen and his arrogant cousins. The whole brood had attended both of Jehoiada's court proceedings since Hazi and Jehosheba had met with Queen Athaliah.

Jehoiada nodded and took his seat behind a low-lying wall, pounding the scepter of Solomon, Judah's ancient symbol of wisdom and justice, on the platform. Zabad stood in place at Jehoiada's right shoulder, and those gathered in the Throne Hall fell silent. A wandering thought took root as Jehoiada glimpsed the golden scepter in his hand. How had it been saved from the Philistines? And another question nagged. Where had Hazi found that golden goblet?

"According to the laws of Judah set forth by our beloved King Jehoshaphat," the royal herald announced with practiced tones, "all matters of Yahweh's Temple are set before the high priest of Yahweh."

The first twenty complainants filed into the courtroom.

"You may begin, sir." Jehoiada trained his attention on the

man before him, refusing to let his suspicions of Hazi or Athaliah rob God's people of justice.

"Your priests required me to bring a female lamb for the sacrifice, but my family is poor. We should only be required to sacrifice two doves."

Jehoiada scratched his chin, letting the man linger under his gaze. Experience told him that liars fidget, unable to stand under the inspection of their accuser. But honest men—

"I believe the man deserves recompense from Yahweh's priests." Hazi's smooth, warm voice stole every man's attention.

With all eyes on the prince, Jehoiada had a moment to quell his fury. How dare Hazi offer a verdict on the day of the Temple's court? Zabad's hand landed hard on his shoulder as the silence forced the crowd's attention back to the high priest.

Mind spinning, Jehoiada stared across the grand hall at Hazi's pleasant smile and lifted brow. Was he anticipating Jehoiada's answer, or did he believe he'd trapped Yahweh's high priest? "If Prince Ahaziah would be so kind as to instruct this man on the specific requirements of the law in question, I would be willing to consider the prince's verdict as *held by God*—Ahaziah." His use of Hazi's full name, weaving its meaning into his answer, drew an appreciative sigh from the crowd.

Not from Hazi. Though his smile remained, it became chiseled granite. "Please forgive me, Jehoiada. I spoke out of turn." He addressed the crowd with the warmth and charm that drew men like bees to honey. "Though I value Yahweh and his Law far more than my reprobate abba, I will never pretend a devotion equal to my saba Jehoshaphat." He nodded in Jehoiada's direction, his hard stare communicating what his words couldn't. Hazi was wholly committed to his ima's purpose.

The first plaintiff got his lamb, and the proceedings continued. After the last complaint was heard, Jehoiada noticed Obadiah enter the Throne Hall, bow to the prince, and then shuffle toward Jehoiada. If the old nobleman hadn't seemed so frail, Jehoiada might have been more pleased to see him.

"We must speak quickly," Obadiah whispered. "Queen Athaliah has assigned me the terrible task of appropriating small

Judean farms into royal lands. She's affixing King Jehoram's seal to the orders so the whole nation believes him the villain."

Jehoiada's temper flared. "But she can't do tha—"

"Shh!" Obadiah clamped his crooked hand on Jehoiada's shoulder. "Keep your voice down. Prince Hazi concocted some excuse to steal me from my duties. Don't squander his efforts."

"Hazi?" Jehoiada cast a confused glance in his brother-in-law's direction but found the prince engaged in more fraternizing. "Where does Hazi's allegiance lie?"

Obadiah looked as if he might throttle the high priest. "Is that why the repeated summons? Surely you can figure that out without endangering me. Hazi is a survivor who loves his wives and his sister. It's that simple. Now, what do you want? Queen Athaliah is becoming suspicious."

Obadiah was weary, and Jehoiada's regrets warred with urgency. "Forgive me, Obadiah. I didn't think about Athaliah intercepting my messages, but I need someone I can trust *inside* the palace."

"Consider anything you send to the palace fodder for the queen. She seems to know everything."

"Does she know about the quarry?" Jehoiada held his breath.

"Yes, but only that Jehoram hid there during the raid. She hasn't mentioned it since."

"How well do you know your way around the tunnels?"

An impish grin creased the old man's face. "Like the back of my hand. Why?"

Jehoiada's hope soared, but he kept his voice low. "They may be our only way to protect Yahweh's sacred items if Athaliah uses the city watchmen to attack. Is there any way to tunnel directly from the quarry into a chamber on Temple grounds?"

"No need. Such a tunnel already exists."

"What?" Jehoiada shouted.

"Shh!" Obadiah chuckled and leaned in. "When you visit the Most Holy Place as new high priest on the Day of Atonement, you will discover more than Yahweh's presence waiting to be revealed."

"But that's four full moons from now."

"I can assure you—Athaliah is conniving, but she's also patient. She lets King Jehoram writhe in pain until Hazi wins Judah's favor, and she steadily builds military and treasury funds to a surplus. You will not need the tunnel until after the Day of Atonement."

Jehoiada caught sight of Zabad signaling him and Obadiah. Their conversation must have drawn suspicion. They needed to return to the Temple, but one last question grated. "If there was a tunnel in the Holy of Holies, why didn't we save the Ark *and* King Jehoram when the Philistines raided the city?"

Obadiah's compassionate gaze offset his urgency. "Remember that night in your chamber when I said we must move the king, but I *asked* if we could move the Ark as well? Amariah chose to move only the king. I knew he meant to keep the Ark's tunnel secret—and it's good we did. Jehoram told Athaliah of the quarry's existence, but if he'd known of the Ark's tunnel, Athaliah would have an unhindered path into the Temple compound." He squeezed Jehoiada's shoulder. "For now, only I know how to navigate the quarry."

Zabad's warnings grew bolder, capturing Obadiah's attention again. "We can't talk here. I'll send word of another meeting through Lady Zibiah." Obadiah walked away before Jehoiada could answer.

Yahweh, keep him safe as he treads among serpents in this dark palace.

32

*On the tenth day of the seventh month you must deny
yourselves and not do any work—whether native-born
or a foreigner residing among you—because on this day
atonement will be made for you, to cleanse you. Then,
before the LORD, you will be clean from all your sins.*

Sheba wound the last length of yarn on her spindle, feeling
an overwhelming sense of satisfaction. She raised a single
eyebrow and issued the challenge. "Ready, Princess Zibiah."
Keilah laid her own spindle aside and lifted Samson from the
goatskin rug—out of the field of play. Zibiah sat on the rug,
legs outstretched, spindle tucked between her feet against two
heavy pieces of leather. Sheba assumed her position—leaning
back against the princess, legs outstretched, spindle ready to
unwind. Keilah sat on a cushion with her elbow propped on
the table to help support Samson as he nursed.

"Don't start until I've settled Samson into nursing. I want
to see who's winning." Keilah nestled Samson into position to
begin his meal and lifted her free hand in the air to begin the
competition. "All right, grab the thread . . ."

Sheba and Zibiah leaned toward their feet, pinching the leader
thread, ready to begin winding their ball of yarn. This little

contest was their favorite part of the day, the moment they wrapped their finished yarn into tight, neat balls, with a strand to draw from the middle. Sheba's hands ached from her daily task, a wonderful weariness born of productivity.

"Okay, start wrapping." Keilah's verbal signal was less than enthusiastic, and though Sheba felt Zibiah's frantic whirling behind her, she was distracted by the concern in Keilah's whisper. "Come on, sweet boy. You've got to eat or this infection will get worse, and then we'll both be in trouble."

"Come on, Sheba. You're not even trying!" Zibiah continued her frenzied pace. Sheba increased her speed but kept an eye on Keilah and the baby.

Watching her friend's intimate moments with Samson piqued the ache in her heart. On most days, Keilah's presence warmed her, giving her a much-appreciated dose of motherhood. She and Jehoiada never discussed children. The subject seemed too painful for him and too confusing for her.

Amid Jehoiada's other lessons, he'd explained Yahweh's promise of King David's eternal ruler. Every woman with a drop of David's blood thought she could bear the Anointed One. Sheba, as the daughter of Jehoram and one of his Judean wives, was a candidate through both parents' lineage. But did she really want to have children? Watching Keilah with baby Samson reminded her that she'd never known an ima's love.

Shame wracked her. How could she be relieved at the prospect of childlessness? Was she evil as Leviathan—or simply thankful for one less opportunity to fail?

"Done!" Zibiah leapt to her feet, holding her ball of yarn aloft like warriors' booty.

Sheba turned her head to wipe tears, hiding emotions that had so suddenly overwhelmed her. She heard Keilah sniff and found her wiping tears as well.

Zibiah fell to her knees between them. "Well, I would have let Sheba win if I'd known you'd both be this upset." They laughed together, knowing Zibiah's humor eased into compassion. She took Sheba's hand. "Has Queen Athaliah called you back for another meeting? Are you and Jehoiada arguing?"

Sheba stared at the ceiling, trying to blink away her tears. It wasn't working. Her emotions had become steadier during the waxing and waning moons, but for Sheba, any tears were too many. What if she couldn't stop them? What if her friends grew weary of her moods? With a frustrated sigh, she smiled and shook her head, sparing them her burdens. Sparing herself the risk of more pain. Would she ever be able to talk as freely about her feelings as Zibiah and Keilah did? *Yahweh, are You weary of my weeping?*

"You can trust us, you know." Zibiah's eyes glistened now.

Sheba nodded, refusing to cry—or confide. "I do trust you. It's me I don't trust." It was partially true.

Zibiah's face twisted, tears beginning in earnest, and Keilah brushed her cheek. "Have we made you cry now?"

"Why haven't I conceived yet?" Zibiah's voice was small.

The nursemaid tilted her head, compassion radiating. "Sometimes it takes awhile, especially when you must share your husband with other wives. How often does he come to you?"

"He visits almost every night now, since all but three of his other wives are with child. But the queen is forcing him to take more wives—ten more noblemen's daughters, I think. And when they arrive, my time with Hazi will again be limited." She paused, as if the words were too bitter to speak. "What if one of his new wives steals his heart from me?"

She wilted into Sheba's arms, sobbing. "Shh, my friend. Don't be afraid. Hazi loves you deeply." She and Keilah exchanged a heartbroken glance, Keilah's pure and innocent, Sheba's entirely too informed. In yesterday's scroll from Ima Thaliah, among other reports of Baal's growing influence came news of Hazi's imminent marriages to ten more noblemen's daughters—from wealthy families faithful to Baal Melkart.

"Sheba, you know what harem life is like. The other wives scheme for Hazi's affection and barter for his time as if he were a trinket in the market. They go to Baal's temple, offering sacrifices to win Mattan's favor, hoping he or your ima will manipulate Hazi on their behalf."

Sheba silently mourned for her friend, a prisoner of palace

intrigue day and night, but she couldn't let her lose hope. "Hazi sees the purity of your love, Zibiah, the love of Yahweh's covenant marriage—a lasting promise that never wanes, never dies."

"But can he recognize it while he continues to worship Baal?"

Zibiah's question escaped on a sob, and Sheba grasped her shoulders, meeting her gaze. "I'm not giving up on him, and neither is Yahweh. You mustn't either."

Keilah whimpered. Startled, Zibiah and Sheba watched her normally calm facade crumble. The nursemaid tried to reposition Samson, who fussed and fidgeted at her breast. Grinding her teeth, she was obviously in pain. Finally, she gave up and hoisted the baby into Sheba's arms. "I'm scared," she whispered and opened her robe, revealing large, red splotches on both breasts. Sheba and Zibiah gasped as Keilah closed her robe just as quickly, tying her belt. "I've had a fever since last night, and Samson doesn't want to nurse because my milk has changed. Both breasts are hard as rocks. I've tried warm compresses, but nothing helps." Tears stopped her words, but she didn't need to explain.

"Have you seen a midwife to get herbs?" Sheba asked.

Keilah shook her head. "I can't pay her, and if Samson's family finds out, I'm afraid they'll find another nursemaid."

Zibiah removed an ivory comb from beneath her head covering. "Here. This will help pay a midwife and maybe even feed the widows until you're feeling better."

Keilah covered the comb in Zibiah's hand, gently pushing it away. "Thank you, my friend, but I can't. If Samson's family sees a midwife, they'll know something is wrong. And if the midwife makes me stop nursing, I'll stop producing milk. Then I'll need more than a comb to feed my widows." She took a deep breath, regaining control.

Before Zibiah and Sheba could argue, Keilah stood and began gathering her things. She lifted Samson from Sheba's lap. "Since tomorrow is the Day of Atonement, I'll have the whole day as Sabbath after the sacrifice. I just need rest and I'll feel better." Zibiah and Sheba stood to offer hugs, and a little mischief crept into Keilah's smile. "I'll see you both tomorrow at the sacrifice, and then I'll be back the day after to show Zibiah how a *real* woman winds a ball of yarn."

This morning's vestments were much lighter than the golden garments Jehoiada usually wore. On the Day of Atonement, the high priest dressed in a simple linen undergarment, tunic, belt, and turban. His ornate ephod, breastpiece, and diadem rested on the wooden cross in the corner of Nathanael's chamber, waiting to be donned after Jehoiada made atonement for himself and the Israelites in the Holy of Holies.

Will the Lord be displeased that my heart is divided in duty, part of me fulfilling the role of high priest, part of me seeking the entrance to the quarry?

"You seem distracted." Nathanael's voice scraped like bone on bone, interrupting Jehoiada's contemplation of the Most Holy Place. The second priest's face shadowed with concern. "You can't have a moment's lapse when you minister before the mercy seat. I don't want to haul out a dead high priest because he was daydreaming about his lovely wife." He pulled on the rope fastened to Jehoiada's ankle—the method by which they would extract his body if he displeased Yahweh in the Holy of Holies.

Jehoiada met Nathanael's teasing with a scowl, but his young friend wasn't easily cowed. Should he confide in Nathanael about the quarry entrance? Surely if the Temple was attacked, someone besides the high priest must enter the Most Holy Place to rescue the Ark . . .

Before he could ponder further, Nathanael began quizzing him—again. "All right, your bath is complete, and you're wearing the white garments only. Are you *sure* we've done this correctly?"

"I prepared Amariah for the Day of Atonement for forty years. I know how to do *your* job. It's my ability with the high priest's tasks that I question."

"Let's go over them again." Nathanael reached for the scroll they'd perused four times this morning. "You've chosen the bull and ram for yours and Sheba's atoning sacrifice. Zabad will open the Temple gates at sunrise, and you'll choose two goats and a ram for the Israelite community's atonement. You'll then slaughter the bull as a sin offering for you and your household, and we'll have Eliab stir the bull's blood in the trough to keep it from coagulating while you cast lots at the Temple entrance to determine which goat will be slaughtered and which will become the scapegoat. Are you listening? The timing is crucial."

Jehoiada grinned at his meticulous second priest and glanced at the eastern sky through the chamber window. Barely a glow. They had time to form a plan. "Nathanael, your schedule must allow me to search for a tunnel entrance in the Most Holy Place."

The shock on his face was worth divulging the secret. "A tunnel? What do you mean, 'a tunnel'? A tunnel leading where? And how do you know—"

Jehoiada lifted his hand, stopping the questions. "For now, let me say that Obadiah is the only other soul who knows the full details. I've told you in case I displease the Lord today and meet His wrath."

Nathanael's eyes glistened. "I can't bear to think of it, but go ahead. Tell me what I need to know."

"The tunnel was built as an escape for the Ark if the Temple should fall under attack. When King Solomon built the Temple, Yahweh warned that Israel would one day turn to foreign gods and that He would destroy His Temple. Solomon believed Yahweh and built the tunnel under the Holy of Holies in order to rescue the sacred articles and protect King David's lineage—and then Solomon destroyed all record of the quarry. I believe if the Temple comes under attack, the Lord will allow consecrated priests to use the tunnel in the Most Holy Place to protect His presence."

"Why didn't—"

"I'm sorry I can't give you more details," Jehoiada said, noting the brightening eastern sky, "but if anything happens to me, Obadiah knows the plan. We've met secretly during these last months. Right now, you and I must decide how to find the tunnel entrance today. When I enter the Most Holy Place for today's three sacrifices, which offering poses the best opportunity for a search?"

Sighing, Nathanael referred to his scroll, studying the order of sacrifice. "Before your first entry, place burning coals from the Holy Place's golden altar into a censer. Add two handfuls of finely ground incense before passing through the curtain to the Most Holy Place. The heavy smoke from the censer will conceal the Lord's presence between the cherubim on the mercy seat atop the Ark."

"That's excellent news to keep me alive in Yahweh's presence but not so helpful to detect a subtle deviation in the limestone floor. How will I see a tunnel entrance if I'm blinded by smoke?" Jehoiada's frustration mounted as the eastern sky grew brighter.

"For your second offering, retrieve the bull's blood that Eliab will have been stirring. This offering atones for your sins and the sins of your household by sprinkling the blood with one finger on the side of the mercy seat and seven times on the *floor* in front of—"

"On the floor! Yes!" His enthusiasm got a chuckle from his second. "I can inspect the floor while I sprinkle the bull's blood."

"Yes, the second time looks promising, but the third offering of goat's blood uses the same method and placement if you need another chance to locate the tunnel. Your third entry atones for the *pesha`* of the Israelites—our deliberate sins and intentional rebellion. The smoke should have cleared by then . . ."

Jehoiada lost Nathanael's final instructions in the overwhelming weight of his final atonement. *For the* pesha` *of the Israelites—our deliberate sins and intentional rebellion.* Images flooded his memory of the night King Jehoram had attended the Temple sacrifice with his arrogant princes—all priests of Baal. Jehoiada imagined the faces of his mortal enemies. Mattan, Queen Athaliah—their wickedness nearly choked him. *Yahweh, how can I atone for their sins?* The familiar anger started to rise, but then nausea swept over him in a wave. He clutched his belly, staggering to a wooden bench.

"Jehoiada!" Nathanael grabbed his arm, helping him sit down. "Are you ill?"

How could he answer? Yes, the burden of unrepentant sin made him sick, but as Israel's high priest, did he get to choose whom the blood atoned for and whom it didn't? He met his friend's concerned gaze. "I'm not ill, Nathanael, but this duty is almost more than I can bear." Inspecting his simple linen tunic and belt, he said, "I would much rather carry the weight of the ephod and breastplate than the sins of the whole nation on this single Day of Atonement."

"May I offer some advice?"

Surprised, Jehoiada nodded.

"Don't worry about the tunnel to the quarry. Concentrate on Yahweh's commands and the purposes behind them. Fill the Holy of Holies with the burning incense of your worship. Make the atoning sacrifice for your own sin, and then your heart will be prepared to atone for others."

Zabad's knock on the door accompanied his summons. "The sun has risen, and Yahweh's people wait at the gates for atonement."

Gaining strength from these faithful brothers, Jehoiada left Nathanael's chamber to cover the sins of a nation.

33

The goat chosen by lot as the scapegoat shall be presented alive before the LORD to be used for making atonement by sending it into the wilderness as a scapegoat.

Sheba stood at the edge of the inner court with Zibiah, keeping one eye on her husband and one eye on the Sur Gate. Keilah hadn't come with her widows for this morning's sacrifices. When Sheba asked Hobah, her favorite among the dear ladies, if she'd seen Keilah, Hobah had answered with a toothless grin. "Keilah didn't bring us food this morning since we're fasting for the Day of Atonement. I'm sure she'll be here soon." That had been before Jehoiada's first sacrifice. Now he'd completed his third journey into the Holy of Holies.

Each time those great golden doors swallowed him, Sheba prayed for Yahweh's favor. *Have mercy, Yahweh. He is but dust.* And each time, her husband emerged, alive but older, paler, more burdened.

Zibiah leaned over, whispering, "Where could she be?"

"I don't know." Sheba tried to keep her voice from shaking. "How long can you stay today?" She glanced at Hazi, standing nobly on the upper porch, observing the ceremony with the few Judean leaders still faithful to Yahweh. As Jehoiada placed his hands on the scapegoat, Hazi pointed as if explaining something to the nobleman beside him. *Yahweh, forgive his hypocrisy.* She had watched her brother become more comfortable lying about Abba Jehoram's debauchery, lying about Ima Thaliah's goodness, even lying about Judah's future. How could he deceive so convincingly?

Zibiah kept her voice low. "I need to know that Keilah is okay."

Sheba nodded and led the princess to the northeast outer courtyard. "When Elan takes the scapegoat into the wilderness, you go back to the palace with Hazi, and I'll ask Hobah to take me into the City of David to find Keilah."

"No, you will not!" Zibiah shouted, drawing the attention of everyone within a stone's throw.

"Shh! I'll take Zabad with me," Sheba whispered, "and I'll wear one of the sackcloth grieving robes I noticed in a storage chamber. No one will recognize me if I keep the hood pulled over my head."

Zibiah stared at her for a long moment and then returned her attention to the altar, her jaw flexing wildly. "Hazi keeps me locked in that palace whenever I'm not with you. Queen Athaliah *requested* my presence at a special Baal sacrifice this afternoon. When I refused, Hazi ordered me to stay in my chamber. He plans to post Zev at my door to ensure I stay there."

"He loves you, Zibiah, and he's afraid."

"I feel like a prisoner." The words were barely a whisper.

"I know." Sheba hugged her and kissed her cheek. "Yahweh will make this right somehow."

Zibiah nodded but seemed unconvinced. Was Sheba convinced? Sometimes Yahweh felt near and His power unquenchable, but when her loved ones suffered, her faith lagged and she needed Jehoiada's unwavering trust to reassure her. *Yahweh, have mercy on my husband. He is Your faithful servant.*

She hugged Zibiah's shoulders. "Let's go back to the inner court so I can say good-bye to Hazi and prepare to search for Keilah."

The two moved through the crowd, Jehoiada's deep, resonant voice drawing them toward the inner court reserved for priests and royalty. "For all these sins, O God of forgiveness, forgive us, pardon us, grant us atonement." He stood high above the assembly on the platform of the brazen altar, beating his chest, tearstained cheeks turned heavenward.

Sheba gasped. "Oh, Zibiah, he looks ill." Her horror escaped on a whisper. The sins of Judah had etched craggy lines on his kind and loving features. Dark circles ringed his eyes, and his lips were drawn down in a mournful cry.

"I see it too." Zibiah covered her gaping mouth.

Sheba reached for Zibiah's hand. "After his sacred bath, he'll change into his golden garments. Perhaps then he'll look more like himself. I need to see that he's all right before I search for Keilah. Do you think Hazi will let you wait with me?"

Zibiah squeezed her hand. "Maybe he'll even wait with us."

They watched the remainder of the ceremony in silence. When Elan finally led the scapegoat toward the Sur Gate, Hazi descended the steps of the upper porch, making his way toward Zibiah and Sheba. Worshipers bowed as he passed, his retreat stirring more attention than the departing scapegoat.

"Let the high priest anoint Prince Ahaziah as king!" someone in the crowd shouted.

"Blessings and long life to Judah's new king, Ahaziah!" another voice added.

"Long live King Ahaziah!" People began shouting and shoving, surging toward the gates of the inner court. Temple guards filed down from atop the inner wall to help the Carites disperse the crowd. In zeal for their beloved prince, the worshipers now blocked the gates, creating a human barricade between Hazi and the palace. Trumpeters summoned watchmen from Jerusalem's walls. Zabad gathered a cluster of Temple guards around Sheba and Zibiah and looked to Zev for direction.

"Take the women to Jehoiada's chamber," Zev said. Zabad nodded, his guards forming a human shield as they moved toward the high priest's chamber.

Zibiah looked over her shoulder, straining to see beyond the priests and Levites in the inner court. "Will Hazi be all right?" she asked when they stopped outside Sheba's door.

"Zev won't allow anyone near Prince Ahaziah, my lady."

Zabad, somewhat breathless, directed his guards back to the fray and then nodded a quick bow. "Lady Zibiah, the people love your husband. I'm just hoping my guards can stop them from making him king before Jehoram breathes his last." He gasped, his cheeks instantly flushing crimson. Offering Sheba a fully repentant bow, he spoke while staring at his bare feet. "Lady Jehosheba, please forgive me for speaking so casually about your abba's condition."

Sheba's heart twisted at the truth of his words, but guilt raised her defenses. How many new moon celebrations had passed since she'd seen him? "My abba suffers Yahweh's righteous judgment, but don't contribute to Ima's schemes with careless comments."

"Forgive me, my lady," Zabad whispered.

Releasing a sigh, she nudged his shoulder, coaxing him out of his bow. "You're forgiven, my friend." He looked up, his neck and cheeks crimson, and she felt sorry for the dear man.

At the sound of more trumpets, Zabad reached for the door. "Let's go inside. They're calling for reinforcements. I can't escort Lady Zibiah back to the palace until the Temple courts are clear."

Zibiah cast a furtive glance at Sheba and then offered Zabad a sweet smile. "If you're sure Hazi will be all right, and he won't expect me at the palace for a while"—she winked at Sheba—"we need to raid a storage chamber and visit a friend."

Sheba gasped and then hid a smile, realizing what Zibiah had in mind.

Zabad's eyes narrowed. "What could you two want from a Temple storage chamber?"

"Grieving robes." Sheba hated using guilt as a weapon, but they needed to find Keilah. "And after that comment about my abba, you owe me a favor."

The widow Hobah led Sheba and Zibiah through the City of David's narrow streets, Zabad providing rear guard. Sheba pulled the sackcloth hood farther forward and tightened the grip at her neck. The chill of harvest was in the air, and it worked its way up Sheba's spine. What if they couldn't find Keilah?

Hobah led them first to the home of Keilah's employer, leaving the three *imposters*, as she called them, standing in the shadows of an alley between two dressed-stone buildings. She approached one of the servants at a side door and returned with heartrending news. "The master threw Keilah into the street last night because she'd concealed her illness. The maid said to check with Gadara. She's the only midwife in town who'll help a woman without silver."

Urged on by waning daylight, they hurried past the market booths. Sheba wondered why some merchants continued their trade on the Sabbath Day of Atonement but got her answer when she glimpsed their wares. Amulets. Asherahs. Even Egyptian gods: Anubis the jackal, Bastet the cat, and Sekhmet the lioness. Had Jehoiada's travail for Judah covered the sins of these Judeans too?

"This is it." Hobah emerged from an alley and pointed to a portion of the southernmost wall of the city. The wall itself stood as tall as six men, and dilapidated chambers were built into its crumbling surface. Sheba remembered King David's family tombs lay carved in the bedrock of Mount Moriah near here. She had been twelve when the royal family made the long trek through the City of David for Saba Jehoshaphat's burial—the keening processional, the acrid smell of the Hinnom Valley near the Dung Gate. The memories of death and mourning rushed in while they gaped at the southernmost section of the city—the brothel district.

"Keilah and I have known Gadara for years." Hobah raised her chin, a glint of pride in her eyes. "Gadara helped Keilah care for us widows when we were ailing. There's not a finer midwife in Jerusalem—but she's got a temper. And she won't appreciate you three barging in, demanding to see Keilah. I'll go in alone and come back when you're welcomed."

Zabad watched her go and nudged the two princesses into a deserted alley across the street. "We shouldn't have come. This is too dangerous. Look around you." He tilted his head toward two surly men who had become quite interested in their presence. "If Hobah isn't back by the time I count—"

"She's here!" Hobah waved at them from the doorway of the brothel.

Zabad squeezed his eyes closed and clenched his teeth. "We must get in and get out. No lingering."

Sheba hurried across the street, Zibiah close behind, and they greeted Hobah, who led them down the brothel's long, dark hall. The passage eerily resembled the quarry where Jehoiada had hidden Abba Jehoram, and Sheba assumed the hall connected living chambers within the city's wall.

"Hey, soldier. Did you bring your ima and sisters to chaperone?" Bawdy laughter came from prostitutes lingering in doorways, their single-windowed chambers spilling light on the packed-dirt hall.

"In here." Hobah entered a tiny chamber, where Keilah lay on a pile of straw in the corner. A weary-looking woman sat beside her, dabbing her head with a wet cloth. The smell of herbs—and death—filled the stifling space.

The midwife turned and, without apology, inspected Hobah's three guests. "Soldier, you were a fool to bring two princesses here, but I'd imagine if they have the vinegar to charge into a brothel, they'll have what's needed to tend Keilah."

She plopped the cloth into the washbasin, slapped her knees, and stood. Then she marched toward Zabad like an army general and appraised him head to toe. "I suppose you'll do. You'll have to carry Keilah all the way to the Temple, you know. She hasn't regained consciousness since we found her on the front steps this morning." She extended her hand and offered her first smile. "My name is Gadara, and I'll need to check on Keilah occasionally after you take her back to the Temple."

Zabad opened his mouth but nothing came out. He tried again. Same result.

Sheba intervened. "We hadn't planned on taking Keilah back to the Temple with us." Whatever goodwill they'd built by coming, Sheba forfeited in that single statement.

"You *will* take her." Gadara's words were sharp as daggers. "Keilah has no hope if she stays. Either she'll die from this infection, or she'll die of a broken spirit when she's forced to earn her living here." The midwife crossed her arms, broaching no further argument.

"It's settled then." Sheba marched past Gadara, straight to where Keilah lay. Her face was the shade of ripe grapes, hair in sweaty clumps across her forehead. Dark circles ringed her eyes, and her lips looked like they'd been dusted with wheat flour.

"She may not make it through the night." Gadara spoke over her shoulder, confirming Sheba's fears. Zibiah and Hobah knelt with Sheba beside Keilah's still form. The heat of her fever radiated like embers of a fire.

Hobah cradled her hand, kissing it. "Shalom, my girl. Peace to you, sweet peace." Weeping overtook her, and she melted into Zibiah's embrace.

Sheba leaned over, kissing Keilah's cheek, and whispered, "You're not allowed to die. Do you hear me? Zibiah and I have much to learn and no one but you to teach us." She cradled Keilah's cheeks, coaxing her friend to wake. No response. "How could her condition worsen so quickly, Gadara?"

"This high fever seems to boil the blood. Frankincense is the most effective herb to break the fever, but it's costly, and only the wealthy patients have access to it."

Sheba remembered one of the market booths they'd passed touting the finest-quality frankincense. "Zibiah, are you wearing that ivory comb you offered to help Keilah pay for the widows' food?"

The princess's eyes sparkled as she slipped the comb from beneath her hood and displayed it to the midwife. "Will this buy enough frankincense to treat her?"

"It should buy enough to get her through the worst of it—if she makes it that long."

Keilah's eyes fluttered, sending a rush of hope through the chamber. Gadara reached for the cool cloth and dabbed Keilah's forehead. "Talk to her. Tell her you're taking her to the Temple. Maybe hope will keep her fighting."

Zibiah scooted closer. "Sheba wants you to live at the Temple with her, Keilah. What do you think?"

Keilah's eyes remained closed, but a slight smile creased her lips, preceding a single word. "Nathanael."

34

⋅➤ DEUTERONOMY 25:5–6 ⬅⋅

*If brothers are living together and one of them dies with-
out a son, his widow must not marry outside the family.
Her husband's brother shall take her and marry her and
fulfill the duty of a brother-in-law to her. The first son she
bears shall carry on the name of the dead brother so that
his name will not be blotted out from Israel.*

The sun was sinking behind Jerusalem's western wall, casting a golden glow on the tawny stone. Jehoiada held the
last yearling lamb for today's sacrifice and made the death
cut. He was exhausted, bone-weary, as he handed off the lamb
to Eliab and lumbered down the altar steps, Nathanael at his
side. The Law's requirements for their first Day of Atonement
together were almost complete. Only a few more details, and
Judah would be as pure and holy to the Lord as possible—on
this day of each year. Even Jehoiada's personal failures would
be forgiven.

The cool harvest breeze carried the ritual cries of Baal's temple to his ears, piercing him with a question. *Can one day of
an animal's blood wash away such deeply rooted sin in human
hearts?*

At midday, Hazi had worshiped at Yahweh's Temple, celebrating

Israel's atonement from sin. Now, Israel's future king worshiped at Baal's temple, condoning the frenetic cutting and spilling of human blood. The irony churned in Jehoiada's belly as he considered the recent rumors of miracles at Baal's temple. Mattan predicted twin boys for a nobleman's wife by reading a sheep's liver, and he'd averted a shady Egyptian potter's thievery by reading the flight of a soldier's arrow. These were the charming miracles chatted about at feasts and celebrations.

But what about Mattan's curses and spells?

Several priestess candidates had been returned to their families as unsuitable—and died of undisclosed causes soon after. Mattan's appetite for bloodier worship, more frenzied chanting, had stirred a terrible intrigue in the people in Judah. Pilgrims came from every corner of the nation to watch the show at Baal's temple in Jerusalem.

"My lord, are you all right?" Nathanael stopped, placing a comforting hand on Jehoiada's shoulder.

Only then did Yahweh's high priest realize tears wet his cheeks. Clearing his throat, he regained his composure and continued walking toward their chambers. "I wanted to thank you for your wise counsel, Nathanael. You said, 'Don't worry about finding the quarry tunnel. Concentrate on your worship, and your heart will be prepared to be God's instrument.'"

"And were you able to worship? Did you set aside duty alone and let Yahweh lead you?"

His satisfied heart radiated through his smile. "Indeed I did, and by my third journey into the Holy of Holies, I realized the utter futility of animals' blood sacrifice as atonement for sin."

"How can you say that?" Nathanael halted, appearing as horrified as Jehoiada had felt. "If there is no atonement through blood sacrifice, then what is there?"

"That question drove me to my knees. I couldn't bear the thought of my futile efforts year after year, pleading for forgiveness for a nation—for myself—that sins without end."

"What did you do?"

"I found the tunnel."

"You found—"

"Shh!" Jehoiada chuckled.

Nathanael's joy was short-lived, however. "Wait, you were telling me sacrifice was futile, and then you found"—he glanced in every direction to be sure they weren't overheard—"the tunnel?"

"When I found the tunnel, I realized God's atonement is vast and beyond my understanding—like the quarry and its tunnels. I am to be faithful in the Law of Moses that He's revealed to me. And when Yahweh provides more information—a secret tunnel under the Ark or the coming Son of David—I will abide by His new plan."

"Ahh . . . so the morning sacrifice will go on as planned?"

Jehoiada chuckled. "Yes, Nathanael. We're on schedule for the morning sacrifice."

The second priest beamed but kept his voice low. "So what did you see? Where is the entrance? Did you go in?"

Jehoiada grinned and raised a single eyebrow.

Within a few heartbeats, understanding dawned, and Nathanael released an exaggerated sigh. "All right, not here, not now." He pursed his lips and lengthened his stride across the inner court straight to Jehoiada's door. "Would you like to divulge the information in your chamber or mine?"

"My chamber, please, and let's remove my golden garments there as well. Jehosheba will also be anxious to hear the news." He pushed open his chamber door. "Shalom, my love."

Jehosheba's head shot up from a huddle of faces in their small outer chamber. Zabad, Zibiah, and a woman he didn't know stared back wide-eyed, as if he might eat them alive. Jehosheba laced her arm in the stranger's elbow and escorted her forward. "Jehoiada, this is Gadara, a midwife from the City of David. She's showing me how to care for Keilah—here in our chamber."

"A midwife? Is Keilah preg—" Nathanael's tone betrayed his pain, but Jehoiada shot him a warning glance, silencing the inappropriate question. Now was no time to announce his feelings.

Jehosheba seemed enchanted by Nathanael's concern, but Jehoiada was still trying to reconcile the day's emotions, an unknown midwife, and the news of Keilah's long-term visit—

which he hadn't approved. *Breathe. The Day of Atonement is a year away. Don't sin in anger. Don't lose your temper.*

"Welcome, Gadara," he said, stepping forward with a curt bow. "May I ask why you can't care for Keilah with your other patients in the city?"

"Jehoiada!" Jehosheba shouted. "We can't move Keilah again. She'll die. Gadara was kind enough to come with us to show me—"

Gadara shoved Jehosheba aside and began her own explanation. "Keilah started with milk fever two days ago and didn't seek treatment right away, so it's gone into her blood. I thought she'd be lying in a sarcophagus, sleeping in Mother Sarah's bosom by now, but when Lady Sheba and Lady Zibiah came to the brothel—"

"The brothel!" Jehoiada exploded, his first target Zabad. "Is she telling me you took my wife and the wife of Judah's crown prince to a *brothel*! Hazi could have you arrested—*I* may have you arrested!"

"Well, some high priest you are." Gadara snorted and disappeared into Jehoiada's bedchamber, leaving him panting with rage.

Zabad met Jehoiada's fiery gaze, unflinching. "When you see Keilah, you'll be thankful Yahweh sent us to retrieve her. Now, if I'm dismissed, I must be sure Micaiah has completely burned the animal hides, flesh, and offal outside the city. And I can't close the Temple gates until Elan has returned from the wilderness after releasing the scapegoat."

He bowed rather stiffly, and Jehoiada realized Zabad must be tired too. If Keilah was as sick as the midwife described, his chief gatekeeper would have undoubtedly carried her—and taken instruction from that bossy midwife with every step.

A surge of pity washed over Jehoiada, and he squeezed the man's shoulder. "I'm sorry, my friend. Thank you for keeping them safe."

"I'd rather face your anger than Gadara's sharp tongue." A wink and a chuckle assured Zabad's forgiveness.

"Would you mind escorting me to the palace before you close

the gates?" Zibiah's voice was small, almost apologetic. "We heard the Baal worship begin. I hope Hazi hasn't missed me yet. I don't want to explain my afternoon to him." Jehosheba hugged her friend, and Zabad escorted her out the door.

Only Nathanael remained, and he was anxious for answers. "How could Keilah be so sick, Jehosheba? We spoke yesterday about finding time during today's Sabbath to talk—alone."

Jehoiada raised an eyebrow. "I thought we agreed you would be cautious, Nathanael."

Jehosheba gasped and planted balled fists on her hips. "Jehoiada ben Jonah! Why didn't you tell me Nathanael and Keilah felt this way about each other?"

"What do you mean, 'about each other'? Did Keilah express feelings for me?" Hope dawned on Nathanael's features, and Jehosheba looked like an Egyptian cat with a mouse's tail hanging from her lips—utterly pleased but afraid opening her mouth might forfeit the prize.

Jehoiada grabbed his wife's tiny waist and pulled her toward him. "You and I need to talk, Princess Jehosheba. I'm sorry I shouted at you—and you're sorry for . . ."

She cupped an elbow with one hand and tapped her cheek with her finger. "Hmm, I'm sorry . . . I'm sorry you were rude to Gadara?"

Nathanael grinned, but Jehoiada scowled at his charming wife. "I'll address my poor manners with the midwife, but where are we supposed to sleep while Keilah is recuperating in *our* chamber?"

"For the first few nights, I'll sleep in our chamber with Keilah to apply Gadara's poultices. When Keilah's out of danger, I'll sleep on our couch in the outer chamber." Jehosheba glanced at Nathanael. "I was hoping my husband could stay with you while I'm tending to Keilah."

Nathanael beamed. "Of course! Jehoiada, you may have my bedchamber, and I'll sleep on the bench in my outer chamber. But please, Lady Jehosheba, tell me what Keilah said that made you think she has feelings for me."

Jehoiada felt duped, like he'd been sold a wool blanket on a summer's day, but Jehosheba snuggled into his chest, her warmth more comforting than a blanket.

She peeked over Jehoiada's arms and gave Nathanael a sweet gift. "When we first saw Keilah, she was too sick to speak, could barely open her eyes. But when Zibiah told her we were taking her to the Temple, she said one word." Jehosheba waited, seeming delighted in Nathanael's growing anticipation.

The second priest nearly shouted, "What word?"

"She said your name, my friend."

A satisfied smile creased Nathanael's lips. "I'm going to marry her, Jehoiada."

"What?" both the high priest and his wife said in unison.

Jehoiada nudged Jehosheba toward the couch and invited Nathanael to join him at the table. "Listen, my friend. You're tired. It's been an emotional day. Do you even know if Keilah's husband had a brother? She may be obligated."

Jehosheba slid off the couch to join them. "What do you mean, 'obligated'? Who cares about her dead husband's brother? Where was he when she was dying in a brothel?"

Jehoiada exchanged a solemn glance with his second. "Would you like to explain?"

Nathanael turned pleading eyes toward her. "Does Keilah have any relatives? Did her husband have family in Judah?"

"She's never mentioned her family or her husband's past." She alternated puzzled glances between the two priests. "Why does it matter? If he didn't help her when she needed it, why does he have the right to take her away from someone who loves her now?"

Jehoiada prodded his second with a lifted brow. Nathanael sighed. "The Levirate law ensures the continuity of every family and tribe in Israel. As long as a man and his family have sons, they will always have heirs to maintain their God-given land. Israelites have always owned their own land, until Ahab began appropriating small Israelite farms into the royal treasury—whether by purchase or seizure. His sin skewed Yahweh's perfect plan for Israel's enduring economy."

Jehoiada saw the implication dawn on his wife's face. "And Ima Thaliah is forcing Hazi to do the same thing in Judah."

Jehoiada reached for her hand, squeezing it. "Yes. The Levirate law may seem silly or unjust until we understand the Lawgiver's love for His people." He turned then to Nathanael, compassion thickening his tone. "You are a priest and an adult, but my authority over you is defined by this breastpiece." He patted the twelve-stoned plate on his chest. "I care about your happiness, and if you love Keilah, I will support your decision to marry her, but I must wait until her strength returns to ask if she has a kinsman waiting to redeem his claim."

While Keilah napped, Sheba stood at her bedchamber door listening to the monotonous droning of her husband and his second priest. Who could guess so many decisions were involved in running a Temple? She'd been trained as a Baal priestess but had no concept of the grand scheme of Yahweh's worship.

Four Sabbaths had passed since Keilah took up residence in the high priest's chamber. Gadara had visited several times and even spent a few nights with Keilah to give Sheba and Jehoiada time alone in Nathanael's chamber. Nathanael had been extremely generous, sleeping in Zabad's outer chamber or on the wooden bench in his outer room. During the day, however, Nathanael remained within the sound of Keilah's voice whenever priestly duties allowed.

"Next on my list . . ." Nathanael unrolled the parchment, revealing yet another issue, offering Jehoiada little time to comment. "May I suggest we employ a different seamstress to sew sleeves into the priest's woven tunics. Our current keeper of the wardrobe has discovered more rips . . ."

Nathanael droned on with endless details while Sheba watched tension pull Jehoiada's handsome features into a scowl. The high priest's patience was waning like the Jordan River in a drought. Perhaps she should intervene.

"Excuse me for interrupting." Sheba squeezed past the two men seated at their small table and pecked a kiss on her husband's cheek. "I'll only be a moment." She set Keilah's waste pot outside the chamber door and hurried to the basin to gather a towel, more bandages, and aloe. She heard Nathanael speaking, but Jehoiada wasn't answering. *Stop, Nathanael, before he—*

"Aren't you listening?" Nathanael snapped.

"No!" Jehoiada slammed his hand on the table, startling his wife and second priest. "How can I listen when everywhere I turn there are people and commotion and clutter?"

"Jehoiada, keep your voice down." Though Sheba hadn't felt that inner trembling in a long while, she still hated his anger. Standing behind him, she laid her hands on his shoulders and steadied her voice. "What can we do about this? Do you have a solution, my love?" *Yahweh, speak peace to Your servant Jehoiada. Give him wisdom . . .* Almost immediately, she felt his shoulders ease, his breathing slow.

"I'm sorry for losing my temper, Nathanael. Please find Zabad and bring him back here with you. I actually *do* have a solution in mind."

Nathanael glanced at Sheba, puzzled, but rose from his cushion and bowed before closing the door behind him. Jehoiada was on his feet before the door clicked shut. "Is Keilah strong enough to answer the Levirate question? Have you asked her yet?"

Sheba covered a giggle. "This is your solution to our cramped living space?"

He grabbed her waist and pulled her close. "It's part of my solution."

"Yes, she's strong enough, but I believe you should ask her about her kinsman. Nathanael looks up to you as an abba, and I think you should secure his future with the woman he loves."

Jehoiada's throat tightened at the thought. *Nathanael looks up to you as an abba.* He certainly couldn't be prouder of a blood-born son. He kissed his wife soundly, missing her more every night spent apart. Begrudgingly, he released her, and she followed him into their bedchamber, where Keilah still lay sleeping.

"Should I wake her?" he asked.

Sheba stifled a grin. "I don't think she'll mind for this."

Jehoiada grinned and knelt beside the wool-stuffed mattress. Touching Keilah's shoulder, he shook her lightly. "Keilah, I must ask you a question."

Lovely brown eyes fluttered open. Looking concerned at first and then utterly confused, she glanced at Sheba and back to Jehoiada. The long illness had stripped her strength, but she lifted herself on one elbow. "Ask it. Anything."

"Did your husband have a brother, a kinsman to redeem you?"

Leave it to a man to blurt it out. Sheba wanted to giggle, but she was too anxious to hear the answer.

As the implication of his question unfolded, Keilah's cheeks pinked. "You mean a Levirate claim? No. My husband and I had no siblings, and our parents died years ago." Her eyes filled. "Dare I ask why you want to know?"

Jehoiada shot to his feet, startling them both. "It's part of a solution to our cramped quarters." Before either woman could ask more, he turned and fled like his feet were on fire.

Sheba exchanged a puzzled glance with her friend and chased her husband out of their chamber and into Nathanael's rooms next door. "Jehoiada? What do you mean, *part* of your plan?"

35

⋙ 2 Chronicles 24:26 ⋘

Zabad, son of Shimeath an Ammonite woman, and Jehozabad, son of Shimrith a Moabite woman.

Jehoiada captured his wife's small waist, stealing this rare moment alone in Nathanael's chamber. "We can't tell Nathanael that Keilah's free to marry until after I disclose the rest of my plan."

She wriggled out of his grasp, seeming distracted. "That's hardly fair. He's waited so long, and I think he deserves to know right away." Jehosheba spotted the dirty dishes he and Nathanael had left in the washbasin this morning, drawn to them like a moth to flame.

She reached for a cloth to wash them, and Jehoiada's eyes lingered on her form. "Nathanael has been distracted enough recently. I need his full concentration to get the benefit of his detailed mind." Jehosheba continued her busyness, puffing tendrils of dark hair off her forehead as she wiped the small table, her gracefulness captivating. How long had it been since he'd loved his wife thoroughly—without her heart and mind consumed with worry for others? In two steps, he captured her again, drawing her close. She giggled, thrilling him. Had she any idea how much he loved her? He lowered his lips to hers—

"What should we do for Nathanael and Keilah's wedding?" she asked just before their lips met.

He dropped his head on her shoulder, defeated.

"What's wrong?"

Annoyed, he released her, turning away before she saw the crimson flame creeping into his neck and cheeks. "I have other things on my mind right now. I don't want to talk about a wedding."

Silence.

"You think Keilah shouldn't have a wedding since she's been married before, don't you?"

The accusation stung, and he whirled on her, instantly defensive. "It has nothing to do with Keilah's previous marriage. Maybe it's because you found her lying in a brothel. Did you consider how *that* reputation would affect the second priest of Yahweh?"

"Surely Keilah's blameless poverty is more acceptable than a Baal priestess. The high priest of Yahweh sleeps with an idolater every night. What has that done to *your* reputation?" Her eyes blazed, and she began trembling head to toe.

He released a weary sigh. How had an innocent kiss spiraled into a verbal battle? "Jehosheba," he said gently, offering his hand. She recoiled. Was that fear again on her face? "Jehosheba!" His command sent her fleeing—headlong into Nathanael and Zabad, who were ambling in.

As Sheba shoved past them, all three men jumped at the sound of a slamming door in the next chamber. Nathanael was the first to venture a word. "Would you like us to come back later?"

Jehoiada wiped his face slowly. Stared at the ceiling. Counted to ten. "No. I'm learning to give Yahweh time to work with her alone before I try again. Please, sit down." He directed them to the small table. They seemed especially cooperative at the moment—which was good. "This may sound odd, but extend your arms straight out, from north wall to south wall." Puzzled, both men did as they were asked, and Jehoiada measured the empty space between Zabad's fingertips and the north wall. "Less than a cubit on either side."

Nathanael fidgeted, a smile lurking. "I think we all agree that our chambers are small. If Zabad or I were to marry, we'd need more space." Hope tinged his tone.

"I'm not getting married." The horror in Zabad's voice lightened the mood, and Jehoiada clapped his shoulder, offering a little brotherly encouragement.

"I thought I noticed a longing look pass between you and the midwife Gadara. Are you sure—"

Nathanael burst out laughing, and Zabad nearly drew his sword on the high priest. "That's not funny!"

Jehoiada chuckled, calming both men with upraised palms. "I'm simply saying we need more living space." And he stopped there, offering no explanation or reason.

Their silent waiting grew awkward. Zabad finally leaned forward, studying the high priest like a map. "The chambers have always been this size. Why change now? You hate change."

Nathanael grinned. "Is someone *else* getting married?"

Jehoiada ignored him. "Zabad, we need to renovate the chambers in the northern wall of the outer court. All five chambers on the west side of the Sur Gate will become my home, connected by adjoining doors with a single public entrance. The same configuration on the east side of the wall will be designated for the second priest." Jehoiada held Zabad's gaze, feeling Nathanael's heated stare. The second priest didn't like being ignored.

"Those chambers haven't been used in years—not since our workforce was depleted after King Jehoshaphat's death. We've moved all the on-site priests to inner-court chambers because none of the priests have families with children." His eyes nearly popped from his head. "Is there something you and Sheba aren't telling—"

Jehoiada's heart tore in two. "No, Zabad. No."

His gatekeeper's neck instantly grew crimson. "I'm sorry, Jehoiada. Truly. Please forgive—"

"I want a tunnel dug under those chambers, Zabad. One like the secret tunnel that already exists—under the Ark."

"Under the Ark!"

Zabad's enthusiasm coaxed a grin from Nathanael, and he

finally rejoined the conversation. "I think it's time you told our chief gatekeeper about Obadiah's secret quarry and your plan for escape if Athaliah attacks the Temple."

Jehoiada reviewed the history of the quarry from the night he discovered it with King Jehoram to the moment he found the tunnel entrance in the Most Holy Place. Then he asked his Kohathite gatekeeper, "You would have been a mere boy when King Jehoshaphat built the expansion of the outer court, but do you remember the name of the Kohathite engineer who supervised the project?"

Zabad's grin foreshadowed Yahweh's hand at work. "His name was Jonadab, and his son, Jehozabad, is my best friend. Our imas were foreign women—Jehozabad's ima Moabite and mine Ammonite—making us outcasts among the children in our clan. We grew up having to prove ourselves, and Jehozabad helped his abba lay every piece of limestone in the Temple's outer court."

Jehoiada clapped his hand on Zabad's shoulder. "If he's half as good a man as you are, he'll be twice the man of most."

Nathanael had grown quiet, distracted again, as Jehoiada laid the groundwork for his news. "It's important that the tunnel is directly under those new chambers by the Sur Gate. I fear we'll have little warning if Athaliah attacks the Temple compound." Nathanael nodded absently, fidgeting with the thread on his sleeve.

Zabad's brow furrowed. A reasonable man with logical concerns, he asked, "Since you're the only one who's married, why not build the tunnel under our current chambers?"

"Two reasons," Jehoiada said, leaning back, resting his hands behind his head. "Digging the tunnel near the outer Temple wall will place our escape route closer to the *city* wall and quicken our flight from Jerusalem if the Temple falls under attack." He glanced at Nathanael. Still no response. "Secondly, someone else at this table will likely be married by then. In fact, that someone should run now to my bedchamber and ask his waiting bride."

"Keilah is—I mean, she's not—" Nathanael half knelt, half stood, paralyzed, it seemed.

"Go!" Jehoiada said, and Zabad laughed at their friend's hurried retreat.

The door of the neighboring chamber slammed amid squeals, and both Zabad and Jehoiada laughed at the happy sounds.

"So, when will this wedding take place?" Zabad asked.

Jehoiada's heart twisted as he remembered the hurt to be healed with his wife. "I'm not sure. That's part of a discussion I need to have with Jehosheba. Why don't you go plan a tunnel, and I'll plan a wedding."

Zabad stood to leave and nearly plowed into Jehosheba, who stood in the doorway. He apologized on his way out, and she closed the door behind him.

Alone again. The sight of her stole Jehoiada's breath. She'd changed into a simple blue robe with a gold-braided belt cinched at her waist, her face freshly washed and her hair neatly tucked under her headpiece. Had she tucked away her emotions too—as she so often did when she felt threatened? *Yahweh, make me a mirror of Your love—giving, serving, honoring my wife, offering her peace and safety unconditionally.*

"Did I hear Zabad mention the tunnel?" Her voice was small, her hands fidgeting.

"May I explain the tunnel after I apologize for my outburst?"

"It was my fault. I was defensive about Keilah's past and didn't give you a chance to explain."

He offered his hand but didn't move toward her. The fear he'd seen earlier was more than he could bear.

Timid but obedient, she took four steps toward him, accepting his grasp but maintaining her distance. No more trembling and no tears. Was it progress or hidden emotions?

Jehoiada rubbed his thumb across her hand. "It was my fault too. I had hoped for a few intimate moments alone—without words."

She looked up then, startled. "Oh, Jehoiada, I didn't realize you wanted . . ."

"I know." He brushed her cheek. "I miss my wife, but my frustration poured out on the object of my desire." Her features softened, and he pushed off her headpiece, revealing the silky, ebony tresses he adored. "I don't sleep with an idolater or a priestess, Jehosheba. You're Yahweh's beloved and my most precious treasure. I will remind you of that every day we're together, but you must also believe it. Let it soak into your wounded soul."

She buried her face in his chest, shaking her head. "Why? Why did Yahweh save me from Baal? Will I ever feel worthy of Him, of you?"

"We can never be worthy of Yahweh, my love, nor can we fully know His mind or the answers to our whys." He gathered handfuls of her hair, drinking in her liquid-brown eyes. "But by our covenant of marriage, an oath taken in His presence, we are worthy of each other. Don't you think I wonder how a beautiful young princess could love an old goat like me?"

He smiled, trying to soften the truth of his own insecurities, but she captured his face in her hands. "No, don't tease me. You're the best man I've ever known, and I love you more than life." She kissed him then, fully, passionately, as they'd known before the days of commotion and crowds and confusion in their chamber. "I'm sure Nathanael will talk to Keilah for a while," she whispered, nodding toward the bedchamber only steps away.

"Don't you want to plan Keilah's wedding?"

"Yes," she said, sending his heart to his toes. Then she brushed his cheek with a kiss and whispered, "Later."

The glowing brazier crackled and popped, sending the scent of grapevine ash into the air, while the three women sat in Sheba's chamber, enjoying their spinning. A light snow had crowned Jerusalem with added splendor, the rare occurrence a lively topic for three friends who had wrung out every drop of chatter about Keilah's wedding day four Sabbaths past.

"I think I was fourteen the last time it snowed in Jerusalem." Sheba whirled her spindle, drafting the wool mindlessly now. All three of them had spun almost enough yarn to weave their first cloth. "I remember trying to catch some of the flakes outside my palace window, and one of the palace guards rushed in with Ima Thaliah screaming, 'Get away from there! You'll fall and kill yourself!'"

Zibiah and Keilah laughed, but the memory rubbed at a raw place in her heart. "Ima Thaliah locked me in a storage closet for three days after that." The laughter died, and Sheba stared into her friends' shocked faces. In truth, she was equally surprised she'd confided anything about her childhood.

Zibiah's pallor matched the limestone walls. "I had no idea, Sheba. I'm sorry."

Keilah, too, appeared ready to lose her morning meal, and Sheba regretted her transparency. "Why dwell on the past? It's not important. I'm sure I'm a stronger person because of Ima's discipline." She noted the unconvinced glance between her friends and felt her stomach roll. "I think I need some mint tea." The spinning could wait.

Before she'd placed the water over the fire, both Zibiah and Keilah had set aside their work as well. "Maybe some mint tea would settle my stomach," Keilah mentioned as she placed her half-full spindle in her shoulder bag.

"Oh no." Zibiah pressed her hand against her forehead. "Are we getting sick? My stomach is upset too." She dropped her hand to her side like a pouting child. "This is my week with Hazi. I *can't* be sick."

"Well, Jehoiada said some of the priests from the southern clans have sent word of a stomach—"

"Ladies!" Keilah shouted, her mouth agape. "Is your red moon late in coming?"

Sheba watched Zibiah do a quick and silent count and then turn to Keilah with joy. The two grabbed each other, giggling and hugging, adding up the weeks since Keilah's wedding and the last time Hazi visited Zibiah's chamber. It seemed to fit. Keilah and Zibiah were with child.

Sheba couldn't breathe. "I have to get some air." She ran out the door into the cold, forgetting her wrap. How could she be pregnant? Jehoiada couldn't have children. He and Anna had tried for years. Sheba didn't even pay attention to the dates of her bleeding because they didn't matter.

Panic welled inside her. "Yahweh, I can't be pregnant. Please." It was a whisper, but the snow amplified the sound, making her words seem all the more horrific. What kind of woman prayed that? *You're Athaliah's daughter, the kind of woman who will lock her child in a closet.* Sheba covered her ears, blocking out the silent voices in her head. "No," she said through tears.

"Jehosheba?" Jehoiada's warm embrace captured her. "What are you doing out here? You'll freeze." He lifted her into his arms like a child, and when he saw her tears, he curled her into his broad chest—so close she could hear his heartbeat.

Somehow he opened the door while still holding her. She heard Zibiah and Keilah gasp but knew they'd understand her need to be alone with Jehoiada. True friends didn't always need an explanation right away. "Come back tomorrow," he was saying to them, and she heard the click of the door. And then silence.

He lowered her to the goatskin rug by the brazier and removed his winter wrap. "I see you have water on to boil. Were you preparing tea?"

She nodded, staring into the brazier. "Mint."

He prepared the tea, a cup for each of them, handed one to her, and sat beside her on the rug. "Are you ready to talk?"

How should she begin? How could she tell him that the one gift he'd yearned for his whole life had finally been given—but she was too afraid to be happy about it?

"Zibiah and Keilah seemed happy when they left. Did they hurt you in some way that you don't want them to know?"

Good guess, but no. He was so wise, so patient. Perhaps he could be a good enough parent for them both.

"I'm pregnant." The words toppled out before she planned how to say them.

Jehoiada looked as if he'd stopped breathing. Completely still.

"Did you hear me?"

He blinked once. Then again. Finally, he breathed deeply and studied his tea. "Are you sure?"

It wasn't exactly the response she'd anticipated. "When women spend as much time together as Zibiah, Keilah, and I, their cycles tend to align. All three of us were feeling nauseous this morning and realized we were two Sabbaths beyond our due time."

He took a sip of tea. "So, you're all three with child?"

Sheba noted his hand shaking as he lowered the cup, and a tiny spark of something eternal lit deep within. "Isn't it amazing that we're all three pregnant at once?"

Gently he reached for her hand but kept his gaze on the tea. "Will you tell me why I found you outside crying while the others were inside rejoicing?"

She tried to pull away, shame searing her cheeks. But he lifted her hand and kissed her palm, holding her gaze. "I love you, Jehosheba, and you have the heart to love a dozen children. Now, tell me why you were crying."

His commanding voice broached no argument, but his tenderness laid bare her deepest shame. *How did you know?* she wanted to scream. Instead, she let the balm of his love soothe the old wounds this news had opened. "I'm afraid I'll ruin your child." Tears strangled her, and she added on a sob, "As I've been ruined."

He gathered her into his arms, cradling her, rocking her, cherishing her. Oh, how she loved this man.

When her tears were spent, he looked into her eyes. "You are no more ruined than I am by this life, my love. I am broken in ways you must help me fix, and I'll help you when you are in need." He captured her chin and whispered, "And together we'll teach our child of Yahweh." He looked almost giddy, his eyes suddenly growing wide as if he'd been struck by some grand new thought. "And it's a good thing our new living chambers are almost finished, because who knows how many children the Lord will give us!"

36

Jehoram was thirty-two years old when he became king,
and he reigned in Jerusalem eight years. He passed away,
to no one's regret, and was buried in the City of David,
but not in the tombs of the kings.

The cases of central court should have been decided earlier
in the day, but Hazi's disruptions delayed proceedings all
afternoon. Jehoiada pounded the scepter of Solomon on
the platform again, resorting to the only nonverbal hush tactic
he knew to quiet the raucous prince, his disrespectful noblemen,
and the spoiled cousins. When their drunken laughter drowned
out the herald's announcements, Jehoiada leapt to his feet, ready
to jerk a knot in someone's tail, as his abba used to say when
Jehoiada was a child in need of a spanking. Hazi was too old
and well protected for physical violence, but the Carite guards
were about to earn their mercenary wages.

"Jehoiada, don't." Zabad blocked his path, moving left and
right with each step as if they were maidens in a dance.

"As the Lord lives, Zabad, if you don't get out of my way, I'll
take your sword and cut you off at the knees!"

"There's a young messenger approaching who resembles Obadiah's aide." Zabad nodded to the back of the sparse crowd.

Jehoiada recognized the lad and motioned him forward. The boy hesitated, his big eyes as round as camel hooves.

"You've scared him to death," Zabad whispered. "Smile a little."

Considering the dispersing crowd and Hazi's drunken inability to form a sentence, Jehoiada conceded the day's end and offered his kindest smile to the boy. "You there. Are you waiting to see me?"

The approximate ten-year-old with deep-set brown eyes seemed to regain a spark of confidence, propelling him against the flow of the exiting crowd. "Yes, my lord. Master Obadiah requests your presence immediately to speak of urgent matters."

"Well, lead us to him then."

"Yes, my lord. Follow me." The boy turned and cleared a path through the crowd like a warm knife through butter. "Make way. Make way for Yahweh's high priest, please."

Jehoiada raised his eyebrows at Zabad, both men duly impressed at the fine young man in Obadiah's employ. They exited the palace and followed him south through the city streets.

"Where exactly does Obadiah live?" Jehoiada asked. Strange, but he had never considered the old nobleman living anywhere except his palace chamber.

"Master Obadiah's home is in the City of David, though he maintains a chamber on palace grounds for late nights."

"And how long have you served Obadiah?"

"I was born in his house. My abba serves as Master Obadiah's stableman."

As they passed through the marketplace, Zabad pointed out the direction of the brothel where they had found Gadara and Keilah a mere eight new moons ago.

Isn't it amazing how life can change so thoroughly in such a short time? Jehoiada thought. Gadara now visited Sheba and Keilah regularly in their new living chambers, checking on their pregnancies and even learning how to spin. Zibiah's child would, of course, be delivered by the palace midwife, but Hazi had given permission for both Sheba and Keilah to attend the birth.

Jehoiada inhaled deeply, feeling the warm, dry air bake him

inside and out. Winter had been cold, the spring cool and damp, but summer descended like a rough camel-hair robe, the skies stingy with rain even before the early grapes ripened. Athaliah's scrolls came to Sheba less often—only two since the last new moon—and seldom held any news they hadn't heard through merchants' gossip or palace rumor.

"Here we are." The boy opened a vine-covered gate and led Jehoiada and Zabad through a terraced garden to a lovely estate overlooking the Kidron Valley. He then stopped, bowed, and extended his hand toward an arched doorway, where a bundle of blankets lay on a low-lying couch.

The bundle jostled—and then coughed. Jehoiada's blood ran cold. "Obadiah?" He knelt beside the frail frame of his oldest friend. "How long have you been ill? I had no idea." Palace gossip said the nobleman had been sent on a journey for the queen.

The boy reached for Zabad's hand, leading him past the archway toward another chamber. The little chatterbox had already begun explaining to the chief gatekeeper all he knew of Obadiah's household guards and security measures.

"That's quite a steward you have there, my friend."

The nobleman tried to smile but used his strength to grip Jehoiada's hand instead. "I won't be able to guide you through the quarry, you know." He swallowed with effort, and Jehoiada was tempted to spout platitudes about a sure recovery and many more years ahead. But what was the point? Obadiah was dying.

"Tell me what to do."

"Focus on preserving David's descendants on Judah's throne. Israel is lost to Jezebel, and Judah languishes in her shadow—for now. You must protect the future at all costs."

Jehoiada squeezed his friend's hand, tried to smile. "You said you'd never give up on Jehoram. Well, I'm not giving up on Hazi."

An almost imperceivable nod. "Yahweh's wrath is a terrible thing, Jehoiada, but He is just." A coughing fit interrupted. After a sip of watered wine, Obadiah settled back onto his couch. "I believe Athaliah knew of the Philistine raid before it happened—perhaps even aided the enemy."

"No! Even Athaliah wouldn't have her own sons slaughtered."

"She had no idea her sons were going to be here, remember? Jehoram summoned them on the morning Athaliah took Hazi and Sheba to Jezreel."

Jehoiada's stomach rolled. Was that why she tortured Jehoram so ruthlessly? "Why do you believe she knew of the raid?"

"Remember the gold that was supposedly stolen from the palace?"

Jehoiada nodded, the image of Hazi's golden wine goblet coming to mind.

"When I annexed the small farms to the royal treasury, I noted large revenues of gold and silver with no explanation of their source. The specific items listed were suspiciously familiar. They returned to the treasury slowly, when foreign trade increased and Hazi began receiving gifts from visiting ambassadors. Hazi wouldn't recognize the pieces because he wasn't involved in politics before Jehoram's illness. And no one would dare accuse Athaliah because every official on Hazi's counsel is there at the queen's pleasure. Even the sons of King Jehoram's dead brothers sold their souls to Athaliah for a seat at Hazi's side when Jehoram finally dies."

Jehoiada squeezed the bridge of his nose, wishing, dreaming, praying that Hazi would find his spine and embrace the faith of his saba Jehoshaphat.

"Equally troubling is Mattan's increasing power among the people. I suppose you've heard of his reported 'miracles.'"

Jehoiada nodded and then teased, "How do you discover these things while you're shivering on your sickbed?"

The question coaxed a weak grin from the nobleman. "Athaliah isn't the only one with spies." But his smile died, and he seemed stricken by a thought. "Jehoiada, I've discovered which of your Temple servants has been giving information to the queen."

Jehoiada's heart skipped a beat. Of course he wanted to know—needed to know—but dreaded the betrayal. "Who?"

"I'm sorry, my friend. It's Eliab."

The name stole his breath. Apart from Nathanael and Zabad, Eliab was the man Jehoiada trusted most. "Are you sure?"

"I'm afraid so. He was evidently disappointed not to be chosen high priest, and then felt overburdened to perform all your duties when Jehosheba needed your comfort."

Jehoiada's hurt roiled into fury, boiling his blood, making him tremble. "He'll never perform my duties—or any priest's duty—again."

Obadiah's hand squeezed his arm with surprising strength. "Your anger, my friend, has become an idol every bit as real as Asherah or Baal. You must choose to destroy it before it destroys you."

Gasping, Jehoiada jerked away. "How dare you? I am Yahweh's high priest, and I have made atonement for my sin and the sin of this nation—"

"And yet you willfully choose anger over reason, anger over prayer, anger over forgiveness—as Hazi chooses his ima's advice over yours, and Athaliah chooses Jezebel's gods over Yahweh."

Jehoiada was frozen, speechless, at the conviction of his friend's words. Could Obadiah be right? Could an idol be more than wood or clay?

Seeming spent, Obadiah closed his eyes and rested his head on his pillow. "We're too old to dance around the truth, Jehoiada. You're my dearest friend, and Yahweh needs your undivided heart."

"My lords!" Zabad ran through the archway, breathless, the young boy at his heels. "A palace messenger arrived with this scroll for Yahweh's high priest. He said it was urgent."

Jehoiada reached for the missive, noting Athaliah's wax seal, not Hazi's. Dread coiled inside, tightening as he broke the seal and unfurled the parchment.

My husband is dead. Take him, or he'll burn in Hinnom.

Jehoiada crushed the parchment, wishing it were Athaliah's neck. *Your anger has become an idol . . . Destroy it before it destroys you.* How could such evil reside in one human being? And how could he not react in anger? If not anger, then what?

Obadiah's words replayed in his mind: *You choose anger*

over reason, anger over prayer, anger over forgiveness. Maybe he could start with reason and work his way up to prayer. Forgiveness was beyond imagination at this point.

Jehoiada squinted up at Zabad, shielding his eyes from the late afternoon sun. "Is the messenger waiting for a response?"

"No. He delivered the scroll and ran." Eyebrows raised, Zabad left his curiosity unspoken.

Jehoiada squeezed Obadiah's shoulder and kissed his cheek as he stood. "Thank you for speaking hard truths to me, friend. Now I must share one with you." Glancing at Zabad and the boy, Jehoiada kept his voice low. "King Jehoram is dead. If I don't retrieve him immediately, the queen has threatened to throw his body into the Valley of Hinnom with the burning trash and dung."

"Go, Jehoiada." Obadiah's voice was breathy, like wind through a reed pipe. "Jehosheba will need you now."

Sheba stood alone in her abba Jehoram's bedchamber, gazing down at a blanket-covered body. She couldn't lift the blanket. The last time she'd seen Abba Jehoram, he was writhing in pain, barely able to speak, breathe, or concentrate—but he was alive. The shell of flesh under that blanket was so small. It couldn't be Abba, could it?

Why had Ima Thaliah summoned her to the palace and then refused to see her? On a whim, Sheba had enlisted palace guards to escort her to Abba's chamber, never expecting his body to still be here. The physician was packing his last basket of belongings, waiting to be escorted to his new home—in Tyre. He'd explained Abba's death in gruesome detail, something about his intestines falling out.

Oh, Yahweh, why didn't Abba turn away from Ima's lies? Why didn't he listen to his faithful abba Jehoshaphat? Tears streamed down her face as questions poured from her heart. And the most troubling of all—why was Hazi still following Ima Thaliah's and Mattan's advice rather than heeding Jehoiada's warnings? He refused to leave the Throne Hall and grieve with

Sheba, and he kept Zibiah locked in her chamber, denying Sheba a comforting visit with her friend.

So Sheba sat in King Jehoram's chamber alone. With a corpse that couldn't be her abba. Could it?

Gathering her courage, she reached for the corner of the blanket—

"You there!" a deep, male voice cried at the same time the chamber door banged open, and Sheba thought *her* intestines might fall out. "What are you doing here? We need to move the body."

She gasped and then steadied her breath, mustering her most commanding voice. "Where are you taking my abba?"

The men—whom she now recognized as city watchmen—drew closer, studying her in the dim light. One offered a cursory bow and slapped the other, goading due respect. "I'm sorry, Princess Jehosheba. We didn't recognize you. We have orders from Prince Hazi—I mean, *King* Hazi—to remove the body and clear the chamber. This room is to be used for storage of bedding and palace furnishings."

A storage chamber? Taming her instant fury, she would save her diatribe for Hazi. The watchmen still hadn't answered her question. "Perhaps I was unclear the first time I asked." Remembering Ima Thaliah's instruction on intimidating servants, she enunciated each word concisely. "Where. Are. You. Taking. My. Abba?"

The watchmen exchanged a worried glance. "To Hinnom?"

It was a question, not a statement, but it knocked Jehosheba onto her stool. "Leave me," she said, breathless. When they lingered, she screamed, "Leave me!" She heard their shuffling feet and buried her face in her hands.

Had Ima Thaliah always been utterly heartless? How could Hazi allow her to treat Abba this way—before *and* after death? If Sheba left the body unguarded to seek Jehoiada's help, would she return too late? She couldn't bear the thought of his body burning in the Valley of Hinnom.

Yahweh! Help me! What do I do?

The guards had left the door cracked open in their hurried

departure, allowing sounds from a Throne Hall assembly to drift up the grand stairway. A rhythmic chant drew Sheba out the door, down the wide stairway, and toward the courtroom— a place usually reserved for men, and never appropriate for a woman large with child as Sheba was now. Still, the chanting drew her, the words becoming clear.

"Bless our new King Hazi! Bless our new King Hazi! Bless our new King—"

The cheering faded as Sheba strode toward Hazi's throne, leaving scandalous gasps and whispered judgments in her wake.

"She shouldn't show herself in public like that," one old commoner grumbled.

Sheba stopped and met the old man's gaze. "Why shouldn't the daughter of a dead king beg for her abba's last shred of dignity?"

The Throne Hall fell utterly silent, and Jehoiada stepped into her path, Zabad at his side. What was he doing among this rabble? Distrust, betrayal, accusation—all silenced when he held out his hand to escort her to Hazi's throne.

Zabad followed them, and the three halted before the new king's elevated dais. Jehoiada bowed. "Your sister and I humbly ask that you allow us to bury King Jehoram in the City of David."

Sheba's heart nearly leapt from her chest. How had Jehoiada discovered Ima's plan to burn Abba's body? She realized Yahweh had already been at work.

"You've heard my advisors' counsel and the people's wishes, Jehoiada. My abba is refused the right of burial in King David's family tombs." Hazi's face was chiseled stone.

Sheba began to tremble with rage. How could he sit on *Abba's* throne so cold, so unfeeling? How dare he—

"And I will not challenge my king's command," Jehoiada replied calmly. "I simply ask that you allow me to take your abba's body, wrap it in spices, and lay it in the tomb of a dear friend, my lord. I will trouble you no further on the matter."

Sheba shot a confused glance at the priest beside her. Who was this man, so eloquent and calm when his fury and bluster were needed?

"Your request is granted, Jehoiada." Hazi nodded condescendingly and waved them away like pesky insects, leaning over to chat with a royal cousin.

Jehoiada gathered her under his wing, hurrying them up the aisle and out the double-cedar doors. "Come, my love, before your ima hears of your brother's decision and forces him to change his mind."

37

The people of Jerusalem made Ahaziah, Jehoram's young-
est son, king in his place. . . . He too followed the ways
of the house of Ahab, for his mother encouraged him to
act wickedly.

Seething, Sheba let Jehoiada lead her out of the Throne Hall
but stopped when they reached the grand stairway. "Who is
this *dear friend* whose tomb will house my abba's body?"
Jehoiada couldn't have looked more surprised if she'd slapped
him. He shuffled her to a quiet corner, away from Carite guards
and watchmen, who had already perked to their conversation.
"I've just come from Obadiah's estate in David's City. He loves
Jehoram, and I'm sure he'll willingly share his family tomb." He
paused, lifted an accusing eyebrow, and folded his arms across
his broad chest. "I know why *I* was in the Throne Hall, but why
were *you* there—with our child in your belly?"

"I was about to scream at my brother, but you didn't give
me the satisfaction." Hesitantly, she considered his eerie calm.
"What's wrong with you?" She stomped her foot. "Why aren't
you yelling?"

He gathered her into his arms, hiding her in his warmth and
strength. "Why aren't you crying?"

322

She gasped and pulled away, startled. "I didn't cry, did I?"

He chuckled and brushed her cheek. "Perhaps we're both proof that Yahweh still works miracles." He drew her close again, resting his head atop hers. "I'll tell you about my visit with Obadiah later, and you can tell me how you're feeling, but for now we must return to the Temple. I'll send several priests to your abba's chamber with spices and cloths to prepare his body for burial. From the reports I heard in the Throne Hall, it's probably best if you don't help with preparations."

She nodded, thankful for his sensitivity. "I'd like to stay and visit Zibiah. Hazi wouldn't let her come to me, but he didn't say I couldn't visit her chamber." Jehoiada gave her a doubtful look, but she pleaded, "She hasn't been able to meet with Keilah and me for over two moon cycles. Hazi is even more protective now that she's pregnant."

"All right, but I'll send Zabad when we're ready to move your abba's body to Obadiah's estate."

Jehoiada insisted on escorting Sheba to Zibiah's chamber. Zabad also appeared—he must have been waiting somewhere discreetly while they talked. At the top of the grand stairway, they faced Ima Thaliah's doors, where twice the usual contingent of Carites stood. Sheba hurried to the left, getting as far away from Ima as possible.

They arrived at Zibiah's double doors at the opposite end of the women's hall, also doubly guarded on this sad day. Sheba pecked a kiss on her husband's cheek and offered a smile to Zabad. "Thank you both for taking such good care of me." The two hurried away, shoulders weighed down with the cares of a nation. *Yahweh, bless them.*

She returned her gaze to the Carites at Zibiah's chamber, raised an eyebrow, and they opened to her. Perhaps no one would trouble a grieving princess today.

"Sheba!" Zibiah dropped her spindle and ran with open arms. Their tummies bumped before they could manage a hug. "I'm sorry about your abba."

They lingered in the long-overdue embrace, soaking in the strength of a true and abiding friendship. "I'm sorry Hazi isn't the man we'd hoped he could be," Sheba whispered, making sure none of Zibiah's eunuchs overheard.

Aching backs forced the hug's end long before their hearts were ready. "Come, sit here on the balcony. There's a breeze." Zibiah shoved aside the spindle and knotted yarn she'd been working.

"Oh no! Should we try to untangle it?"

Zibiah waved away the concern. "It's fine. I've got cubits of yarn. It's all I do these days." She smiled, the corners of her lips quivering. "So tell me. How's Keilah? And Gadara? Do you like your new living quarters?"

Thankful not to talk about Abba Jehoram, Sheba spoke of happier things. "Keilah has a cute, round belly twice our size! Of course, I'd never tell her that. She eats like a bird, so it's not her weight."

"Do you think she'll have a big baby? Maybe a big, strapping boy?" Zibiah's eyes misted immediately. "Hazi has six sons now. Six sons and three daughters." She began rocking, trying to quell her tears, but finally turned away, burying her face in her hands.

"Zibiah, what is it?"

"I think it would be best for you to go, Sheba. I'm thankful you came, truly, but . . ." She shook her head, unable—or unwilling—to finish.

Sheba studied her friend more closely. Dark circles shadowed wary eyes, and she trembled from head to toe. Two eunuchs lingered on either side of the doorway, failing any attempt at subtle spying. Four more shuffled pillows and dusted trinkets. Why eunuchs, rather than serving maids?

Seeing the chamber with fresh eyes, Sheba noted a tray with only one goblet and a plate of food—both untouched. The meal resembled prison rations rather than princess fare. "How long since Hazi has visited you, Zibiah?"

"Not long, really." Her shaky smile betrayed the lie.

"Out!" Sheba shouted at the eunuchs, startling poor Zibiah. "All of you, out now!"

The chief eunuch, branded with a god of Tyre, bowed repeatedly as he approached. "But my lady—"

"Would you like me to report your rebellion to Ima Thaliah or King Hazi?"

The eunuch backed away without further protest, herding the others out of the chamber.

Alone now, the two women fell into each other's arms, and Zibiah's nightmarish existence unfolded. "I'm a prisoner in this chamber. Athaliah's eunuchs never leave me alone—*never!* They feed me bread and watered wine. They relay terrible threats from the queen—awful plans if my child is a girl. My balcony is my only source of fresh air, and I don't remember the last time I saw Hazi." Hysteria was taking hold, her words erupting in despair.

"Zibiah, Zibiah, shh!" Sheba held her tightly, trying to soothe, for fear the guards would charge in at the sound of her wailing.

When Sheba stood to get the goblet of wine, Zibiah clutched at her robe. "Don't leave me!"

"I won't leave. I'm right here." Sheba returned to the couch and drew Zibiah close, singing a Levite psalm:

> Hallelu Yah.
> Hallelu Yah, O my soul.
>   I will praise Yahweh all my life;
> I will sing praise to my God as long as I live.
> Do not put your trust in princes,
>   in human beings, who cannot save.
> When their spirit departs, they return to the ground;
>   on that very day their plans come to nothing.
> Blessed are those whose help is the God of Jacob,
>   whose hope is in Yahweh their God.
> He is the Maker of heaven and earth,
>   the sea, and everything in them—
>   He remains faithful forever.
> He upholds the cause of the oppressed
>   and gives food to the hungry.
> Yahweh sets prisoners free . . .

Zibiah began humming the tune with her, peace seeping into their spirits. Repeating those opening lines, they sang together and watched the sun sink over the western ridge.

Sheba helped Zibiah stand and guided her to the bed. Hazi's wife was exhausted, but she clutched Sheba's hand. "You're not leaving, are you?"

"Zibiah, you know I must return to the Temple, but I'm going to talk with Hazi about—"

"Why don't you talk to Hazi now, Sheba?" Hazi had slipped into the chamber and was closing the door.

Zibiah's grip tightened on Sheba's hand, terror in her eyes. "Sheba, don't."

"I'm going to ask why your wife is cooped up like a bird in a cage, Brother." Sheba untangled herself from Zibiah's clutches, leaving Hazi's wife cowering on her bed.

Hazi's smug air crumbled. "Zibiah, my love! By the gods, what's happened?" Dashing past Sheba, Hazi cradled his wife in a tender embrace, burying his face in her neck. His whispered words were undecipherable, the tender moment too intimate for anyone to observe. Was she telling him of the cruelty she'd suffered, or did he know Ima Thaliah well enough to assume the worst?

One glimpse, and Sheba knew—Hazi had no idea Zibiah had suffered so. Only two people were capable of this brutality—both were queens of destiny.

Fire in her veins propelled her out the door, down the women's hall, and straight to Ima Thaliah's chamber. Six Carites stood guard, but only one blocked her entry. "I'm sorry, Princess Jehosheba. The Gevirah of Judah has asked not to be disturbed."

The Gevirah. No longer the queen, she officially became mother of the reigning king today. She'd been well trained for the role.

"You *will* disturb her, and I will see her now."

The Carite paused only a heartbeat before tapping his spearhead on the door and disappearing behind it. Moments later, the door opened from within. No invitation. No welcome. It was enough.

Steadying her breathing, Sheba straightened her spine and rolled back her shoulders. She hadn't seen Ima Thaliah since she'd humiliated and crushed Hazi over a year ago. If Sheba was to match wits with Ima, she'd need to employ every strategy of the queens of destiny—beginning now. She lifted a condescending brow, waiting for a guard to announce her presence.

Two guards fumbled their spears in a hurried bow, and finally, the highest-ranking officer opened the door wide. "Princess Sheba to see Gevirah Athaliah." He bowed, let Sheba pass, and closed the doors behind her.

Sheba's knees shook beneath her simple blue robe. Ima would undoubtedly be offended. *I should have worn my festival robe.* But would it have mattered? Ima Thaliah always found something to criticize. In every written message, she included some reproach that Jehoiada encouraged his wife to ignore.

"Sheba?"

The chamber was dark except for a few lamps in the wall niches. The Gevirah's couch was empty. *She must be in her bedchamber.* Walking toward the dividing curtain, Sheba had a harrowing thought. What if Ima had been sleeping? But it was too early for bed . . .

"I'm in here. What are you doing?" The impatience in Thaliah's voice was too fresh for recent slumber.

Suddenly rethinking her rash visit, Sheba felt the familiar panic begin to rise. What had she hoped to accomplish by subjecting herself to another round of Ima's face-to-face abuse?

Silently, Sheba maintained her steady pace, making the new Gevirah wait. When she arrived at the curtain, she yanked it back decisively, causing Ima to jump like a desert hare.

"Sheba! By the gods, girl. I forbid you to skulk like a bandit." Speechless, Sheba stared into the haunted, sunken eyes of a woman who looked ten years older than she remembered. Squirming under the scrutiny, Thaliah looked out her balcony. "So, Jehoiada plans to entomb Jehoram in the lower city?"

"Yes, no thanks to you and Hazi."

Her head snapped back, a wicked smile creasing her lips. "Has our queen of destiny found her spine?"

Sheba raised a single eyebrow, remaining silent. Neither of them flinched, but Sheba was determined that Ima blink first. She did. Sheba grinned and spotted a stool not far from the bed.

She placed it at her ima's right hand. "I haven't come to discuss Abba Jehoram. I'm here about Hazi."

"Ah, I assume it's really about your poor, sweet Zibiah."

Sheba dropped her genial tone. "You *assume* nothing. You know I've just come from her chamber. I'm sure the Carite told you when he announced me, and you've probably heard that I ordered your eunuchs out of Zibiah's chamber earlier this evening."

Delighted laughter preceded the Gevirah's applause. "Excellent, my dear. I feared my training had been wasted, but you do have a sharp mind, don't you?" Ima Thaliah's smile dimmed, and her facade fell away. Cold, black eyes nearly stole Sheba's courage.

Yahweh, please help me. The psalm she and Zibiah sang replayed in her mind, and the words soothed her as she listened to Ima Thaliah's plans.

"Hazi can't be distracted by Zibiah's Yahweh fascination. I've lost you to Jehoiada and his Temple—you never visit me. By the gods, I'm not going to lose Hazi to Zibiah." The tremor in her voice revealed uncharacteristic emotion.

"I didn't know you wanted me to visit you, Ima." Sheba's softly spoken words splashed like cold water in her ima's face.

Awkward and silent, Thaliah turned her head, examining everything in her chamber but Sheba's face. "I'm not Leviathan, you know."

Realizing Athaliah's emotional plea could be just a convincing ploy, Sheba answered with her only certainty. "My childhood is filled with wonderful memories, Ima."

Sheba watched the Gevirah's eyes grow distant, the door of her emotions slam shut. "I received word yesterday from Jizebaal that Elisha is using the wealth he's compiled from favorable Aramean prophecies to mount an army of Israelite prophets."

Sheba shook her head, knowing even as she heard the report that it was false. "We've heard nothing from the northern prophet for months. Elisha's wealth came before Hazael usurped the throne, and he used it to build the prophets' schools, not an army."

"Jizebaal says the three schools are where the army trains."

Sheba laughed. "Jizebaal knew a year ago that the schools had formed in Jericho, Bethel, and Gilgal, but I'm telling you—they're not forming an army. Elisha would have sent word if that were the case, because such a move would affect Yahweh worshipers in Judah."

"You seem quite knowledgeable, my girl." Respect shone from her eyes. "Did you know that General Jehu now sides with Gevirah Jizebaal, urging King Ram to seize the border town of Ramoth Gilead before Aram marches across Israel?"

"No, Ima. I only know the political news from Israel that you share in your scrolls."

"My ima Jizebaal has summoned Hazi and his loyal Carites to Ramoth Gilead to join Israel's troops in fighting the Arameans. Ramoth Gilead!" she screamed. "The place where my abba Ahab died!"

Sheba sat stone silent, back straight, gaze unflinching, the psalm of the Levites resounding in her mind.

Athaliah straightened her already perfect blanket. "You came in here to chastise *me* about pretty little pregnant Zibiah, but I'm worried about the lives of my brother, my son, and two nations." She leaned forward, daring Sheba to speak. "What was it you wanted to say?"

Without hesitating, Sheba matched her posture. "If Hazi is going to war in Israel, he cannot be distracted with worry about how you're treating Zibiah in Jerusalem." She stood, replaced the stool where she found it, and returned to issue her own stare. "Hazi loves Zibiah. I want to believe you once knew that feeling."

Sheba turned to go, but stopped when Athaliah grabbed her arm. Tears glistened on the Gevirah's bottom lashes. "I want you to visit me."

The request sent a wave of pity through Sheba. "All right, Ima. I'll come each week when Jehoiada judges at central court." Seeing her opportunity for bargaining, she pressed, "And I'll visit Zibiah after I see you." She raised an eyebrow, standing her ground.

"Agreed." Ima released her, and Sheba felt as if a camel load had been lifted from her shoulders. "One more thing, Daughter."

Sheba stopped at the curtain, turned, waited.

Athaliah's tears had disappeared, her kindness gone. "If your child is a girl, she's mine."

38

But I trust in you, LORD; I say, "You are my God." My times are in your hands; deliver me from the hands of my enemies, and from those who pursue me.

Jehoiada lumbered down the altar steps, accepted a linen cloth from Nathanael, and wiped away the blood from the evening worship. He started toward the basins as they walked. "Let's wash our hands and feet on the north side tonight. I want to be sure Micaiah feels comfortable assuming my duties when Jehosheba begins her travail."

Three new moons had passed since they'd peacefully entombed King Jehoram on Obadiah's estate—and then buried Obadiah a few days later. The old nobleman, true to his character, left all his holdings to his stableman and the young steward who had so impressed Jehoiada and Zabad.

Since so many priests had come into contact with the two dead bodies, Jehoiada waited until after the mandatory days of uncleanness to publicly reveal Eliab's treachery. Jehoiada announced Eliab's betrayal during the weekly change of duty and became so enraged Zabad had to restrain him. Obadiah's warning about his temper blared in his spirit, and the cleansing of the Day of Atonement was too quickly marred. Athaliah had breached their walls—not with guards and swords, but with the dark stain of sin and treachery that stripped human nature to its ugliest essence. Only time and Yahweh's healing could rebuild what had been lost among His servants.

Climbing the three stairs to the separate place, Jehoiada surveyed the priests gathered around the five basins. No Micaiah. Nathanael dipped his hands into the fourth basin, but Jehoiada moved to the last. He'd try to find Micaiah tomorrow morning and use tonight for friendly banter with others—as was often his practice to keep morale high. Worshipers were few and offerings continued to dwindle, which meant offerings for priests were low and spirits sagged.

"How's Lady Jehosheba feeling, my lord? My wife is due to deliver any day as well." A young priest beside him splashed his hands, initiating conversation. A welcome change.

Jehoiada's heart warmed to a man faithful to his duty even with a wife so close to term. "My Jehosheba is tired of this heat. How about your wife?"

"My Sarah must have her nap during midday, or she's more dangerous than a she-bear with cubs."

Jehoiada laughed, clapping a wet hand on his shoulder. "How long will it take you to get home when your Sarah begins her travail?"

"Not long. She's in Bethlehem with her parents while I serve at the Temple." He covered Jehoiada's hand on his shoulder, kindness radiating from his smile. "We're all in Yahweh's hands, are we not?"

Jehoiada nodded, barely able to speak past his emotion. "What is your name?"

"I am Zechariah."

"Thank you for reminding me of that, Zechariah." The young priest bowed, and Jehoiada cleared his throat, hurrying down the steps before he blubbered like a maiden.

How tender and sweet was a willing heart. *Zechariah—remembered by the Lord.* He had an uncle by that name. Perhaps Jehosheba would be agreeable to naming their son Zechariah.

Nathanael fell in step beside him, and they dragged their

weary bones into the holy chamber now used to robe and disrobe Jehoiada's golden garments. The two top priests could live in the outer court chambers, but the sacred garments could not.

"Close the door behind us, will you, Nathanael?"

"But we'll roast!"

Jehoiada slowly turned to face his second priest, having almost mastered his temper—on most days. Nathanael closed the door.

Jehoiada motioned Nathanael forward two steps to whisper, "I believe it's time we tell Keilah about the quarry entrance." Nathanael remained silent, eyes narrowed, waiting. He wasn't making this easy. The high priest pushed up one corner of a smile, trying to appear pleasant. "Perhaps then Keilah could convince Jehosheba to deliver our child in the quarry."

"Absolutely not!" Nathanael recoiled as if he'd stumbled on a serpent.

"What do you mean, 'absolutely not'? Why do you care where my wife gives birth? If Jehosheba has a daughter, Athaliah will send an army through our gates to steal *my* child!"

"Jehoiada, you're missing the point. We must trust our safety to Yah—"

"My family's safety *is* the point! Yahweh gave us wisdom and strength to build the tunnel under our living quarters. Why does Jehosheba refuse to use Yahweh's provision to deliver our child?"

Nathanael waited in silence, unmasking Jehoiada's soul. Since Obadiah's death, his second priest had become the friend who reflected truth like freshly polished brass.

Regaining control, Jehoiada squeezed the back of his neck. "Nathanael, I'm frightened. When Jehosheba told me three months ago that she'd confronted Athaliah, I wanted to strangle her—and then applaud her. Her courage is astounding."

"Yes, it is." Nathanael barely blinked. "But . . ."

"But she's come so far, and I don't want anything—or anyone—to hurt her again."

"Yahweh is her protector—not you. Yahweh protects His Temple, His people, His nation."

"I know all that! But why doesn't He *do something*?" In a

surge of anger, Jehoiada picked up a clay lamp and threw it against the wall. *Forgive me, Yahweh, but hear my complaint!* The prayer felt compulsory. At the moment, he wanted to be heard more than forgiven.

Nathanael kept his head bowed, focusing on the broken pieces of clay on the floor.

Jehoiada still panted with pent-up fury while the oil trickled down the wall—like teardrops raining down. Was Yahweh grieved by his sin? Obadiah had been grieved by King Jehoram's sin. Jehosheba was grieved for Hazi. Why was Jehoiada's first response always anger?

"We cannot win this battle in our own strength, Jehoiada." Nathanael's eyes glistened, his tone steady, firm. "The tunnels, the Temple guards, Jehosheba's relationship with Athaliah—none of it will save your child or the Temple. Only Yahweh can protect us."

Jehoiada set his jaw, working to walk the fine line of passion without crossing over to anger. "Worshipers flock to Mattan's temple, showering the Baal stone with silver and gold while performing all manner of indecent acts. And somehow Mattan convinced the people he prayed down a miraculous rain over that cursed stone—nowhere else, only on the stone in the courtyard."

Concern softened Nathanael's stare. "I hadn't heard about the latest 'miracle.'"

"Impressive in the middle of a drought, hmm? And how will Athaliah use Mattan's power and the people's support? I'll tell you!" he said when Nathanael drew a breath to answer. "If the queen comes for my daughter, we do not have the strength—in the Temple or through the people's support—to stop her. Athaliah and Mattan will take my daughter and put her to work scouring waste pots with parchment pieces of Moses's Law."

"Don't give up, Jehoiada."

"I'll *never* give up!" Rage burned in his belly, and he considered throwing another clay lamp. *Yahweh, forgive me, but . . .* His prayer echoed as if spoken in a cavern of his mind, mocking. *Forgive me, but . . . ?* When had qualifiers to forgiveness become acceptable practice? Anything after "Forgive me" nullified his confession—like bringing a crippled lamb to the altar. Nothing but perfect repentance would suffice.

"Jehoiada?" Nathanael placed a hand on his shoulder, concern etched on his features. "Are you all right? You're perspiring terribly. May I open the door?"

Jehoiada patted his friend's hand and then directed his gaze to the oil-stained wall. "My tantrum left oil streaks, much like my anger leaves tear streaks on the cheeks of those I love. I've harmed many with my sin—perhaps as many as Athaliah." He saw sympathy on the second priest's face and felt his anger ebbing as the truth soaked into his soul. "You were right when you said only Yahweh can protect us, Nathanael. And only Yahweh can help Jehosheba decide where she will deliver our child." He shook his head, emotion nearly closing his throat. "Why is it so difficult to trust our God when He's proven Himself faithful again and again?" He asked the question but expected no answer. Rather, he submitted himself to Nathanael's ministrations.

After removing Jehoiada's golden garments, the second priest anointed his burdened friend with a little mischief. "You should try the waste pot argument with Jehosheba. That one might get her to deliver in the quarry."

Jehosheba ladled a spoonful of lamb's broth into her mouth, checking the temperature. Still warm. But Jehoiada needed to arrive soon or their evening meal would grow cold. She'd wanted to share the meal alone in their chamber rather than with the community of priests as usual. Their small table was decorated with a flowering desert cactus placed in the center of the tiny blanket she'd made for their babe. Tonight, she would refuse—for the final time—Jehoiada's ridiculous request to make the quarry her birthing chamber.

How could she make him understand? When Gadara came for her weekly visits, she and Keilah talked about which of their chambers should be designated for birthing. Sheba, of course, would never disclose the existence of the quarry or the tunnel to the two women, but when describing the perfect setting, both Keilah and the midwife said the room should be relaxing, a place where she could focus on the loving friends around her.

They'd bemoaned poor Zibiah's plight. Hazi had refused to give Zibiah the title *queen*, but neither would he allow Gadara—a brothel midwife—to attend his favorite wife's birth. Sheba and Keilah had simply been grateful he'd allowed them to attend, even if they had to endure the old palace midwife. They'd secretly prayed they wouldn't be having their babies at the same time—Zibiah needed her friends.

"Jehosheba?" She jumped at Jehoiada's whisper in her ear, plopping the wooden spoon back in the broth. He chuckled, his warm hands lifting her by the elbows to stand. "I'm sorry I startled you. I called your name at the door, but your thoughts were elsewhere." He lifted an eyebrow, waiting.

"Should we eat the lamb broth before it gets cold?" Heat began rising in her cheeks.

"I don't mind cold soup. It's hot outside." He leaned down, pressed a gentle kiss at the bend of her neck. "Why don't you tell me what's bothering you?"

She'd almost completely mastered her emotions in Gevirah Thaliah's presence, playing the cunning lioness, a worthy opponent for Jezebel's daughter. Why couldn't she hide her emotions from Jehoiada? She swallowed the tightness in her throat, trying to maintain control—all of it extending the silence that confirmed her husband's instincts.

"Come, my love." He nudged her toward the cushioned couch. "You sit there, and I'll wait until you're ready to tell me." A lamb's wool pillow lay by the table. He grabbed it, placed it at her feet, and sat down. Waiting again.

Suddenly annoyed by his tenderness, she swiped at her eyes. "Why are you doing this?"

"Doing what?" His grin flung her past annoyance to fury.

"Do you think if you bow to my every wish, I'll agree to have this baby in the quarry? Well, I won't."

"Why don't we talk about that?"

"You mean, why don't *you* talk while *I* listen. You have all these reasonable arguments, but you haven't listened to any of my concerns, Jehoiada. Not one!"

His smile disappeared, deep creases etching his brow. "I'm listening now, Jehosheba." And he was—intently—his eyes unveiling her deepest fears.

"What if we get down there and can't find our way out? No one knows the tunnels like Obadiah. You, Zabad, and Jehozabad have done some exploring, but what happens if your torches fail?" She paused, but he waited, drawing unrealized fears into the light. "What if Gevirah Thaliah attacks the Temple grounds during my travail, and no one comes to retrieve Gadara, Keilah, and me? Our child will die with us in a dark hole in the ground."

Jehoiada finally looked away, releasing a long sigh. "It seems neither of us is willing to trust Yahweh with our child, are we, Jehosheba?"

Her breath caught, the question stabbing her. Of course they trusted Yahweh. They lived three courtyards away from a madwoman intent on destroying them.

When he returned his gaze, his tone was as gentle as the hand on her cheek. "All right, my love. In which of our five rooms will Gadara set up the birthing chamber?" Where was his fury, the angry arguments she'd prepared for?

Sheba searched his eyes. Clear. Peaceful. She should have rejoiced. So why did she feel all the more like weeping? "And that's another reason the quarry would never do. We'd have to tell Gadara and Keilah about it. You've always said, 'The fewer people who know, the better.'"

"Yes, I've always said that, and Gadara would undoubtedly instruct me on a better way to build the tunnel." He chuckled and brushed her cheek.

"But Gadara wouldn't tell anyone, Jehoiada. She knows how to hold her tongue when she must."

"Where would *you* like to birth our child, beloved?"

What had come over him? *Neither of us is willing to trust Yahweh with our child.* The words dug into her heart like a plow into fresh soil. When had he realized their error? But he was right. If they couldn't trust Yahweh with their child's life before the child was born, how could they trust Him for protection after?

"Gadara resigned her responsibilities at the brothel today and moved in with Nathanael and Keilah so she could be close when either of us begins our travail. And then she can help us with the babies after they're born."

Jehoiada's expression darkened, but he recovered quickly with a grin. "I'll pray for Nathanael's patience."

She nudged his shoulder, chuckling at the ongoing feud between her husband and the sassy midwife. "Will you go to Nathanael's chamber and ask them all to come over here?"

Confused, he drew together his wiry gray brows.

"If I'm going to have a baby in the quarry, *you* must explain the reason to our friends."

The surprise on Jehoiada's face was worth the concession. He cradled her hand, turned it over, and kissed her palm, never taking his eyes off her. "Are you sure? Yahweh can keep you safe here or there. We can trust Him."

"We will trust Him in the quarry," she said, covering his lips with a gentle kiss.

39

*The LORD said to Moses, ". . . A woman who . . . gives birth
to a son will be ceremonially unclean for seven days. . . .
On the eighth day the boy is to be circumcised. Then the
woman must wait thirty-three days to be purified from
her bleeding. She must not touch anything sacred or go to
the sanctuary until the days of her purification are over."*

Jehosheba and Keilah supported Zibiah's back and shoulders as she sat on the birthing bricks. "Push, my lady!" the midwife shouted between Zibiah's knees. "I see her head!"

"I. Refuse. To. Have. A. Girl." Zibiah gritted her teeth.

"Keep pushing! Push harder!" the midwife commanded.

But Zibiah fell back into her friends' arms, soaked in perspiration, pale as goat's milk. "I can't. I've got to rest, Keilah. Tell her. Just for a moment."

Sheba watched with wide eyes, utterly silent. She'd never witnessed a birth and certainly wasn't qualified to arbitrate the decisions between Keilah and the midwife. Every part of her ached. If Keilah's baby or hers came within the next day or two, neither would have the strength to deliver after helping Zibiah with her two-day ordeal.

Keilah stroked their friend's forehead. "Your body will tell you when to push, Zibiah. You'll know—"

"I'm telling her to push!" the midwife groused. The old woman had started delivering palace babies before any of them were born—she'd told them so repeatedly.

"Let's give her a few moments." Sheba intervened—making another decision she felt unqualified to make.

Zibiah gripped her friends' hands, making the next decision without consultation. "I've got to puuuush!"

Together, Keilah and Sheba pressed her back and shoulders forward as Zibiah pushed with all her strength. A soft *whoosh*, and then a whimper-turned-squall announced a healthy baby. The three friends whimpered and giggled, shedding tears and sharing kisses.

"Another boy," the midwife mumbled, working salt and watered wine into the natural emollient that covered his body. "Queen Athaliah won't like this, not one bit." She washed the little one with warm water and then rubbed him with olive oil before wrapping him firmly from waist to neck with strips of swaddling cloth.

Sheba watched in awe, each detail a fascinating new discovery. "Why didn't you wrap the rest of him?"

As if on cue, Sheba's new nephew sprayed the midwife, who grabbed a small clay pot readied for the occasion. All four women burst into laughter, draining the tension between them as the baby gave his offering.

"You did a fine job helping your sister and friend." The midwife nodded a curt bow and stood, the compliment resounding like trumpets from the tough old bird. She halted at the door, her expression almost regretful. "I'll give you a moment alone before I send the king to take his son." And she was gone.

Panic stole Zibiah's smile and washed her cheeks white again. "What did she mean, 'take his son'? I thought if I had a boy, I kept him. Athaliah takes only the girls to her nurses and leaves the boys with their imas."

"Shh." Both women tried to calm her. "Hazi won't take him, Zibiah." Sheba tried to sound confident, but the midwife's announcement surprised her too. "I'll talk with him."

"He listens to you, Sheba. You have to convince him." Tears streamed down her face, and the baby's minimal protests became wails.

"Zibiah, my friend, you must calm down." Keilah took the crying babe, stood, and began bouncing with him, her own unborn child proving a handy shelf to support the bundle. "Yahweh makes these little ones sensitive to their ima's turmoil. He won't nurse while you're this upset."

Zibiah turned pleading eyes on Sheba.

What was she supposed to do? *She* was usually the one with runaway emotions. A quick assessment of Zibiah's discomfort made the first decision easy. "Come. We're taking you back to your chamber."

Keilah instructed them on wrapping Zibiah's abdomen tightly, creating a sort of sling that the two friends used to support the new ima as she walked to her chamber two doors down.

If Hazi finds the birthing chamber empty, perhaps his panic will soften his heart for my request. Sheba took charge of Zibiah's eunuchs, keeping each one too busy to slip a message to Hazi or Athaliah. "You there, clean sheets on the bed. And you, a cup of wild carrot-seed tea for Lady Zibiah." The others scrubbed and tinkered with projects she invented.

When Zibiah was tucked safely into bed, Sheba handed her the cup of tea. "Drink it all."

After one sip—"Ew! That's awful!"

Sheba laughed. "You have to drink it." Keilah nodded.

"Why? I've never even heard of it."

"It helps control your bleeding." Sheba hoped her friends wouldn't ask how she knew. The training from Baal's temple seemed to be of good use at odd times. Mattan forced all the priestesses to drink the tea on the morning after the Awakening Festival. The high priestess then took the girls who began with abdominal cramping to another temple. A shiver worked its way through her, and she was thankful she'd never been subjected to the festival, amazed once more at Yahweh's protection.

Sheba found a nice fluffy pillow and pulled it closer to the bed to rest. Keilah did the same and sat down with the baby in her lap—and began chewing her bottom lip.

Zibiah spotted it too. "All right, Keilah. What do you want to say—but you're afraid to say it?"

Releasing a long sigh, their quiet friend kept her eyes on the baby while she spoke. "Babies are born knowing how to suck, but some need help learning to latch onto their ima's breast. When my son was born, I was too weak to nurse him right away, so one of the experienced imas nursed him while I ate a meal and gathered my strength. Since your little one is still so fussy, would you mind if . . ." She looked up at Zibiah, almost apologetic.

"Oh, Keilah." Relief swept over Zibiah's face. "I think it's a wonderful idea. I was the youngest in my family, so I've never really cared for a baby. I have no idea . . ."

Keilah seemed relieved as well and began loosening her belt.

"Wait!" Sheba shouted. "You haven't had your baby yet. Do you have milk to nurse him?"

Keilah smiled. "Sheba, all three of us have the newborn cream of an ima's first milk. The regular milk comes later."

Gasping, Sheba said, "So I could nurse him too?"

"Hey!" Zibiah protested. "I'm next!"

The three giggled, and Sheba and Zibiah learned of Yahweh's miraculous plan of nourishing a babe.

"Does it hurt?" Sheba asked.

"A little, at first." Keilah stroked the baby's oily hair as he nursed, and Sheba noticed a tear fall. She placed a comforting hand on Keilah's arm. Sometimes she forgot that Keilah had had another life before Nathanael. They seemed so in love and excited about their new arrival, but watching Keilah now and witnessing the travail of Zibiah's birth, Sheba understood in a profound new way—the wounds of losing a child would never completely heal.

A soft rumble rose from the wool-stuffed mattress beside them. Zibiah had finally settled enough to sleep. Sheba winked at Keilah, feeling a sweet exhaustion seeping into her bones too. She ached to see Jehoiada, share this moment with the one she loved most. What would their baby look like? Would it be a girl? A boy?

The chamber door swung open, and Hazi appeared with Zev on his heels—panicked, as Sheba intended.

"Shh!" She tried to rise from her cushion quickly, but her cumbersome belly slowed her progress and tickled her brother's funny bone. Her humiliation was worthwhile if it softened him for the kill. She waddled into the hallway, inviting her brother and his Carite to follow.

Hazi hesitated when he glimpsed Keilah nursing his newborn son but held his tongue until they were in the hall. "Thank you, Sheba." His hug nearly suffocated her. Upon release, he held her at arm's length and fairly glowed. "I don't know how you did it, but thank you."

Sheba looked at her belly and then back at her brother. "I didn't have the baby. Your wife did."

He laughed hysterically and hugged her again, talking over the top of her head. "I don't know how you talked Zibiah into letting Keilah nurse our son, but I approve. I so approve! It's brilliant!"

Startled, she could only stare when he released her again. First at Zev and back at Hazi.

"What?" he asked. "Why aren't you celebrating with me?"

"Because I'm—" She stopped. *Careful, Sheba. Why would he want Keilah to nurse the baby? Think!* "Because . . . I'm . . . tired, Brother. Of course I'm pleased you approve of my plan." Her mind raced. If Ima Thaliah took the girl babies and Hazi took the princes, why would he be happy about a plan that left the boy in Zibiah's care without requiring her to nurse? What benefit . . . ? *More children! He wants her to bear more children right away!*

"Sheba, you look a bit pale. I believe you *are* tired. Would you like Zev to escort you back to—"

"Hazi, you realize that Zibiah *needs* to nurse the baby until her purification ceremony, don't you?" His face clouded, suspicion and disappointment candidates for the cause. "Yahweh's Law says for seven days she is unclean, and on the eighth day, your son must be circumcised." She lifted an eyebrow. "King Jehoshaphat's great-grandson *will* be circumcised, won't he?"

"I don't see any need for these archaic traditions when—"

Sheba clutched Hazi's fox-fur collar, drawing him close and keeping her voice low so the guards wouldn't hear. "Zibiah is to be untouched for forty days—seven days before the circumcision and thirty-three days after. During that time, she *must* be allowed to nurse your son, Hazi. She needs that time to be his ima. Please." She released his collar and straightened his robe, smiling as Ima Thaliah had taught her.

Hazi grabbed her arm, fingers digging into her flesh, and ground out his words against her ear. "My wife will do as *I* say, Sheba. She has to bear more sons quickly so she can secure the position of first wife—queen. It's the only way I can secure her power to defend herself against the other wives—defend herself against *Ima*."

Sheba jerked her arm away, rubbing the throbbing spots that would undoubtedly be bruises tomorrow. "I know you love her, Hazi, but this is not the way to protect her."

"It's the only way, and you know it."

Sheba squeezed her eyes shut. *Lord God, will this madness ever end? Give me wisdom.* She heard the newborn cry from Zibiah's chamber and watched Hazi's features soften. He did love her. "For now, Hazi, promise me that you'll let Zibiah nurse the boy during her forty days of purification. Give Keilah and me time to have our own babies, and then I'll talk to Keilah's husband about her nursing both the prince and her own babe." What was she saying? How could Keilah be Zibiah's nursemaid?

"Can a woman do that?" He looked as incredulous as Sheba felt.

"Of course," she said, hoping it was the truth. "Yahweh made women capable of miraculous things, Brother."

"You promised him what?" Jehoiada lay beside Jehosheba the next morning, propped up on one elbow, eyes wide. "How can a woman nourish two babies? Nathanael will never agree, and I don't blame him!" Crimson tinged his cheeks, restraint sifting his anger like winnowed wheat.

"Nathanael may not have a choice, Jehoiada. Hazi is king, after all." She sounded harsher than intended, but she'd hoped for more sleep before having this conversation. Zev had escorted her and Keilah home after the moon's zenith, and Jehoiada had been sound asleep. She must have slept through the morning service because she vaguely recalled trumpet blasts, and Jehoiada now lay beside her in his golden garments.

"You surely don't agree that Keilah should leave her husband and household to become a royal wet nurse."

"No, my love, I don't agree, but she wouldn't *leave* them. She'd be gone part of the day and return at night." Sheba's back had begun aching during Zibiah's labor and had grown worse through the night. She turned away from her husband, curled into a ball, and pointed to her lower spine. "Rub," she instructed.

Massaging gently, he continued his argument, undaunted. "Did you ask Keilah what she thought? Surely she has enough sense to know that one woman can't—"

Incessant pounding began at their chamber door, and Nathanael's voice accompanied it in an unusually high pitch. "My lord—Jehoiada—I need you to open this door now. Right now. It's very important that you open the door immediately."

Sheba bolted upright while Jehoiada leapt out of bed and ran to the outer chamber. Nathanael's incessant knocking and pleading seemed to aggravate Jehoiada's foul mood. "As surely as the Lord lives, Nathanael, if you don't stop knocking, I'm going to—"

Sheba heard the door creak open and then—silence. She jumped out of bed, throwing her robe around her shoulders. When she reached the outer chamber, she saw Gadara and Nathanael supporting Keilah between them. Jehoiada was as pale as his under-tunic.

"Is it time?" Sheba had barely spoken when a gush of water rushed from her body, wetting her feet. Shocked, horrified, she gaped at the four faces that undoubtedly mirrored her own.

"It's definitely time." Gadara laughed and startled both couples. Jehoiada frantically helped Sheba to one of the lamb's wool cushions. Gadara, still amused, shoved her fists to her hips and shook her head. "Well, Priest, you'll never use *that* cushion again."

"Gadara, please!" Jehoiada shouted. "If you don't have helpful instructions, keep silent!"

Sheba wasn't sure whether to laugh or cry at the feud her husband and midwife had begun at their introduction almost a year ago. As stubborn as two rams at one trough, neither Jehoiada nor Gadara were likely to relinquish command.

Gadara commandeered another lamb's wool cushion and positioned it and Keilah beside Sheba, while the men scooted away the table and rug that covered the tunnel opening.

Sheba squeezed Keilah's hand as the pain in her back grew suddenly more intense. Keilah breathed in slowly and blew out through pursed lips. Was Keilah teaching her to manage or having a birth pain of her own?

While Gadara gathered more strips of cloth, linens, wine, oil, and herbs, she instructed the men to bring twice the food. "We're going to have two babies tonight, by the looks of it." They'd been stockpiling supplies in the quarry for three days, and with each visit to the world below, Sheba's fears diminished—a little.

A knock silenced all but Jehoiada. "Yes?"

"It's Zabad. I have urgent business to discuss."

Jehoiada nodded to Nathanael, who opened the door, inviting Zabad and Jehozabad inside.

"I don't really have urgent business." The gatekeeper grinned. "I saw Keilah and Gadara come this way and wondered if you need me to escort them."

"No, Zabad, but thank you." Sheba relished the men's shocked faces. "Our husbands will escort us and assist the midwife."

"Jehosheba . . . I . . . we . . . but you . . . " Her high priest husband seemed unable to complete a thought.

Feeling the next pains beginning in her back, Sheba had no time for arguments. "Keilah and I can't help each other, and Gadara can't do it all. Jehoiada, this is your child and your tunnel. You're helping. Ohhh!" She tried to breathe slowly, tried to relax as instructed, but her back felt a thousand daggers thrust into it.

Keilah extended her hand to Nathanael, nodding agreement though unable to speak through pained breaths.

Zabad and Jehozabad offered blessings and hurried out the door, promising to take care of the Temple responsibilities while the two top priests tended their wives.

"Sheba, you've scared those poor gatekeepers out of marriage for good." Gadara chuckled as Jehoiada helped her descend the first steps into the tunnel.

Offering her a clay lamp, Jehoiada pointed to the inky blackness below. "You can use this to light the torches we've placed at the bottom."

"Thank you, Jehoiada." Gadara's voice echoed from the passageway. "See how well we're working together? You and I are going to bring your child into this world—and you're going to really appreciate my *helpful instructions*."

Jehoiada glared into the tunnel and then at Sheba. She wasn't sure who was more frightened now—her or her husband.

40

*In the twelfth year of Joram son of Ahab king of Israel,
Ahaziah son of Jehoram king of Judah began to reign.
Ahaziah was twenty-two years old when he became king,
and he reigned in Jerusalem one year. His mother's name
was Athaliah. . . . He followed the ways of the house of
Ahab and did evil in the eyes of the LORD.*

Jehoiada waited at the door of their chamber, trying to be patient. "Jehosheba, my love, we don't want to keep Hazi and Zibiah waiting."

Baby Zechariah had been awake half the night, and Jehosheba napped with him all morning, skewing the whole family's schedule. Nathanael's son, Joshua, wreaked equal havoc with the second priest's household, and both top priests arrived breathless and weary for the morning sacrifice. Who could imagine that two month-old boys could disrupt the whole Temple complex?

"Jehosheba, please!" Frustration seeped into his tone.

"I'm coming!" She hurried into their outer chamber, tucking unruly curls beneath her headpiece. "I finished feeding Zechariah, and Gadara will stay with him and Joshua until we get back from our nephew's ceremony." Jehoiada stared at her like a besotted shepherd boy. "What's the matter now?" She planted her hands on her hips, her cheeks flushed the color of roses.

"Four more days." He hadn't touched his wife since Zechariah was born. As high priest, he was considered sacred, separate unto the Lord, and could not touch his wife until after her purification. "Four more days," he repeated, and her cheeks went from roses to grapes.

"Now who's making us late?" She winked and walked past him, the sway of her hips a promise.

"It's cold." He reached for her winter wrap.

"Jehoiada, no!" She lunged at her shawl, scooping it away from him and around her shoulders. "It's unclean."

At times like these, Jehoiada admittedly battled discouragement at God's laws. His frustration must have been evident.

"Only four more days," she whispered, eyes sparkling. "Surely if Yahweh helped Hazi keep his word, He can help us."

The reminder helped Jehoiada walk the Law's prescribed arm's length from his wife across the courtyard toward the southern portico. He wanted to ask if Jehosheba was as surprised as he that Hazi planned to attend Zibiah's firstborn ceremony. But shouting a question like that across the outer Temple court seemed unwise. Zabad and Nathanael were confident that Eliab was an isolated betrayal, that all other priests and Levites could be trusted. *Yahweh, let it be so.* But Sheba's visits to Gevirah Thaliah were scheduled to begin again after her purification, and he couldn't risk any hint of the dangerous role Sheba was playing.

Nathanael met them at the outer court's southern portico, jittery and stammering. "Please hurry! The king is most anxious to begin." Ushering them into the third door on the right, he pointed Sheba toward her waiting friends. "Lady Zibiah is near to tears, pleading with King Hazi not to send his guards searching the holy places for you."

"I'm sorry we're late, Nathanael." Jehoiada squeezed his shoulder, feeling sorry for his second. It was a thankless job. "Shalom, King Ahaziah!" Using the king's full name always chafed Hazi's tunic, but Jehoiada was the only one bold enough—or foolish enough—to chance it.

"We're glad you could join us, Jehoiada." The king's grace-fully arched brow issued a silent rebuke, as did the cool nod to his sister. "Sheba."

Jehosheba was oblivious, already intently talking about Keilah's nursemaid arrangement and Zibiah's purification end-ing a single day before her friends'. Zibiah asked about their births, and Jehosheba expertly tiptoed that narrow wall of in-tegrity—wise without lies. This tiny chamber sanctioned no secrets, making every whisper a shout.

Zibiah had invited only the three couples for the service, but Zev and Zabad lingered near the door, neither willing to trust his duty to the other. The harvest air was crisp outside, but inside the cramped chamber, the smell of bodies, braziers, and sacred incense overwhelmed the senses.

And then the young prince began to wail. Zibiah turned to Jehoiada, looking stricken. "I'm supposed to hand him to you, but do you want him if he's crying?"

Chuckling, Jehoiada reached for his squalling nephew. "I'm afraid Yahweh requires our first and best—no matter the objec-tion." Bouncing the babe, he began the redemption ceremony. "The Lord said to Moses, 'Count all the firstborn Israelite males who are a month old or more and make a list of their names.' Lady Zibiah, do you vow that this is the firstborn son of your womb?"

"I vow it."

Turning to Hazi, Jehoiada paused slightly, searching the win-dows of his soul. "King Ahaziah, you have presented your son in Yahweh's holy Temple to be listed by name among the Lord's firstborn. What is the child's name?"

"His name will be listed as Joash." Hazi spoke without flinch-ing, but Zibiah gasped at the name devoid of reference to Je-hovah. Even Jezebel's children bore names indicating Yahweh's presence.

Jehoiada felt the affront like a dagger in his side. "If your son is to be redeemed in *Yahweh's* Temple, he will bear a form of Jehovah's name." Without waiting for an answer, he pronounced, "The prince of Judah will be named Jehoash—'given by God.' Do you, as his abba, bring the five shekels for his redemption?"

The grapevine in the brazier sparked, its crackling almost deafening in the stillness. Hazi stood like granite, unyielding, disobedient, arrogant. Had Athaliah suggested the baby's name, or was it the king's doing? Where did the Gevirah's evil stop and Hazi's begin?

Baby Jehoash cooed, finally at peace against Jehoiada's large chest. The sound seemed to startle the king as if from a dream, and he nodded to Zev, who stood at the chamber door. Jehoiada watched Zev signal to another Carite waiting outside. Together they retrieved a large myrtle-wood chest and laid it at Jehoiada's feet.

Hazi extended his arms, demanding his son before the high priest opened the chest. "The redemption price for a firstborn is five shekels. I give you three times my son's weight in palace gold."

Jehoiada kissed Prince Jehoash's downy black curls. "On this day you have redeemed this firstborn child of Zibiah." He stepped forward, placing him in Hazi's arms. "King Ahaziah—held by God—this son of David is yours to protect as Yahweh's gift: Jehoash, given by God."

When Jehoiada stepped back, empty-handed, he saw the unshed tears in Hazi's eyes moments before the king shouted, "Out! All of you."

Startled and confused, the celebrants of this happy occasion exchanged glances and obediently moved toward the door.

"Not you, Jehoiada," Hazi said.

Zibiah stood quietly beside Hazi, obviously desperate to leave with her son. Hazi wiped his face on the babe's blankets and kissed Zibiah's forehead, relinquishing their firstborn with a tender smile. She mouthed, "I love you," and hurried to catch up with Sheba and Keilah. The exchange offered Jehoiada some hope.

The door clicked, and Hazi's face clouded as he looked past Jehoiada's shoulder. "Out, Zabad."

Jehoiada nodded, but Zabad maintained a humble bow. "I'm sorry, my king, but I must refuse. I answer to a higher authority. As chief keeper of the threshold, I cannot leave anyone other

351

than a Levite unsupervised on Temple grounds—even in the outer courts." Zev stood beside him, stone-faced, eyes focused on a window on the opposite wall.

By the time Jehoiada looked back at Hazi, he was squeezing the bridge of his nose, teeth bared. "So, Jehoiada, let's review. I'm the king of Judah, but I can't name my son or order one of your guards out of the room?"

"In Yahweh's Temple—"

"Do you trust Zabad, Jehoiada?" Hazi's quick temper seemed to be more than just arrogance today.

Jehoiada sensed near panic in the young king. "I trust Zabad with my life—with Jehosheba's and Zechariah's lives."

"Both guards stay. No interruptions."

Zev and Zabad blocked the door, hands clasped behind them.

"Ima Thaliah received word from Jezebel that in the spring, when the season of war begins, Israel will engage King Hazael's Arameans in battle at Ramoth Gilead." Hazi sighed as if he'd hoisted mud bricks off his shoulders. "She's *ordered* me—the Gevirah of Israel has ordered *me*, king of Judah—to bring my elite royal guard and join forces with Uncle Ram and his Isra-elite army."

Jehoiada was silent, waiting to see how transparent Hazi would be. Jehosheba had confided Jezebel's plans to combine Judah and Israel under Baal and make Hazi king, but Hazi had no inkling Jehoiada knew of the queens of destiny. "Why would Jezebel ask for only you and your Carites? Why not the whole Judean *army*, as Ahab requested Jehoshaphat rouse the whole nation to fight at Ramoth Gilead?"

"Why indeed? Ima Thaliah wouldn't be the first Gevirah to 'help' her son, the king, to an untimely death."

And there, Hazi let it rest. But Jehoiada's horror reached new depths. Would Athaliah—whose rumored conspiracy with the Philistines caused her other sons' deaths inadvertently—now send her last son *intentionally* into harm's way?

"Hazi, I can't believe that even your ima is that wicked."

"I can't take that chance, Jehoiada. I need you to protect Zibiah and Jehoash—no matter what happens to me."

"But you aren't actually *going* to Ramoth Gilead!"

"I have no choice, Jehoiada."

"But you *do* have a choice. You're the king of Judah! Choose Yahweh, Hazi, like your saba Jehoshaphat and his abba Asa before him."

"Ima has the loyalty of Mattan, the Judean commanders, at least part of the Carites, and the noblemen. One man's choice— even a king's choice—to follow Yahweh can't change a nation."

"Yahweh will change the nation if you take the first step, believing—"

"Here's what I believe, Brother. If my Carites and I don't fight in Ramoth Gilead, Jezebel will muster Israel's army and take my throne. Ima Thaliah may not be wicked enough to send me to my death, but I assure you—Jezebel is wicked enough to murder us all."

Sheba, Zibiah, and Keilah left the Temple after morning worship, ambling down the garden path and through the palace's Horse Gate. Life had developed a comfortable rhythm since Keilah began daytime wet-nurse duties with Prince Jehoash. Gadara cared for both Zechariah and Joshua between feedings, allowing Sheba and Keilah to travel between the palace and the Temple as needed.

"You look tired, my friend." Zibiah placed a loving arm around Keilah's shoulders. "Hazi's been in Ramoth Gilead almost four Sabbaths. Since he let me continue Jehoash's nighttime feedings, maybe I could take over daytime too. Who would know?"

"Who would know? Really?" Sheba looked from beneath shuttered eyes, glancing around the main palace entrance. Zibiah rolled her eyes, but Sheba couldn't let it go. "I fought hard with the Gevirah to replace your chamber eunuchs with handmaids from your hometown. Please don't do anything foolish, Zibiah."

"I could nurse all three of our sons." Keilah winked at them both. "If Sheba would let me have Zechariah."

Chuckles eased the tensions, but Zibiah's gaze grew distant

as they ascended the grand stairway. "Why won't either of you bring your sons here? Athaliah never comes to my chamber."

Keilah looked at Sheba, brows arched, eyes bulged, mirroring her aggravation. How could Zibiah ask the delicate question here, where it echoed off the marble steps of the palace's main thoroughfare? Sheba's hesitation coaxed yet another question from her careless friend.

"So, has Gevirah Thaliah asked to see Zechariah yet?"

Horrified, Sheba gasped as they reached the top step—directly in front of Ima Thaliah's door.

Zibiah let out a disgusted, "Well, what is she thinking? He's almost five months old!"

Sheba grabbed her arm, shoving her toward her chamber, Keilah keeping pace. Sheba leaned close, grinding out a whisper. "Not another word until we're inside your chamber."

Zibiah, utterly contrite, hurried past two Judean watchmen posted at her door. "Sheba, I'm sorry. What did I—"

"You can't be that ignorant."

Once they were inside her chamber, Sheba's words tumbled out like unwinnowed wheat, and poor Zibiah flinched as if she'd been slapped. Keilah dropped her gaze, studying her hands. Trembling with rage, Sheba worked to remember her friends hadn't been steeped in deceit all their lives. They hadn't been taught to think first and speak falsely. The chamber maids Sheba had trained pretended to be deaf—ignoring the conversation, continuing their duties.

"I'm sorry, Sheba." Zibiah retrieved Jehoash from his cradle and then sat on one of three cushions gathered in a circle.

Keilah occupied a second cushion, still silent, and Sheba sat on the third, completing their daily circle of friendship. The sight of her nephew in Zibiah's arms drained Sheba's fury. She planted a kiss on Jehoash's downy head. The awkward silence felt ugly. Unusual.

"I didn't mean you were stupid. I meant you didn't think before you spoke, and it could endanger—"

"I know." Zibiah's eyes glistened as she stroked Jehoash's cheek. "You're right. I didn't think. I'm lonely, and I didn't consider the danger to others." She looked at Sheba, pleading. "But how could a savta not wish to see her grandson?"

"Surely you realize Ima Thaliah's attention would not be like a doting savta, Zibiah. I consider it Yahweh's protection that she's never acknowledged Zechariah's birth."

"Let's spin some wool!" Keilah's clear attempt to change the subject prompted Sheba to reach for Zibiah's hand. A little squeeze, a silent truce, and Keilah jumped to her feet. She retrieved the basket of spindles from the corner. "We haven't had our spindles out since the babies came."

Keilah and Sheba began their work while Zibiah rocked Jehoash, but a knock at the door stilled them all.

Sheba's first thought was Zibiah's careless remark. Had the Gevirah heard and now demanded to see Zechariah?

"Do you think it's news about Hazi?" Zibiah's face was as white as Egyptian linen.

Sheba hadn't even considered news of Hazi. Her brother and his Carites had joined Israelites in battle at Ramoth Gilead—and she was worried about bringing her baby to a palace? Maybe she was becoming too cautious, too selfish. *Yahweh, forgive me.* She placed a soothing hand on her sister-in-law's arm as a maid answered the door. "I'm sure it's fine."

Two burly watchmen entered, eyes straight ahead, their expressions betraying nothing. "The Gevirah summons Lady Sheba. It's urgent."

41

→ 2 Kings 8:28–29 ←

Ahaziah went with Joram son of Ahab to war against Hazael king of Aram at Ramoth Gilead. The Arameans wounded Joram; so King Joram returned to Jezreel to recover from the wounds. . . . Then Ahaziah . . . went down to Jezreel to see Joram son of Ahab, because he had been wounded.

Sheba's legs trembled so violently she stumbled into the watchman leading her to Ima's chamber.

"My lady! Are you all right?" The guard behind steadied her before she went to the floor, and she hung suspended between the two men.

The watchman on her right eyed the guards at Athaliah's doorway but kept his voice low. "It's good news, my lady. Don't be afraid." Clearing his throat, he righted her roughly—undoubtedly a show for the Gevirah's watchmen.

Relief washed over her, and she gathered her tattered courage, straightening her robe and tucking stray curls beneath her headpiece. Why did the palace feel so foreign under Judean guards? Was it because Hazi's Carite mercenaries resonated loyalty and brotherhood no matter where they served? She glared at the swaying Judean watchmen as she walked through Ima's door. At least the Carites stood for honor. The four men at Ima's chamber could barely stand at all.

"It would appear your guards mixed too much beer with wine last night, Ima," Sheba announced as she strolled confidently toward the Gevirah, who sat on her balcony couch. "The two who escorted me seemed competent, but your chamber guards stink of horse manure and vomit. Surely the Gevirah of Judah should have the finest watchmen, not the dregs."

"Ha!" Ima Thaliah clapped her hands, appearing delighted. She elbowed Mattan, who stood at her right. "Isn't she splendid? I told you our training wasn't wasted."

She motioned to the guard on her left—his brass and leather breastplate distinguished him as a commander. Ima stared at Sheba while whispering to the man. He focused on the tiled floor, his neck and ears crimson, jaw muscles dancing to some rhythmic beat.

"Yes, Gevirah. It will be as you say." He nodded, gave Sheba a sideways glance, and exited.

Before the door closed behind him, Sheba watched the commander withdraw his sword. The door clicked shut, and a blood-curdling scream pierced the air. Then another. Two thuds jarred the chamber door, and indistinct shouting erupted in the hall.

Sheba's heart raced, and she cast a disbelieving glance at the Gevirah. A serene smile was firmly fixed on her face, and Mattan's features were set like granite. Unable to hide her disgust, Sheba at least curbed it. "If you kill every watchman that displeases me, we'll be defending the walls with women by morning."

The Gevirah chuckled, but Mattan's frown deepened. Sheba's stomach rolled as silence was restored outside the chamber.

Finally, Ima Thaliah sighed and smoothed her purple linen robe over her knees, adjusting the emerald and pearl brooch at the center of her gold belt, precisely in the center of her waist. "Now, my dear. I have news of Ramoth Gilead."

Sheba worked to keep her expression passive, prepared for anything. *Yahweh, please let Hazi be safe.*

"My brother Ram was injured."

"Oh, Ima. I'm sorry." And she truly was. "Is he all right?"

The Gevirah seemed unsettled by the display of compassion. Clearing her throat, she glanced at Mattan, readjusted herself on the couch, and continued as if Sheba hadn't spoken. "Ram and his driver retreated to Jezreel, where his wounds will heal before he returns to battle. Hazi, however, proved himself a noble warrior and a capable leader among the Israelites. General Jehu was reportedly quite impressed." She was fairly beaming—in spite of her only brother's injury.

"That's good news." Sheba's tone betrayed her disapproval.

"It is *very* good news, young lady. The Israelites took the city with few losses, and Hazi is a hero. Jehu remains in Ramoth to secure the city while Hazi has gone to Jezreel to comfort his uncle Ram. Don't you see? It's the first step in unifying the nations under Hazi's rule and Baal Melkart's great power!"

"Yes, Ima. I'm happy for Hazi. That's wonderful." Sheba glanced at Mattan, whose gaze nearly burned a hole through her. Why was he here? He never attended their meetings anymore. "May I ask, what does Mattan think of Hazi's victory?"

"I have counseled the Gevirah to seize the victory for Baal Melkart," Mattan said. "We plan to celebrate the Festival of Awakening even though our king—"

"Yes, since Hazi is away," Ima interrupted, "we want *you* to attend the Festival of Awakening as a representative from Yahweh's Temple—"

"No." The word clattered like a clay dish on a tile floor.

The Gevirah's eyes narrowed dangerously. "What did you say to me?"

"Send word for Hazi to return from Jezreel." She'd learned gentle distraction swayed more effectively than blatant rebellion. "The Awakening is still two Sabbaths away, Ima. That's plenty of time for messengers to ride to Jezreel and bring Hazi back." She sensed a slight softening, so she added with a smile, "We made the trip in less than two days. Surely Judah's king hasn't become so soft he can't make the trip in two *weeks*?"

The barb wrenched a smile from the Gevirah. "As usual, Sheba, I'm a step ahead of you. I've already sent Hazi's royal cousins to tell him of the festival, but I still want you to attend the Awakening."

Sheba allowed a pause—only a few heartbeats—to cushion her reply. "I'm sorry, Ima, but no. Jehoiada will celebrate the Passover Feast at the same time, and I cannot—I will not—jeopardize the relationship I've built to make an appearance at one Baal festival. You commissioned me to make myself indispensable to the man you chose as my husband. Well, I am becoming his right arm. Now, let me complete the task for which I've been called." Sheba's heart was pounding. Had she lied? *No! I didn't lie!* Wise without lies, Jehoiada always said.

"You see, Mattan," the Gevirah said, elbowing the priest, "I told you we could trust her."

"You're beautiful in the morning." Jehoiada brushed an ebony curl off his wife's forehead, mesmerized by Yahweh's gift of life and love. Zechariah stirred in his goatskin-lined crib, and Jehoiada scooted off their bed to retrieve the little one who had stolen his parents' hearts.

When Jehoiada returned to bed with the babe in his arms, Jehosheba lay on her side, inspecting the stone seal Athaliah had given her with Jezebel's insignia. "Will we ever be free of Jezebel's shadow? Or will evil reminders forever bind our necks?"

Her questions intrigued more than troubled him. He placed Zechariah between them and then reached for the seal, rolling the intricate cylinder between his fingers. "I suppose we'll always remember her evil because we live with its consequences daily, but we need not live in Jezebel's shadow unless we let her block Yahweh's light." With a quick jerk he broke the leather tie, removing the seal from her neck.

She covered a small gasp, but then wonder laced her tone. "I think I finally believe that nothing will stand between us and Yahweh's love." She leaned across Zechariah, brushing a gentle kiss on Jehoiada's lips. The baby squawked in protest. Jehosheba giggled and then offered him the first nourishment of his day. "I love waking up with both of you beside me." Her smile mirrored Jehoiada's contentment.

"Wait right there," he said, determined to imprint this moment on their hearts forever. Jehoiada scooted off the bed and retrieved a hidden dagger from behind the loose stone in their chamber wall—a weapon he kept close since they lived nearer the city gate. He placed the hated seal on their limestone floor and crushed it with the dagger's handle.

Jehosheba gasped. The sound pricked his heart. Did she regret his irrevocable act? He looked up and recognized the once-common fear etched on her face—quickly replaced by a beaming smile and confident nod.

Peace. It was his wife's most beautiful adornment—more lovely than her gold and jewels on their wedding day. He hoped she could wear it more often. The news of Hazi's safety had provided more comfort than their wool-stuffed mattress. His wife had snored most of the night, but he dare not tell her, lest she turn red as roses and never sleep another wink.

The sound of their chamber door scraping the limestone floor startled them both. Jehosheba paled. "No one enters without knocking."

"Shh." Jehoiada donned his robe, pressed a finger against his lips, and winked. Best not to appear rattled, but his wife was right. Zabad would never let anyone into their chamber unannounced. Not even Nathanael entered without knocking. Jehoiada secured the dagger in his belt, inhaled a steadying breath, and soundlessly opened their bedchamber door.

Zabad was crouched over a filthy soldier, so animated in their conversation that neither noticed his approach.

"What's the meaning of thi—" Jehoiada's sudden presence startled the soldier—his face heart-stoppingly familiar. "Zev?" A thousand questions swirled into a single whisper. "Where is Hazi?"

Zev seemed dazed, muted, unable to sort out details. Zabad shook his head and then shook the king's guard—gently but firmly. "Zev, talk to me. Where is the king?"

"Jehoiada, who is—" Jehosheba arrived at the doorway, but she paused at the sight of Zev. "What are you—where's Hazi?" she shouted, rushing toward him.

"Keep her quiet!" Zev came alive at the sight of Jehosheba. "Hazi said no one can know!"

Jehoiada grabbed his wife, who was already growing hysterical. Zabad seized the exhausted Carite by his breastpiece, shaking him. "What do you mean, 'no one can know'? Where is King Hazi?"

Zev began to weep, burying his face in Zabad's shoulder, sobbing like a child. "Hazi said I must tell Lady Sheba first. No one can know he's dead until I tell his sister."

Zabad met Jehoiada's gaze, sharing the horror. Jehosheba buried her face in Jehoiada's shoulder. "No! I can't lose Hazi. Please, Yahweh, how much more must I endure?"

Jehoiada held her close, wishing he could shield her from the pain—knowing only one could truly comfort her. "This life is a wilderness, my love, but Yahweh leads us through it, offering His strength, His light, His love to bear the journey. We will endure this together because He'll carry us when we can't take another step."

Her quiet tears turned to heaving sobs, grief wringing her heart in its merciless grip. Jehoiada carried her to the couch, rocking her until her crying ebbed.

Zabad ministered to Zev, pouring fresh water into a basin, then offering him a wet cloth. The warrior had returned to his dazed state, unable to move or speak. Helpless, Zabad looked to Jehoiada and shrugged.

Jehosheba noticed the exchange, inhaled a ragged breath, and joined Zev on the floor. She took the rag from Zabad and knelt beside the Carite, dabbing blood and dirt from his face. Jehoiada remembered with piercing clarity serving his wife in much the same way when her inner wounds grew too severe to express. With every rinsing of the cloth, Jehosheba ministered quiet . . . peace . . . healing. And Zev seemed to drink them in like a desert wanderer at an oasis.

Finished cleaning the Carite's face and neck, Jehosheba lifted his left hand—and gasped. Hazi's signet ring sparkled on his little finger.

Her reaction seemed to stir him. He removed the ring, placed it in Jehosheba's palm, and folded her fingers over it. "Hazi asked that you give this to Jehoash someday—when he's old enough."

Jehosheba clutched it to her heart, nodding, tears streaming down her cheeks. "Can you tell us what happened?"

Zev dropped his gaze and nodded. "Yes, my lady. If I could trouble you for a glass of watered wine, I'll tell you what I know."

Zabad grabbed the wineskin from its peg, filled a wooden cup half full, and placed it on the floor beside the parched soldier. Zev's hand trembled, but he lifted the cup quickly and downed the full serving in a single gulp. "Thank you," he said, wiping his lips with a dirty sleeve.

Jehoiada pointed to two cushions. Zabad tossed one to the high priest, and both men huddled near the Carite to listen.

"During the battle for Ramoth Gilead, King Ram took two arrows, one each to the left arm and thigh. When it became clear the Israelites would roust the Arameans, King Ram placed General Jehu in charge and retreated to Jezreel to recover from his wounds." Zev examined his wooden cup and then hurled it at the wall. "That's when the general and his men began celebrating."

Jehoiada exchanged a troubled glance with Zabad. "Where were Hazi and the Carites?"

"After the battle, we set up a separate camp west of Ramoth Gilead. The Israelites made it clear from the beginning—they wanted nothing to do with us."

"What do you mean?" Jehosheba interrupted. "Ima Thaliah read me the letter saying Jezebel and General Jehu agreed that Ramoth Gilead must be retaken. Jezebel summoned Hazi to help fight."

Zev's features softened as if addressing a child. "Neither you nor young Hazi understands a soldier's mind, my lady. General Jehu agreed Ramoth should be retaken, but he and the Israelites resented interference from a foreign king and his mercenaries. The Gevirah ordered Hazi to the battle to prove Jehu could be replaced."

Jehoiada's heart ached. *If only Hazi had chosen Yahweh.* "So, did Jehu kill Hazi?"

The hardened Carite nodded—disbelief, wonder, fury mixed

on his face. "I saw this with my own eyes, and I can hardly believe it . . . Hazi ordered the Carites to break camp and ride for Jezreel. We arrived late one night, and the next morning, a watchman shouted that a madman was approaching in a chariot, and another identified the driver as Jehu."

"Jehu came alone?" Zabad's military senses seemed offended by the thought.

"No, but the dust he kicked up by his driving hid the few troops he brought with him. King Ram sent a horseman down to ask if Jehu came in peace. Something seemed amiss to the king." Zev shook his head, his eyes misting. "I wish he'd listened to his instincts." Clearing his throat, he continued with a ragged voice. "When the first horseman didn't return but instead fell into rank behind Jehu, King Ram sent a second horseman. But the second horseman also fell into rank. King Ram ordered his own chariot hitched, and of course Hazi wouldn't be left behind. I drove his chariot, following Israel's king . . ." His voice trailed off, and he wiped his hand down a weary face.

"What happened, Zev?" Jehosheba's voice was small. "I need to know everything."

"Jehu stopped his chariot on Jezebel's herb garden, reminding King Ram that his abba Ahab had stolen that ground years before from the vineyard owner Naboth. Then he condemned idolatry and Jezebel's witchcraft—calling her a pile of dung, though he knew she listened from the palace balcony. I think that's when King Ram realized Jehu meant to kill him, because that's when he tried to warn Hazi—but it was too late."

Jehoiada gathered Jehosheba into his arms as Zev unfolded the most difficult details. "Jehu shot King Ram first. The arrow pierced his heart, my lady. He didn't suffer. I wheeled King Hazi's chariot up the road to Beth Haggan with Jehu and two other chariots swift on our heels. As we neared Ibleam, I heard Hazi cry out and saw an arrow in his back. Jehu and his men abandoned their chase then and turned back toward Jezreel." He stared into Jehosheba's eyes like a man haunted. "My king died in my arms at the Megiddo fortress with three requests: 'Save my signet for Jehoash. Protect him and Zibiah. And Sheba

363

must tell Ima Thaliah of my death—or there will be more blood. Too much blood.'"

Jehoiada's arms tightened around his wife even as he began shaking his head. "No, Zev."

"No, I can't," she agreed, panic in her voice. "Hazi was right about the blood. Whoever tells her will die, and others too—" She gasped. "Zibiah!" Jehosheba leapt to her feet, her brow creased, hand covering her mouth while she stood deep in thought. "Hazi was right, though. I must tell Zibiah and then get her out of the palace before anyone else knows. We must hide her and Jehoash in the quar—" She clapped her hands over her mouth and glanced at Jehoiada as if she'd released a wild beast from her lips.

"Zev knows about the quarry, my love. Remember? We hid there together with your abba." Jehoiada purposely left out the new tunnel entrance hidden by the goatskin beneath them. Though he trusted Zev, wisdom dictated keeping some secrets from the top Carite.

Zev cleared his throat, drawing their attention. "I've placed Hazi's wrapped body in the quarry."

"You carried him all this way—alone?" Zabad asked, his tone laced with respect.

"The soldiers at Megiddo helped me wrap and prepare the king's body for burial. I left there at dusk and traveled all night on a dromedary, arriving at the quarry just before dawn this morning." He lifted his chin, regaining his warrior's mettle. "I welcomed Hazi into this world. I taught him to walk, to drink, and to fight. I protected him in life, and I held him in death. He *will* be safely buried in Jerusalem." The Carite's features hardened, and he pushed himself to stand. "And I *will* protect Zibiah and Prince Jehoash. Come, my lady," he said, offering his hand to Jehosheba.

"No!" Jehoiada stood, intercepting her hand before she could seal the pact. "I admire your determination, Captain, and I'll pray for Zibiah's and Jehoash's protection, but I will *not* allow my wife to meet certain death."

"I'm going to fulfill Hazi's last wishes." Jehosheba's quiet voice crashed like cymbals in Jehoiada's ears. She stood behind him, laying her head against his back, arms around his middle. "Yahweh is my strength and my shield. My heart trusts in Him, and I am helped."

Jehoiada bowed his head and held his wife's arms tightly around him. *Yahweh, forgive my doubt and fear. Strengthen my faith to trust You without question—no matter what comes next.*

42

➤ 2 KINGS 9:27 ⬅

When Ahaziah king of Judah saw what had happened, he fled up the road to Beth Haggan. Jehu chased him, shouting, "Kill him too!" They wounded him in his chariot on the way up to Gur near Ibleam, but he escaped to Megiddo and died there.

Sheba and Keilah stood with Zev, ready to exit the moment Zabad opened the Temple gates at dawn. "Yes, I remember the signal," Sheba assured her husband for the sixth time, kissing his cheek.

"Tell us again." This time Zabad quizzed her.

She reached into her pocket for the unique multicolored priests' linen, exposing only a peek of it. "If we're in trouble, I'll hang this swatch of fabric from a north window of the palace. Now open the gate!"

Zabad glanced at Jehoiada, who reluctantly nodded his approval.

The lump in Sheba's throat grew. "I'll be back soon." She rose on tiptoes and kissed her husband's cheek—for the seventh time—and left the Temple grounds.

"Are you all right?" Keilah squeezed Sheba's hand as they walked down the garden path toward the palace, Zev leading them.

She nodded but couldn't speak. In truth, the inner trembling had returned. Zechariah had sensed it, refusing to nurse, and Keilah had soothed him with her milk supply. Probably for the best. Sheba might have to nurse both Jehoash and Zechariah tonight. Who knew how Zibiah would react to the news about Hazi?

Pressing a breath between pursed lips, she tried to staunch her stubborn tears. "How do I tell her, Keilah? What do I say?"

"Yahweh will give you words." Another hand squeeze, and they followed Zev through the servants' quarters, fear chafing at Sheba's nerves like the sackcloth she and Keilah wore. Though most attendants would be away from their quarters, they hoped their plain robes would avoid suspicion.

Yahweh, I'm frightened. Please calm my fears and prepare the way.

Nearing the southernmost end of the barracks, they ascended the guards' spiral stairway to the women's hall on the second floor. Zev opened the hall door, surprising the Judean watchmen on duty. Abruptly, Zev closed the door behind him, leaving the women waiting in the stairway.

"What's he saying?" Keilah whispered.

Before Sheba heard a word, Zev opened the door and led them past six contrite watchmen, straight to Zibiah's door. Sheba caught his shoulder as he reached for the latch. "What did you say?"

"I told them Hazi is dead, but unless they want to face the Gevirah's wrath, they'll keep quiet until you've had a chance to inform his widow." He leaned close to whisper, "Athaliah's watchmen have no honor, but they're not stupid." He opened the door and stood aside, allowing Sheba and Keilah to enter first.

"Sheba? Keilah, what are you doing—" Even in the dim glow of dawn, Sheba saw Zibiah's sleepy face—and recognized her fear at the sight of Zev.

Sheba lunged toward the bed, covering Zibiah's mouth before her wail escaped. Keilah held her in a ferocious embrace, both soothing as best they could while keeping her silent.

Sheba cried too, whispering in her ear, "Hazi was killed in battle, Zibiah. I'm sorry. I know it's awful, but we can't weep and wail. Ima Thaliah can't know until we've hidden you and Jehoash, Zibiah. You must be silent."

Her words seemed to sink in slowly, calming their friend's flailing and grief. And then confusion. "Why are we in danger?"

Sheba's heart nearly broke at the innocence of that question. How could an aristocratic sheep farmer's daughter fathom Athaliah's plan for the queens of destiny, when Sheba herself didn't know it completely? Zibiah had been raised at her ima's knee, helping servants with spinning, weaving, and baking bread, with little exposure to bloodthirsty political scheming. "Anyone with a drop of royal blood is in danger until it's clear who will sit on Hazi's throne."

The handmaids. Sheba turned to find Zibiah's maids huddled around Prince Jehoash's cradle. Pinning Keilah with a stare, she nodded in the baby's direction. Understanding, her friend ambled toward the cradle, gathered Jehoash in her arms, and placed him in Zibiah's embrace.

Sheba slipped Hazi's signet ring from her pocket, keeping it hidden for only Zibiah to see. With a quick glance over her shoulder, she ensured the handmaids couldn't hear her whisper. "Jehoiada will keep this at the Temple, but someday this will be Jehoash's."

"But he's a baby. How long must Jehoash wait to be ki—"

Sheba clamped her hand over Zibiah's mouth, patience waning. "Shh! Just trust me."

Zibiah squeezed her eyes shut, nodded, and lowered her voice. "I'm sorry, of course. What must I do?"

"Keilah will stay here with you and Jehoash while Zev and I tell Gevirah Thaliah about Hazi. Gather only the things you *absolutely* need, and when we return . . ." Glancing back at the handmaids, Sheba added quietly, "You and Jehoash will come with us, but don't let your maids leave the chamber to slip a message to anyone. I think we can trust them, but . . ."

Word of Hazi's death had traveled down the women's hall to the watchmen stationed at Ima Thaliah's door. "I'm sorry about your brother, Princess," one of the guards whispered from a bow, the same man who had been kind to her yesterday.

Sheba placed a hand on his shoulder. "Thank you. Is the Gevirah awake yet?"

He stood to attention but kept his voice low. "Yes, my lady. She broke her fast and has already called for the priest Mattan to begin plans for the festival."

"Thank you again. You may announce my arrival." He lifted his spear to pound on the door, but Sheba stopped him. "Only *my* arrival. I'll introduce the Carite."

"Yes, my lady." The spearhead hit the door, and the big guard disappeared inside.

Zev turned a slow, stunned look her direction. "Making friends, I see."

She lifted only one corner of a smile. Hazi would have been proud too, no doubt. The thought pierced her anew. She sniffed fresh tears and rolled back her shoulders. "Walk behind me, Zev. I know you're too big to hide, but Ima will know about Hazi the moment she sees you. We need to get as far as possible into her chamber before dealing with her reaction—whatever it is."

He nodded as the door opened wide, and then did as she asked.

Relieved to see the outer chamber lit dimly with niche lamps, she heard Ima's voice from the bedchamber. "By the gods, Daughter, why have you come so early?" As Sheba realized her ima might not be dressed yet, the Gevirah stepped around the dividing curtain in full splendor.

And then she spotted Zev.

Stumbling backward, she grabbed the curtain, bringing the heavy tapestry down to the floor with her. Sheba rushed toward her, but Thaliah held her off, arm extended, eyes fixed on the Carite. "Tell me." No tears, her voice cold and dead. When Sheba tried again to approach her, she screamed, "No! Tell me now!"

Sheba recoiled, but Zev knelt, head bowed. "The traitor General Jehu drove like a madman to Jezreel, killed your brother, King Ram, and chased King Hazi and me in the chariot to

Ibleam. Your son took an arrow to the liver and died at the Megiddo fortress. I've wrapped his body and await your command, Gevirah. I have no word on the fate of Queen Jizebaal."

Silence.

Standing by the Carite, Sheba tried to still her ragged breathing. She hadn't even considered Jezebel! Zev's report had been masterful. Concise. Truthful. Yet no hint of his real feelings or purpose. Could she ever be as proficient? She heard a sniff and glimpsed a distinct quiver on Ima Thaliah's lips, tears gathering on her lower lashes.

Four eunuchs continued their morning work in the bedchamber, exposed after Ima pulled down the dividing curtain—one arranging the cosmetics, another making the bed, the others at the washbasins. None of them dared pause and risk her wrath.

"Ima, may I send one of your eunuchs for warm honeyed wine? Perhaps I should stay with you." Sheba kept her distance, not willing to be rebuffed again.

Surprisingly warm, Ima softened her features and extended her hand for assistance. Both Zev and Sheba hurried to help her stand. "Thank you, my dear, but no." She wiped tears, smearing the kohl already applied, and then huffed when she noticed it on her hand. "Ohhh, I'll have to retouch my eyes. Don't put away those cosmetics," she shouted at her eunuch. Wiping away another sniff, she took a deep breath and addressed Zev. "Thank you, Captain, for bringing my son's body home. King Hazi will be buried in King David's tombs—the last of David's sons on Judah's throne. We'll make sure his memory lives forever."

Warning shofars sounded in Sheba's head. *The last of David's sons on Judah's throne.* "Ima, I'm sure Zev is capable of arranging the burial details. I'll stay so we can discuss your plans for Judah."

"Forgive my boldness," Zev interrupted, winning a wicked stare from Ima, "but my duty now lies with you, Gevirah, and my talents lie with sword and dagger, not in women's work with burial spices."

"Your duty and your talents lie wherever I command them." The Gevirah's tone was unpolished granite. "Deliver my son's body to the palace garden. We begin the processional into the City of David at dusk."

Zev stood and bowed once more. "Yes, Gevirah."

"Sheba is leaving as well," she called after him. "You may escort her back to the Temple before you make the arrangements." Ima cradled Sheba's hand, her expression pleasant. "I will send for you later today, my dear. We'll talk then about our plans for Judah's queens of destiny. I must find a messenger who knows something of Ima Jizebaal's fate. If she's hiding in Tyre as I suspect, we must continue the work already begun. Go back to your husband for now, but be ready to take action, my girl." Sheba lingered, and the pleasantry turned to a hiss. "I said go!"

Sheba bowed and then hurried to catch up with Zev at the chamber door. *We must get Zibiah and Jehoash to the quarry!*

As they exited, Ima called out behind them, "Send in all the watchmen from the women's hallway immediately. I want them in my chamber *now*!"

Zev bowed, and Sheba walked out the door as Judah's watchmen filed in.

It was the longest walk of Sheba's life. Her steps slow, gait steady, she strolled down the long women's hall as Zev informed every watchman at each door of the Gevirah's immediate summons. Every guard showed terror, glancing at Sheba as if she'd undoubtedly instigated his execution—as she'd inadvertently done to Ima's chamber guards yesterday.

When Sheba and Zev arrived in Zibiah's chamber, they immediately dismissed the maids. Zibiah sat nursing Jehoash while Keilah fidgeted beside her, not knowing what to pack. Sheba lost all patience. "Zibiah, let Keilah nurse the baby, and *you* fill a shoulder bag!"

Sheba thought the maids had gone, but one of them tapped her on the shoulder. "My lady, I know we've been dismissed, but if we're seen in our rooms in the middle of a workday—"

"I don't care! Just get out!"

The girl dissolved in tears and ran, the other maids following. They were gone only a few moments when Sheba's conscience assaulted her. She paused at the door, casting a lethal stare at Zibiah. "I'm going to apologize, but when I return, we're taking you and Jehoash out of here—packed or unpacked."

She calmed herself before opening the door and then peeked into the hall. The maids were descending the grand stairway—a silly way to go unnoticed. She rolled her eyes, then gasped. Two watchmen exited one of Hazi's wives' chambers, wiping blood from their swords. Then two more from across the hall, swords also dripping blood. The guards exchanged wary glances, shook their heads, and entered the next two chambers.

Sheba closed the door, clutching her stomach and covering a sob. Zev noticed her horror. "What? What did you see?"

"The guards." She stared at Zibiah and Jehoash. *Lord God, please no!*

Zev shook her. "Sheba, what about the guards?" He reached for the latch, but she fell against the door, keeping him from opening it. "We can't let them know we saw them."

"Saw them what?" Zibiah asked in a panicked whisper.

Sheba's eyes locked on Zev. "I saw the guards leaving the wives' chambers with bloody swords."

"Ohhh!" Keilah and Zibiah stifled their cries, and baby Jehoash began to wail.

"Shh," Sheba whispered. "You must keep him still!"

Zibiah handed the babe to Keilah, who hid him under her robe and began to nurse the little prince. She was the one most apt to succeed amid the tension.

Zev drew Sheba close, whispering so only she could hear. "They're likely killing only the boys—and the imas if they resist. I'll stay here with Zibiah, but you must get the prince out of this chamber. Can Keilah keep him under her robe all the way to the Temple?"

Sheba considered her resourceful friend. Hiding Jehoash while seated on the bed wasn't hard, but keeping him quietly nursing while strolling to the Temple . . . "No, Zev. We can't make it that far without being seen." Tears started to form. Panic began chewing at her, crumbling from the inside out. "Hazi's sons! All of Hazi's sons!"

He held her face—and her gaze—until she calmed. "We're going to save Zibiah and Jehoash, but we can't march Zibiah out of this chamber unnoticed. You and Keilah can leave together—as you came—hiding the baby under Keilah's garment. I'll stay here to guard Zibiah." When she nodded, he released her. "Since you can't make it back to the Temple, you must think of somewhere in the palace no one would search for Keilah and Jehoash."

"Maybe—"

"Don't tell me." He clapped his hand over her mouth, startling her.

The intensity of his stare nearly rekindled her panic. He didn't want to know in case he was captured—and tortured. The thought chilled her. She nodded and he released her.

Sheba hurried toward her friends and whispered instructions. "Zev will stay here to guard you, Zibiah, and I'll hide Keilah and Jehoash." When Zibiah started to protest, Sheba cupped her cheeks and kissed her forehead. "I love you, my friend."

She grabbed Keilah's arm and nudged her toward the door, snagging Zibiah's basket of spindles on the way. "Hold this over one arm to hide your little bulge." She patted her nephew's warm body. "Stay close behind me, and keep Jehoash nursing. Don't stop for anyone, and act like you're afraid of me."

"Acting afraid won't be difficult." Keilah adjusted the baby and the basket. "All right. We're ready."

Sheba released a deep breath, steadied her nerves, and prayed for protection. She swung open the door with purpose and, without a pause, turned left, slipping into the guards' spiral stairway. Keilah closed the door behind them and followed Sheba up. They exited the door near Hazi's chamber on the third floor.

The watchman on duty nearly dropped his spear. "My lady, I—" Gathering his senses, he bristled. "You're not allowed on the king's hallway—"

"How dare you!" Sheba shouted, producing tears at near hysteria. "My brother is dead, and you dare challenge—"

"The king is dead? I had no idea . . . I'm sorry, I—"

Sheba glared through her tears, shaking her head dangerously. "Why aren't you and the rest of these watchmen in the garden helping with preparations for the burial processional? I'm astonished you would hesitate to carry out the Gevirah's orders. She's in no mood for incompetence."

"We'll get down to the garden immediately!" He issued a deafening whistle, summoning every guard on the king's hall—and then apologized when Sheba winced and covered her ears.

Feigning affront, she lifted her chin, heart pounding. "Please inform the Gevirah that I'll gather a few things from Hazi's chamber to place in his tomb before I return to the Temple. I'll meet her in the garden at dusk for the processional."

"Yes, my lady. I'll send word to the Gevirah." He bowed and led the entire floor of watchmen down the spiral stairs.

Sheba hurried toward Abba Jehoram's chamber, Keilah whispering behind her, "I thought we were going to Hazi's chamber."

"I'll retrieve a few keepsakes from Hazi's room *after* we find a comfortable hiding place for you and Jehoash in Abba's chamber. I'll return for you tonight after the processional."

43

But Jehosheba . . . took Joash son of Ahaziah and stole him away from among the royal princes, who were about to be murdered. She put him and his nurse in a bedroom to hide him from Athaliah; so he was not killed.

With each progression of the morning's service, Jehoiada glanced toward the palace, pleading for Yahweh's protection of those he loved. So far, no priestly fabric waved from a window.

The sacrificial lamb was slain and the salting of the offering complete. Nathanael had assigned another priest to trim the wicks on the lampstands and offer incense on the golden altar in the Holy Place. Only the Levites' psalm and the blasting of silver trumpets remained, and then this morning's service would be over. *Yahweh, forgive my preoccupation.*

From where he stood atop the brazen altar, he saw Zabad hurry across the outer court and through the portico. Jehoiada caught his eye as he entered the priests' court. Disappointment was scrawled across the gatekeeper's features. *No Jehosheba or Keilah.* The Levites continued their worship, and Jehoiada turned to Nathanael, who was stationed at the northeast corner of the Temple porch. The high priest relayed the silent message and recognized his own angst on the second priest's face.

Melodic voices accompanied by harp and lyre ended precisely on a single note. Jehoiada intoned Aaron's ancient benediction, praying the words over his wife's circumstance in this moment. "May Yahweh bless you and keep you; may Yahweh make His face shine on you and be gracious to you; may Yahweh turn His face toward you and give you peace."

The silver trumpets blasted as he descended the altar steps. Nathanael met him before he reached the northern basins. "You didn't see them return?"

"No."

"Where could they be?"

"I don't know." Jehoiada kept walking, Nathanael following as quickly as his bare feet would carry him, through the portico, down the steps, across the outer court, and into the high priest's chamber—

"Jehosheba!" both men shouted at once, startling her and interrupting Zechariah's peaceful meal.

The baby cried, and Jehosheba fumbled to close her robe, plopping Zechariah in Gadara's lap. The midwife already held Joshua, who appeared to be content and well fed.

Nathanael's eyes were alight as he walked past them into the next chamber. "Keilah?" When she didn't answer, he stepped back into the room. "Where's Keilah?" His smile began to fade. "How are Zibiah and Jehoash?"

Jehoiada saw his wife wilting and gathered her in his arms. "Jehosheba, what hap—"

"Where's Keilah?" Nathanael grabbed Jehosheba's arm, trying to wrench her from Jehoiada's grasp, but the high priest shoved him away.

"Nathanael!" Zabad walked in just then and grabbed Nathanael as he was lunging toward the high priest.

"That's enough of that!" Gadara shouted at the men. Both babies started to wail. "Keilah's safe, thanks to Jehosheba, and she did it all without acting like an ox in the market! Oxen in priests' robes, that's what you are!" She gathered both babies, soothing them as she left the room. "Shame on those silly men for upsetting our day."

Jehoiada wanted to ignore Gadara, who too often resembled a polished brass mirror—reflecting every blemish of his character. But, as usual, she was right. "Forgive me, Nathanael," he said, watching Zabad steady his fearful friend. Jehoiada pulled his wife into a fierce embrace. "Can you tell this ox in the market what happened?"

"Keilah is hidden away with Prince Jehoash in my abba's bed-chamber." She melted into Jehoiada's embrace, and he guided her to the couch as she gathered her composure.

Zabad and Nathanael sat on cushions at her feet, waiting.

"Ima has planned Hazi's burial procession for this evening," she began, "and I plan to retrieve Keilah and Jehoash after-ward. It was the only solution I could think of when I saw Ima Thaliah's guards killing Hazi's sons."

"You watched them kill . . ." Zabad said, horrified.

"No, no. I saw the guards leaving the wives' chambers with bloody swords . . ."

Jehoiada watched his wife's face drain of color. "Jehosheba, what's wrong?"

"There was no sound." Before he could clarify, her panic poured out. "There was no sound! If the guards had killed only babies, as Zev said, surely at least one ima would have wept or moaned." She was crying now, ranting through tears. "But there was nothing, Jehoiada. No sound. Zev said if I escaped with Jehoash, he'd stay with Zibiah. But he knew, didn't he? He knew it was the only way to save Jehoash. Zev and Zibiah should have been here by now!"

Jehoiada gathered her in his arms, speechless, exchanging a despairing glance with Zabad. Nathanael dropped his head and wept. When Jehosheba stilled, Jehoiada tipped her chin and searched the windows of her troubled soul. "After you left Keilah in your abba's chamber, did you go back to find Zev or Zibiah?"

She laid her head against his chest. "No, I came straight back here to feed Zechariah and Joshua. I thought Zev would bring Zibiah here—"

"How did you enter the Temple gate without me seeing you?" Zabad interrupted.

"I used the Corner Gate at the back of the complex. I knew if anyone saw me return without Keilah, worship would stop, and the whole city would realize something was wrong."

A loud pounding on the door launched Zabad to his feet, Nathanael not far behind him. Within a few racing heartbeats, the gatekeeper had drawn his dagger and signaled the second priest to open the door.

Jehoiada held his wife tighter still. "Yes, who is it?"

"I have word from the prophets," came a strangled whisper.

Warily, Nathanael backed away as Zabad opened the door. A man barely larger than a child stood at the threshold with smudged face and wild hair. He wore a camel-hair robe and leather belt. No sandals. "Elisha sent me with word of Yahweh's victory." His eyes sparkled when he smiled.

Zabad grabbed his wrist and yanked him inside, closing the door before he drew more attention. "Did anyone see you?"

"I'm sure anyone that was looking saw me." The simple answer confounded Zabad and tickled the prophet.

Feeling a grin threaten, Jehoiada left his wife's side, inviting the man-child to join him at the table. "Tell us about this victory."

He knelt across from the big high priest. "Jezebel is dead, eaten by dogs. Not enough left to bury." He leaned over and spit on the limestone floor. "And that was merely the first of General Jehu's—excuse me, *King* Jehu's—housecleaning."

"Are you sure?" Jehosheba breathed—relief, wonder, hope playing at the corners of her mouth.

"Are you the princess?"

Startled, she slid off the couch and took shelter behind Jehoiada, seeming somewhat rattled by the strange little man. "This is my wife, and yes—she is King Hazi's sister. We heard he was also killed in Jehu's slaughter, but didn't realize the rebellion was at Yahweh's command."

The prophet peeked over Jehoiada's shoulder, inspecting Jehosheba like a fig in the market. "I've heard she's a descendant of David—not the family of Ahab. Is that true?"

Annoyed, Jehoiada leaned across the table, using his size to intimidate. "True. But we're talking about Yahweh's victory, not my wife or her family."

The little prophet rose to his knees and leaned across the table, mimicking Jehoiada's tactic with a grin. "Yahweh's victory is the *destruction* of Ahab's family. Jehu killed the seventy princes and even slaughtered King Hazi's cousins since they happened to wander into Israel." His face shadowed, and he seemed suddenly dismayed by a thought. "Jehu overstepped his calling when his bloodlust reached into David's line. I hope your King Ahaziah produced offspring to maintain God's covenant on the throne."

The realization toppled Jehoiada back to his cushion. "Jehu has killed the seeds of Ahab *and* David in Israel . . . Athaliah has killed the princes in Judah." *Lord God, we must save Jehoash.* Regaining the breath knocked from him, Jehoiada whispered, "How could Jehu kill everyone so quickly?"

"King Jehu didn't have to kill them all himself. Jezebel's own eunuchs threw her off her balcony, and the seventy princes of Ahab were killed by their own tutors—to prove their loyalty to the new king. Jehu is a wild man—unpredictable—but one man obedient to Yahweh can turn the course of a nation."

The words pierced Jehoiada's heart like a dagger. Hadn't he tried to convince Hazi of that very thing? "What will Jehu do next?"

"Our new king is preparing for war, High Priest, and has already commissioned Jehonadab the Rekabite to build more chariots."

Jehosheba leaned over Jehoiada's shoulder. "Excuse me, sir, but will he use King Hazi's Carites as soldiers? They accompanied my brother to Jezreel." Jehoiada stared at his wife, confused by her sudden boldness.

She planted her fists at her waist. "Zev will want to know what happened to his men."

"All those associated with the house of Ahab—chief men, close friends, and priests—are dead. Including those loyal to your brother." The prophet recited his answer like a market list.

Just then, the shofars blew, wresting everyone's attention from the strange little man.

Memories of the Philistine raid made Jehoiada's heart race. "Has Jehu come south? Will he attack Jerusalem and begin Yahweh's reforms in Judah?"

"Hmm." The prophet paused, rubbing the patchy whiskers on his chin. "That would seem a wise strategy . . . but no. Yahweh commanded Jehu to clean out his own waste pot and prepare for further abuse from King Hazael's Arameans." Without warning, he leapt to his feet. "I must return to the school at Jericho. Elisha will send word if Yahweh's plan affects the Temple in Jerusalem or the people of Judah." The prophet whisked from the chamber, leaving Jehoiada and the others gawking when the door clicked shut.

"That was the strangest man I've ever seen." Zabad was the first to voice the shared opinion.

A second shofar sounded, and Jehosheba donned an amazing calm. "Royal heralds are probably announcing Hazi's death in the streets. While there's increased activity at the palace, I could use the prophet's report as an excuse to see the Gevirah again and then search for Zev and Zibiah."

"I'll escort her," Zabad said.

Jehoiada squeezed his eyes shut. He knew Sheba must continue her pretense with Athaliah, and he must trust Yahweh with her safety—again. *Is this how faith grows, Lord? Challenging it repeatedly?*

Silver trumpets blared from the palace, the signal of court convened in the Throne Hall.

Zabad chuckled. "I suppose we should have expected the Gevirah to call a special session. It appears I'll escort the high priest to the palace instead of his wife."

Thank You, Lord.

Jehosheba was on her feet before Zabad finished speaking. "Yes, Zabad! You escort Jehoiada while I get Keilah from Abba's chamber, and then we'll search for Zibiah." She was halfway to the next chamber when Jehoiada heard, "Gadara, I need a gourd and a small blanket to take to the palace!"

The story of Abraham offering Isaac on the altar was suddenly too real. Must he really be willing to give up everyone he loved if Yahweh asked it of him?

Sheba lingered in the palace garden, hiding behind a caper bush, far from the processional preparations but near enough to watch Jehoiada and Zabad enter the Horse Gate. After they disappeared inside, she tightened the blanket around the gourd and nestled it against her chest. The perfect size for a baby.

Strutting as arrogantly as the queen herself, Sheba entered the main hall of the palace. Watchmen shouted threats at the overflow of court spectators in an effort to quell raw emotions. Sheba shouldered past the crowd toward the grand stairway, tilting her bundle toward her chest to keep prying eyes from its true content. Nodding condescendingly to every servant and guard, she ascended the stairs and finally reached the third floor. Relief washed over her. No guards. *Of course not, when the chaos is by the Throne Hall. Thank You, Yahweh.* Hurrying toward Abba's chamber, she slipped in without a sound, surrounded by used palace furnishings.

"Keilah?" Nothing. A little louder, she whispered again, "Keilah, are you—"

"We're here!" Her friend emerged from behind a tall stack of mattresses, her face registering instant concern. "Why did you bring Zechariah?"

"I didn't. See?" Sheba separated the blanket from the gourd and held both proudly aloft. They giggled together. "I simply needed people to *think* I brought Zechariah so I could walk out of the palace with a baby." She took Jehoash in her arms and swaddled him in the blanket she'd brought from the Temple.

"How's Zibiah?" Keilah's hopeful eyes dimmed at Jehosheba's silence. "What happened?"

"I don't know. She and Zev never returned to the Temple. I came to get you first, and then—"

The door banged open. Two watchmen entered—one of them the man Sheba had deceitfully sent to the garden this morning.

"*Queen* Athaliah has deemed this chamber off limits." He paused, examining Keilah from head to toe. "I thought you came in here alone, Princess . . . ?"

Sheba's heart thundered like racing horses, her thoughts keeping pace. "What do you mean, '*Queen* Athaliah'?"

"I mean the Gevirah will assume Judah's throne in a few moments, and you didn't answer my question." He moved to seize Keilah's arm, but Sheba blocked his path.

"You're not much of a *watchman* if you miss a beautiful woman like Keilah walking into Abba's bedchamber with me. She's the baby's nursemaid." *Wise without lies.*

His eyes narrowed. "I'm a very good watchman, Princess, and I'll prove it by taking you both to the queen. As you so rightly reminded me this morning, Queen Athaliah's in no mood for incompetence."

Sheba sensed she'd spent her last shekel of intimidation on this man. Tears were her only recourse. "I'm sorry I tricked you this morning." She sniffed, allowing pools to form on her lower lashes. "The truth is, I never said good-bye to my abba or my brother, and I'm grieving. Can you understand that?"

The second guard handed her a dirty piece of linen to wipe her nose, but the threatening one remained stoic and silent.

"Ima Thaliah has never seen my son," she continued, causing both men to instinctively look at the babe in her arms. *Wise without lies.* She squeezed her eyes closed, releasing a stream of tears down her cheeks. "Perhaps today, during the specially convened court, my ima should see her grandson. Isn't he the only one she has left?" It was a terrible risk. She wasn't sure Ima had murdered *all* the princes. And if she was forced to present Jehoash, would Ima kill him, thinking he was Zechariah?

"All right, Princess, I'll gladly present you and your son to the queen—and tell her I found you in King Jehoram's bedchamber. I suppose she'll kill your son like the rest of her grandsons."

She heard Keilah gasp. Ima *had* killed all of Hazi's sons. Sheba forced indifference—and then a slow grin. "I have a better idea, Watchman. You go right now and tell Ima Thaliah that her daughter, a queen of destiny, can't honor the spirits of the dead in Yahweh's Temple. Then you ask her if she forbids me to have a private *Marzeh* ceremony with my son in Abba Jehoram's chamber. Go ahead. Ask her if she forbids worship of Baal Melkart in Abba's chamber." *Wise without lies. Wise without lies.*

Her new argument confounded the threatening guard, and Sheba attacked his confusion. "With all the sons of David dead and Ima Thaliah on the throne, you would do well to court my favor, Watchman. Have I not always been the queen's treasure?"

Fear washed both guards' faces white as a tomb, and Sheba knew she'd won the battle.

While the men debated silently, Sheba hoisted Jehoash into Keilah's arms and lifted a trembling hand to her forehead. "I'm too upset now to appear before the queen. Come, Keilah, we're returning to the Temple. Get out of my way!" Plowing forward, she split the guards like freshly turned soil and called over her shoulder, "I've got to rest before tonight's processional. If I faint on the way to King David's tombs, I'll tell Queen Athaliah it's your fault!"

She heard Keilah's faint footsteps behind her but dared not look back. *Lord God, get us back to the Temple safely.*

44

→ 2 Chronicles 22:10-12 ←

When Athaliah . . . saw that her son was dead, she pro-
ceeded to destroy the whole royal family of the house of
Judah. But Jehosheba . . . hid the child from Athaliah so
she could not kill him. He remained hidden with them
at the temple of God for six years while Athaliah ruled
the land.

Zabad and Jehoiada again used the shortest route to the Throne Hall, hurrying along the dimly lit corridor of the northern stable. They emerged through a side door into the teeming courtroom and found Athaliah seated on Hazi's throne, Mattan standing at her right in full regalia, and—

"Jehoiada, it's Zev!" Zabad spoke over the high priest's shoulder, pressing him faster through the crowd and closer to the throne. "Look at his face. He's badly beaten."

Jehoiada noted the deep cuts and fresh bruises on Zev's face and his slightly swayed stance. The Carite captain was definitely in pain and had met with violence since coming to the palace. How many guards had attacked him to inflict such damage on a soldier so skilled? Had he been injured while trying to save Zibiah? Would Athaliah trust him to guard her if he'd shown loyalty to Hazi's wife? Jehoiada had given up trying to understand Athaliah's scheming, but Yahweh knew.

Lord, give me wisdom to discern truth and courage to protect Your people.

Watchmen separated a scuffle between spectators in the back corner, and the whole room throbbed with angst. Jehoiada and Zabad continued their slow progress toward the front, wincing when Athaliah began pounding the platform with the ancient scepter of Solomon. When her signal failed to settle the mob, she motioned to Zev, who called a watchman to the platform and relayed the Gevirah's message.

Without warning, the watchman grabbed the nearest spectator and sliced his throat. A collective gasp joined Jehoiada's horror, and utter silence fell with the dead man.

"You two," Zev shouted from swollen lips, "out with him." Two watchmen dragged the dead body from court, trailing a testimony of Athaliah's ruthlessness up the center aisle and out the grand cedar doors.

"Thank you for your attention," the Gevirah began.

Jehoiada's stomach lurched when he felt Zabad's hand pressing him forward. "Keep going! We should be at the front of the crowd so we can obey if Yahweh calls us to act." Zabad must have been Yahweh's infusion of courage. Jehoiada commanded his legs to move, praying he'd be able to hear Yahweh speak over his pounding heart.

"As you heard from the royal heralds in the streets, my son and your king, Hazi, was brutally murdered by the traitorous General Jehu of Israel's army. And as you can see, Captain Zev fought bravely to return his king's body to Judah." A murmur began, but Athaliah lifted the scepter and quieted the room like a tomb. "A messenger from Israel arrived moments ago with news that both King Ram and the Gevirah Jizebaal are also dead."

Jehoiada and Zabad arrived at her throne as she delivered the news. "Jehu didn't do that to Zev!" Zabad whispered over his shoulder.

Jehoiada shushed his gatekeeper, realizing Athaliah meant to use Zev to gain the crowd's sympathy.

"My high priest, Mattan, has divined the meanings of these dire events and will interpret their impact on our nation."

Mattan signaled six of his priests out of the shadows, each holding a gold basin containing bloody entrails. "The blackened goat heart is the sign of death and destruction . . ."

Zabad leaned over again. "I think I could have divined death and destruction after hearing of Hazi's, Ram's, and Jezebel's deaths, don't you?"

Jehoiada ignored him.

"In the sheep's stomach, I found an unground kernel of wheat, whole and complete. Baal Melkart has promised a new reign, a whole and complete ruler for Judah." Receiving a flask of oil from a seventh priest, he lifted both hands. Athaliah slid from the throne onto her knees and removed her silken headpiece. "Athaliah, blood-born daughter of Jizebaal of Tyre and Ahab of Israel, chosen daughter of Judah's great King Jehoshaphat and Gevirah of our noble King Hazi—by the divine power of almighty Baal Melkart, I anoint you queen and sovereign of Judah." Mattan emptied the small flask of oil over Athaliah's head. "Let all of Baal's people rejoice."

Halting applause pattered, crackled, and died. The new queen resumed her throne and raised a linen cloth to blot the oil dripping down her cheeks. In the looming silence, she lowered her head, allowing Mattan to place Hazi's crown atop her plaited black and gray hair.

Scanning left and right, the new queen appraised her subjects and then rested her gaze on Yahweh's high priest. "As I am now the whole and complete ruler of Judah, I decree that every household bow their heads and hearts to my lord Baal Melkart."

Zabad squeezed Jehoiada's shoulder, and Jehoiada squeezed his eyes shut. *Yahweh, I know You're at work in Israel, but what about Judah? What will become of Your Temple and Your people here?* A plaintive rumble spread through the gathering, and guards pressed in on all sides. Someone shoved Zabad, sending him into Jehoiada, whose eyes were now wide with fright. The crowd began to surge, roiling its disapproval.

Mattan, visibly unnerved, approached the front of the dais.

"Hear me! Hear me, citizens of Judah! The queen's order does not *prevent* the worship of other gods in our nation!"

The queen pounded her scepter on the platform again. The Carite beside her stared at Jehoiada—held his gaze long enough to reveal the captain's spirit, as badly beaten as his body.

The Judeans quieted to the pounding of Athaliah's scepter, and Mattan took up his plea once more. "Every household will maintain an altar to Baal Melkart, uniting us in worship of one god—the mighty Rider of the Clouds—but this in no way *limits* whom you may worship." Baal's high priest signaled for another golden basin and reached in with both hands, drawing out two bloody entrails. "The gods revealed their will this morning, when two livers were found in a single yearling lamb. Judah's gracious queen won't limit her people to one god, but she mandates that every household worship a god that recognizes *all* gods."

"It's a lie," Zabad ground out between clenched teeth. "Can't the people see that he's manipulating them with sheep guts? You must say something, Jehoiada—do something."

"What would you have me do?" he asked amid the sea of confusion. "If I confront Mattan or Athaliah now, will it stop this?"

Zabad had no answer, frustration shading his neck crimson.

"Change must take place at Yahweh's command and in the *people's* hearts. Have you received a call like Jehu's? Have we won the people's loyalty like King Jehoshaphat?"

"So, it's hopeless." The defeat on Zabad's face was more terrible than his fury.

"Yahweh has begun the fight in Israel." Jehoiada lowered his voice and leaned close. "The reaction of this crowd tells me Athaliah doesn't have enough support to mount a war effort. Wisdom says wait. We must save Jehoash, teach him of Yahweh, and wait on Yahweh to move in Judah."

Athaliah stood, increasing her command over the gathering. She pointed at Zev's swollen face and shouted, "Captain Zev bears the wounds of Jehu's zeal for his *one god*. Israel's traitorous general annihilated Ahab's entire family—King Ram and even his seventy sons—to impose Yahweh's archaic rules. Why serve a god who demands only blood and discipline when you can enjoy many gods that promise pleasure and abundance? Baal offers you freedom, Judah! Freedom!"

"Long live Queen Athaliah!" came a feeble shout from the back.

"Long live Queen Athaliah!" another man echoed, this voice stronger. Soon the Throne Hall swelled with the chant. "Long live Queen Athaliah! Long live Queen Athaliah!"

Those standing near Jehoiada cast furtive glances and stepped away from him, leaving a noticeable divide between the mob and Yahweh's servants.

Athaliah pounded her scepter again, and the room instantly grew still, her earlier lesson well learned. "With freedom comes sacrifice, my people, and I have sad news to share. My son was betrayed by his wives." She lifted a linen cloth to kohl-rimmed eyes, stirring the emotions of her newly won crowd. "I was forced to act quickly when I discovered the treachery in my own palace. Now that the evil has been purged from Jerusalem's walls, we can move forward in unity and harmony."

Jehoiada heard murmurs, questions about the fate of Hazi's wives, but none were courageous enough to interrupt the new queen as she rushed forward with her plans.

"Captain Zev now stands beside me as he stood beside Hazi. He will return to his homeland, recruit and train a new force of Carites, and bring them back to Jerusalem to guard me and the remaining royals." Zev stood like a crumbling statue, stooped but immovable.

Finally, someone shouted, "How many remain from the house of Judah?" Watchmen swarmed the man, dragging him from the hall as he pleaded for reprieve.

The queen's voice lowered to a sultry purr. "There is no longer a house of Judah, my people. I will fashion queens of destiny, transforming Judah from a nation to a *kingdom*."

Silence. The queen's power was complete, effective, and thoroughly binding.

Smiling, Athaliah again signaled Zev to bend close for her whisper. Every spectator near the throne backed away—all but Jehoiada and Zabad. She noted their stand and offered a cursory nod as Zev stepped to the front of the platform with a labored gait.

Wincing in pain, the captain announced with a voice strong and clear, "King Hazi's burial processional begins at dusk and will proceed from the palace garden through the City of David to the ancient tombs. Let no man or woman, slave or child be found on the streets when the royal procession passes by."

Trumpets blared, declaring the session's end. Mattan escorted Athaliah up the center aisle—their robes smearing the blood of the man the queen had ordered silenced.

Zabad stood, unmoving, while spectators hurried away from this new reign of terror. "So, Judah is bullied into silence, and Baal Melkart shoves Yahweh into a list of other gods." He turned to Jehoiada, cheeks mottled crimson. "Why did we come? You didn't even speak."

"Sometimes prudence must temper zeal, my friend. Perhaps we came not to speak but to listen. We now know Judah's burden—fear—and Yahweh's Temple can become their refuge." Jehoiada braced his gatekeeper's shoulder. "And perhaps we came for Zev. It appears our dear Zibiah is gone, and his countenance conveys a loss greater than I first realized. Yahweh may have plans for the captain of which we know nothing yet."

Sheba sat with Keilah and Gadara in her chamber, door barred, each woman with a babe in her lap. Gadara had wept for joy at the sight of Keilah, the two like sisters since the midwife had come to help raise the Temple babies, as Joshua and Zechariah were known to other priests. Gadara adored Prince Jehoash instantly, and all three women prayed for Zibiah, not knowing her fate but hoping somehow Zev had secreted her to a safe location.

They'd settled onto their cushions around the low-lying table when trumpets announced court adjourned.

No one had spoken since—not even chatty Gadara.

How long had they been waiting? Long enough to nurse two babes and let Keilah begin feeding the third.

Perhaps Jehoiada and Zabad had stopped to talk with Nathanael about tonight's evening worship. But would there be an evening service? Or would they cancel it because of Hazi's processional? *Or will we flee to the quarry and never worship in Yahweh's Temple again?*

Fear grabbed Sheba's insides and shook her, robbing her breath. Her thoughts spun in circles—all ending in death for her husband, her son, her friends.

No! She took a deep breath and released it slowly. *I will wait in hope for the Lord; He is my help and my shield. I will wait in hope for the Lord; He is my help and my shield. I will wait in hope—*

The door latch turned, and a hard *thump* hit the barred door. All three women jumped, letting out a faint cry.

"Jehosheba?" Jehoiada's voice!

"Yes, yes! I'm coming!" She plopped Zechariah in Gadara's lap and raced to open the door.

Jehoiada rushed in, nearly smothering her in his embrace. "Thank the Lord you're safe."

"I was going to say the same about you!" She peeked over her husband's arms and saw Zabad followed by Nathanael, who barred the door behind them. *No Zibiah.*

Nathanael hurried toward Keilah, circling her waist with a possessive hug, showing her off like a new pair of sandals. "I got my wife back—thanks to Jehosheba." Keilah's cheeks grew pink, and the whole chamber filled with love and laughter.

Zabad offered a quick wink to Gadara—the only two in the room not hugging. She squeezed the two babies in her arms, burying her face in their necks.

Sheba could hold her tears no longer. "Zibiah?"

Jehoiada glanced at Zabad before brushing his wife's cheek. "I'm sorry, my love. Zev was guarding Athaliah at court. He'd been badly beaten and seemed . . . defeated. Athaliah hinted at her savagery—trying to justify it—by saying Hazi's wives betrayed him. She confirmed the house of Judah is no more."

Sniffs and quiet sobs filled the room. Sheba clutched at her husband's sleeve. Another loss. She squeezed her eyes closed and laid her cheek against Jehoiada's chest, feeling the jewels of the sacred breastpiece. *The twelve tribes—Yahweh's covenant remains.* The sacred garment that once condemned her now reminded her of Yahweh's faithfulness to generations past and future. Glancing at Jehoash, she nudged her husband toward their newest proof of Yahweh's protection. "You should get to know your nephew."

Jehoiada lifted the babe from Gadara's arms. "Shalom, young prince. Yahweh has great plans for you."

Jehoash began to wail, unaccustomed to the big man with shiny clothes.

"Don't worry, little prince." Gadara took him back, juggling Zechariah on one hip and Jehoash on the other. "The high priest is big and grumpy, but his character is improving." She winked at Sheba.

Jehoiada grinned at his favorite adversary and then sobered when he returned his attention to Sheba. "Do you realize what you've done, Wife?"

Suddenly anxious, she wondered if the court session had uncovered something she'd done wrong. Had she betrayed Yahweh somehow? Or Jehoiada? Revealed too much to Ima Thaliah? "What did I do?" she asked, ready to make amends, not flee or hide.

"You've saved the only male heir to Judah's throne." He brushed her lips with a kiss. "Remember when you heard Yahweh's voice? His call to a greater purpose?"

"David's covenant," she breathed.

Her husband's glistening eyes became the familiar mirror of love, but this time something more. She saw respect, admiration.

Zabad cleared his throat, interrupting the intimate moment and rousing nervous giggles.

Jehoiada reached for Sheba's hand and faced their friends. "We must find a way to protect Prince Jehoash until he can lead Judah back to Yahweh—"

"Wait! What happened in court?" Gadara blurted the question. "Will Athaliah take us to war against Israel?"

"I don't think she has enough public support to challenge Jehu." He glanced at Zabad, inviting his comments.

"Jehoiada's right. Judeans would protect their homes if Jehu attacked, but they won't rally to Athaliah when they're ruled by cruelty and fear."

"Athaliah rules with fear, but she also seems ruled *by* fear. She's ordered Zev's return to Caria to recruit and train a new royal guard who will protect her and the queens of destiny."

"Wait!" Sheba said, startled by the report. "Ima publicly revealed the queens of destiny? Did she explain its origin, its purpose? Did she say if any of Hazi's daughters remain?"

Jehoiada drew her close again. "She explained very little. We *know* very little." Then, glancing at their friends, he shook his head. "For now, we must continue as if nothing has changed. Sheba must play the loyal daughter, and we will continue to worship Yahweh. Wise without lies."

He lifted his son from Gadara's arms but held him close to the prince. "Our Zechariah resembles Prince Jehoash enough to be his twin, so as long as only one of them is seen with little Joshua, we should avoid suspicion. Everyone on Temple grounds knows two infant boys live in these outer chambers."

Gadara snuggled Prince Jehoash close. "You've had a rough start, little one, but no army can breach General Gadara's walls."

Warm laughter was healing balm after a painful day—and sweet elixir for whatever bitter herbs they must swallow this evening.

45

[Ahaziah's] servants took him by chariot to Jerusalem and buried him with his ancestors in his tomb in the City of David.

Though Sheba longed to melt into Jehoiada's arms, she matched Ima Thaliah's posture atop her royal white donkey. The two women led Hazi's burial processional to King David's tombs. Zev followed in Hazi's chariot, which he'd ordered converted to a funeral bier. Judean watchmen lined Jerusalem's high wall, standing guard over every street along their path.

When Sheba's donkey reached the bottom of a hill, she reined him to a halt and stole a glance behind her at the processional winding through the City of David. Jehoiada and his Temple guards descended the hill at the end of Hazi's processional, her husband's golden garments glistening in the last rays of this wearying day. Mattan, royal counselors, and Judah's military commanders surrounded the king's bier, followed by rows of soldiers and every Baal priest and Astarte priestess in the city.

Prodding her donkey gently, she hurried to catch up with Ima Thaliah and pondered the day's events. Had it only been this morning that Zev arrived unexpectedly in their outer chamber?

How could so much change in a single day? Hazi and Zibiah dead. Jehoash hidden at the Temple. Ima Thaliah queen. And Baal the legally mandated god of Judah. *Yahweh, deliver us from evil.*

"Captain! Control that horse!" Ima's stately facade cracked when the chariot stallion spooked their white donkeys. Zev strained at the reins, his muscles and veins bulging with the effort.

Sheba found brief solace in the undignified frenzy. The stallion's stomping mirrored her inner battle, and she masked a smile, cheering him on.

Don't let them take your heart. They'll try, but don't let them, Hazi had warned her in Jezreel. He'd watched her heart rage against Ima Thaliah's restraints, Jezebel's wickedness, and Baal's deception.

No one took my heart, big brother. I gave it freely. The thought made her smile. Jehoiada hadn't taken her heart, nor had Yahweh. She'd given it willingly—each time a lamb's blood was spilled, each time the sacred incense wafted heavenward. Sheba's fighting was over. Her heart had been won, not stolen.

"How can you smile, Sheba?" Ima Thaliah's tone was laced with pain, a dangerous threat in her glare. "Did you love Hazi so little that you can smirk at his burial?"

"I loved him so much that I can enjoy the antics of his horse." She held her ima's gaze, pressing into her heart. "Don't you think Hazi would have used his stallion to make this moment bearable for us?"

The queen's hand trembled on the reins, her eyes filling relentlessly while the muscle in her jaw danced to a silent dirge. Turning away without a word, Thaliah kicked her donkey, hurrying their pace to the tombs. Within moments, they arrived. Ima slid off the small creature before a guard could assist and nearly dragged Sheba from her own donkey's back.

"Come, Sheba. Don't dawdle." Ima looped her arm in Sheba's, hurrying her toward the stone-walled courtyard of King David's tombs.

At the entrance, Sheba stopped. "I'd like to wait for Jehoiada."

Mattan arrived just then. "What's the delay?"

Zev and five Baal priests carried Hazi's body on their shoulders, followed by Judean commanders.

"Jehoiada isn't going into the tomb." Ima Thaliah ignored the others and pierced Sheba with her words—brow raised, battle lines drawn.

Sheba's throat went dry. "Why?"

"Mattan will send Hazi's spirit to Mot's underworld without any interference from your high priest or his god."

Sheba felt a wave of panic when she saw Jehoiada and Zabad shouldering their way through the rows of soldiers, approaching the tomb's entrance. Both men were a head taller than most guards, but they were unarmed, while Judah's soldiers wore full battle armor and fidgeted with their swords.

"Choose, Sheba. Your priest returns to his Temple, or both he and his guard join Hazi."

Sheba glimpsed the watchmen perched atop Jerusalem's wall, lining the streets, and now forming double rows around the Temple guards behind the processional. Ima had planned this. Too many watchmen separated her from Jehoiada and Zabad. They would die before they reached her.

"Stop, Jehoiada!" Her loud cry rattled the solemn stillness.

Her husband gasped, halted, fear shadowing his face before the familiar anger crawled across his features.

She prayed as she spoke, hoping to save all their lives. "Since I know you cannot yet embrace the mighty Baal Melkart, we cannot allow you to participate in King Hazi's burial. Return to your Temple, and I will return after the Marzeh is complete."

"No! I won't leave you." Jehoiada took two steps before Zabad pulled him back, and the watchmen drew their swords. The pain in his eyes was unbearable.

"Go back to your God." Sheba held his gaze, pressing her meaning into his soul. "I go now to bury my brother and fulfill my own calling." Her knees nearly gave way when she saw Zabad turn him around, leading Yahweh's high priest back to the Temple.

An iron grip bit into her arm. "You were destined to be a

queen." Ima Thaliah's whisper felt hot on her cheek and stunk of day-old garlic.

Sheba ducked through the low entrance and emerged into a large, torch-lit tomb connected by an endless corridor to smaller chambers. In this main sepulcher, shelves lined the right wall, and a low-lying rock slab served as a center table, where Zev and the priests laid Hazi's wrapped body. The smell of death and sweaty men grew unbearable as Judean commanders squeezed in and priests filed out.

"Where are the priests going?" The realization awakened Sheba's senses and weakened her knees. Ima Thaliah ignored her, whispering to Zev and Mattan—but a queen of destiny would not go unheeded. "I assume you've prepared Judah's watchmen for Mot's vengeance should their sacrifices during the Marzeh ceremony displease him, Ima." Her indignation received more than one concerned glance from the guards and seized the queen's attention.

"Your quick mind pleases me, my dear, but you will address me as Queen Athaliah now." A simple nod to the guard beside Sheba sent his fist into her left cheek. Light exploded with the pain, and Sheba fell into the arms of a second man, dazed. She felt herself supported between two watchmen as Ima continued. "Don't ever forget that you are alive at my pleasure and for my purpose."

Sheba regained her footing—and her senses. Cheek throbbing, she offered a stately bow. "Forgive me, Queen Athaliah."

Athaliah returned a curt nod. "It is my pleasure to forgive you, Sheba, and my purpose that you serve as high priestess."

Sheba swallowed hard, trying to tamp down rising panic. "High priestess?"

"Yes, that's why you're here. I had to keep you safe while I send the watchmen to raid Jehoiada's precious Temple. I couldn't risk your husband using you as a hostage or a shield."

With every shred of control, Sheba trained her features. "I had a visitor today who confided information from Jehu's camp. Raiding Yahweh's Temple would be a critical error, my queen." Looking at the watchmen on her right and left, she played the bluff. "I know without doubt you do not have the loyalty of the military or the people of Judah. In fact, I have reason to believe at least one person in this room is faithful to Yahweh."

"Who?" Athaliah's rage boiled quickly. "Tell me who and I'll kill him myself."

An empowering peace surged through Sheba. "I will not divulge anything else until this chamber is cleared."

"Out! Get out or I'll have you all killed for treason!" The queen's fury blazed hotter than the torches. Even the commanders fled like haunted spirits from Hazi's tomb. "Mattan and Zev will stay. No one else."

The two men looked as if they'd been sentenced to death.

Sheba touched her throbbing cheek, waiting for the tomb to grow quiet. "You once asked me to win Jehoiada's heart in order to unite Judah with Israel, to restore the glorious days of David and Solomon." Seeing she'd gained their rapt attention, she lowered her voice, drawing them in. "I've won Jehoiada's heart. Now we must have time to rebuild Judah. Jehu ruined Jizebaal's plan—"

"Don't you think I know I'm ruined?" Thaliah seethed.

"*Jizebaal* is ruined, Ima. *You* still have choices." The comment seemed to startle Thaliah, and Sheba glimpsed her vulnerability. Jehoiada was right—she was ruling with fear because she herself was afraid. A lump lodged in Sheba's throat, making it impossible to speak.

Ima Thaliah lifted her chin and forced her resolve. "I have lived in the shadow of *Jezebel* all my life. The world has not yet seen *my* strength." Quick as an Egyptian cat, she grabbed Mattan's jeweled dagger and sliced her forearm, drawing a steady stream of blood. "Almighty Melkart, lead us to victory!" she cried.

Mattan immediately began chanting, and Ima turned on Sheba with the blade.

"No!" Sheba screamed, jumping out of her path.

Zev blocked the queen's advance. Incensed, Ima Thaliah raised the blade over her head, but Zev snagged it and twisted her hands behind her back, blood smearing both him and the queen. "I cannot let you harm yourself further, my queen."

His statement was respectful but firm, seeming to jar Thaliah from her frenzy.

The dagger fell to the dirt floor, and both Sheba and Mattan lunged to retrieve it—Sheba snatching it from the bloodthirsty Baal priest.

"You must cut yourself," he challenged, eyes fixed on Sheba. "You must prove your devotion to Baal Melkart."

Sheba aimed carefully crafted words at the queen once more. "I prove my allegiance to the Almighty God every day. If I return to Yahweh's Temple with cuts on my body, the trust I've built with Jehoiada will be lost. You fight your war and I'll fight mine, but know this. Jehu conspires with the sons of Rekab to build chariots, and he fights for Yahweh. Consider *that* before you shed blood in the Temple where your queen of destiny woos the high priest."

Zev released Ima Thaliah, and the queen straightened her robe, casting an impatient glance at Mattan. "Well, get me something to staunch the bleeding!" She held her hand over the wound, blood seeping between her fingers, and walked around Hazi's wrapped body to face her daughter. "You speak with poise and conviction, my dear. I have raised you well."

Sheba forced a smile and kissed her ima's cheek. "I must return to the Temple before Jehoiada becomes suspicious. May I have Zev escort me?"

Without answering, Queen Athaliah turned her back, nodding her approval to the Carite. Mattan began chanting his Marzeh, and the Baal priests waiting outside the tomb joined the eerie dirge. Zev and Sheba crept through the City of David in lengthening shadows of the coming night.

Jehoiada paced a flat limestone path in the quarry near the pool where he, Zev, and Obadiah had once hidden King Jehoram. A lifetime ago. He released a sigh and turned abruptly to retrace his steps. The pitch-covered torch swished, dropping pieces of charred cloth and singeing his gray hair and woolen robe. He'd left behind his golden garments in case . . .

He glanced at the other side of the pool, where Keilah and Gadara tended the three babies. Zabad had remained in their living chamber above to direct Jehosheba if—*when*—she returned from Hazi's tomb. *Yahweh, I will serve You faithfully no matter what happens, but please . . .*

After Zabad had nearly dragged him away from the burial site, Jehoiada had returned to the Temple with a keen sense of urgency to hide the children in the quarry. Nathanael waited above with Zabad to rush into the Holy of Holies if the Ark needed to be lowered through its secret passage. Surely Yahweh would show mercy if someone other than the high priest entered the Most Holy Place to save the Ark.

Laying the torch aside, Jehoiada fell to his knees, weeping. "Yahweh, protect Your Temple, Your Ark, Your priests, Your people. I don't have an army like Jehu. No horses or chariots. I am one man who strives to be obedient. I have only my love for You—and for my wife."

"Jehoiada!" Gadara shouted in a panicked whisper.

His head snapped toward the brightening tunnel entrance. Someone—or an army of someones—approached from the city. Had Athaliah discovered their secret?

Two silhouettes appeared, piercing him with relief. "Jehosheba! Zev!"

He grabbed his torch and staggered across the quarry's uneven floor, his wife and the Carite meeting him halfway. Jehosheba fell into his arms, weeping.

But Zev grinned and shook his head. "Your wife has the tactical mind of a general. You should have seen her handle the queen, and she knew you'd be hiding here—all of you." He gasped when he glimpsed the babies.

Jehosheba raised her head at the pause, and Jehoiada noticed her bruised cheek. Instant fury caused him to clutch her head in his hands. "Who hit you?"

"Jehoiada, I took a risk—and lost. But I won when it mattered."

"Your life is not a game, Jehosheba. What if you had *lost* when it mattered?"

She cupped his cheeks and planted a gentle kiss on his lips. "Yahweh is God. You and Zechariah are safe. My heart is at rest, my love. *These* are the things that matter."

Jehoiada's throat tightened, silencing any attempt to reply. He drew her close again but noticed Zev's shoulders shaking, head bowed. Jehoiada drew Jehosheba's attention to their friend. "Zev, my friend, thank you for all you've done to keep Hazi's son—our future king—safe."

The hardened Carite pressed both thumbs against his eyes, regaining control. "I tried to save Zibiah, you know."

Jehoiada released his wife and steadied the Carite's shoulder. "Do you want to tell us what happened?"

"The watchmen must have sent Zibiah's maids back upstairs. When we heard them knock, I told her not to let them in, but she wouldn't listen. As soon as the maids entered, the watchmen rushed in with them, and the guards got to me before I could defend Zibiah." Zev closed his eyes and shook his head as if disgusted with himself. "Ten of them pinned me to the floor before everything went black. I awoke in the prison, staring at Athaliah herself, eye to eye. She said all Hazi's wives and sons were dead, and I had two choices: join them in Mot's underworld or go to Caria to train a new royal guard to protect her." He lifted his gaze and offered a slow, sinister smile. "I've never believed in Mot."

Jehoiada's blood ran cold. "Does this mean you're truly loyal to Athaliah?"

A satisfied grin lit Zev's features. "A servant of Yahweh could never be loyal to Jezebel's daughter."

Jehoiada and Jehosheba gasped in unison. "Servant of Yahweh? You, Zev?"

He chuckled and nodded, seeming almost shy. "It's not something I announce publicly." The sparkle in his eyes told Jehoiada it had been a well-kept secret for quite some time.

"Did Hazi know?" Jehosheba asked, her voice quaking.

"I prayed with him as his life ebbed away, Princess. Only Yahweh knows a man's heart in those final moments of life. Only Yahweh."

Jehosheba hugged the man so tightly he winced, his recent injuries still painful. Jehoiada gently patted his wife's shoulder. "Come, my love. Let's share our joy with the rest of the family."

Keilah and Gadara had set aside their spindles while Zechariah, Joshua, and Prince Jehoash kicked and cooed on a veritable cloud of goatskin rugs. "I thought you'd never get over here," Gadara grumbled as they approached. "Now you'll have to repeat all the news."

Zechariah squealed the moment he saw Jehosheba. She scooped him off the rug, weeping with joy at their reunion. Keilah gathered Joshua into her arms, leaving Prince Jehoash lying on the soft white curls. Gadara's wary eye warned Jehoiada away like a bear from her cub—no doubt she recalled the prince's reaction at Jehoiada's last attempt.

But Zev heeded no warning and needed no invitation. His warrior-calloused hands lifted the infant prince with the care of a master potter. "Shalom, my lord Jehoash," he whispered. "I am Zev, your protector. Yahweh our God has kept His covenant to David and will someday place you on your abba's throne. I will guard you on that day and rejoice in Yahweh's victory." Zev's tear dropped on the prince's cheek.

Gadara raised a skeptical brow. "Well, I guess that covers part of the news, doesn't it?"

Zev smiled, weary but radiant. "I leave at sunrise for Caria and will return to Jerusalem with a new royal guard—loyal to me and to Yahweh." He placed the prince in Jehoiada's arms. The babe remained still, seemingly infused with the Carite's peace and strength. "Guard Hazi's son with your life and teach him to walk in the ways of David. When the time is right, we'll place him on Judah's throne and destroy Athaliah's reign."

Jehoiada studied Prince Jehoash's innocent face—the face of a king. Then he reached into his pocket and extended his clenched fist, holding it out to Zev without a word.

Jehosheba gasped, drawing Zev's attention. Her eyes filled with tears, and she nodded enthusiastically, coaxing the Carite to accept Jehoiada's unseen gift.

Looking confused but intrigued, the captain opened his hand. Jehoiada dropped Hazi's signet ring onto his palm. "Keep this with you always. The day I summon you to the Temple will be the day you place this ring on Jehoash's finger—the day we place King David's descendant back on Judah's throne."

Epilogue

2 Kings 11:4, 9–11

In the seventh year Jehoiada sent for the commanders of units of a hundred, the Carites and the guards and had them brought to him at the temple of the LORD. He made a covenant with them and put them under oath. . . . Then he showed them the king's son. . . . He gave the commanders the spears and shields that had belonged to King David and that were in the temple of the LORD. The guards, each with weapon in hand, stationed themselves around the king—near the altar and the temple.

Queen Athaliah ruled her people as she had raised her daughter—cold, distant, and ruthless—and the fear she wielded against Judah sliced her own soul. Within four years, the threats on her life grew so numerous she became a prisoner in her own palace. By her sixth year, she could no longer appear in the Throne Hall. Keeping to her private chamber, Athaliah valued only Mattan's counsel, and Sheba alone brought her comfort.

This day dawned bright and clear, as if Yahweh Himself had arrived for the coronation. Sheba sat on the frayed embroidered couch beside Ima Thaliah, heart pounding with joy and sorrow, waiting for the imminent sound of Temple trumpets.

Ima was completely unaware.

"I think Mattan has betrayed me. I've seen a great swell of Judeans enter the city during the past few days, but Mattan says he didn't summon them or declare a special feast." She stared out her open balcony doors, addressing no one—or perhaps she spoke to the gods who had failed her.

"It wasn't Mattan." Sheba's words, spoken so softly, echoed through the chamber, mocking years of carefully crafted phrases.

The queen's eyes flashed, and then a wicked grin creased her lips. "Ah, my girl. You've always exceeded my expectations."

Sheba reached for her ima's hand and knelt before her, stubborn tears gathering on her lashes. "We're not playing a game now, Ima. You must listen. We haven't much time."

"Our lives are always a game to the gods, Sheba. We're nothing but ants on a hill, tormented by gods with big sticks."

"No, Ima, Yahweh is not like other gods. He is the one true God, and He loves His people, cherishes them—cherishes us. He will forgive—"

"Forgive?" Athaliah ripped her hands from Sheba's grasp. "You think Yahweh will forgive *Jezebel's* daughter? Don't be a fool. I hate Judah's god, and He hates me." Her sharp black eyes had grown dull. Like pounding swords against a boulder, Ima's intensity was blunted against Yahweh's constancy, and Sheba felt more pity than revulsion for the woman she once thought great.

Trumpets blared from the Temple grounds, and a mighty shout rose in unison. "Long live the king! Long live the king!"

Athaliah shot to her feet and hurried to the balcony for a glimpse at the outer courts of Yahweh's Temple. Sheba followed, arriving in time for Ima's accusation. "What have you done? What about the queens of destiny?"

"Yahweh made a covenant with David that his descendants would reign forever on Judah's throne." Sheba wiped a triumphant tear, not even trying to hide it. "Hazi's son lives. My nephew, Jehoash, is now Judah's king." Sheba held the queen's gaze, waiting, hoping her ima would somehow accept—

"Nooooo!" Ima Thaliah fled from her chamber, screaming, leaving her double cedar doors ajar.

Sheba wondered if Ima noticed the absence of Carites, then shook her head, returned to the balcony, and scanned the sea of people flooding the courts of Yahweh's Temple.

"Long live the king! Long live the king!" they cried, the sound like waves crashing against a crumbling sea wall.

Sheba watched from the palace balcony as the queen's lone figure dashed into the Temple courts she'd avoided so long. The irony chilled her. Ima Thaliah would die on the only day she visited Yahweh's Temple.

Jerusalem fell silent.

"Treason!" Ima's bloodcurdling screech split the air. "Treason!" she cried, suddenly trying to retrace her path toward the palace.

Jehoiada, having vowed not to shed blood on Yahweh's holy grounds, raised his hand in the direction of the Horse Gate. Temple guards followed his command, descending on Judah's queen like hawks on prey. Sheba turned away, unable to watch the execution of the only ima she'd ever known.

A great shout ascended, drawing Sheba's attention to the Temple grounds again. There, on the porch between the pillars Jachin and Boaz, stood Jehoiada with their new king—Jehoash, only seven years old.

Yahweh had blessed the high priest's family with two sons now. They stood with their abba and the king, wide-eyed and frightened. Her heart ached at what these little ones had seen in their brief lives—ached with an ima's heart. *Thank You, Yahweh, for showing me how to love my children.*

A wave of peace flowed over her. *Perhaps now Jerusalem will enjoy peace as well.* Even as the thought formed, she watched the Temple courts empty like a stream of grain pouring from a great silo. Frenzied, people raced from the Eastern Gate, past the palace grounds, toward the city . . . No, toward Baal's temple. From Sheba's vantage on Ima's balcony, she glimpsed only Baal's outer courts, but she need not see more. Mattan would die by the sword he'd sharpened. Renown. Power. Wealth. Could any of these save him now?

Returning her attention to Yahweh's Temple, Sheba watched as her husband and sons were escorted by Carites down the garden path toward the palace entrance. Zev carried Jehoash proudly in his arms, fulfilling his promise to Hazi.

And I am free. Sheba's heart swelled at the thought. Her fears purged. Tears unleashed. Love realized.

Lifting her face to the cloudless sky, Sheba sent a prayer heavenward. "Let the shadow of Jezebel never darken Judah again, O Lord, and may Your kingdom endure forever and ever. Amen."

AUTHOR NOTE

The Book That Gave Me the "Feel" of Jezebel

The idea for Jezebel's seal came from a fabulous book titled *The Jezebel Letters: Religion and Politics in Ninth-Century Israel* by Eleanor Ferris Beach. The stone seal from the ninth or eighth century BC is an authentic archaeological find, housed at the Israel Museum, Jerusalem. Though Beach presents *The Jezebel Letters* as a novel, the depth of her research, maps, charts, plant and animal life, and so on testifies to the level of her expertise. Ignoring the areas in which Professor Beach veers from scriptural truth, I embraced the amazing insights she offered into the lives of Jezebel and Ahab.

Incredible Insight into Solomon's Temple

Out of all the research books I've seen, *Tabernacle and Temple* by Thomas Newberry is the most thorough explanation of the biblical descriptions and significance of Solomon's Temple. Every nook and cranny is documented with its corresponding scriptural reference, and then the author comments on its spiritual symbolism. A truly amazing resource—from 1887.

Solomon's Quarries

A large series of caves lay beneath the city of Jerusalem, causing a variety of legends to arise. Some suggest Solomon quarried the stones for Yahweh's Temple from the special meleke limestone on which David's city stands. Solomon's Temple was destroyed by the Babylonians, and two temples after it were destroyed as well. Jesus stated clearly that no stone of the Temple would be left on top of another (Mark 13:2) after Rome's destruction in AD 70, so no indisputable proof is likely forthcoming to support or refute the theory of Solomon's quarries.

Others have deemed the 330-foot-wide and 650-foot-deep cavern "Zedekiah's Cave," attaching the legend that King Zedekiah attempted to escape his palace when the Babylonians broke through Jerusalem's walls (2 Kings 25:4). Again, no evidence has been found to support the story that Zedekiah escaped through a tunnel under his palace and traveled partway to Jericho in the underground maze.

The fact is, the closest point of the current cave excavation is still 105 meters—the length of a football field—from the Temple Mount (what would have been the Most Holy Place). At times like these, I'm thrilled I write fiction! We know from 2 Chronicles 20:5 that King Jehoshaphat built a new courtyard on the Temple grounds, so *what if* the tunnel reached into Jehoshaphat's outer courtyard? Well, that makes a fun twist in a novel, eh? *What if . . . ?* I love those words.

Jehoiada's Age

The high priest's age—as compared to his young bride—was one of the most delicate details in the story. As my first task in plotting a biblical novel, I create a timeline with the characters, their dates of birth and death, and significant events. It's fascinating to see who bumps into whom along the way! The kings, queens, and their offspring were so confusing in this story that I overlooked poor Jehoiada in the initial process, neglecting to factor in the dates of his birth and death until after I'd written the first chapter. Big oops. Here's why:

> King Jehoram was thirty-two when he became king (2 Chron. 21:20), and he died eight years later, at age forty.
>
> Jehoram's youngest son Hazi became king at age twenty-two (2 Chron. 22:1–2), which means Jehoram would have had his youngest son when he was eighteen.

Those facts are true because they're stated in Scripture. Now, if Jehosheba was younger than Hazi (as in my story), she would have been a teenager when marrying the high priest.

The high priest Jehoiada died at age 130 (2 Chron. 24:15)—sometime during Hazi's son Jehoash's forty-year reign (2 Chron. 24:1). We know that Jehoash reigned for a period of time after Jehoiada died because Jehoash turned away from Yahweh during the latter part of his reign (2 Chron. 24:2, 17–18). So even if Jehoash reigned only five years after Jehoiada's death, the high priest would have been in his nineties when he married the teenaged Jehosheba. Do you see my dilemma? The truth of Scripture must be told—but I tried to tell it gently because our cultures are so very different.

ACKNOWLEDGMENTS

Each book takes on a life of its own—a rocky road, smooth sailing, or somewhere in between. The consistent thread through every project, however, is the tribe of folks necessary to finish the work. And the Lord always surrounds me with amazing people!

First and foremost, to the whole Revell team—thank you beyond words for listening to the Spirit's direction as you make decisions. To the three dear women I work with most closely— Vicki Crumpton, Jessica English, and Michele Misiak. You make writing fun! Some of the hard things about publishing become a labor of love because of your wit and wisdom. (And you are all three lightning-fast on that "reply" button!)

Thank you to Suzanne Smith, Research Librarian at Multnomah University, who streamlines my research time considerably.

My critique partners, Meg Wilson and Michele Nordquist, have again been so faithful to read, edit, comment, and encourage.

Thank you to my literary agent, Karen Ball, who is an amazing cheerleader, coach, and "Ball" of fire!

I'd also like to thank the great folks at Jones House Creative—

Matt and Tracy Jones and Emily Scifres. You have worked so hard to establish a professional presence with my website and social media. Thanks for being in my corner.

To Eric and Deanna Rice, thank you for opening your home to me as a quiet writing retreat when I needed it.

To three new friends, Mark and Teri Mayerstein and Raelene Searles, who gave me a new perspective into Jewish culture and challenged me to go deeper into the Temple.

Thanks to my niece, Joni Reeves, who gave insight into the deep emotional struggles of some of these characters through her counseling training at Indiana Wesleyan.

Thank you to my prayer team for the faithful prayers when my "red flag" requests appeared in your in-boxes! Only heaven can fully appreciate the battles you've won for me and my family.

This story hit very close to home. While I was researching and writing, my dad went to be with Jesus, and both my daughters gave birth for the first time! Thanks to all who sent notes of sympathy and encouragement at my dad's passing. And thanks to my daughters and sons-in-love, who allowed me to attend the births of my grandbabies—and to my whole family, who let me retreat for weeks into my writing cave.

As always, to my beloved husband, Roy. I couldn't do this without you. Spiritually, physically, emotionally—you give me yourself, and I'm refreshed, so I can pour out my passion on a page.

Mesu Andrews's deep understanding of and love for God's Word brings the biblical world alive for her readers. She and her husband, Roy, enjoyed fourteen years of pastoral ministry before moving to the Pacific Northwest to pursue the next step in God's calling. They have two married daughters and enjoy visiting their growing tribe of grandkids. Their Rottweiler–pit bull, Bouzer, snuggles at Mesu's feet while she writes, and both enjoy the cozy warmth of a fire on rainy Northwest days. Mesu loves movies, waterfalls, and travel. You can keep up with her news at www.mesuandrews.com.

Meet

MESU ANDREWS

at www.MesuAndrews.com

✢ ✢ ✢

Read her blog, sign up for devotions, and learn
more interesting facts about her books.

Connect with her on

f Mesu Andrews

🐦 MesuAndrews

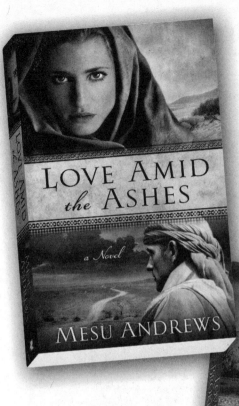

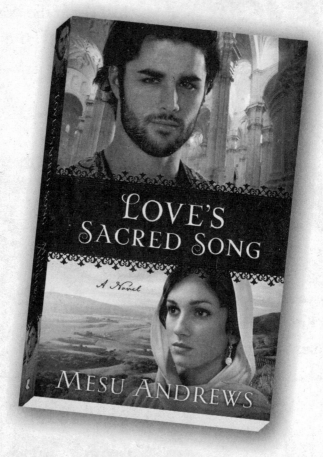